The Arm of Gold

The Arm of Gold

BY
RALPH CONNOR

INTRODUCTION BY
JOHN LENNOX

Formac Publishing Company Limited
Halifax

© 2007 Formac Publishing Company Limited
Introduction © John Lennox, 2007

Formac Publishing Company Limited recognizes the support of the
Province of Nova Scotia through the Department of Tourism,
Culture and Heritage. We acknowledge the financial support of the
Government of Canada through the Book Publishing Industry
Development Program (BPIDP) for our publishing activities. We
acknowledge the support of the Canada Council for the Arts for our
publishing program

Cover Illustration: *Cape Breton Nova Scotia: The Unspoiled Summerland
of America*, published by the Cape Breton Tourist
Association, circa 1930

Library and Archives Canada Cataloguing in Publication

Connor, Ralph
    The arm of gold / Ralph Connor ; introduction by John Lennox.

(Formac fiction treasures)
Reprint of the ed. published Toronto : McClelland & Stewart, c1932.
ISBN 978-0-88780-729-9

    1. Cape Breton Island (N.S.)--Fiction. I. Title. II. Series.

PS8463.O58A7 2007   C813'.52   C2007-904142-6

Formac Publishing Company Limited
5502 Atlantic Street
Halifax, Nova Scotia
B3H 1G4
www.formac.ca

Printed and bound in Canada on 100% recycled paper.

Presenting Formac Fiction Treasures

Series Editor: Gwendolyn Davies

A taste for reading popular fiction expanded in the nineteenth century with the mass marketing of books and magazines. People read rousing adventure stories aloud at night around the fireside; they bought entertaining romances to read while travelling on trains, and curled up with the latest serial novel in their leisure moments. Novelists were important cultural figures, with devotees who eagerly awaited their next work.

Among the many successful popular English language novelists of the late 19th and early 20th centuries were a group of Maritimers who found, in their own education, travel and sense of history, events and characters capable of entertaining readers on both sides of the Atlantic. They emerged from well-established communities that valued education and culture, for women as well as men. Faced with limited publishing opportunities in the Maritimes, successful writers sought magazine and book publishers in the major cultural centres: New York, Boston, Philadelphia, London and sometimes Montreal and Toronto. They often enjoyed much success with readers at home, but the best of these writers found large audiences across Canada and in the United States and Great Britain.

The Formac Fiction Treasures series is aimed at offering contemporary readers access to books that were successful, often huge bestsellers in their time, but which are now little-known and often hard to find. The authors and titles selected are chosen first of all as enjoyable to read, and secondly for the light they shine on historical events and on attitudes and views of the culture from which they emerged. These complete original texts reflect values that are sometimes in conflict with those of today: for example, racism is often evident, and bluntly expressed. This collection of novels is offered as a step towards rediscovering a surprisingly diverse and not nearly well enough known popular cultural heritage of the Maritime provinces and of Canada.

Ralph Connor

INTRODUCTION

When he died in October 1937, the Reverend Charles W. Gordon was the most famous Canadian of his generation. As "Ralph Connor," he had been for many decades (from the publication in 1898 of *Black Rock: A Tale of the Selkirks*) the author of a series of best-sellers that sold by the millions in Canada, the United States and the United Kingdom.

They were formulaic romances that combined fast-paced adventure, larger-than-life heroes, inspirational heroines and evangelical Protestant Christianity in equal measure. In their pre-World War I heyday, Connor's action-filled narratives answered to a moralistic climate and culture whose enthusiastic readership encompassed a large part of the English-speaking world. The popularity of his novels made Ralph Connor a household name, and his public role as a prominent and respected religious leader with an international reputation gave him an unprecedented profile in the Canada of his day.

Charles Gordon was born in 1860 in the pioneering community of Indian Lands, Glengarry County, Canada West, the fourth son of Reverend Daniel Gordon, a Presbyterian Highlander who had immigrated to Canada in 1853. At the age of ten, Charles Gordon and his family moved to Oxford County in southwestern Ontario, where Gordon completed his primary and secondary education before leaving for the University of Toronto. He graduated in classics and English in 1883, then took training for the Presbyterian ministry at

Toronto's Knox College, completing his course in 1887.
The year following he spent at the University of Edinburgh.

Gordon then went west to take charge of the church mis-
sion at Banff, where he began to establish an enviable reputation as a dynamic and charismatic clergyman. He took up
duties as the incumbent of St. Stephen's Church in Winnipeg
in 1894 and, apart from a period during World War I, spent
the rest of his life there. In 1914 he went overseas as chaplain
of the 79th Cameron Highlanders and was for a time chief
chaplain of the Canadian forces in England. At the end of
1916 he returned to Canada and became active in two cam-
paigns. The first aimed at encouraging the United States to
enter the war, and Gordon took an active part in speaking to
American audiences. The second was Gordon's involvement
in the run-up to the December 1917 federal election on
behalf of a proposed Union government, committed to con-
scription and to be led by Sir Robert Borden.

When contextualizing *The Arm of Gold* it is important to
note that for nine weeks prior to the election, Gordon travelled to the Maritime provinces campaigning in support of
Borden. Maritimers knew him as the world-famous author
of the Glengarry tales. In return, Gordon had what he
described in his 1937 autobiography *Postscript to Adventure:
The Autobiography of Ralph Connor* as "the immense advantage of knowing those Maritime people by the heart, the
only way to know them. Was I not born and bred among
their stock in old Glengarry? I knew every quirk and turn of
their theology and their consciences."

Among his destinations, Gordon travelled to Antigonish
in a violent snowstorm and there — at St. Francis Xavier
University — he met and came to admire the Catholic

Reverend James Tompkins. Tompkins informed Gordon of the support of Scottish Catholics for the war, in spite of the position of the Catholic Church in Quebec. He invited Gordon to make an after-dinner speech to a group of male students. Gordon was accorded a very positive reception by "a hundred or so wild and rugged young men, mostly gathered from the farms of Nova Scotia."

Gordon's public role continued to grow after the war. He was chair of the Manitoba Joint Council of Industry for its three years of existence following the Manitoba General Strike of 1919, and was much sought after as a mediator in industrial disputes. In 1921–22, he was moderator of the Presbyterian Church of Canada and subsequently campaigned in favour of the establishment of the United Church of Canada, which was formed in 1925 from the union of the Methodist, Presbyterian and Congregational churches. Gordon was active in the initiative for world peace and preached at the inauguration of the League of Nations' general assembly in 1932. He spoke out against fascism in the 1930s and advocated public ownership of certain industries, nationalization of banks, unemployment insurance and government pensions for the elderly.

His writing career as Ralph Connor had begun in an effort to awaken and encourage interest in the Presbyterian church's ministry in the Canadian west. Although his subject matter varied, the ethics of personal probity and moral courage remained at the heart of his storytelling. Over almost four decades he published a novel every two to three years, which gave him constant exposure to the reading public. In the pre-war world Gordon's books had been written to celebrate and encourage exemplary behaviour; in the social

and cultural upheavals of the post-war era the predictability
and piety of his plots became more and more dated.

He continued to write in the aftermath of World War I,
producing a stream of fiction that played up the nostalgia for
simpler times, although the climate for popular fiction had
changed. The reading public had a diminished interest in
stories celebrating a moral order that had been pulverized
on the battlefields of Europe. Didactic narrative had become
an outmoded literary vehicle, even though it remained the
means by which Gordon consistently reaffirmed his spiritual,
social and literary vocation. In terms of the overall reach of
his life and his impressive accomplishments, it was a limita-
tion that he accepted. It is interesting to note that of his 23
works of fiction, nine were published before the war, two in
the war years and twelve in the post-war period.

The Arm of Gold appeared in 1932 and was among the last
of Gordon's stories. Except for 1930, the last decade of his
life saw the publication of one work of fiction each year and
two books — one of which was a study of the life of Christ
— in 1936, the year of Gordon's death. His autobiography
appeared posthumously in 1937.

The plot of *The Arm of Gold* is the romance story of personal and communal transformation within the idyllic
pastoral and spiritual world of rural Cape Breton. Its ethnic
community of Highland Scots represented a cultural environment that Gordon had known intimately in his youth and
celebrated in his early fiction. Of Cape Breton Island's four
counties, only Victoria County was predominantly Protestant
and it provided the sectarian setting for *The Arm of Gold*.

The wealthy Americans who come to holiday on Cape
Breton Island echo the Maritime holiday pattern of their

famous real-life counterparts from the United States and urban Canada, like Alexander Graham Bell whose summer home was in Baddeck; William Van Horne who had a vacation residence in St. Andrews; the Franklin D. Roosevelts who made their annual summer pilgrimage to Campobello Island; and other wealthy families who spent their holidays in small oceanside villages like Chester.

The fictional American visitors in *The Arm of Gold* are Russell Inman, a stock promoter from New York, his daughter Daphne, her physician fiancé Dr. Fritz Wolfe and their chauffeur Steve. They have come to the village of Ravanoke on the Bras d'Or Lakes for a fishing holiday. They are rescued by Reverend Hector MacGregor when their large automobile becomes mired in mud, and subsequently meet his sister Logie and their friends. These two groups represent the meeting of national values — the individualistic Americans whose free-enterprise economy has grown robust from the war, and the ascetic, contemplative Scots-Canadians who live in the Maritime post-war economic depression. Ravanoke is the scene of their cultural interchange. The Americans come to realize the virtues of domestic and spiritual simplicity while the Canadians acquire some of the benefits of the American spirit of enterprise and self-reliance.

Two major events of international significance mark the world of *Arm of Gold*: World War I and the stock market crash of 1929.

Ravanoke is full of war veterans. Hector and Jock MacGregor were soldiers, their younger brother Alistair was an airman killed in action and their sister, Logie, was a VAD (Voluntary Aid Detachment), as was her friend Vivien

Marriott. Jock's wasting illness is evidence of the lingering effects of the war, a war that left the American visitors largely untouched. Dr. Wolfe, however, was overseas during the war and recognizes the precariousness of Jock's health. The Inmans generously put their car and chauffeur at the MacGregor family's disposal to convey Jock to a Boston hospital for surgery.

In an effort to raise money for Jock's operation, and much against his religious principles, Hector is helped by Mr. Inman to invest his money in the stock market, communicating by means of telegraph. The village telegraph operator, unknown to Hector, is soon investing for most of the villagers.

In the event, both initiatives ultimately fail. Jock is brought home after the operation and dies shortly afterward. Although Hector cashes out successfully, the stock market collapse wipes out the savings of the other members of the community and Hector quickly reimburses their losses.

Midway through the narrative, the American values of self-reliance and enterprise come together with Canadian self-help movements to enact real change in the community. Hector is the animator and Inman is the catalyst. Here again the historical context is important, and it is rooted in two Canadian social reform movements — the "Social Gospel" and the "Antigonish Movement."

The "Social Gospel" was a form of social involvement and activism that had its origins in the Protestant churches of Western Canada in the early twentieth century. The Rev. Charles W. Gordon was among its most ardent proponents, popularizing social issues in his series of best-selling novels.

The "Antigonish Movement" was begun at St. Francis Xavier University by two Roman Catholic priests: Dr. James

Tompkins (1870–1953), whom Gordon had met during the 1917 federal election campaign and who later became vice-president of the university, and Tompkins' cousin and protégé Dr. Moses Coady (1882–1959). For its time, *The Arm of Gold* demonstrates a shrewd and broad-minded ecumenism in its dramatization of the tenets and practices of the movement. Tompkins, much admired by Gordon, was determined that the university should be open to the common man and directed much of his career to that end and to the improvement of people's lives through adult education. His principles were continued by Coady, under whose aegis the Extension Department at St. Francis Xavier was established in 1930. Coady emphasized the imperative of working with adults where they lived, and the need for study and enlightenment in order for them to obtain control of the instruments of production. "In a democracy, it is the privilege of the people to work overtime in their own interests — the creation of a new society where all men are free," he wrote.

The Maritimes — and especially Nova Scotia — had experienced dramatic changes of fortune in the nineteenth and early twentieth centuries. The economic prosperity assured by the era of wooden ships and abundant forests in the early nineteenth century disappeared as the age of steam and steel emerged. An economic hiatus prevailed during the years of this transition, but soon Cape Breton's vast reserves of coal and the demands for coal-generated power by an exponential growth in industry, especially in Ontario and Quebec, began to usher in a dynamic new era of prosperity. Coal and steel became the economic foundation of the Cape Breton economy. The population of boom town Sydney Mines more than doubled between 1901 and 1911.

The promise of employment and steady wages drew individuals and families from overseas and from the rest of the
Maritimes. Trade unions were established. Many of their
members actively espoused socialism and some joined the
communist party. The coal and steel industries also became
the scene of bitter disputes between unions demanding a living wage and proprietors fixated on low wages and high
profits. There were several mine disasters involving large
losses of life. In this highly volatile setting, unrest, intimidation, strikes and sometimes violent confrontation took place.
The situation was exacerbated at the end of World War I as
the coal and steel industries, facing competition from more
cheaply priced American coal, found themselves in serious
financial trouble.

Almost immediately following the end of World War I,
the Maritimes experienced an economic depression that was
to last two decades, resulting in the economy of the region
falling seriously behind that of the rest of the country.
Vicious coal mine strikes contributed to a general climate of
defiance. Dawn Fraser, the popular Cape Breton poet, captured the mood in his *Echoes From Labor's Wars* published in
1926. The Great Depression that began with the stock market crash of October 1929 served only to intensify the considerable economic hardship that people in the Maritimes
were already experiencing.

In this troubled and highly charged climate, the Antigonish
Movement was designed to meet, challenge and change the
status quo. Its *modus operandi* involved mass meetings in
farming, fishing and coal-mining communities, featuring a
hard-hitting speaker — sometimes Coady himself. The
meetings were followed by the immediate establishment of

study clubs that met regularly in people's homes with a view to setting out and implementing a course of action with an emphasis on economic co-operation. *The Arm of Gold* fictionalizes this course of action. Hector and Russell Inman talk about the advantages to the community of co-operation in production and marketing. A meeting is held in the church, Inman speaks on the need for co-operative action and a Co-Operative Association is established, with each study group responsible for its own success.

Two additional elements in the novel — domestic and doctrinal — are noteworthy in the context of the Victorian world in which Gordon grew up.

The first element is the cult of the sacrificial mother, so dear to the domestic ideal of the period and celebrated throughout Gordon's fiction — specifically in *The Arm of Gold* in the person of Mrs. MacAskill. She also identifies a distinctive Maritime family pattern of the day: the out-migration of the younger generation to the detriment of the overall well-being of the region.

The second, doctrinal element is captured in Hector's sermon on scripture. He conveys to the shocked congregation his conviction that the Bible is a book of figurative rather than literal truth. This liberal approach, as opposed to the fundamentalist belief in the Bible as the literal word of God, became the hallmark of the United Church of Canada, which Gordon had long advocated. He pointedly avoids identifying the denomination of Hector's church since the story is set after church union. The tolerance of Hector's theology, however, is consistent with that of the United Church of Canada, although the ethnicity of his congregation underscores their, and Gordon's, historical Presbyterianism.

In the range of its concerns, *The Arm of Gold* reflects important historical issues particular to its setting. There is in its telling an admiration for Cape Breton and its people, as well as a broad-minded awareness and social conscience. There is also the sympathy generated by Gordon's experience as a labour arbitrator in several strikes and his understanding of the anxieties and frustrations attendant on social upheaval.

John Lennox
York University
June 2007

JOHN LENNOX is Professor of English, York University, and a specialist in Canadian Literature. In 2000 he was awarded the Governor-General's International Award in Canadian Studies, which is given annually for outstanding service to scholarship and to the development of Canadian Studies internationally.

CHAPTER I

A man tall, slender, enveloped in a mackintosh, stood on a little wooden pier, jutting out some fifty yards from a ledge of rock, glistening black, which formed a sea wall for the little harbor. Behind him a tiny village of half a dozen houses straggled along a road which meandered northeast and southwest over ramparts of wooded hills. Upon the slopes of the hills small farms, with their homesteads and orchards lay like a patchwork quilt. A bleak enough landscape, and yet under the rampart of wooded hills the farms—such as were occupied, for numbers were abandoned —possessed a certain sheltered cosiness.

Such was the hamlet of Ravanoke, loveliest of all the lovely hamlets that adorn the shores of the Bras d'Or, which, a veritable arm of gold, thrusts itself some sixty miles into the heart of the Island of Cape Breton. At one end of the village, upon a little green plateau, behind a line of firs, a tiny church of white clapboard raised its pointed spire above the trees, and beside the church, with flower garden in front and an extensive kitchen garden at the rear, a manse also of white clapboard, a spot of cloistered loveliness and peace. About the front windows and over the little front porch hung vines, which in summer would give the house a cosy, kindly aspect.

Before the man on the pier, blue water, a deeper blue than of the sky, stretched a mile away to low hills crowned with pines, rugged and wind-blown with Atlantic storms, eastward opening to the sea. Across the bay a half-gale was kicking up rough water and driving white-maned sea horses hard upon the rocky shore.

Gallantly riding these white-maned sea horses a small

fishing boat, under full sail, was making for land. Leaning
far over the gunwale, sheet in one hand, tiller in the other,
with foot braced hard against the thwart, taut yet full of
virile grace, a girl was driving the boat over the wave crests,
with an air of gay unconcern, scorning to reef sail or tack,
but taking the full drive of the sou'-easter as if she enjoyed
it.

"She is the crazy one," growled the man, with grudging
admiration of her seamanship.

Straight for the pierhead the girl drove, her leaping little
craft now in the trough, now battling the white crests, taking
full in the face the drenching spray. A clean-cut face it
was, strong, yet for all its strength lovely in its contours,
and now alight with the rapture of battle. A mass of gold-
brown hair, bobbed and whipping in the wind, lent to her
face a touch of gay wildness. *Joie de vivre* was thrilling
through her taut slender body to her very finger-tips. Nearer
she came till the man could see her eyes, green-grey he knew
they were, now steady and fearless fixed on the pierhead.

Straight at him she came, missed the pierhead by inches
and swept head-on for the sea wall of black glistening rock.

"Huh! Showing off!" he grunted, and stood breathless,
watching the boat, waiting for its swing into the wind.

Forty yards from the rocky wall—thirty yards—fifteen!
"God bless my soul! Is she mad?" He rushed down the
pier shouting at the girl, "Stop! Stop!"

Suddenly the sail flew from her grasp, the boat plunged
head-on at the wall, swung with the wind and crashed—a
slanting blow. Headlong the girl was catapulted into the
water and disappeared.

"God's mercy! She's gone!" cried the man. Tearing off
his mackintosh he dived into the smother of foam and reappeared holding the girl's head above the water. Turning
over on his back he fought his way through the backwash
toward the pier. A few moments of struggle and he had
her on the pier, choking, gasping for breath.

"My boat! My boat!" she muttered.

"Your boat be damned!"

"And—me—too—I guess?" she gasped with a faint smile.

"And you, too!" he said angrily.

"Oh—Hector! A minister!"

"Minister? You'd make an angel from Heaven swear! I'd like to shake you!" he answered in a fury and went to salvage her boat, which was battering itself against the rock.

While he was so engaged the girl sat up, took off her reefer fishing coat and jersey, revealing a silk blouse whose flimsy material offered but slight cover to her girlish form. Hastily she wrung out her jersey, and with painful difficulty struggled into it, groaning the while.

"What's the matter? Broken an arm or something, I suppose, and serves you right," said Hector, bringing the boat to the pier and mooring it.

"You're cross, Hector," she said, a slight quiver at her lip while still struggling for breath.

"Cross? You made me swear! You scared me to death!"

"Did I, Hector?"

"It is no smiling matter! Crazy idiot!"

"My tiller jammed, Hector," she said with sweet humility.

"Your tiller? What sort of way was that to come to your mooring? You just love to show off, don't you?"

"My fish, if you would be so very good," she said with unabated sweetness, pointing to a sack lying in the bottom of the boat.

"Fish? Oh, confound you and your fish! Look here, Vivien, you ought to be spanked, pulling such a fool stunt as that."

"I'd love to have you do it, Hector."

"Oh, you—" As he went after her fish a heavenly smile spread itself over her lovely face.

"There's your fish," he said, flinging the sack at her feet. "But you are a fool kid."

"Kid? Just twenty-four last week, Hector, and you are twenty-eight. But do put on your coat, Hector," she said. "You are so—so—oh! so funny!" Her voice rang out in a chime of silvery laughter. His ministerial garb, his dog collar all wet and clinging to him, gave him a rather ludicrous appearance. "Why, you're—you're—awfully wet!" Her lips were twitching.

Without a word but evidently still very angry, he put on his mackintosh, picked up the sack of fish and set off along the pier.

"Oh, Hector, forgive me!" she said penitently, catching up to him, "but I haven't seen you so—so—natural for years and years. Confess now you haven't sworn since before the War. Have you now?" She stepped out beside him, her face radiantly happy. "You know you have been so terribly good ever since—since—since you began wearing that—that collar."

"It's all your fault! You might have been killed on that rock!"

"Huh, huh! And gone to hell, eh?"

He made no reply, striding on before her.

"Would you mind going a little slower? I feel—a bit—upset."

Swiftly he faced her.

"You are hurt, Vivien? I'm a brute," he said. "Let me help you. Take my arm."

"What, before your congregation? There's Mrs. MacTavish sweeping out her porch. Not if I died for it! Just walk a little slower. It's my—my—arm. Let's admire the scenery a bit. No—please—don't touch me—or I shall scream —and then think of the scandal. How lovely the bay looks!" Her hand swept the bay as she stood panting, her face toward the water, her back toward Mrs. MacTavish.

"Just a minute, Hector. It's only a little way home."

"Let me help you, Vivien."

"Hector, don't touch me!" she ordered. "Give me a

couple of minutes. Then I shall get safely past dear Mrs. MacTavish, whose porch seems to require an extra touch this morning. There—I'm all right. Now a gentle saunter. Oh! your hat! Hector, it's gone!"

"Come on!" he said roughly, "or I shall pick you up in my arms and carry you," he threatened. "You are like a ghost."

"Don't you dare touch me! Oh, good morning, Mrs. MacTavish! Looks like rain, don't you think? I'm just back from my nets and Mr. MacGregor insists on carrying my fish for me. He is such a burden-bearer."

"Indeed then, whatever he is, it is yourself might be carrying your own fish," said Mrs. MacTavish, severe disapproval in her voice.

"Oh, it is nothing, Mrs. MacTavish. I was at the pier for a breath of air when Miss Marriott came in with her morning catch," explained MacGregor.

"And it is the meenister she would be putting her feesh on." Mrs. MacTavish's voice was eloquent of scorn.

"He is so very kind, you know, Mrs. MacTavish," said Vivien, sweetly penitent, "and—and so very firm. But there's the rain. We must hurry, or you will get wet, Mr. MacGregor. Good morning, Mrs. MacTavish."

Mrs. MacTavish's only answer was a vicious thump of her broom against the side of her porch, and a bang of her door.

"Wait—wait a little—Hector—oh, I am so sorry. Mrs. MacTavish is evidently puzzled by your appearance—your —your—hair. Hector!" Once more she was struggling with her laughter.

Mr. MacGregor made no reply. He was anxious only to get her safely to her home.

"There! Oh, thank you so much, Hector. I won't ask you in. The rain is really coming on, and you will get wet."

"Wet? Funny, eh? Well, I'm glad it strikes you that way. But some day you will do some fool thing with that old tub of yours and—"

"What matter after all, Hector?" The girl's voice was suddenly bitter.

"What matter? Vivien, I wish you would not act the fool," said Hector angrily.

"There now, you are angry again, Hector. But—oh—well, I love to see you so. As I was saying, it is years and years since—"

"Good-bye, Vivien. I hope your arm is not badly hurt." He waved his hand in farewell and turned away.

"Hector!" she called softly.

He turned and stood looking at her. "Yes?"

"Come here a moment."

Reluctantly he came back to the door.

"Hector," she said, her grey-green eyes darker than usual, "I think—you saved—my life—this morning. I was dazed —and—one arm was helpless—and—oh, Hector"—her voice grew husky, her words came with a rush—"would you have cared very much?" She was slightly breathless.

For a moment or two his eyes held hers with an intent gaze. Then brusquely he made reply,

"What nonsense are you talking? Of course I would have cared—we would all have cared—all of us—Jock and Logie and everybody—your father," he ended rather lamely.

The light faded from her eyes.

"Good morning!" she said with a hard little laugh. "Of course you would—all of you. You are a great minister, Hector."

As he was turning away, the door opened and her father appeared.

"Ah, Mr. MacGregor! You were caught in the rain."

"No, Dad, he has just pulled me out of the drink."

"What do you mean, Vivien?" exclaimed her father. "You are so very erratic in your speech."

With face growing white he listened to her account of the accident.

"My dear Vivien, you should think of other people, if not

of yourself," he said gravely. Then he turned to the minister. "Words are poor things, Mr. MacGregor," he said in a husky voice. "May life bring me an opportunity to show my gratitude!" He took the minister's hand in a fierce grip.

"It was God's mercy I was there," said Hector. Mr. Marriott said nothing to that.

"Mighty lucky for me anyway," said Vivien.

"I am not arguing to-day, Mr. MacGregor, I am only very, very grateful."

"I wish you could see it as I see it," said Hector. " 'Not a sparrow falleth without your Father,' " he quoted. "If God is, that is the kind of God He ought to be."

"Yes, I will grant you that. And yet—but no, Mr. MacGregor, not to-day. You have come too near my heart to-day for arguments. As your dear father did that dreadful day—" He paused abruptly, his eyes full of an unspeakable sorrow.

"Victor was a good boy. He is with God," said the minister in a voice of quiet assurance. "So brave, so good, so loving a spirit must be with God, Mr. Marriott. Surely all those noble spirits are with God."

"Don't, Mr. MacGregor," said Vivien in a voice sharp with pain.

"At least let me think so," said Hector.

"Yes, yes, Vivien. Let him think so. If only I could think so, too! Vivien, why do you risk your life so foolishly?" he said in a piteous voice. "I have only you—" His arm went about her shoulder.

"Come, Mr. MacGregor," he said, "take breakfast with us. These fish will be fine."

"Logie will be waiting for me, sir."

"Send a fish or two, then, Vivien, to my dear little friend. Ah! if all people were like Logie it would be easy to believe."

The minister took his departure, leaving behind him a sad and silent home. The threat of death to his daughter had brought back the memory of that dread day two years ago when the news of his only son's death had pierced his heart.

Vivien set herself to bring her father back to normal by retailing in humorous style the incidents in connection with her ducking, making light of the danger, picturing the minister's ludicrous appearance in his ministerial attire, and Mrs. McTavish's indignation. By the time she had finished her narrative there was a tap at the door and a young girl some two years her senior burst in upon them.

"Logie!"

"Vivien!" They were instantly in each other's arms.

"I wanted to be sure you were all right, Vivien," she said, "and your father too," she added, kissing the old gentleman. "Hector is cooking the fish. So good of you to send them over. He told of your accident, but he is so difficult. You never know just how to take his stories. He seems to regard your accident as a huge joke. You aren't hurt, Vivien?"

"Not a bit. That is, not much. My arm is a little sore, that's all."

"Are you sure now? Should you try to do your work? I can easily run over after breakfast and look after everything."

"Tut, nonsense, Logie! As if you hadn't enough work of your own. But that's you all over. I'm quite all right. Run back to your fish. Hector will have it burned to a cinder. Go! You are a dear." She took between her hands the girl's lovely face with the clean-cut beauty of an old cameo, and kissed her.

"Oh, I am so glad." The clear brown eyes were soft with tender light. "Anyway I'll run over after breakfast. Goodbye, Mr. Marriott."

"Good-bye, my dear," he said, patting her shoulder. "You are so kind."

"Now, Father, the fish is done to a turn, and I am ravenous." The little incident of Logie's visit had brought light into the room.

"A rare girl! A wonderful girl," her father said.

"Well, so all the boys at the front used to say. They were all mad about her." And Vivien kept up a stream of reminiscences of Logie's War service, thankful to see the shadow quite gone from her father's face. Logie's visit had done its work.

CHAPTER II

HURRYING home Logie found Hector waiting impatiently for his porridge, with the fish perfectly browned in the oven.

"Well, how did you find the patient?" he asked. "Taking nourishment, I hope."

"But she might have been badly injured. But here is your buttermilk for your porridge."

"Buttermilk? Hurrah! Where did that come from?"

"Pheemie brought it over last night."

"God bless her dear heart," said Hector fervently.

"But she is a good creature, Hector, and so good to her mother."

"She is full of good works. She is sure of a high place among the saints in light."

"Hector!"

"I mean it. She is tireless in her ministrations to the halt, maimed and wounded."

"She is good enough to you, Hector."

"Better than I deserve. Somewhat oppressive, I must confess. But her buttermilk is something to talk about. And with this porridge! Wonderful! Fish and bacon, too, eh? You are far too lavish, Logie."

"I thought that after your ducking— But you must go after breakfast and see how Vivien is?"

"Not me. She will be all right."

"But the shock?"

"Shock? The shock was mine."

"Then her arm? She has hurt her arm. Indeed, I think you ought to send Dr. McQueen up."

"And have her slam the door in his face? Look here, Logie, what's the idea? Why should I go up, after you have just been there?"

"Someone should really go, and I shall be busy with Jock."

"I'll look after Jock. No, no, you go. I would look funny looking after her arm. Besides, she is a nurse."

"She is rather hard to manage. She is very rash. Someone should speak to her father about her. She won't take care of herself, but she might mind her father. Suppose you speak to her father, Hector."

"Her father? What good would that do? He would likely get me into a discussion over molecular reactions and the freedom of the will. No. Why are you fussing over Vivien? You go and see her, I'll look in on Jock."

What Logie really desired was that Hector should pay a pastoral call upon the Marriotts. This she considered a golden opportunity to win old Mr. Marriott's confidence. Perhaps he might begin attending church again. The general impression abroad in the congregation was that Mr. Marriott was an atheist, and his daughter but little better. For this reason the Marriott house was shunned by most of the faithful. Logie gave up her attempt, however, and after hurrying through her morning chores, she put on her rain coat and tam and ran off to see what she could do for her friend.

Hector went slowly upstairs to his brother's room.

"Well, how goes the War, Jock, old boy?"

"Most damnably."

Jock's once handsome face was now pale and worn with lines, deepened by pain. The masses of light brown hair hung in unruly tangles above eyes that in their deep sockets seemed larger than they really were.

With heart torn with pity which he knew he dared not express, Hector sat by the bed.

"Not much sleep, eh?"

"Sleep? Lord God, what does it feel like to sleep? Don't speak that word. It is like a cup of water in hell."

Hector rose and began to move quietly about the room straightening things out.

"Did you try aspirin?"

"Aspirin? I've been chewing tablets all night as if they were peppermints."

"Shouldn't do that, Jock boy."

"Why not?" shouted Jock.

"Bad for you—bad for your nerves—kill you."

"Kill me, eh?" He laughed wildly. "Kill me? Not a bad idea. Kill me?" he repeated to himself in a low voice.

"Yes, kill you in the long run."

"Kill me, eh? All right. Damned good idea—why live? What's the use? I'm getting worse every day—nuisance to myself and to everybody else."

"Stop that!" said Hector. "That's not true."

"It is true. I am worse than I was a month ago. My pain is worse, my stomach is worse. I hate food. I can't sleep. I can't control myself. I am like a petted child. I'm a blight on this house. McQueen's medicines are simply narcotics. Why should I live?"

"Because," said his brother, speaking quietly, "it is the will of God that you should carry on."

"Will of God? How do I know? How do you know? Did He tell you?"

"Yes. His last order to every living soul is to keep living till the word comes to quit."

"Last order to live like this? What good am I to God or any of you?"

"Don't know. Headquarters secret. Haven't seen the plan. No orders here come to quit. Got to play the game, old man. Remember those shell-holes at Hill 60? Mud to the thighs. Shelled every day. Remember?"

"Do I remember? Hell!"

"But we had to stick. Headquarters' orders. We had to stick. Tough! Awfully tough! Didn't know why, but we stuck. Guess we've got to stick it, whatever it is, till new orders arrive, eh?"

"Damned rot! What do you know about it? Got a private line, eh?" There was a sound of madness in his laugh.
Hector scanned his face swiftly. There was a glitter in the
hazel-brown eyes.

"Private line?" he said in a slow, quiet voice. "Yes. I
have a private line. I know—at least I think I know. I'm
sure Father knew, and Mother too. Can't explain very
well. But we can't funk. Don't, don't, Jock! I know you
think it is easy enough for me."

"Easy for you? For Logie? No! That's the hell of it.
It's worse for you both. Damn it all, Hector, can't I read
your faces? Pardon me, Hector, I can't help cursing.

"Well, I won't—but—" Suddenly his voice broke. "Oh,
Hector, I'm afraid." His voice sank to a whisper, "I'm
afraid! Oh, I'm afraid." He clutched at his brother's hand.
"I'll go mad! And you'll have to send me away. Oh, Hector, don't send me away! Oh, promise me—promise me,
Hector—kill me first—give me a pill—promise me!" His
voice sank to an agonized whisper. His eyes were glittering
with the light of madness.

Hector dropped to his knees, took his brother's hand in
both of his. "Listen, Jock. Did you ever know me to
break my word?"

"No, no, Hector! No, never! Never!"

"Then listen to me talk to God." He closed his eyes, released one hand, held it high and said in clear, solemn voice:

"Hear me, God. Hear me when I pledge my honor to my
brother Jock here, that I will never do anything he does not
want me to do." He paused a moment or two. "Is that
enough, Jock?"

"Yes! Yes!" sobbed Jock, kissing again and again the
strong hand that gripped his. "That's enough, Hec. Oh,
Hec, I am ashamed of myself! But I can't talk to God any
more. I'm bad—bad. God help me! I don't know anything about Him." The words came rushing forth in a

broken torrent.

"Never mind, Jock, old boy, you're not bad—you are ill. You may not know Him, but He knows you all right, all about you, and He'll stick by you, old chap."

Instantly Jock's mad frenzy passed. His whole body relaxed. He lay with closed eyes, pale and panting for a few moments. Then opening his eyes he said, with a boy's smile:

"Damned baby, eh, Hec?"

The smile broke Hector's calm. His arms went round his brother in a strong grip.

"Captain Jock! Old boy Captain Jock!" he said brokenly. "There was never a soldier like you! I wish I could take your place. You carried me out of hell once. I wish I could take your place."

"I just bet you do. But you are right. I guess we'll just wait orders from Headquarters and carry on," said Jock.

He lay quite still, and in a few minutes, exhausted by his sleepless night and by his recent nervous explosion, he was breathing quietly in sleep. Hector listened to his breathing, not daring to move for some minutes. Then quietly he stole from the room and went to his study resolved to find some plan by which he could have his brother examined by a specialist.

CHAPTER III

In his study Hector stood looking out of his window across the blue waters of the bay, now full of dancing sunlight. He was still shaking from the scene through which he had passed. To have Jock break like that! Jock, Captain Jock, who had fought his way up from the ranks, who had been through it all from Hill 60 to Vimy, with never a shiver, who had won his M.C. and Croix de Guerre and had been decorated by his King! For the first time he realized how terrific must have been the suffering through which his brother had been passing these last six months. Some remedy must be found and immediately.

He sat down at his desk and looked about him. This had been his father's study. On the wall were enlarged and colored photographs of the family, artistically atrocious, but humanly heart-moving. Over the desk on the wall facing him, his father's strong face, softened with masses of red-brown hair, darker than Jock's, and with kind blue eyes. Strength of heart there rather than of intellect. Next his mother, not beautiful in feature—her mouth was too large and with crooked lips. He remembered her crooked humorous smile. But there was a fragile serenity and strength in the face that spoke of inner resources illimitable, and in the dark eyes a mystic fire, eyes like Logie's inherited from Highland seers. She had been both the heart and the mind of the family.

It was a fatal bullet that had reached the heart of her aviator son Alistair, her baby boy, twin brother to Logie. Her heart, too, it had pierced. Three months later she had died, to be followed by her husband within a month.

Two young soldiers, gloriously splendid in Highland kilt

and bonnet, were side by side on the east wall. Captain Jock and himself. Hector could only glance at them. On the west wall the twins, Logie in her special V.A.D. uniform, and Alistair in his smart Royal Air Force uniform. The boy was the image of his father, but of slighter mould and of gayer air. A brilliant wild young medico, he was only seventeen when the War broke out, but he was neither "to haud nor to bind." He wangled an appointment to the Royal Air Force and was away. Six times wounded, decorated with many honors, he had fought through the War till the very last month. A week before the Armistice, leading his Squadron hard on the heels of the retreating enemy, too eager, too daring, he had been trapped in a cloud by a group of desperate enemy aces. These heavy losses, together with a general disgust with the sordidness of materialistic post-War living, had changed his life for him. Hector stood long before the gallant, smiling picture of the young aviator.

"My God, why was all this?" he groaned. "Is there any meaning or purpose? Any guiding, foreseeing vision in this awful mad swirling mass of unregulated humanity?"

He threw up his hands. "God, God, if You are there, help me to find out something of what You mean, or are!"

He sat down, his face in his hands, and so remained for some minutes. Suddenly he lifted his head, his eyes rested on his father's, and then on his mother's face. He drew a long breath.

"Yes, there must be something in it. God is, or nothing is," he said. Now what was to be done about Jock? A specialist should see him. That meant money. He had a few hundred dollars in the bank, saved from his year's salary of $1,800. That would not go far. He could borrow some on a note. He ran over in his mind likely prospects for a loan. All his personal friends were poor. Those who had money had drifted away from him. His congregation too consisted of poor people. From their little farms they were making a bare living. There was only one man among them who might be called well off, James Cameron. Perhaps he would lend him a thousand. He hated asking him. James Cameron was a hard man. He was one of his elders, orthodox, his theology a fantastic mixture of a pagan fatalism which he mistook for Calvinism, and an unctuous emotionalism, which he considered evangelistic fervor. He was shrewd enough to suspect that his religion nauseated his minister, whom he admired for his intellectual ability, his sincerity and his courage. But he was gravely doubtful of his minister's soundness, especially in his attitude toward the Bible. James Cameron was a "cover to cover" Bibliolatrist, a valiant and violent defender of the Faith in the matter of the inspiration of the Book *verbatim et literatim*. With him it was the Book, the whole Book and nothing but the Book. But withal James Cameron was an honest man, hard-working, self-denying and with a kind heart if it could be reached. He had little use for the easy-going, "daddling" habits of the small farmers and fisher folk of the community. He lent them small sums, but he took care to collect his interest from the proceeds of their small output, which he handled for them. Hector frankly did not like his elder. He strove against, prayed against this feeling, but not with complete success. Still, James Cameron was the only man to whom he could apply. He knew what this might involve: "The borrower is servant to the lender." But what could he do? Jock must be considered before all else. He would go to James Cameron after dinner.

Logie had returned from her visit in the meantime. It turned out that Vivien had a badly bruised arm, making it difficult for her to do her work.

"I suppose you swept out the house," said Hector.

"What else could I do, Hector?" Logie's voice was full of reproach.

"And what was her father doing meanwhile? Gave you a screed from Bertrand Russell, doubtless."

"Well, poor old man, it pleases him and doesn't hurt me."

"No, it doesn't hurt you, Logie—no fear. You are too busy doing things for people to bother with his cheap Socialistic atheism."

"But I am sorry for Vivien. She has no one to talk with but her father. And he is quite clever, isn't he?"

"Diabolically. If he would do a little more digging in his garden it might help him."

"Well, I am sorry for him anyway."

"Not by any means as sorry as he is for you—and indeed for all of us."

"Poor Vivien! She has no one to talk to. Why don't the people go in and see her? You might, Hector. You could help her."

"Me? She pities me too profoundly. I am hopelessly antique."

"You are wrong, Hector. She admires you immensely. And she is terribly grateful for what you did for her this morning."

"Pulled her out of the drink. What else could I do, the little idiot?"

"You are too hard, Hector," said Logie, turning away with a grieved face from her brother.

"How is Jock?" she asked anxiously.

"He fell asleep. He was quite done up, poor chap. We must do something, Logie, we must, we must."

It was an old subject with them. There was no use telling Logie his plan. Besides she had her housework to do, and he had his sermons for Sunday. But before sermons there were the chores to attend to. Wood for the fires, water for the cooking and washing. Then, too, there were his boots to clean, which Logie would gladly have taken on, but which Hector had strongly forbidden her to touch. In Logie's mind there was a growing conflict between the duty owed to her brother and the duty owed to her minister. To brush her brother's boots might be beyond the sphere of duty. But the minister's boots? That was different. This would always put Hector in a rage, so Logie stayed her hand at the boots.

Never would Logie acknowledge to herself that she had been a little disappointed when her eldest brother Hector had given up the law, in which he had made a brilliant beginning, and had taken up theology. Often had Hector poured forth his soul to his wise and sympathetic sister.

The War had done something to him. Its first effect was the shattering of all the home ties. Alistair's tragic death was to them all a heavy blow over the heart. His mother's death following so soon, and his father's almost immediately, and now Jock's illness, which he attributed to war effects, had awakened him to the real meaning of war. War, whose main and immediate purpose was to shatter as many homes in the world as possible.

Synchronizing with war was the destruction of so many of humanity's nobler ideals. The finishing touch to his disillusionment was the ghastly exploitation by people in high places of the horrible results of war, both to victors and to vanquished.

His vision of life became that of an army of huntsmen driving a scurrying, terrified mass of furred and feathered things to sure destruction. The whole world was mad after material things. From all this his soul turned in loathing and horror.

"Of course, Hector," had said his wise-hearted little sister, into whose ears he had poured forth all his soul anguish, "you are not seeing things quite sanely."

"Sanely? My God, how can I?"

"Perhaps in a year or two you will see other aspects of life," she suggested.

"That is what I fear. No doubt I shall. That is war's greatest curse, its power to blind the soul's sight and deaden the heart's sensibilities. No! I see clearly now. I shall make my choice now. This at least is a profession which definitely turns from the pursuit of personal advantage."

Logie shook her wise little head.

"I am not so sure that all ministers do."

"All right ministers do—Father did."

"Yes, yes, oh, yes!   Father did.   And so will you, Hector," said his sister, eager conviction in her voice.

Thus Hector had made his choice.   He was now finishing the second year of his ministry in Ravanoke, to which little, remote and poor congregation he had been called after his ordination.

CHAPTER IV

ONCE resolved upon an unpleasant duty, Hector was unhappy till it was done. The money for Jock must be found and James Cameron was the only available source of supply.

"You wouldn't call at the Marriotts' on your way?" Logie suggested timidly.

"Not I."

"I only thought that Vivien—"

"Woman, you fair upset me at times," said Hector, shaking his stick at her.

"Oh, go on with you," said Logie.

Without further word Hector took his way to the village and up the muddy road. The road indeed was well-nigh impassable with the breaking of the frost and the spring rains, but Hector took to the banks alongside.

As he was surmounting the second rise, he observed an automobile making its way down the incline toward him.

"Now, my mannie, you will need to have a care, I doubt," he said and stood watching the car make the descent down the slithery clay road. "Taking it with a rush, eh? You are certainly a stranger in this land. Well, your fate is before you." He waited a few moments. "There! I told you so—"

The huge car came careering down the muddy clay road, reached the bottom of the hill and began to wobble from one side to the other, slowed up, and then, quietly but definitely, settled down into the deep clay ditch and there remained hopelessly bogged.

"Hope you have your nighties with you," said Hector to himself. "What sort of fools are you, anyway? Ah, Americans! And you won't be thinking much of Canada, I war-

rant you. Well, let us hope Hughie Heggie is at home.
Hughie will be delighted to help in getting you out."

Back and forward, twisting and turning, the chauffeur attempted to operate his car. But all in vain. Deeper and
deeper sank the spinning wheels into the red slimy clay. At
length out came the chauffeur in his natty uniform, viewed
the car from various angles and finally in despair turned his
gaze upon the landscape generally. As Hector drew near
he could hear from the car a voice raised in a series of sul-
phurous expletives.

"Good day," said Hector pleasantly, as he came up to the
car. The chauffeur preserved a gloomy silence. Not so the
occupants of the car.

"Say, what the hell kind of a road is this, anyway?" came
a voice at him from the interior.

"Not so good, I fear, especially at this time of the year,"
replied Hector gravely.

"Why the devil don't they warn people at the crossing,
about this road?"

Hector paid no heed. "Let us get a couple of fence rails,
and some rocks," he said to the chauffeur.

Through the muddy ditch they proceeded to the fence, selected a couple of rails, and gathered a heap of stones from
the roadside.

"Now I'll pry this up and you pack in the stones under
that wheel."

The chauffeur obeyed directions and similarly with the
other wheel, making a little causeway.

"Can someone in there take the wheel?"

"I'll take it, Daddy," said a girl's voice.

"You can't do it, Daphne."

"Well, if I can't I'm darned sure *you* can't."

The girl clambered into the chauffeur's seat.

"All right! Say when," she cried, getting the engine
going.

"You pry up the other wheel," directed Hector. "All

ready. Now wait for the word, and take it easy."

"O.K."

"Lift! Now let go."

The powerful engine clutched the machinery with a mighty jolt, and the wheels gripped the stones, jerked the car forward a couple of feet, flung the stones into the ditch, spun violently and slithered back into the mud.

"Say, what sort of a driver are you?" roared the father's voice. "Why didn't you let that power on easy?"

"Say! Come and try it yourself, if you're so smart."

"Shut up! You get out of that! Let me have that wheel."

Once more the causeway was carefully built and the pries set in place.

"All ready?" asked the driver.

"Let her go easy now!" said Hector.

Once more the wheels gripped the causeway, and the car began to climb.

"Let her go," shouted the chauffeur.

An excess of power and the car climbed out of the ditch, mounted to the comb of the road, over the comb.

"Left! Left, Daddy!" shrieked the girl.

In vain. The impetus of the car carried it right over the comb and into the ditch on the other side.

"Why didn't you swing her?" cried the girl.

"Swing her *hell!*" roared her father.

"We will get her next time," said Hector. "The comb gives very little grip. You've got to swing her quickly."

"Swing her quickly," the man echoed. "Say what you want— These damn roads is a lightning conductor."

"We will try it again," said Hector to the chauffeur.

"Damned if I do," said the father. "How far is the next town in this God-forsaken country?"

"The village is about a mile and a half away," said Hector quietly. "But I think we can with care do it next time."

"With care, Daddy," said the girl. "Get that."

"Oh, will you keep your mouth closed!"

"I only want to be helpful," replied the girl sweetly.

"Helpful?" the man glared round at her, but remained speechless for a few moments, then ejaculated, "Well, get at the blasted thing."

"Daddy, the man—the gentleman is trying to help you."

"What? Well—what the—I say I hope you don't mind me—I—"

But Hector and the chauffeur were again building the causeway, this time with more elaboration and care.

Once more the attempt was made.

"Now, Daddy, watch that wheel," warned his daughter.

Again the car made the comb.

"Now! Now, Daddy, swing her!" shrieked the girl wildly. And swing her he did, to such purpose that the car slid off to the right toward the ditch at such an alarming angle that the girl's voice rose again in agony of terror.

"Look out! Look out! We're going over!"

And over they would have been had not Hector and the chauffeur both hurled themselves at the machine and clung for dear life. Once more the car came to rest in the ditch.

"Here! I'm through! Get out! We'll walk to this blasted village."

"Not me!" said his daughter. "It's beginning to rain. I'll get soaked and ruin my new shoes!"

"Get out, I tell you," ordered her father.

"I will not!"

"What do you propose to do?" said her father in a voice of sarcastic calm. "Stay here till this damned country dries up?"

"There's lots to eat in here," said the girl.

"If you don't mind waiting, I think I can get a team, sir," said Hector.

"How long will you be?"

"That, of course, I can't say, but I shall be as quick as possible."

"Oh, thank you, Mr.—" began the girl.

"MacGregor," said Hector, lifting his hat.

"Well, that would be splendid of you, Mr. MacGregor. I hope you don't mind?"

"Oh, not at all," said Hector and set off for Hughie Heggie.

He found Mr. Heggie reposing, pipe in mouth, upon a lounge in the kitchen. Mrs. Heggie was busy with her cooking.

"Good day, Mrs. Heggie. Busy as ever I see. Where's Hughie?"

"Indeed then, where he is most of his time."

"Ah, Hughie's not very well, eh?" said Hector.

"No, he is not well except when the table is set," said Mrs. Heggie. "Can you not rise and speak to the minister?"

"Oh, it is you, Mr. MacGregor? Indeed the rheumatism is sore on me," said Hughie with a groan, struggling to his feet.

"All but his jaws," said his wife.

"Can you come with your team and help an automobile out of the mud?"

"An autymobil? And whatna autymobil is it?"

"What difference will it be what kind it is?" asked his wife indignantly. "Is it not the minister that is wanting your help?"

"Ooh, ay! And where will the autymobil be?"

"Just down the road a bit."

"Ooh, ay! And will they be strangers?"

"Oh, they'll pay you for it, Hughie, if that's what you mean. It is a grand affair."

"Ooh, ay! And—"

"Man alive! Will you not hasten!" exclaimed his wife. "The roads will be drying up on you and you will lose your chance."

Hughie glanced out of the window.

"No likely," he said with a cheery smile, "with yon rain on them."

"Come on, Hughie. We mustn't keep them waiting."

"Ooh, ay! But indeed then, the horses are round the stack down at the other barn."

"And why not the oxen?" said his wife. "The first thing you know someone will be coming along and pulling them out before your nose."

"Ooh, ay! Bless my soul, that's so, that's so." The terrifying suggestion quickened Hughie's movements.

With Hector's assistance he yoked his oxen.

"Bless my soul!" exclaimed Hughie. "The wagon's down back and a load of wood on it."

"Can't wait for that, Hughie. I'm afraid you may lose your salvage. We don't need the wagon. Come along."

"Yonder is the stone-boat," said Hughie doubtfully. "But that wouldna dae, I doot."

"Fine, Hughie—hitch on. Bring your logging chain along, but hurry up."

Nearly an hour had elapsed since Hector had set out for help when the bogged travellers saw him returning.

Hughie and his oxen made a weird picture. Hughie was a small man with a large head, goggle eyes, red hair and beard, and very bandy legs. His tam, set at a rakish angle upon his bushy red hair, gave him the appearance of a man returning from the night before. Grave deliberation marked his every movement. He carried a long elm gad with some of the small branches still attached, so that every stroke of the gad came down with an alarming swish. The oxen were young, rather undersized, gaunt and wild-eyed, and obeyed none too readily the tug of the rope lines round their horns and the guiding touch of the gad.

"Holy Moses and all the prophets!" exclaimed the man at the wheel. "Will you look at what's happening to us!"

Daphne looked out through the window and went off into a shriek.

"Oh, what darling cows! Just look at them, Fritz. And what in the world are they dragging?"

"A stone-boat," said her father. "Used to ride 'em when I was a kid! Used to draw stones with them. Saves lifting—great scheme. But say! What crowbait they are? Those oxen can't draw their own weight."

With difficulty Hughie guided, prodded, led and swished his team past the car and brought them to a stand. Then slowly he came, chain in hand, to the car window.

"Good day, sir," he said.

"Mr. Heggie," said Hector. "Hughie, this is—er—"

"Inman's the name. Russell T. Inman from New York."

Hughie stood silent, allowing his eyes to wander slowly from face to face, then said solemnly:

"You will be wanting a tow?"

"I damn well do."

Hughie glanced hastily at Hector.

"Whisht, man, the minister will be hearing you."

"The minister?"

"Ay. Yonder." Hughie's thumb over his shoulder indicated the minister. "Many's the man hae I extricated frae this verra place."

"Regular trap, eh?" said Mr. Inman grimly.

"Ooh, ay! You may say that," replied Hughie cheerfully. "There was yin last fall. He broke his axle. Ooh, ay, yon was a guid yin." Hughie's voice became gleeful. "I towed him backwards to the blacksmith's. Ay! Yon was a guid yin. There would be the-r-r-ty in that yin."

Hughie proceeded without further words to hitch his chain from the axle to the stone-boat.

"This will be precarious, I'm thinking," he said. "Ay, it will be precarious. There will likely be an upset to it indeed."

"Upset!" exclaimed Daphne. "But, Dad, I'm not going to stand for any upset."

"I should say not," said Mr. Inman with emphasis.

"Look here, Mr.—"

"Heggie," said Hector. "No, Hughie, there must not be any upset."

"It is as well," said Hughie calmly, "to be prepared for eventualities." Hughie had a predilection for long words.

"Look here, Mr.— Dammit, what *is* your name, anyway?"

"Heggie," supplied the minister.

"Look here. I'm not going to have any upset, you make up your mind to that."

Hughie proceeded to unhitch his chain.

"Here, what the devil are you doing?"

"Whisht, man! Yon's the minister," said Hughie.

"Come, come, Hughie," said Hector. "Leave that chain alone. There must not be any upset. And there won't be. The chauffeur and I can hold this side down, and if you are careful we can prevent any upset. Go on, Hughie."

"Very well, sir. I am only warning you. It's as well to prepare for—"

"Go on, Hughie. Get your team going at once," said Hector.

"Just as you say, sir. But I am no accepting any responsibilities," replied Hughie, respectfully but firmly.

He moved toward his team, picked up his rope lines and gad and gave the word.

"Hup there, Buck! Hooish, Bright! Sober now! Haw there, Buck!" He applied the gad circumspectly. The oxen moved forward. Hughie stepped on the stone-boat. "Hup there!"

Slowly the car began to move forward, the minister and chauffeur holding on for dear life to prevent the "eventuality" of an upset. At this moment Mr. Inman gave the engine power. There was a series of loud reverberations. With a snort and a plunge, the oxen hurled themselves upon the yoke, the car leaped free of the ditch, lurched violently —a wild shriek from Daphne—a fresh series of explosions from the engine—up went the tails of the oxen—the car made the comb of the road in safety—and away went the oxen at a mad gallop. In vain Mr. Inman threw on the powerful brakes. The four wheels, though deadlocked, slipped over the slithery clay as if it had been ice.

"Whoa! Buck! Whoa, I'm telling you! Sober now!" But Buck and Bright paid no heed to their master's commands. With heads low and tails high they madly careered down the sloping, slippery road, the stone-boat pitching and sliding, Daphne shrieking at the top of her voice.

With all its mad pitching and sliding, the car, under the steady drag of the chain, held the comb of the road. At ever-quickening pace the oxen went careering down the greasy slope, never slackening speed till checked in the ascent of the next rise, where at length they came to a halt.

"Whoa then, ye devils!" cried Hughie, and rushing forward he took a turn of the rope around Buck's nose. "Now I have ye," he cried and brought the ox round with a savage jerk.

"Ooh, ay!" said Hughie gravely. "It was yin o' the eventualities."

"Oh, damn your eventualities!"

"Whisht man! The minister is comin' yonder," said Hughie in a shocked voice.

"The minister!" shouted Mr. Inman. "What the hell—"

"Whisht now! Man, your language is most reprehensible! And you on the verge o' eternity!" said Hughie in a shocked voice.

Hector and the chauffeur came up breathless, the former choking with suppressed laughter, the latter with the face of a graven image.

"It was yon engine!" Hughie explained apologetically to the minister. "The beasties are no accustomed to siccan a commotion. Aweel, we will jist be going."

"Hold on!" said Mr. Inman, who had recovered his nerve. "Can't you control those devils of yours at all?"

"Ooh, ay, I hae them noo, if ye can control yon engine,"

said Hughie calmly. "We will be going on."

Mr. Inman glanced at the minister doubtfully.

"I think everything will be all right now, Mr. Inman," said Hector with a glance at the girl's face.

"Daddy, you had better let Steve handle the wheel. Besides, it is raining again." Her eyes were twinkling mischievously.

Without further word Mr. Inman stepped into the car leaving the wheel to the chauffeur.

"Hup! Now, Buck! Sober now, beasties!" Again Hughie stepped aboard the stone-boat, and the procession advanced, the minister acting as rear guard. Without further incident the cavalcade reached the manse gate and there halted.

Hector stepped to the window.

"What are your plans, Mr. Inman, may I ask?"

"Plans?" said Mr. Inman, who had regained his equanimity. "Is there a hotel in this—this—village? The fact is, we have come here for the fishing. By the way, this is—what is the name, Doctor? Ravanoke?"

"Yes, sir, this is Ravanoke," said Hector. "There is a tavern of sorts, but I'm afraid I can't guarantee the accommodation."

"We have our tents with us, and our provisions, as a matter of fact, but in the rain—"

"This is my manse, Mr. Inman. We live very simply, but we have abundance of room. I shall be glad if you will stay with us till the rain is over, at least."

"But we can't pile in on you like this, Mr.—"

"Mr. MacGregor, it is awfully sweet of you," said the girl. "Me, I can't see myself camping out in this rain, so if it won't be too much trouble—"

"Not at all. We shall be glad to give you such as we have to offer. At least you will be protected from the rain," said Hector.

"Well, then, thank you, we will go in—for a while any-

way," said Mr. Inman. "Of course, I'll make it all right
with you."

"Let us go then," said Hector.

"All right," said Mr. Inman, stepping from the car.
"Here, Mr.—er—"

"Heggie," said Hector.

"Heggie. What's your charge?"

Hughie scratched his head under his tam, glanced hastily
at the minister and said, "Weel, the gentleman last fall made
it the-r-r-ty. Of course, there was a broken axle—and the
drag—"

"Tut, tut, Hughie!" said the minister sharply.

"Aweel, I will jist leave it to yersel'. However, it was a
precarious—"

"Hurry up, Dad," said Miss Daphne impatiently.

"Here's twenty-five," said Mr. Inman.

"Hughie!" Hector's voice was stern.

"That will be a wee bit too much, sir," said Hughie, "although it might hae been—"

"Here you are. It was indeed 'precarious,' as you say,"
said Mr. Inman with a slight smile. "And darned if I don't
think we are well out of it."

"Aweel, if you insist, sir," said Hughie, pulling off his tam
and making a most profound bow. "Of course, it was—"

"Come away in," said Hector.

"Mr. MacGregor, this is my friend Dr. Wolfe," said Miss
Daphne, stepping from the car.

"Glad to meet you, sir!" said the doctor. "Awfully good
of you to take us in."

"Not at all," said Hector, leading the way into the manse.
"Hughie, help Steve in with the luggage. The car can go
into the stable."

"Yes, sir," said Hughie, bowing with all reverence to the
minister. "I will see aboot everything. It was indeed a—"

"Here, get a move on!" said the chauffeur sharply. "Open
that stable door."

CHAPTER V

"This is a real imposition, Miss MacGregor," said Mr. Inman as Hector introduced the party to his sister.

"Why, no," said Logie, a bright smile irradiating her dark, lovely face. "People always come to the Manse in trouble."

"Well, we were certainly in trouble this afternoon when your brother came along, and he helped us out most efficiently."

"With Mr. Heggie's assistance," murmured Dr. Wolfe.

"And don't forget the beasties, Fritz!" laughed Miss Daphne. "Never while I inhale the breath of life shall I forget them."

"Oh, Hughie helped? Isn't he priceless? We are very fond of Hughie," said Logie.

"But how far off is this fishing, Mr. MacGregor?" enquired the doctor. "I have heard it is the most wonderful lake and river in Nova Scotia."

"Oh, and who told you that?"

"Well, as a matter of fact it was one of my young nurses about a year or so ago. A Miss Marriott."

"Miss Marriott!" cried Logie. "Oh, you were her chief. She is my best friend."

"She lives here? She is at home now?" the doctor's voice was eager.

"Yes. I saw her to-day. Indeed she had an—"

"Yes," said Hector, rather abruptly breaking into the conversation. "She lives just across the village. You can see her house from here."

"Splendid! I must see her!" The doctor's interest was unmistakable.

"Here, what's all this?" exclaimed Daphne. "Do I see

32

the apex of a triangle? Look here, young man, we came afishing up here. I want you all to know that this attractive young man is at present my fiancé."

Miss Daphne's face was smiling but in her voice and her bright eyes there was the ring and flash of steel.

"You will like Miss Marriott, my dear. A very charming, very bright and modern—oh, quite modern young lady," said the doctor.

"Well, let's get on. I'm dead!" was Miss Daphne's only reply to this.

They were all still standing in the hall.

"Won't you take off your things and wait till the rain is over?" said Logie.

Reluctantly Miss Daphne laid off her motor coat, glancing round the bare and cheerless hall with a bored air.

"Come into the living-room. I'll get a fire going. It is quite chilly, isn't it?" Logie was humbly apologetic for her country and its climate.

She went out into the woodshed and began to pick up some kindling wood. Here Steve, loaded with baggage, found her.

"Let me do that for you," he said. "I know all about fires. Besides, it's my job. I do anything and everything except wash babies."

"Oh, no. I don't like your lighting my fire."

"Quite all right, if you don't think it butting in—"

"Not a bit, but—"

"All right then," said Steve, and in ten minutes he had a blazing fire going in the big living-room grate.

"Perhaps you can wash your hands here," said Logie, setting basin and towel on the sink table.

"Thank you. I hope you will let me help you with the tea. For instance, cake." He opened a large hamper, took out a cake-box and produced a fruit cake.

"But we shouldn't use that cake," protested Logie.

"Why not? It's for them." With quick clever fingers he

cut and set the cake in order in the cake basket which Logie brought out.

"What lovely old Wedgwood!" he said, handling with reverence Logie's hundred-year-old china.

"Yes, isn't it? My great-grandmother brought that from Edinburgh to Halifax. I love it."

"Please let me serve," he said, setting the teacups upon a tray. "I am used to this."

"But really—do you mind?"

"I don't mind anything—for the right sort of people."

"And they're the right sort?" Logie could have bitten out her tongue.

"You are," said Steve almost brusquely.

Miss Daphne acclaimed the tea with a scream of delight.

"Oh, Logie—may I call you Logie? It's a lovely name. And this tea is the next best thing to a Manhattan."

"We can't give you a Manhattan, but—"

"Much better for her, Miss Logie," said Dr. Wolfe. "There's altogether too much Manhattan going round with these young people."

Daphne made a face.

"Now he's aboard," she said. "He'll pull the throttle in a minute. That's his job. Nerve specialist."

"Nerve specialist!" exclaimed Logie, with a quick look at Hector.

"Oh, he's a top-notcher—best in New York! They all run into the corner and watch him when he comes into a room. You needn't make faces at me, Fritz. He hates to have me toot his sax. He's one of those modest people—strong, silent stuff, you know."

The doctor ignored her and busied himself with the serving.

"Say, now, this is solid comfort—eh, Doctor?" said Mr. Inman, stretching out his legs toward the fire. "You know, that rain was chilly."

"I didn't notice you were chilled at all, Dad," said his

daughter, grinning impudently at him.

"Well, now, I guess I did get slightly heated. You know, nothing gets my goat like anything going wrong with my car, Mr. MacGregor. I've got a good car, the best there is, and when I start I like to keep going. I must apologize to you for my temper and language. The truth is, when I get mad I seem to kind of let go."

"Let go? Well, I should say so!" exclaimed his daughter. "Almost everything except the wheel. And it would have been better if you had let that go, too."

"Well, perhaps so, though I didn't notice much improvement in our gait when *you* had hold! Isn't that a great fire, though? Pine knots, eh? Used to burn those back in Michigan."

"Oh, Michigan?" said Hector, making conversation.

"Yes, sir. Born in Michigan, worked in the lumber woods —drove oxen too. Say, that man this afternoon—what's his name?"

"Heggie, Dad," said his daughter. "Heggie, Heggie! Shall I ever forget his red hair and bow legs!"

"Well, he made me think of the ox-teams I drove in Michigan. Yes, sir, that's where I began. Lumber, then railroading, then stocks."

"Stocks? You mean stock-broking?" asked Hector.

"Stock-broking? No, my brokers do that. I do the promoting."

"They seem to be running rather wild just now. I know nothing about stocks, but I understand a lot of poor chaps will lose money."

"Serve 'em right, too. No business going into a thing they can't finish."

"I'm afraid I don't know much about it. I confess I have always had the notion that there was a certain amount of fraud in connection with the buying and selling of stocks," said Hector.

"And you are right on the green, Mr. MacGregor," said

Miss Daphne.

"Like everything else, stock-broking is what you make it," said Mr. Inman. "There's fraud in stocks just as in doctoring or anything else," and thereby precipitated a lively three-cornered tilt between the doctor, Mr. Inman and Miss Daphne, to which Hector listened with great interest.

"Am I right, then, in saying," he asked as the discussion appeared to die down, "that one can play the game quite according to the rules and still rob a man of his money?"

"Rob? No," said Mr. Inman.

"Take a man's money without a *quid pro quo?* Yes," said the doctor.

"Play a sucker? I should *say* so!" said Miss Daphne emphatically.

"Could I rightly put it this way?" asked Hector, a deeper note coming into his voice. "Eliminating the word 'rob,' which is a legal term, could a man without losing caste on the Stock Exchange break the Second Commandment?"

A silence fell upon the company. Then Miss Daphne in a low voice enquired of Logie, "The Second Commandment? What's that?"

"Well, I guess we don't bring that in exactly, Mr. MacGregor," said her father. "But the rain seems to be over. What about a fish or two, Doctor?"

"I'm game. Two miles, eh?"

"About two."

"In the car?" asked Miss Daphne.

"No, I'm afraid not," said Hector.

"Count me out then. I'll stay with you, Logie, if you will keep me," said the girl. "This suits me."

"Why, certainly," said Logie, a sincere hospitality in her voice. "Hector, would you take a look at Jock? Our brother upstairs has been quite ill for some months," she explained to the doctor quietly. "Some nerve trouble, the doctor says."

"Nerve trouble?" cried Miss Daphne. "Why, Fritz, this

is your show."

The doctor looked annoyed. "Is he improving?" he asked quietly.

"We are afraid not," said Logie, her eyes full of pain. "Indeed, we— I'll run up, Hector, for a minute." She hurried from the room.

"Yes, my brother has been under the weather for a long time," Hector explained. "We don't seem to know just what the cause is. As a matter of fact—" He paused abruptly. He would not be guilty of a breach of the laws of hospitality by asking aid from this stranger now a guest in his home.

"Mr. MacGregor, if your physician agrees, I should be delighted to consult with him," said the doctor, with the quiet courtesy characteristic of his profession.

Hector hesitated.

"Well, it hardly seems right to take advantage of you—"

"My dear fellow, let's not stand on ceremony. The patient is always the first consideration. I might have a look at him anyway."

Logie came running down.

"Hector, he wants you. He is rather—"

"Let me go up with you," said the doctor. "No, don't ask him. Just a moment. My bag, please. Where is Steve?"

"I'll get him," said Logie, and ran out into the kitchen. "The doctor's bag," she said with trembling eagerness. "It's for my brother, my sick brother."

Without a word Steve vanished and returned almost immediately with the doctor's bag.

"Miss Logie, you can trust the doctor. He is a great nerve specialist."

"Oh, thank you, thank you. I'm so glad you told me. He looks kind."

"He is a good doctor, none better."

She took the bag and ran back into the hall, stood watching the two men go up the stairs, then turned back into the kitchen. She could not face the others.

Steve placed a chair for her in front of the blazing kitchen stove. "You need not worry, Miss Logie. The doctor will find out what is wrong and will tell you just what should be done."

His voice was quiet, kind and with the well-bred intonation of a gentleman.

She put her face in her hands and waited, praying. Steve brewed a fresh cup of tea and took it to her.

"Take this, Miss MacGregor," he said.

Without a word she took the tea and drank it. He was a strange chauffeur. She glanced into his face. Thin, hard, almost cruel, she had thought it, with cold grey eyes. But now, she wondered. The face was kind, the eyes soft and pitiful.

"Oh, thank you! How good you are!" she said.

To Logie people were not classified by their work or social standing. They were just people. She took them at their real value. Her dearest friends in the War had been among the "other ranks"—orderlies, drivers, and such.

"No. You need not worry about the doctor. He is a good doctor, and awfully keen on his job."

"Sit down, won't you, please?" said Logie.

"Thank you," he said, "I must go and look after some things."

He slipped out into the stable. It seemed hours to Logie while she waited there alone. What would the report be? How wonderful that this doctor should have come to them! It was God who had sent him. Secondary causes were nothing to Logie's simple faith. God had always been very real to her, as to her father and mother. She was not unfamiliar with the jargon of modern science. During her war service she had listened by the hour to the chatter of nurses and doctors, and the smart and cheap cynicism of young officers. But all that had flowed over her as water over rocks. God was friendly and strong, so why worry? A tap came to the door. The doctor in hat and coat was at the door.

"You are to take me to Dr. McQueen," he said.

"How is he?" she said, standing before him with tightly clasped hands. "Have you found out?"

"Yes, I know what is wrong." How sure he was! "He is very seriously ill. He must have suffered terribly."

A rush of tears came into the dark eyes. "Oh, he has! He has!" she said. "And he's been so brave!"

"But I hope—yes, I do hope we can do something for him," Dr. Wolfe said slowly.

She put out her hands to him.

"Oh, Doctor, thank God for you!" she cried, sinking into her chair and breaking into wild weeping. The terrible load of anxiety and uncertainty was suddenly lifted. Here was someone that knew.

"Now I must get the history from Dr. McQueen, and you are to go with me." The doctor's voice was calm and matter of fact.

"Oh, yes, yes! I am foolish." She sprang up, wiped her eyes. "What a silly fool I am! Forgive me! But we have all been so very anxious." Her tears were flowing again.

"You must have suffered agonies. But—shall we go?" The quiet, efficient, authoritative voice steadied her. She ran into the hall, and in a few moments returned ready.

"But your friends, and your fishing?" she said.

"My friends are mighty lucky to be as comfortable as they are. And as for fishing—" He waved his hand. "We will go."

The interview with Dr. McQueen revealed nothing new but confirmed Dr. Wolfe in his diagnosis. There was a slow-growing tumor on the brain of the patient which would necessitate an operation, and at the earliest possible moment.

"And is it a dangerous operation?" enquired Logie with paling face.

"It is a serious operation, undoubtedly, but one that is being done and with satisfactory results."

"And will he be as well as ever again?"

"There is no reason, if the operation is successful, why your brother should not be as good a man as ever he was."

"And would you do it?"

"No, I am not a surgeon. But my friend Dr. Whitney of Boston has been very successful in this particular operation."

Logie was treading air. Jock would be well again. Dr. Wolfe, glancing at her face, was amazed at its beauty. He had thought it a quiet, not to say dull, face. But the face of this girl, walking with springing step, was vivid with the loveliness that overflows from a pure and radiant spirit.

Their way led past a little cottage set back from the street and in the midst of appletrees. It would be lovely in spring.

"May I just run in and speak to my dearest friend? I want to tell her of Jock. I promise I shall only be a minute."

"Don't hurry. I shall sit on the rock and look at the sea," he said. "Look how wonderful!"

She let her eyes rest on the blue water twinkling now in the sun, for the rain had ceased. "Yes, wonderful!" she said, a deep light in her eyes. "Like the face of one you love. Now, since you love it too, I am going to take more than a minute."

"Take as long as you like. Only," he pointed to some rain clouds, "you don't want to get wet."

"Pooh!" she said and ran off to the house.

"What a lovely, sweet girl she is," he said to himself, looking up at the trees. "Like an apple-blossom, lovely and fragrant too." A dark shadow settled upon his face as he watched the sea, and remained there till she came out from the door. Down the gravel walk she danced, dragging her friend with her. "I insisted that she should come and see our doctor, who has done so much for us all. Miss Mary Murray, Dr. Wolfe. The very best woman in the world."

"A large order, is it not?" said Miss Mary, giving her hand. "But I am thrilled with the news about our dear Captain Jock. Of course you can't understand. But Captain Jock we all adore." She was tall, handsome, finely made, dark-haired, dark-eyed and with a face of noble serenity.

"A woman to trust," the doctor said to himself.

"We shall all be so grateful to you," said Miss Mary. "You can't understand what it will mean to this village and this country to have Captain Jock well and with us again."

"You owe it to Miss Logie here and her brother. They treated a lot of trippers as if we were friends."

"But they always do. It is the tradition of the house. The MacGregors have never failed in the custom of truly great and good people."

"I am quite sure of that, Miss Murray," said the doctor earnestly.

"You must not call her 'Miss Murray.' She is 'Miss Mary' to all her friends. And she is coming up to-night and bringing her music, unless Jock can't bear it. Sometimes he can't, poor dear."

"He will have a good night," said the doctor, bowing his farewell to Miss Mary.

"But you will be going up to your fishing perhaps. I heard Hector planning that Hughie should come and take you up."

"With the stone-boat?"

A peal of laughter burst from her lips. She glanced hastily about. "Do you know, I haven't laughed for six months like that! Oh, I can't tell you how different everything is now that Jock is to be better." She seemed almost to be dancing on her toes.

"You poor child! What a crime."

"How about the fishing?" she continued. "Hughie has a

team of horses and a light wagon."

"We won't mind the fishing just now, I think. I want to watch my patient to-night."

She looked at him with adoring eyes. He had made her world a new world, this marvellous doctor.

CHAPTER VI

"MR. MacGregor, it looks as if you can't get rid of us. This rain looks like an all-night business."

"But we don't want to get rid of you. Besides, the doctor has placed us already in your debt beyond what we can ever repay," said Hector.

"Yes, indeed," said Logie. "Far, far, beyond what we can ever repay. Besides we have plenty of room in this house. You see we were a large family before the War. We can easily put you up, and we feel as if we had friends visiting us."

Mr. Inman's hard eyes softened as they rested upon the girl's face.

"Well, you certainly are real folks. And since you put it that way we will just camp right here for the night."

"And then, Mr. Inman, the doctor is good enough to say he is going to observe his patient during the night. Oh, you are *so* good!" said Logie, a rush of emotion throbbing in her voice as she offered the doctor both her hands.

"My dear young lady, this is a matter of professional interest and duty, and I couldn't possibly leave my patient to-night."

"Yes, that's Fritz all over. He is more doctor than anything else," said Miss Daphne, making a face. "He forgets everything and everybody, even me, when he gets interested in someone with nerves."

"Well, we will try to do what we can to keep you from being too bored. I have asked a friend in. Are you fond of music, Mr. Inman?"

"Is he?" exclaimed Miss Daphne. "He's crazy about it, especially music with whiskers. He hates jazz and the high-

43

brow line. But give him sob stuff, the 'old home' songs and a handkerchief, and Dad's happy for the night."

"Well, we will do our best to let him have both," said Logie with a gay laugh. "Miss Mary is quite wonderful with both the old and the new."

"Dr. Wolfe is a great music-lover, too," said Miss Daphne.

"Oh, splendid!" said Logie. "Now I hope you feel at home. Hector's library is upstairs. He can furnish you with the latest things in philosophy, psychology, theology and science. My books you will find in that bookcase in this room, from detective and murder stories to sociology and economics. So I'll just leave you now." And Logie went after the very important, and to her rather appalling, business of planning and preparing the evening meal.

In a few minutes Hector joined her, sorely perturbed.

"Now, Logie, don't let them fuss you. Boil some eggs and—and that sort of thing."

"Pooh! Dinna fash yourself, laddie. Run away and keep them going in talk. Show them your coins. Go now and keep that girl out of here."

"No fear of her. But can't I help?" Hector was quite anxious for the good name of the family.

"Now, Hector, do run away, please," said Logie, pushing him bodily out of the kitchen, and donning her work apron.

In came Steve from the stable.

"I understand we are here for the night, Miss Mac-Gregor," he said. "Will you let me help? We have quite a variety of meats, soups, and sweets. Let me show you our stock."

"Oh, but, Steve—"

But already Steve was unpacking his hamper. "Perhaps you would allow me to suggest." And he proceeded to sketch his idea of an evening meal. "Very simple, and quite good enough."

"Why, it is splendid, Steve. But should we take your stores that way? I can make a pan of hot biscuits in no time."

"Quite unnecessary, Miss MacGregor. But if you prefer to do so I can take care of the rest."

Making no fuss, asking no questions, but going at his work with swift efficiency, Steve with Logie's help prepared a sumptuous meal of soup, meat, a cheese omelette, with hot biscuits, cake and coffee.

"Indeed it is more elaborate than is necessary, Miss Mac-Gregor. And if you will allow me I should like to take charge of the serving from the kitchen. You will be needed at the table."

"Steve, you are a wonder! A perfect treasure! I was a little disturbed, I confess, but you have just taken the whole load off my shoulders."

"Glad to do it, Miss MacGregor. And I shall attend to the washing up afterward. Please. It's my job."

The tea was a marvellous success. The guests were ravenously hungry, the dishes were beautifully cooked and served with smooth precision. Hector was filled with amazement, Logie with delight.

"What else are you besides chauffeur, cook and butler?" she asked Steve, when she had got her guests safely into the living-room again.

"I've knocked about a bit and have kept my eyes open. If you would just keep the door shut and allow no one to come in here I shall soon put this straight."

"I hate to do that, Steve. I want to get you your supper."

"No, Miss MacGregor. I could not allow that," he said with an air of calm finality that made it impossible for her to do anything but obey.

"You will have your guests to attend to. That will be quite enough responsibility for you this evening. And I would suggest serving some lemonade and cake a little later. I suppose you would not care for cocktails?"

"Cocktails! We never have them."

"Pardon me. I judged you would not, but lemonade will

be quite simple."

"But, Steve, I can't have you doing all this. We are going to have some music. Miss Mary is really a remarkable player, and—don't you like music?"

"Some music, yes. I shall hear it quite well, if I may open the door slightly."

"Why not come in, Steve? We are all friends here."

"Friends? I am Mr. Inman's chauffeur, butler, valet and a few other things." His manner was cold, almost repellent.

"But not mine, Steve," said Logie with quiet dignity. "Only friends come into this house."

"I did not mean to be rude, Miss MacGregor. But I shall be much happier here, where I belong."

"Very well, Steve, but I do thank you for your help tonight. It would have been a little difficult without you. You have really helped me amazingly."

"Thank you, Miss MacGregor," he said quietly, beginning to busy himself with the dishes.

The company sat about the fire replete with food and purring with content. Miss Mary, with her fine air of calm serenity, took command. It was she who, without seeming to do so, placed and kept Logie in the foreground of the picture.

At the first touch of her fingers on the piano the doctor came to her side.

"What a lovely tone?"

"It is really a very lovely piano. This is one of Logie's war trophies."

"What do you mean, war trophies?" asked Daphne, who had followed the doctor to the piano.

"It is quite a story, a beautiful story indeed. This piano is a gift of Logie's devotees at Étaples, the great hospital camp in the north of France, you know. Patients, orderlies, doctors, Tommies. It began at Étaples, but her train extended from Ypres to Albert. Hundreds of the boys begged to be allowed to share in this gift."

"What did she do? What was she? A nurse?" asked the doctor.

"No, no," said Logie hastily. "Nothing at all. Just amused the poor dears. They were so grateful."

"That's all," said Miss Mary. "Amused them, sang to them, danced for them, told them stories, organized things, made them forget their broken bodies and bruised hearts and jangling nerves—that's all. But hundreds, thousands of them begged to have a share in Logie Mac's music box. A very great musician in London chose it, the War Office saw about the transport to France and afterwards home. No wonder it has a lovely tone. It carries the heart throbs of thousands of soldier boys back from the front, and going home or going up again."

Logie put her hand on Miss Mary's arm.

"Miss Mary, that will do," she said softly.

"What did she sing? Jazz?" asked Daphne.

"What didn't she sing? Everything from 'The Long, Long Trail' to 'Keep the Home Fires Burning,' from Harry Lauder to Wagner, from 'They Didn't Believe Me' to 'The Land o' the Leal' and the Hebridean lilts." As Miss Mary talked, her fingers were wandering over the keys in a medley of the old war songs.

Logie's eyes were shining, her dark oval face was suffused with the soft glow of tender memory.

Miss Mary's fingers came at last to the lovely old Song of the North, "Land o' Heart's Desire."

"The boys all loved this one. She had it from Mrs. Kennedy Fraser herself. Sing it, Logie."

And without hesitation Logie sang. Sang with the artless simplicity of the mavis. It was not a great voice, but it had the rare heart-moving power that great artists always have, that gift of the gods that no art can bestow.

"And this one," said Miss Mary. "Different, but the very loveliest of old English songs." And from her fingers there flowed the limpid, exquisite melody, "My Mother Bids Me Bind My Hair." She nodded at Logie, who once more without protest or apology sang.

With face filled with amazed wonder the doctor stood gazing at the singer.

"My God!" he said in a low voice, when the song was finished. "Lucky devils! I don't wonder they gave you this piano."

"Hello, Steve! What's the matter with you?" cried Daphne with a laugh. "Seen a ghost?"

They all turned and saw at the kitchen door set ajar the face of the chauffeur, pale and rigid, his hard grey eyes fixed upon the singer's face.

Softly the door closed.

A quick flush came to Logie's dark face. "I declare I quite forgot Steve. It's a shame! I have left all the work to him."

"Well, why not?" said Daphne. "Now let's have something lively!"

"Miss Logie," said her father, "I don't know what you're singing, but the doctor's right. I know now how that piano got here all right, just where it belongs."

With a gay laugh Miss Mary went off into a rollicking bit of the newest jazz.

"Sacrilege, eh?" she said to the doctor.

"Damned right," he muttered, and turning away took a seat by the fire with Hector.

Under Miss Mary's skillful manipulation the music went lightly on, now a bit of jazz, now a popular march, now one of Mendelssohn's "Songs Without Words."

"You sing, Miss Daphne?"

"Oh, I croak a bit."

"What would you like to sing? Perhaps I can play for you?"

"Oh, the doctor plays my accompaniments."

"Good heavens, Daphne, we haven't practised for ages,"

said the doctor hurriedly.

"Oh, that's nothing. You don't need any practice. What about 'Climbing Moonbeams' or 'Blue Eyes and Red Gold Hair'?"

"Can't remember a note," protested the doctor. "Miss Logie, may I run up and take a look at my patient?"

"Certainly come. He seems quite quiet. He says he is enjoying the music."

"Say, Miss Murray, your music suits you, and it suits me too," said Mr. Inman. "Seems like real music, not like the terrible stuff we get at the shows."

"Oh, Dad, go on! You know you just love peppy music. Hot stuff, and the hotter the better."

"Well, that's so. It is kind of exciting noise. But somehow this seems more like music. I mean—you know—makes me think of the stars and running water in the Michigan woods in the spring."

Miss Daphne gave a shout. "Dad, you're sure getting goofy! Stars and running water! Good Lord!"

"Well, I'm no hound on music, but I know what I like."

"Something like this, Mr. Inman," said Miss Mary, slipping into the first movement of "The Moonlight Sonata."

"Oh, that's all right," said Daphne, flinging herself into a chair beside Hector. "But look here, don't *you* like something a little hotter than that?"

"But this now is really something special, you know," said Hector, laying his hand on her arm. "Listen to that movement. Lovely, eh?"

"Oh, of course, I suppose so, but—"

"Daphne, keep quiet, I want to hear this," said her father in such a tone that his daughter subsided into gloom, her restless eyes upon the door.

When the doctor and Logie came down from their visit to the patient they found Miss Mary dashing off jazz with Miss Daphne singing at intervals in a somewhat thin and nasal tone, but with the utmost enthusiasm. Immediately she pulled the doctor over to the piano, planted him down upon the bench beside Miss Mary.

"Go to it," she insisted, and the doctor, with a grin at Logie, "went to it" with brilliant improvisations in truly movie style.

"Isn't he a bird?" cried Miss Daphne.

"Splendid! Wonderful!" cried Logie, with genuine enthusiasm.

The jazz demonstration continued till the door from the kitchen opened and Steve appeared with a tray of refreshments.

"Oh, boy!" cried Daphne. "Here you are! Cocktails an' everything."

She helped herself to a glass, tasted it and made a face.

"What's the matter, Steve? What sort of stuff do you call this? Have you no cocktails?" she cried in disgust.

"No, Miss Daphne. I am serving no cocktails to-night," Steve replied quietly.

"I am afraid we haven't the makings in the house, Miss Daphne," said Hector. "We never have any."

"And quite right too, my girl," said her father. "I'd hate to see cocktails in this house." Something in his tone checked the outburst which was evidently upon the girl's lips.

"Me, too," said the doctor. "Cocktails and 'The Moonlight Sonata' don't mix somehow."

"Have you seen these Hebridean things?" Miss Mary asked the doctor. "Probably not. They are really quite new."

The doctor turned over the leaves of Mrs. Kennedy Fraser's latest publication and began playing.

"Extraordinary good stuff. How weird! Do you sing them?"

"Does she?" cried Logie. "Come along, Miss Mary. Let me play for her, Doctor. They have a rhythm all their own. You know how these were got? No? Wonderfully interesting. Mrs. Kennedy Fraser spent years in the north of Scotland and in the Hebrides, taking down these songs from the lips of the old folk and getting the Gaelic words to them. Then she composed the accompaniments. They are unique."

"Never heard of them. You will think me a barbarian. But I come from New York, you see."

Miss Daphne soon grew weary of "that slow stuff" and dragged the doctor away from the piano and demanded the program for the next day.

"I had an idea we came up to this country to fish?"

"It is still early in the season," said Hector, "but you can get fish up at the Lake. It is about two miles off, inaccessible for a day or two by car, but I have arranged with Hughie Heggie to take you up."

"On the stone-boat?" cried Daphne. "Not me!"

"He has a light wagon and horses of sorts, but entirely safe. There is a little cabin which will give shelter in case of rain, a stove, table and bedsteads. I can't guarantee comfort, I'm afraid."

"We can get comfort at home," said the doctor. "Give me a chance at the fish."

When the discussion had ended, Miss Daphne with a wide yawn declared for bed.

"Come on, Fritz, and see what sort of a day we're going to have to-morrow," she said.

"I must be off," said Miss Mary. "I think the rain is over. Why cannot the doctor and you see me safely home?"

"Well! You ladies have given us a great evening," said Mr. Inman, shaking hands with Miss Mary. "That Moonlight thing was marvellous, and those songs. We must have them all again, eh?"

"Now," said Mr. Inman when the others had gone. "I want to talk to you about your brother. I have a plan to submit to you. The doctor says that the sooner he is in the hands of Dr. Whitney the better. My plan is that you take my car. Steve will drive you to Boston. The train would be a little quicker, but you would have the night on the train and the changes from car to train and from train to hospital, and all that. The doctor can make him quite comfortable in the car. After you strike the highway the going will be very smooth, and Steve will take him right to the door of the hospital."

For some moments the brother and sister looked at each other in silence, then Hector, in a voice deep with emotion, said:

"But, Mr. Inman, we could not allow you to do this for perfect strangers."

"Perfect strangers!" exclaimed Mr. Inman. "I thought Miss Logie here called us something else a little while ago. She said something about 'friends.' Didn't she mean that?"

"I did. Oh, Mr. Inman, I did, I did," cried the girl, her dark eyes bright with tears, "but—still—you know—"

"There's no 'buts' between friends. So the thing is settled. The doctor agrees—I asked him."

Again there was silence. Then Logie came to him, offering her hand.

"Dear Mr. Inman, Hector is a dumb man at times like this, but from all of us let me say we are very—oh! so very thankful! I wish I could tell you how thankful. But I really can't—" Her voice broke suddenly.

"Pshaw!" exclaimed Mr. Inman, wiping his own eyes. "Why talk about it? Now that that part is settled, I want to ask you—if a friend might—what about the expenses connected with this operation?"

"Oh, I think we can arrange that all right, Mr. Inman," said Hector hurriedly. "I'm afraid I don't know what they will amount to. But we can arrange—er—some way."

"All right. That's fine. I was talking to the doctor about that too. Ordinarily the cost of hospital—you might have to keep him there for some weeks—and the doctors' fees, and travelling, and so on, would mount up."

"Did the doctor suggest a possible sum?" asked Hector.

"Two thousand."

Hector's face showed his dismay.

"Of course if he went into the public ward it would be a great deal less. You get attendance of doctor and nurses free, you see."

"Jock would not stand for a private ward, Hector," said Logie. "Besides, it would be better than what he had at Albert, and you at Étaples."

"No, Jock would prefer the public ward," said Hector. "Of course, for the first day after the operation a private ward would be better."

"Of course," said Logie.

The discussion was continued with the doctor after the women had retired for the night. The doctor, of course, could give no definite assurance that his friend Dr. Whitney's fee would be purely nominal. Ordinarily the charge would be very much higher than that suggested by Mr. Inman.

"If it were my friend Mr. Inman, now, the fee would probably be anything up to $10,000. These specialists lay the burdens upon the backs that can bear them."

"Don't public ward patients get free treatment?" said Mr. Inman.

"Not often free operations from the top-notchers. You see, their time is fully taken up. The operation would be handed over to a smaller man."

"Do you mind telling me, Mr. MacGregor, man to man, just how much you can put up?"

"Well, to be quite frank, Mr. Inman, five hundred dollars is all I have in the world. My salary is eighteen hundred."

"Good Lord! A man of your ability?" Mr. Inman was indignant.

"But," continued Hector, "I believe I can raise a thousand dollars. I must, that's all—and I can."

Mr. Inman glanced at Hector's set face.

"Darned if I don't think you can! Say, if you ever want to change your job you come to me."

"I'll remember that, Mr. Inman," said Hector quietly.

"And let me lend you a thousand or so. Pay me when and how you can."

"Mr. Inman, you have already laid me under a debt of gratitude. But I cannot do that," said Hector with quiet dignity.

Once more Mr. Inman's eyes searched the strong set face.

"Huh!" he grunted. "Well, let it rest just now."

"Let me show you to your room," said Hector. "Six o'clock comes early in the morning."

CHAPTER VII

WHEN Logie came down to the kitchen next morning she found breakfast ready, the house tidy from all signs of last night's party, and Steve outside gazing seaward.

"Why, Steve, you are a perfect wonder."

"Lovely view, Miss Logie," he said, waving his hand toward the blue water over which banks of white cloud, shot through with rose and saffron, hung low swathing the tops of the encircling hills.

"Yes, a lovely view!" said Logie, standing beside him. "I have seen it a thousand times and never twice the same. Do you know the sea?"

"Yes, I know the sea. It is always new. Like a living face." He turned and faced her suddenly. "You had a bad night. The Captain is not so well?"

"No. He had a bad night—he was quite ill. But how did you know?"

"Your brother told me. He is coming up with Heggie. Miss Logie, it will be a very simple thing to drive to Boston. The car can make fifty miles with the greatest ease, sixty when the road is clear, and the Captain will never feel it."

"You think so? You know?"

"Yes, I know. I have driven an ambulance. I know how to handle a wounded man."

"Steve, you are wonderful! Where did you—?"

"I used to take them down from the front. Sanctuary Wood and Valley Cottages—and that was a bad spot—and Contalmaison—that was worse—"

"Back to Albert—I know—and Courcelette," said Logie. "You saw them come in?"

"I drove them sometimes. From Albert to Contay—in

55

the big push in 'sixteen.'"

"Drove them?" The hard grey eyes flashed upon her. "In 'sixteen! Some driving, eh?"

His face suddenly changed.

"I think you will find everything quite right, miss," he said, touching his hat as Miss Logie's guests came to the door.

"Hello, Logie! My! That is a good smell!" cried Daphne. "And I could eat tin cans."

"Oh, good morning, all of you. Come along, breakfast is waiting. It's Steve's doing, not mine. And here is Hector and your baggage man. Good morning, Mr. Heggie. How will the roads be this morning?"

Mr. Heggie pulled off his tam. "Aw, no sae bad in spots," said he cheerfully.

"Oh, come in, or I shall die," cried Daphne impatiently. "I only hope there is lots of grub. Yum, yum—that coffee!"

"Haven't felt like this for years," said Mr. Inman. "Not since I was a lumber-jack."

"It is this wonderful air," said the doctor. "I'd like to build a sanitarium on that hill."

"Not me!" said Mr. Inman with emphasis. "I want it just like that. Great Jupiter! What a picture!"

"Oh, come in, folks! I'm dying!" called Daphne from the dining-room window.

The whole company seemed suddenly to be in a like condition and hurried in to breakfast.

Porridge, eggs, smoked haddock, toast, and coffee constituted the menu.

"Oatmeal! I never eat it at home, but I'm going to begin with it or I'll never get full," said Daphne. "But, Logie, what sort of porridge is this anyway? It isn't like what we get in New York. Oh, boy! Have you any more? Say, Dad, why can't they give us oatmeal like this?"

"It's the sauce," said her father.

"Sauce?"

"Yes, hunger sauce. Beats even Oscar's all to bits."

It was a glorious breakfast.

"You are a wonderful cook, Miss Logie," said Mr. Inman.

"Not me. You must thank Steve. He had everything ready for me when I came down."

"Steve's a peach," said Daphne.

The breakfast was more or less of a rush meal. The fishermen were eager to be off.

"I should like to have a look at my patient, Miss Logie," said the doctor.

"He had rather a bad night, an attack of nausea."

"Ah! nausea?" The doctor's tone was grave.

It was quite half an hour before the doctor and Logie rejoined the others. He found Hector ready to accompany the party to the fishing.

"You are coming with us? That's fine."

"I want to get you settled, to show you the best pools and that sort of thing."

"I am riding with Mr. Heggie," said Daphne, climbing up into the spring seat beside the driver. "What about you, Fritz?"

"Walk."

"Me, too," said Hector.

"Well, daughter, I think I'll go with you," said Mr. Inman.

Steve sat upon the blankets in the rear end of the wagon.

"This whole town's asleep still. When do they get up?" asked Daphne.

"Asleep? My dear Miss Daphne, do you think our people would so forget their manners as to stare openly at their neighbours' private ongoings?" said Hector.

"Not openly," said Logie, "but if you could look behind those muslin curtains!"

"Hup there, Prince! Go on with you," said Hughie, and the party was away.

"I only wish you were coming with us too, Logie," said

the doctor.

"We will see you when you come back," said the girl, a smile struggling with the trouble in her face.

"Damn shame!" said the doctor as they set out on their journey. "She is a brick."

A tightening of his lips was Hector's only response as he walked on in silence, turning at the winding of the road to wave to his sister.

"He had a bad night, Doctor," he said in a troubled voice.

"Yes, I don't like his appearance to-day, and that nausea is a bad symptom. We must get him away immediately."

"I am taking steps to-day."

"I wish you would let Inman help you," the doctor ventured.

"No, I could not do that," replied Hector sharply, his head going back a little.

"Well, you know your own business, but—"

"Jock would not like it, nor any of us."

Hector's tone put an end to further discussion.

Their road wound up through wooded hills by a series of gentle ascents from bench to bench, crossing at intervals a little river that came singing and chattering to meet them. Already the birds were busy with their love-making. Black squirrels and red frisked up and down the trees with noisy clamor.

"It is fairly easy to believe that God's in His Heaven in this environment," said the doctor.

"Yes, I find it easier here."

"Easier?" The doctor glanced at the strong set face beside him. "For you?"

"Did you see the War?"

"No, couldn't get away. But—"

"In that hell Browning's optimism was not so easy."

"Nor in New York. Nor anywhere in my life," said the doctor. "There's a lot of hell about."

Hector halted. "Yes, a lot. *That* helps a bit, though."

He pointed up through the trees.

The doctor's eyes followed his stick. "What?"

"That bit of blue. The long view. That keeps us going. But let's not think too much to-day."

In silence they walked for some minutes.

"I'm sorry, Doctor," said Hector. "I have no right to shadow this lovely walk with my affairs. Six years ago the MacGregor Manse was the jolliest spot on earth. Six of us full of work and life and fun. To-day—three of us, and— as you see."

"We'll get your brother right again, MacGregor. But we must not delay."

"I won't. I shall make arrangements to-day." There was a note of desperate resolve in Hector's voice.

"Ha! See that!" A splash from a pool, in which the little river had paused in its rush toward the sea, had caught his ear. "You might remember this spot. It is quite a famous pool. 'The Salmon's Leap.' A little early for them yet. You stand on that rock. See? And cast across the pool. Look out for that log jam. They always make for that."

"Delightful spot. I'll remember."

In due time they reached the fishing ground. The little lake lay a gem of sapphire in a dark green setting of spruce and pine; a half-mile wide by some two miles in length it stretched, wooded to the water's edge and surrounded with low hills, a very haven of rest and beauty.

Hector took some minutes to point out the best casting spot, and then with Hughie and Steve went to work. There was the cabin to clear out, the roof and floor to patch up, balsam for the bunks to get, the old boat to make watertight with gum and pitch, the fireplace to rebuild, wood to get. By the time the sun stood half-way to the zenith Daphne had tired of her luckless sport and had thrown aside her rod in disgust.

"I don't believe there's a single fish in this beastly lake.

Not one. The only suckers are the ones on the shore."

"Well!" said Hector, who was putting the finishing touches to the old boat, "perhaps they don't know that you are here. They haven't had a look at you yet."

She glanced at him sharply.

"They don't like my style, I guess."

"Oh, I can't believe that," said Hector. "Shall we try the boat?" With the help of Steve and Hughie he slid the boat into the water.

"We will try that point over there. Perhaps we may have better luck with the troll. It is a most unsportsmanlike thing to do. But desperate situations call for desperate measures. Now I shall row, and you let the line out slowly."

They had not moved more than twenty yards from shore when Daphne sprang to her feet with a piercing shriek.

"Sit down!" said Hector sharply.

She paid no attention, but continued shrieking. "Oh— oh—oh, I've got him! I've got him! What'll I do?"

Hector reached forward, caught her ankle and gave her a sharp jerk. "Sit down! Do you hear me? Sit down at once."

"Here! You stop that! Let go my ankle!"

"Sit down!" His voice was sharp and stern. She at once subsided into the stern seat with a wrathful face.

"But I have something on my line!" She began rolling it up.

"Heavens and earth, it's a fish!" she yelled. "It's a fish, I tell you! Oh! He's coming in right here!" She made again to spring from her seat.

Hector's hand closed upon her arm with a vicious grip.

"Sit down, you little idiot!" he ordered, pushing her back with a thump into the seat. "Stay there or I'll throw you into the lake!"

"Darn you—you almost broke my arm!"

Hector paid no attention but continued rolling up his line till he had his fish, a good-sized trout, at the gunwale.

"Oh! Don't let him touch me!" shrieked Daphne.

Hector with a quick lift deposited the fish in the bottom of the boat, where it began flopping about in a lively manner.

"Don't move!" he said sharply, once more gripping her ankle. "Sit just where you are or I'll put this fish right into your lap."

In speechless rage and fear the girl remained on her seat while he released the hook and tossed his fish into the bow. Then he turned his attention to the girl.

"Have you ever caught a fish before?"

"Never!" she snapped.

"Ever seen one caught?"

"Never in my life!"

Without a word he picked up his oars and headed for the shore.

"What are you going to do now?" she asked.

"What I ought to do is take you on shore and spank you."

"Sp— Oh, you beastly brute!" she sputtered.

"Were you ever in a boat before?" he asked.

"You go to hell!" she said. "I won't speak another word to you."

He stopped rowing, dropped his oars, looked at her steadily a few moments. Then his face broke into smile.

"Listen to me!" he said quietly.

"I won't! I won't! I won't!"

"You know every year scores of people get drowned by doing just what you did. What's worse, they drown other people. The one law of a boat is never stand up. Never move, no matter what happens. I never suspected that you were so ignorant of boats. I ought to have asked you. It was my fault. I apologize."

Swiftly the red flamed in her face.

"Oh, don't be an idiot!" she said. "I ought to be spanked all right. You can do it right here now."

"You deserve it, but—well, a boat is a poor place for

spanking." His smile drove the last remnant of wrath from her.

"You are a darling," she said impulsively. "I'd love to kiss you right now. Still, a boat is no place—I've never tried it in a boat—" She made as if to rise from her seat.

"Sit down!" he said, terror in his tone.

Her voice rang out in a gay laugh.

"Ha! Afraid!" she cried in triumph.

"What are you going to do now?" he asked.

"I'd like to catch another of those darned fish."

"Word of honour, you won't move?"

"Do fish ever bite?" she inquired anxiously.

"Often—but only hooks."

"You're a devil, aren't you? Go on!"

"You won't move?"

"I won't move—not even if he jumps down my throat!"

Once more he dropped the troll into the water, handed her the line and turned the boat toward the open water. Within a dozen strokes she announced quietly, "I think—yes, I know—I have one."

"Pull him in."

Hand over hand she pulled her line. Twenty feet from the boat the fish leaped clear of the water.

"Jove! It's a whale!" he cried.

"A what?" she returned anxiously, but steadily pulling on her line.

"A whopper!"

"Oh! all right!"

Nearer and nearer came the fish, leaping, flipping, splashing. Steadily she pulled till he was within a few feet of the boat.

"What shall I do?" she asked. Her face was pale and set, her eyes wide and staring.

"Let me land him!" said Hector.

"Don't you dare touch him!" she said.

"Then bring him right close up, and lift him clear into

the boat. We ought to have a net. My fault."

Without a moment's hesitation she hauled the fish bang against the side of the boat, then with a mighty heave lifted him clear into the boat, doubtless a much surprised fish.

"Great Cæsar's ghost! A salmon! A ten-pounder!" cried Hector, throwing himself on the fish and holding it down till he had stunned it with his club. "Oh, he is a splendid fellow—and so are you!" He stretched out his hand and gripped hers. "I take it all back! You are a perfect brick. By Jove, I didn't think it was in you."

"You don't want to—to spank me now?" she asked breathlessly, in a low soft voice.

"No, by Jove, I'd like to hug you!" he exclaimed with enthusiasm.

"But—in a boat—?"

"Well—perhaps—in a boat . . . You see— By the way, can you swim?"

"Not very well, but—you can. Of course—there's the fish."

"Ah, yes—there's the fish," said Hector regretfully.

There was no more fishing. Daphne was too eager to show her catch. Besides, she declared, she was dying of hunger. The others were waiting on the landing for them.

"Well, what was all the row about?" asked Mr. Inman. "What did you catch? Must have been a whale at least."

"Hector said it was," said Daphne demurely, as she was handed out by the doctor.

"Jumping Jemima Jane! What is it?" cried her father, lifting the salmon from the boat. "Wait till I get my scales." He dashed off to the cabin and came back with the scales. "Six—eight—eight pounds and a half. Eight and a half pounds. Well, I'm— Well, well, well! Good girl! Didn't think it was in you."

"Nor I," said the doctor, a look of admiring surprise in his face. "Did she land it herself?"

"She certainly did—wouldn't let me touch it. Oh, she's a

fisherman. Wait till she gets one on a rod," said Hector in warm admiration.

"Will you show me, Hector?" she asked quietly.

"Glad to! I should love to see you do it."

The girl made no reply but went and sat on a rock near by and there remained, her chin cupped in her hand, a new look on her face as her eye wandered toward the minister.

"Now I must be off," said Hector. "I have business to attend to."

"When are you coming back?" said Daphne, springing to her feet and glancing up at him through veiling eyelashes.

"That I cannot say," he replied, turning to Mr. Inman to point out again the best fishing points. "The evening will be better for the rods. Of course you can always use the troll. But there is no sport in that, of course. It's the hungry man's resort. But if you do go out in the boat"—he turned to Daphne again—"you will be careful."

"I'll nail myself to the seat," she said. "Word of honour. Not if they climb into the boat at me."

"Well, good luck."

"Can't you run up to-night?" said the doctor. "I shall want to know your plans, you know."

"Yes, yes, I will come up to-night," replied Hector. "We must do something at once."

"Right," said the doctor. "Good luck."

As Hector strode off Daphne suddenly sprang to her feet. "I'll go a bit of the way with you," she said.

"I'm afraid—I mean I'm rather a fast walker."

"So am I when I want to—come on—"

"Daphne, you will only keep Mr. MacGregor back," said the doctor.

"Let Mr. MacGregor speak for himself," said the girl with a lift of her chin.

"You can come to the first turn," he said with a little smile. "Good luck, all!"

"Why not take Heggie with you? Save you the walk,"

said the doctor, observing Heggie with Mr. Inman manœu-vring about his team behind the shack. "By the way," he continued, "I shall give you some tablets for the Captain in case the nausea should return." Hector walked with him toward the cabin.

Meantime Mr. Heggie was busying himself with his harness when Mr. Inman appeared with a flask and cup in his hand.

"Here you are, Heggie!" said Mr. Inman.

"Whisht, man!" said Mr. Heggie, with a mysterious gesture, moving with quite unwonted speed to the rear of the cabin.

"He's a teetotaller!" he said with a jerk of his head toward the minister, "a awfu' teetotaller."

"What? Who?" said Mr. Inman, gazing about.

"Whisht, man! Be canny!" Hidden from observation Mr. Heggie waited, a pleased, expectant look lighting up his countenance.

"Ay, he is a noble man, and a mighty preacher, but a wee bit circumscribed in his principles."

He took the mug in his hands and while Mr. Inman began to pour allowed his gaze to wander off toward his horses. "They beasts now, they are— Hut tut, Mr. Inman, ye are unduly liberal—na, na—nae mair!"

He lifted the cup to his nostrils and inhaled deeply.

A glow of seraphic peace settled upon his face.

"This will no be frae New York," he said with a shake of his head. He took a careful sip.

"Ay! There is nae prohibeetion aboot this, I doot."

"Prohibition! Not a smell. I got this at Halifax."

"Halifax?" said Mr. Heggie, again sampling. "I cud hae telt ye that. It is a sad restraint yon."

"Restraint? Oh, prohibition? Well, not so that you'd notice it," said Mr. Inman cheerfully.

"A terrible infringement on a man's liberty," continued Mr. Heggie. "Noo, *I*'m for moderation in a' things." He put the cup to his lips and slowly drained to the last drop.

"I dunna haud wi' drunkenness an' coorse leevin'," said Mr. Heggie, waving the empty cup, "but in moderation. Ay, it's a sair deprivation," continued Mr. Heggie, shaking his head sadly. "Man, yon's a fine blend. That'll no be Glenorchy? Na!"

Mr. Inman glanced at the label. "G-l-e-n-l-i-v-e-t!" he spelled.

"Dods! Of course! I should ha' kent it. But it's awhile—ay, awhile since—na, na!—nae mair, Mr. Inman, I'm a moderate man. Aweel, since ye are sae kind, Mr. Inman," said Mr. Heggie, turning his back upon him. "Hoots, man! What are ye daen'? That's borderin'—ay, it's borderin'—and I'm a moderate, ye micht say an absteemious man, Mr. Inman. Ma Goad! Now he comes!" With two gulps he emptied the cup and threw it behind a bush.

"Pit it awa', man—oot o' sight," he whispered fiercely. "Ay," he continued in a loud voice, "I'll be coming up the morn's morn in case ye'll be needin' me tae row yer boat for ye. Ay, I ken a' the hidie-holes o' them. Well, guid day, sir."

Mr. Heggie proceeded with deliberate pace toward his team, mounted his wagon and with a bare glance at the minister drove off, singing cheerily, "It's a wee deoch an' dorris." At a safe distance he turned and called to the minister: "Ye'll na be comin' wi' me, sir?"

"No, Hughie. I'm walking. You're a bit slow for me."

"Ay! I'm a wee bit slow for ye," said Mr. Heggie with a chuckle. "It's as ye say! A wee bit slow! Ay! Just a wee thocht! He ha!" The sudden and quite unusual explosion of laughter galvanized the minister into swift activity. He turned upon Mr. Inman.

"Have you been giving anything to Heggie?" he demanded.

"Well, a bit of a snort," said Mr. Inman with a grin.

"Any money?"

"Only a five."

"Enough for him to get a glorious drunk on."

And without further word the minister set off on a run after the disappearing wagon, on whose spring seat sat Mr. Heggie, waving his whip over the back of his team in an effort to quicken their pace, while from the woods there floated back the refrain:

"If ye can say it's a braw bricht munelicht nicht,
Ye're a' richt, ye ken."

"Say, what the devil is he after, anyway?" wailed Daphne.

"The devil, I guess," said Mr. Inman with a wide grin on his face.

CHAPTER VIII

"And where's the twenty-five you got yesterday?" sternly asked the minister. They were at the manse gate.

" 'Deed an' ye can ask her that."

"Well, I will keep this five for you meanwhile. And now you are to go straight home."

"An' wi' this breath on me?" inquired Hughie aghast.

The minister realized the gravity of the predicament. "Well, then, you will come in to dinner with me and likely Logie will have onions."

To this, but most unwillingly, Hughie agreed. He had planned a quite different and more hectic afternoon, but an evil fortune in the pastoral supervision of his minister had intervened and he must just make the best of it.

After dinner Hector spent some time in dressing himself in his ministerial garb, and in screwing up his courage to the necessary tension for his interview with Mr. James Cameron. In this latter operation he was taking counsel with his sister in whose courage and wisdom he had come to confide. A quiet soul she had, sweet, kindly, patient, but with a quality of steel in it. There was, moreover, in her moral make-up, uncompromising and invulnerable, the element of conscience. The heavens might fall, but Logie would quietly, gently, sweetly but unswervingly pursue the path of right going.

"I hate the business, Logie. James Cameron is a stony-hearted old hypocrite.

"Not hypocrite, Hector—more Pharisee, perhaps."

"Well, Pharisee then. He is so sure of himself. If I could only get him drunk or something . . ."

"Now that would be much harder than getting money out

68

of him. But he is kind too. I am sure he is awfully good to his old mother."

"But to no one else in his family," Logie returned. "Look at Willie George. Almost my age, and scared to call his soul his own."

"I know, a wobbly weakling—but who made him so?"

"If you can only make him see the necessity? And that his money will be sure. Can't you sign a note or something? There's your coin collection—and—and there's my piano. It is worth—"

The brother flared up fiercely. "Your piano? I'll see him in blazes first!"

"But he may be quite nice to you, Hector. Don't be too quick. Give him time. And don't be too proud. You know you *are* proud. And don't hurry him. And when he says 'No' wait a bit. Don't just turn on your heel. You know he is really fond of you and he admires you immensely."

"He thinks I'm a heretic. Nearly as bad as old Marriott himself."

"Well, aren't you?" said Logie with a little laugh.

"Poor old Marriott," said her brother. "It is people like 'Jimmie Hannah' that make heretics."

"Don't let him hear you calling him 'Jimmie Hannah.' They say nothing enrages him like that. He is a modernist in that regard—he can't bear the custom of calling men after their mothers that way: Jimmie Hannah, Johnnie Kate, and Bella Johnnie Big Duncan, and so on."

"Oh, I shall be most respectful."

"But not too respectful. He can stand a little jollying. Man-of-the-world stuff, you know. 'Hello, Mr. Cameron! How is the world treating you?' and that sort of thing."

"Oh, I shall jolly him along. I wish you were doing it."

"Now you are jollying me. But you know what I mean, Hector."

Her brother could hardly bear to look at her anxious face.

"I know I must get the money, and I shall get it too,"

he said. "Well, I am away. I need your prayers, I guess."

"You will have them, dear. I will be sayin': 'O Lord, make him patient, but not too patient; make him cheery and friendly, but not so familiar as to lose his dignity.' The Lord will have some difficulty in knowing what He ought to do to answer my prayers!"

The minister found Jimmie Hannah—which is to say James, son of Hannah Cameron—in a none too favourable mood for his purpose. He was in his grand new barn, all fine and clean. But upon his soul lay heavy the thought of payments made or to be made. Furthermore, he had just finished his annual computation of the outlay necessary for his spring operations in machinery, wages and fertilizer and the like. This procedure always exasperated him, and convinced him that he was headed toward financial ruin. He greeted his minister with gloomy respect.

"Good day, Mr. MacGregor. I hope I see you well."

"Fine and fit," said the minister in a cheery voice, remembering his sister's advice.

"And how is all your care?"

The opening seemed propitious and without further preparation the minister plunged.

"Not so well, Mr. Cameron. In fact we have just had serious news," and he proceeded to give a detailed report of the condition of Captain Jock as diagnosed by Dr. Wolfe.

Mr. Cameron listened with sympathetic interest.

"And he says there must be an operation forthwith. And —a wonderful piece of luck—his friend Mr. Inman has kindly offered his car and chauffeur to drive him right away to Boston."

"To Boston? Man, that is fortunate. It will save the expense."

"Yes, and we shall need to save. The expense of hospital, doctors and all will be very heavy."

"How much?" inquired Mr. Cameron.

"It is hard to say. Perhaps fifteen hundred dollars, and

it might run to two thousand. And that, Mr. Cameron, is what brings me here to-day. I am here to ask your help."

"My help! Indeed—"

"I only want a loan from you." Hector forgot all his finesse. He saw his Elder's face grow harder and harder every moment. He went at his plea in a passion of abandonment. He described his brother's suffering, the utter hopelessness of recovery without operation. It was operation or a terrible death. The present opportunity seemed too good to be lost, indeed it seemed providential. He could put up five hundred dollars himself, he would pay any interest desired. He could repay at the rate of nine hundred a year. His sister and he could live on half his salary, there were only the two of them, but he needed—he must have two thousand dollars; not all of it at once, but the pledge of it at once. He came to Mr. Cameron as a friend, and as his minister.

Mr. Cameron caught at the phrase. "My minister? That is just the difficulty. I do not believe in business transactions between a minister and the members of his congregation."

"But why not, Mr. Cameron? To whom else could I better come than to one of my own session?"

"No, it is a principle with me." Mr. Cameron was mildly reproachful. "The relation between a minister and his people, and especially his session, is a sacred relation, a spiritual relation."

"But does this relation preclude the exercise of Christian charity?"

"Charity? Are you asking charity of me, Mr. Mac-Gregor? I understood—"

"You know, Mr. Cameron, I use the word in a Pauline sense, not in the debased sense in which you have used it now. I am putting this on a business basis. I am asking you for a loan. I will give you my note at any interest you ask. It is not a gift, it is a business proposition."

"A business proposition?" Mr. Cameron's voice grew cold as chilled steel. "A purely business proposition? Well then, what security can you offer?"

"Security?" The minister's eyes flashed fire. "Security, sir? I give you the security of my word."

"We are talking of a business proposition, Mr. MacGregor. For your honesty it is ample, Mr. MacGregor. For your ability it is nothing. Honest men die."

"Against dying, Mr. Cameron, I can give you no security."

"Exactly. You cannot make a business proposition. That is why I object upon principle to any business transaction between a minister and a member of his congregation. No, no! That relation is upon a spiritual basis and should be preserved as such."

"Mr. Cameron, your argument is sound. I cannot give you security. But I am a healthy man." The minister, remembering his sister's injunction, was patient.

"Healthy men get killed."

"I see you do not want to lend me the money," said Hector, flinging all patience to the winds. "The proposition is withdrawn. Let us say no more about it. But you have spoken about the relation between minister and congregation. I am your minister. You have disappointed me. Believe me, I cherish no ill feeling—but I want to leave with you a message from God. I have a vision of you—of your soul." The minister's eyes were flaming fires, his hand was lifted high. "A poor and shrivelled thing from which all the tender compassions of God have disappeared. I solemnly warn you to repent and turn to God, if haply He may forgive you ere it be too late."

The minister's voice rang out in solemn denunciation. The man before him, with the blood of God-fearing, minister-reverencing ancestors in his veins, could not shake off the sense of fear, of awe from his soul.

"Good day, sir! And God be merciful to you."

The minister turned and left him.

"Wait a minute, Mr. MacGregor. Wait a minute. Perhaps I—I—might—"

"No, Mr. Cameron. I can have no business dealings with you. I cannot wait with you—but God will wait with you. How long I cannot say. May He have mercy upon your soul!" The minister turned and with head high, looking very stiff and tall, strode from the barn and down the lane.

He had intended making some pastoral calls in the neighbourhood, but he was in no mind for pastoral calls. Nor could he face his sister in this mood. And besides, he must think. So he took the road over the hills, and with him his problem. Somehow he must raise two thousand dollars or at least fifteen hundred. No other man had enough money to spare the amount. A hundred dollars here, and a hundred there he might borrow. No! He would not peddle his misery from door to door. There was Mr. Inman's offer. But to take the money from a stranger—that, he could not, he would not do. But if there were no other source of help he might be forced to swallow his pride.

He made up his mind that he would consult with Mr. Inman.

By making a detour of about three miles and taking a cross road he could come upon the fishing camp on his way home. He resolved to do so. They were pleasant people, the doctor evidently a man of education and some culture. The Inmans had lots of money, but nothing else—neither education nor breeding. The father was a good-hearted chap apparently, with some instincts for finer things, but the girl was a sophisticated modern of the most impossible type. How the doctor could stand her he could not imagine. And yet there might be something in her. He remembered the fishing incident. She certainly had nerve. And besides, there had been for a moment a gleam of soul. And she had disturbing eyes, soft, but with a glint of the devil in them. Well, that was her own concern and the doctor's. He had no interest in her, no responsibility for her soul.

Yet the warm shy welcome in those eyes when he walked in upon the camp at supper hour made him not so sure. The girl in her present rôle of *ingénue* possessed a certain charm that awakened interest, if not a sense of responsibility in him.

"Come and try our fish. Steve has done wonders with it," cried Daphne, running to meet him.

"Not Steve, I guess, altogether," he said. "I can contribute some of that sauce your father was speaking about."

"No, it is in the fish, Hector—our fish. Come and see."

The supper began on a hilarious note, but somehow it ended almost in a minor key, the cause of which lay in Hector's face. For his valiant efforts at mirth were like upthrusts of flame from a wet fire: they quickly died down into deeper gloom.

Hector was waiting for the inevitable question which would elicit the confession of his failure.

"Well," he said, postponing the dreaded moment. "The first thing in every well-ordered camp is getting ready for night. 'Picking up, laying down,' so that if a bear comes along you will know exactly where the things are that you want and that the bear does not."

"A gun," said Mr. Inman.

"No, no—not in our woods. Boots and matches! Boots to run away in, and matches to show the bear where not to go."

"Wouldn't you shoot him?" inquired Daphne.

"Never. He is not cross; he is just curious. He is hungry, but he is not after you—he is after anything sweet."

"Ha! Ha!" came from the doctor in an explosive burst.

"Never mind him, Hector. I know just what you mean," said Daphne. "Fritz is very smart now and then."

"I was about to add 'not already appropriated,'" said

Hector gravely.

"Nice little short-arm Fritz," said the girl, with a grin at the doctor. "Besides, you can't always be too certain of that 'appropriated' stuff, you know."

When the men were settled pipe in mouth about the fire the doctor abruptly broke the silence.

"When do you expect to get away? Pardon me, but time is an extremely important element in this matter." No need to ask what he meant.

"God help me—I cannot say!" Hector said, leaning forward and gazing with desperate eyes into the fire.

"Look here!" said Inman. "I've got a proposition. Don't reject it without careful thought. I was all set to launch a move in International Oil in two weeks. Give me your five hundred dollars. I'll start the thing to-morrow morning at nine. You'll get your two thousand—well, say within a few months sure, probably within a few weeks. No! Don't refuse till you understand. This is straight, on my word of honour. As straight as buying and selling."

"I confess I am prejudiced against all stock market operations. I have only the vaguest reasons, but—"

"Now, boy, listen to me. Just give me twenty minutes and if I can't make clear where the crookedness in stocks begins then I'll quit."

It took more than twenty minutes for Mr. Inman, speaking in simple terms as to a child, to make clear to the minister how necessary were the stock market operations to all the great industrial enterprises of America and of the world; how without the stock market, the great railways and telegraph systems, the mighty steel, coal, and packing industries would have been impossible. He frankly acknowledged that the stock market lent itself to crooked, ruthless and destructive financing. But he pledged his word of honour that in this enterprise there should be nothing that the Presbyterian General Assembly wouldn't approve.

"If ever there arises an occasion for some quick turning

I'll let you know in time. The stock will go at the very least to one hundred and fifty dollars—it is at fifty now."

"I don't want that. Tell me, will it be absolutely sure value at par, say?"

Mr. Inman curbed a smile as he glanced at the doctor. This man's ideas of stock manipulation were infantile.

"You bet! Why, my dear fellow, we don't get busy till it gets above par. No, no, you are as safe as if you were dealing in—in—"

"Fish!" said Daphne.

"Yes, fish. And listen! Any time you want to get out I'll take your entire holdings. That's my solemn promise before witnesses."

For some minutes the minister sat gazing into the coals. Then rising to his feet he offered Mr. Inman his hand.

"Mr. Inman," he said with solemn deliberation, "I am not sure that I know just what I am doing, but I am trusting in you. I will give you my five hundred dollars to-morrow morning."

"Steve! Here!" Mr. Inman's voice was like the crack of a whip.

"Yes, sir," said Steve, coming from the other side of the fire.

"You will take a wire for me down to that telegraph office. By the way, will your office be open? Yes? All right. And see that it is sent right away."

"Yes, sir," said Steve. "Do I understand the car starts for Boston to-morrow, sir?"

"Yes," said the doctor.

"At what hour?"

"Let me see. There will be certain preparations necessary—say at one."

"Very good, sir," said Steve.

"I shall put down a few things for you to get," said the doctor, going to the cabin.

"All right. I must send one or two wires," said Mr. Inman, following the others into the cabin.

"Good night, Miss Daphne," said the minister. His face was overcast with doubt.

The girl seized his hand in an impulsive grip.

"Oh, I am so glad! Now everything will be all right."

"All right? I don't know. But anyway I am going through with it."

She slipped her hand through his arm. "Oh, pshaw! Don't be a silly boy. They are doing it every day, the very best people. Why, lots of ministers do it—our own minister, Dr. Humphrey, gets Dad to do this sort of thing often."

"Dr. Humphrey?"

"Sure thing! Oh, I am glad!" she gave his arm a quick squeeze. "Your face to-night almost broke my heart. I could have just bawled right out if it hadn't been for the rest of them."

Hector turned his eyes upon the upturned face. Her eyes were like stars in the firelight. He was conscious of a queer thrill at his heart.

"Oh! I want you to be happy!" she said in a quick soft whisper. "I can't bear to look at your face when it is sad."

"What—? I mean—thank you ever so much. You are very kind. You are all very kind." The minister stammered in his confusion.

"Kind? Oh, hell!"

His face grew grave.

"Forgive me! I am a bad girl. A bad girl," she said hastily, still holding his arm in a tight grip.

"Good-bye," he said. Then, in a lower tone, "No, you are not a bad girl. That is impossible."

The doctor came out from the cabin.

"Good night then!" she said, giving him her hand. "And the best of luck for Captain Jock and for all of you."

"Thank you," he said quietly, and went off with the doctor down the trail into the dark woods.

The group at the fire stood watching them till the shadows swallowed them up.

"What a child he is," said Mr. Inman.

"Child? Child? My God, Dad!" She turned hastily toward the fire and, shivering, cried: "For heaven's sake stir up this fire."

"But, Daphne, it's not cold to-night. Are you cold?"

"Cold? I'm chilled! Chilled to the—the heart," she said, with a shiver, stretching out her hands to the blaze.

CHAPTER IX

THE spring bell on the door of the little shop, which was also the telegraph office for Ravanoke, disturbed Miss Mary Bella MacRae at the exciting moment when the cool and fascinating sleuth was about to lay his deadly hand upon the equally cool and fascinating villain in the "Mystery Murder of Malvern Manor." Miss Mary Bella finished the paragraph and appeared, yawning.

"Good evening. Sorry to wake you up. Will you please get these off as quickly as convenient?"

The young man pushed two somewhat crumpled sheets of paper across the counter. Miss Mary Bella preferred wires written on forms provided by the Company. They were more convenient for filing, and also for reference. With disapproval in her languid movements she proceeded to decipher the messages.

" 'Moran, Ellis, and—H-u-s . . .' This is some writing. 'H-u-r- . . .' "

"No, no, little one. *Hirsch—H-i-r-s-c-h.* Get it?"

Miss Mary Bella ignored the flippancy. " 'Moran, Ellis and Hirsch, Wall St., New York. Assign Hector Mac-Gregor—' Say, is that our minister?"

The young man shoved up his cuff. "Look here, sweetheart, it is near my bedtime. I'll come round and sit up with you any time you say, but not to-night."

"You sure ought to be abed about now."

"Now, now! Late hours are spoiling your temper, though not your good looks, my dear."

"Some people are mighty smart. This is awful writing. Left school too soon, I guess. 'Assign Hector MacGregor.' That *is* our minister. An awfully fine man, a little solemn and holy perhaps."

The young man leaned over the counter and touched her arm. "About this message? Would you mind?"

Miss Mary Bella drew her arm away haughtily.

"'Assign Hector MacGregor ten International Oil.' International Oil—say, what's that?"

"Removes warts, corns, and lipstick. I always insist on my customers—"

With a toss of her bobbed hair Miss Mary Bella proceeded.

"'Assign Hector MacGregor ten International Oil at fifty stop ten margin on my account stop pyramid till par stop wire me situation before twelve to-morrow.' We-ell, whatever does it mean?"

"Never mind now, honey. You'll get it to-morrow morning. Here's another."

"Say, he's real polite too," murmured Mary Bella.

"'News Editor, *New York Financial Review*, Wall St., New York.' This is better. 'We understand recent developments in Oklahoma oil fields reflected in International Oil—' M-m, what's this? G-u-a—?"

"No, no, sweetheart, you've missed a step. That's not a g. It's a q. Q for quinine. See?"

"Not for 'cutie,' eh? Q-u-o-t—quotations."

"Right on the green."

"Signed, T. K."

"No, no, my dear. T. R. I. 'Try,' see?"

"Ain't he real bright now?"

"Here's another." The young man drew a pad toward him and wrote rapidly.

"Say, you sling a dandy quill. He ought to make you secretary."

Rogers, Barker & Co., Wall St., New York. Buy fifty International Oil at fifty stop ten margin stop Pyramid till further orders.

Drew.

"Drew, eh? That's your name?"

"Yes, dear, my own—not my first, though. It's my father's name too. Also my mother's after marriage—you understand?"

"Ain't he the smartest thing?"

"Listen. Get these wires right. They are important. I'd hate to see you lose your job. Better read 'em out."

His tone sobered Mary Bella instantly. She read the wires aloud.

"Correct. Get them right off." He threw a five-dollar bill on the counter. "Keep the change, honey, till I see you again."

Mary Bella flushed a little as she opened her cash drawer.

"Excuse me, Mr. Drew, here is your change," she said with quiet dignity.

The young man removed his cap. "My mistake—awfully sorry. Pray forgive me." His tone was both earnest and respectful.

Mary Bella flushed a deeper red.

"It is quite all right, Mr. Drew," she said with a brilliant smile that gave her tired face a distinct touch of beauty. "I guess it was my own fault."

"Not a bit. All mine—too fresh."

"But I really don't understand what they are all about," said Mary Bella, her curiosity once more getting the upper hand. "Oh," a light dawning on her face, "it's about stock. Your boss is the New York man fishing up the Spray."

"Hole in one. Good night, my—Miss—"

"MacRae is my name—Mary Bella MacRae."

"Good night, Miss MacRae. Please keep any wires that may come for 'Steve Drew.'"

"I sure will, Mr. Drew. Good night."

Hector's great news threw Logie and later Miss Mary into wild excitement. He did not explain just how he had arranged for the necessary funds, except that the arrangement had been through Mr. Inman.

They spent a long time discussing the coming journey, poring over maps and time-tables. Both Logie and Miss Mary were busy making the necessary preparations. There were all Jock's things and Logie's things to be got ready, for they settled between them that Logie must go and that it would be unnecessary for Hector to accompany them. He was rather helpless in looking after things. Long into the night they were busy washing and ironing, for Logie's wardrobe was none too elaborate. The doctor's directions and preparations too demanded attention.

The following morning while seated at an early breakfast they were startled by a loud halloo from the gate.

"Daphne! That's her hunting call," said the doctor.

"Sure enough, and Mr. Inman," cried Logie, running to the door followed by the others.

"We've had breakfast, Miss Logie, so don't worry about us," said Mr. Inman.

"But I've walked two miles since. This is the *hungriest* country in the world! I positively can't fill up so as to stay full. That fish, now, Logie—have you any left?"

"I'm sure Steve has. Oh, yes, Steve is in charge."

"Well, we thought we would like to see you off," said Mr. Inman.

"Sure thing! Fond farewell, sob stuff, and all the rest of it, you know," said Daphne with a steady look at Hector.

"Awfully good of you. We have not settled yet who are going," said Hector. "The doctor has very kindly offered, but we couldn't break in on his holiday that way. I guess Steve and I can manage quite well."

"Oh, Hector, Jock will need me," cried Logie.

"By the way," said the doctor, "didn't someone say that Nurse Marriott was in this village?"

"Vivien?" joyously exclaimed Logie. "Splendid!   The very person! She is so very capable."

"I can vouch for that," said the doctor heartily.

"Go and get her, Hector. Oh, that is the very thing.

Run, Hector! She will need all her time to get ready."

Hector found her in the garden, rake in hand, her face glowing wholesome and radiant in the morning sun, her hair a golden aureole about her head.

With succinct clarity Hector told the whole story and presented his plea.

"But how wonderful! And the doctor says Captain Jock will be well again?"

"He says there is a fair chance. Mr. Inman says Dr. Wolfe's a great authority on—"

"Dr. Wolfe? Of New York?" The girl's face flushed red and then grew pale.

"Yes, he is responsible for the whole thing. By the way, it was he that suggested that you might go. Indeed you are responsible for his being here. He says it was you that told him about our fishing."

"He is not going?" asked Vivien slowly.

"No. He offered, but of course we would not hear of that. Besides, he says that if you go there is no need of him. He is very sure of you, apparently."

"You want me to go, Hector?" said the girl in a low voice.

"I certainly want you to go if you can."

"When do we start?" she said, dropping her rake, and moving with him toward the house.

"My dear Vivien! You are going. Oh, you *are* a trump. I knew you would. You are really a brick."

"I would do a lot for you, Hector—and for Jock—and for you all."

"Oh, you are a dear good girl, Vivien."

"Good? Do you think so? I don't know."

"Most certainly I do. You are a brick. I shall never forget this. I can never repay you." His voice was deep with emotion.

"Can you not, Hector? I wonder. Now we must have a word with Dad," she went on. "But do keep off theology and all that. I am rather fed up with theology and Higher Criticism, I confess.—Here's the minister, Dad, and he wants me to take charge of Captain Jock, who is going to Boston for an operation to-day. Dr. Wolfe—my old chief, you remember—has ordered him off."

Mr. Marriott was a man of few words and fewer questions, but his mind worked swiftly.

"Very well, my dear. We are always glad to help Mr. MacGregor. When do you go?"

Vivien flung a look at the minister. She was proud of her father.

"When, Hector?"

"Right after dinner, if you can be ready, and if your father can spare you? Mr. Marriott, I can't tell you how grateful we are to you and Vivien. The truth is the whole thing has come with a rush." And he proceeded with a full account of the events leading up to this sudden move. "It is really a wonderful thing, quite providential."

Mr. Marriott listened with keen attention.

"Providential? The sequence of events is enough, Mr. MacGregor," said Mr. Marriott drily.

"Now, Dad, no theology!"

"Well—very true. But, Mr. MacGregor—you will pardon me for asking—but this must involve expense, heavy expense, and on short notice too. Can I be of any assistance? I mean—an advance?"

The minister was deeply moved. "Mr. Marriott, as to your theology and psychology I am more than doubtful, but as to your heart—" Hector's voice choked abruptly.

"Nonsense! Why not, Mr. MacGregor? I am your friend, and your father was my friend. His theological presuppositions—well, the less said about them the better. But when the days were dark he stood very near to me. Can I help?"

"I thank you, Mr. Marriott, more than I can say. I thank you—but I have been able to arrange the matter."

Mr. Marriott's face expressed disappointment and doubt. "Very well, sir. I wish for you all, and for my special friend Captain Jock—and Vivien's friend—I can only wish the very best of good luck."

The manse party were still about the dinner table when Vivien walked in upon them, in a suit of powder blue that threw up the color of her glorious eyes and her golden hair. With a cry Logie rushed at her.

"Vivien, how marvellous!" Her arms went round her neck in a rapturous embrace. "I knew you would come. Dear people, let me introduce my friend, my everlasting friend, school chum, War comrade and all and all, Vivien Marriott! Best girl in the world!"

Dr. Wolfe rose quickly and came to meet her with warm welcome.

"No one needs to proclaim the many and varied endowments of my old friend and assistant, Nurse Marriott," he said, offering both his hands.

"Why! How delightful to meet my old chief!" said Vivien, shaking hands with frank friendliness. "So you did come for the fishing! I hope you are not disappointed."

"You never disappoint," said the doctor with enthusiasm.

But Vivien's casual friendliness somewhat dashed the suggestion of intimacy in the doctor's words.

Daphne's greeting was coolly critical and more than slightly superior.

"You were one of Dr. Wolfe's staff," she said with a somewhat casual air. "How lucky you can take over this case."

"Lucky! You may say so," said Hector warmly. "We know now that Jock will have the very best that can be done for him."

Daphne's hard keen eyes were searching Hector's face.

"A well-trained nurse is really quite a comfort," she said.

"Can I do anything for Jock, Logie?" said Vivien, ignoring the girl.

"Yes, Nurse, there are tablets to be given before he sets

out." The doctor's manner was strictly professional.

"Very well, Doctor," she said and ran upstairs to her patient.

With efficient capability she aided the doctor in steadying and guiding the patient's slow and uncertain steps down the stairs, and out to the car, in the back of which the doctor had improvised a couch. Deftly she arranged the cushions. "There, Captain Jock," she said with a little pat on the shoulder. "You will hardly know you are going till you are at the hospital door."

"Say! This is swell, Vivien! If only you could climb in here beside me!" he said, touching her cheek with his pale fingers.

"That will be enough from you, young man," she said, giving a final touch to the arranging of the cushions. "Let me remind you that you are under the care of a very authoritative and very proper nursing attendant."

"I shall do my best, Nurse," said Captain Jock, impudently winking at her.

"This is your itinerary, Steve," said the doctor, handing the chauffeur a road map with rests and stopovers marked. "And there are the instructions for you, Nurse."

"Very good, Doctor," said Vivien in her best professional manner.

"Everything all ready? Let me see," he referred to a card in his hand. "This is a letter for Dr. Whitney, Miss Logie, which you will give into his own hands."

Logie's dark eyes were bright with tears which she was resolved should not overflow.

"Doctor Wolfe, the words just won't come," she said as the doctor held her hand in farewell. "And if I cry I know I shall just make a baby of myself."

"Good-bye, Miss Logie," said Mr. Inman. "Now don't hurry home too soon. See Boston, eh? We won't need the car for ten days or so."

Logie kept her eyes steadily on his face for a moment.

"I hope I shall live to be an old lady that I may be able to show you how grateful I am," she said softly.

"Oh, shucks!" said Mr. Inman and became voiceless.

"Hector dear, don't worry." Her brave lips trembled. "We shall be all right. Steve is so careful, and Vivien is with us. And the doctors—and everything." She ceased abruptly. Then she put her arms round her brother's neck and kissed him again and again.

"All right, Steve," said the doctor sharply.

But Steve waited. He had caught sight of Hector moving toward his brother. It was one of the great moments in their lives. From boyhood they had been as halves of a single entity. Captain Jock's face was little whiter than his brother's. Both were as if cut in stone.

"Good-bye, old chap," said Captain Jock, affecting an air of gay nonchalance as their hands gripped.

"Good-bye, Jock boy. God—" Hector's lips came together in a thin hard line, cutting off further words.

"Don't be afraid, Hector. We will bring him back to you," said Vivien, leaning out to him from the front seat.

A swift spasm shook Hector's face out of its iron calm.

"God bless you, Vivien!" he said in a husky voice and kissed her on the lips.

"There!" she said, triumph in her voice. "I was afraid he wouldn't!"

"Drive on, Steve!" ordered the doctor.

In Daphne's face there was a look of cold scorn.

CHAPTER X

WITH face tortured as if by pain, Hector watched the car climb the first rise of the hill till it disappeared behind a clump of trees. For some minutes he stood with his eyes upon the road, silent, motionless, rigid.

Daphne touched the doctor. "Speak to him," she murmured.

"They have a fine day for the run. The car will make good time to-day," he said.

Hector turned to him and regarded him stupidly as if he had not understood.

"He will make the journey quite comfortably," said the doctor, "and in Nurse Marriott's hands he will have the best of care."

"The best of care?" said Hector. "Yes. Will he come back again? Shall I see him again? No, Doctor. You cannot promise that. Twenty years ago I took him out of that gate to school. He was afraid. I had to take his hand. He was a little chap. Since that day we have met every phase of life together." His eyes were away over the hills. His voice was that of a man speaking in a dream. "We fished that river together. I remember his first fish. He was wild at it. He was rather a timid little chap. Always together. At college together. He was quicker at his work. We went to the War together. The Cape Breton Highlanders. He went in the ranks, rose to Captain. He was a great boy with the men. They adored him.—Will he come back?"

"Sure, he'll come back," said Daphne, moving swiftly to his side and taking him by the arm. "Come along with us up to the camp."

"What? I beg your pardon. The camp? No, thank

you! No, I must—I have work to do. I must get at my work."

"Mr. MacGregor," said Mr. Inman, "will you be good enough to walk to the telegraph office with me? I am expecting a wire."

"Certainly, sir."

They all moved toward the village. At windows and doors faces could be seen, but no one spoke to the minister. They understood. At the door of the little store which housed the telegraph office Daphne halted the doctor.

"Let's wait here," she said. "Say, Fritz, he's had an awful jolt. What about it? Has his brother a chance?"

"A chance? Yes. But not much more. Can't tell. He certainly takes it hard."

"Well, he just breaks my heart. He's so helpless. Not a soul to look after him. And he's so darned stubborn." Daphne was on the verge of tears.

The doctor eyed her sharply. "He'll be all right," he said. "Wants to be let alone, I guess. Don't fuss over him. He'd hate that."

Daphne turned away impatiently. "Fuss over him? Who's fussing over him?"

Meantime Mr. Inman had received his wire, and was having a friendly chat with Mary Bella.

"I hope I took your wire correctly," she said. "It is so very queerly worded. I can't understand it. But that's the way it came over."

"Quite all right. Guess you're new to this kind of talk."

"About stocks, isn't it?" ventured Mary Bella, whose curiosity was consuming her.

"Here, I'd better explain this to you," said Mr. Inman, "or you'll be getting all balled up."

"Thank you, sir," said Mary Bella demurely. "It will be a great help if any more come."

"They will be coming every day, perhaps twice a day. And I want you to send them right up to camp. Now listen here." And Mr. Inman proceeded to enlarge Mary Bella's knowledge of the jargon of the stock market, while Hector listened absent-mindedly.

"Oh, I see! It's just like selling apples, or potatoes."

"Well, something like, only different."

"A point up or down is one dollar more or less for a share."

"You get it."

"My, that is an easy way of making a dollar!"

"And of losing a dollar."

"That is so—and not so good," said the shrewd Mary Bella. "But," she mused, "if you could only get them when they are going up! That International Oil now. It is going up, Mr. Inman." Mary Bella's big blue eyes were lifted in shy appeal, her voice was lowered so that her minister could not hear. "I have three hundred dollars and I want Angus John—my brother, sir—to be a doctor. He is that clever! He has his B.A. already." She was all atremble with fear and excitement so that her Highland speech supplanted her fine English.

"Leave it alone, young lady. You'll get your fingers burnt."

"But you are doing it, and the minister," she whispered with frightened eyes.

Mr. Inman drew a pad toward him. "How much do you need?"

"Oh, another three hundred would do, with what I could spare."

Mr. Inman wrote a few words.

" 'Accept order from M. B. MacRae at sixty pyramid till further orders.' Send that," he said, "but keep it to yourself."

"Yes, yes," she whispered in fervent gratitude. And thus Mary Bella with timid daring broke into the stock market.

"Well, Mr. MacGregor, let's go. The fish are calling us," said Mr. Inman. Together they left the office.

"Better come up to camp with us, Mr. MacGregor?"

"I have work to do, and I am company for no man to-day."

"You can't work to-day. Come along. By the way, I have news for you already. So you need not worry about the financing of the operation."

The minister was hardly interested.

"I hope it is all right," he said dully.

"I guess we can make it all right. Don't worry. Come with us."

"Do come with us," pleaded Daphne. "You need a change. Who will look after you here? Your grub? Oh, come on, be a sport."

"A sport? I am no sport. I have work to do!"

"Work, what work?"

"There is an old lady to see. She has been more or less crippled with rheumatism for two years and more. I must look in on her."

"But she has her people."

"Her people? Not much good to her, I fear. A son who is a doubtful asset, and a granddaughter of sixteen trying to work her way through school. I must look over her papers. I must give her a hand," replied Hector with a smile.

"And you? What about you? You look like a ghost." The mother in all women God ever made was stirring in the girl's frivolous heart.

Hector considered her with new eyes.

"Thank you, Miss Daphne," he said with grave kindness. "I will look in on you some time soon, but now I must get at my sermon this afternoon. This is Friday."

"Sermon? What about?"

"The folly of making fortunes," he said, smiling at her.

"You don't mean it! You're all wet! 'Folly of making fortunes'—the folly of *not* making fortunes, you mean."

Hector shook his head.

"I'm coming to hear it. When and where does this folly come up?"

"Sunday morning, eleven, in the church there."

"I'll make Dad come down. Fritz has no use for that sort of thing."

"Come, come, young lady. Leave my sins alone. Your time might be profitably occupied in dealing with your own," said the doctor.

"The Lord knows that's true all right," said Daphne.

"Good afternoon," said Hector. "I am keeping you. You ought to have a good evening's fishing."

Mary Bella appeared in breathless haste.

"Mr. Inman," she said, "let Angus John drive you up. He has his wagon here. It won't cost you a thing," she added shyly.

"Thank you," said Mr. Inman. "We want the walk."

"Send him along," cried Daphne. "Me, I'm all for that wagon!"

In a few moments Angus John, with a wild and shaggy team of colts, drove up in a more or less ramshackle democrat wagon.

"But how do I get up there?" cried Daphne. "And what about those bronchos?" She surveyed the colts with dubious eyes.

"Whoa there, Jim! Stand still, I tell you!" Angus John admonished his team. "Now, if you give a jump when they are quiet, you can do it easy."

Daphne waited her opportunity, gave a jump and by the aid of Angus John's sinewy arm landed upon the spring seat. The others managed to achieve lowlier seats in the back of the wagon, and at full gallop the colts were away.

With slow steps the minister made his way to his home, followed by many friendly eyes, ascended to his study and was alone with his heart and its agony.

In his mind he followed the car with its burden along the hill road winding by the Bras d'Or. Jock would perhaps be suffering. "But it is a lovely day," he reminded himself. "And the Bras d'Or and the islands and the hills across will be gorgeous. Jock will love it all, poor chap. He hasn't seen much but the four walls of his room for six weeks. Will he be able to stand it? There's Vivien—she will know when to give the tablets. But will he tell her? Not he. Not till the pain drains the soul out of him. He is a proud devil. When they put the sixteen stitches in his back did he give a cheep? Not till the last stitch was in. And then they found him dead to the world. Oh, Jock lad, you are the stuff, but you are the darnedest fool God ever made."

He walked over to the east wall of the study and stood gazing at the gallant figure in its Highland uniform, gazing till he could not see for the tears flowing from his eyes. "Oh, but you were the brave lad," he said aloud, falling into his Highland speech. "Will you come back, Jock boy?" He lifted his clasped hands over his head. "O God," he cried, "bring him back to me!" Then as if ashamed he sat down to his desk and went resolutely at his sermonizing.

But no consecutive thinking was possible. He was ever with the car, humming smoothly along the curving road, following the contours of the hills. He gave up in despair, and took his way to the Widow MacAskill. A steep climb by a wooded path brought him over the rampart of hills into another valley more rugged and wild. Here the little farms were more unkempt, the buildings more tumbledown, the stone dykes and log fences more hopelessly inadequate to their purpose. But not all the marks of neglect and shiftlessness could take the glory from the blue of the sea, the dark green of the woods, the soft azure haze of the distant hills. Nothing that man could do, or might neglect to do, could mar that perfect beauty which held these people to their primitive dwellings and their narrow lives. But were they so narrow? Some half-dozen farms lay before him. Poor enough were these people, and hard their fight for bare living. Yet from almost every home had gone forth to school and college a son, a daughter—from some, more than one—to arrive finally at positions of influence and honour in the life of the nation. Some secret urge, some divine unrest stirred within the family circle so that while some remained at home to save and scrape and toil, others went forth to win name and fame, and set on high the family honour. Nor did they forget the homes that sent them forth, or those who suffered and saved that they might achieve.

There was the Widow MacAskill in her unpainted, unlovely shingle-sided house. The farm with its ragged, broken outbuildings was a very picture of misery and poverty, yet within the house were the marks of comfort, even of refinement, in furniture and draperies, in table linen and dishes, in the pictures on the walls and the books in the shelves and the gramophone in the corner with the glories of Beethoven and Wagner and Brahms, Debussy and Tschaikowsky, waiting release from their mechanized cold storage.

The minister was met at the door by the granddaughter, a girl of sixteen, whose dull, heavy face flamed into a sudden glow in her welcome of him.

"You came over the hill," she said, almost in reproof.

"And how did you know, Peggy?"

"I was watching the road. This is your day. I will go in and tell her you are come. But indeed she will know it already," said Peggy, hurrying into a bedroom at the rear of the living-room.

The minister sat down and waited. It was a pleasant room, well lighted, comfortably furnished, its whitewashed walls adorned with good copies of the great masters. And with these were large photographs framed in oak, of members of the family arrayed in the gowns and hoods of their graduation day—one a famous surgeon in the city of Buffalo, another the principal of a boys' academy in the same city, a third a nurse, the head of a hospital in Vancouver in her matron's garb. Hector knew them all by name. They were not of his generation, but their achievements were writ-

ten in the imperishable living epistles that formed the annals
of the parish.

"Come in, Mr. MacGregor," said Peggy, reappearing at
the bedroom door, and the minister entered the room.

On a bed, propped up with gaily coloured cushions, the
Vancouver matron's handiwork, reclined a truly remarkable
woman. A great wealth of white hair, of which she was in-
ordinately proud, was confined in her lace widow's cap
adorned with gay ribbons of pink and blue. A soft Shetland
wool shawl was held in place over her shoulders with a large
silver brooch. Two hands knotted and curved into bird-like
talons lay on the gay coloured hand-woven bedspread before
her. The face was a marvellous network of tiny wrinkles,
dark as the pitch pine of the walls of the room. Those walls
had their story. This room had been built years ago by her
sailor son. The scrollwork on the window frames and on
the heavy cornice round the ceiling were the work of his
hands. When the other parts of the house were painted in
delicate greens and blues, this room retained the deep yellow
tint of its native pine, deepening year by year to a richer
hue. "It will be as he left it, so long as my eyes shall look
upon it," the mother had decreed.

Pictures adorned the walls. On the right of her bed, King
Edward VII, on the left Queen Alexandra. Over the bed
just above her head hung the debonair and gallant John A.
MacDonald, the old lady's political prophet, and in front of
her a coloured photograph of her sailor son in his white and
blue of the Royal Navy. These constituted her Lares and
Penates, the dominant passions of her heart.

But the dark and wrinkled face in its frame of soft white
hair was redeemed from sheer forbidding ugliness by her
eyes. Dark in dark caverns, large and full, they glowed with
a brilliance, soft, almost tender, and yet with the piercing
fierceness of a caged eagle.

Under their penetrating glance the soul's secrets lay bared
to the owner of those eyes. All evasion and subterfuge was

vain. Only truth would avail.

"Come away, minister!" she said in a voice hoarse and deep as a man's. "Sit you down. No, not in that chair— here!" The chair faced the full light of the window. "I want to see my friends."

With a brief word of greeting the minister sat down in the chair indicated.

"What is it?"

"I beg your pardon," he said, startled.

"Never mind begging my pardon. Just tell me what it is."

The minister retreated to the only refuge available from those soft penetrating eyes: silence.

"Is it anything in your congregation? But no, that would not go as deep. Is it Jock?"

The minister nodded. His power of speech was suddenly gone.

"He is worse?"

Then Hector unburdened his soul to her.

"And this doctor, does he know?"

"Mr. Inman—that is the American gentleman—says he is a great doctor, a specialist in nervous disorders."

"An American? Hum!" With an eloquent distrust that even her expletive could not express.

"Vivien says he is at the top in New York. She nursed for him."

"Vivien? Well, at least she is no fool, whatever her other defects. Then, what is the matter? The doctor knows and he advised the operation, and Jock is in the hands of a good nurse and his sister. And what better could you have? And yon Boston doctor?"

"They all say he is one of the best."

"And the lad will be in Boston the day after to-morrow. And Logie with him, and that Vivien girl?" The question mark against the name was more than apparent. "She is a good nurse, I am hearing, whatever. Now what is the matter, will you tell me?"

For the life of him the minister had no answer to give. His fears somehow seemed to be ill-founded.

"I don't know, Grannie. I guess I am a fool."

"A fool?" Her eyes wandered to the face of the jolly sailor lad on the wall before her. "Ay, laddie, our brains are not in our hearts."

She waited some moments, her soft, searching eyes still upon his face. He waited in fear of her next question. But it was inevitable.

"And the pay for this operation?" There was no hint of apology for the probing into his family affairs. Had she not been a friend of his father and of his mother before him? Was he not her minister? "I know these doctors," she continued. "Is not Aleck telling me himself? And the bigger they are the bigger the charge."

"Not with Aleck, Grannie," said the minister, hoping to escape.

"Indeed he can charge with the best of them. Didn't he charge a millionaire last fall five thousand dollars for taking the bladder out of him? I told him he was a worse reiver than his great-grandfather along Galloway side with the cattle. But he just laughed at me. He said he was making the millionaire pay for a thousand patients who could not pay." The minister was not to escape. "And what about the pay for Jock?" asked the old lady, her eyes steadily boring into his.

"I've arranged it, Grannie," said Hector.

"Indeed! Well, well, I can see a door when it is shut as well as the next one."

"No, no, Grannie, not that."

"Man, man, do not let an old woman trouble you. Peggy, bring the tea."

"Grannie, it was an arrangement with the American," said Hector.

"And quite right, I doubt. Only it was in my mind that you had friends of your own people to whom you might have

applied. But no more of it." She raised her claw-like hand
to silence further words.

"I tried some of my people, or at least one of them," said
Hector with a touch of bitterness.

"Ay, and Jimmie Hannah could not accommodate you."

"Grannie, you are a witch."

"They would be putting fire to me in the old days," she
said with a cackling laugh. "But you might have remembered that though some of your friends are poor they can
arrange things also."

"I might have thought of you, Grannie, and the doctor,"
said Hector penitently.

"Tut, tut! Here is the tea and Peggy to go over her
algebra with you. Come, Peggy, show him your a's and
x's."

But Peggy was shy and would show nothing in Grannie's
presence. No—later, when her father came in.

Sandy MacAskill was what was known as a quiet man. A
man with little force and less spirit. Sixteen years ago he
had laid in the grave with the mortal remains of Peggy's
mother what of spirit and force he had, and since that day
he had dragged out a colourless and negative existence.
"Poor Sandy," his mother would say. "He has little brains,
and just as well, for what could he do with them? Now
Mary Rory Over" (to wit, Mary Mackenzie, daughter of
Rory *over* the mountain), "there was a woman for you. He
would have dragged the heart out of her." However that
might have been, when Mary Rory Over laid herself in her
last resting-place she took with her the best that was in her
adoring young husband, and left but the pale shadow of a
man to care for her baby girl. Not that he was gloomy or
morose—he was rather a "chatty" man, full of the good-
natured gossip of the neighbourhood, but with the vital
forces of manhood drained out of his soul.

"And where have you been with yourself all the afternoon?" asked his mother of her son.

"Oh, over at Johnny Up's." (To wit, Johnny *up* on the hillside as distinguished from Johnny down below the hill.) "Man, but it's the drove of young ones that's running in and out of that house. Ten of them and all under twelve years."

"Ach, leave them alone. They will all be good Tory votes some day," said Grannie. "And now Minister will take the books."

"And what shall I read, Grannie?" asked Hector, taking the Bible from the table.

"First we will be having the Psalm," said Grannie, who would have no shortened form of family prayers, but a full dress parade.

The singing was weird enough. Sandy, who had a clear but rather light tenor voice, took the lead. Hector supplied the bass. Peggy followed the words in a dull monotone, the old lady joined Sandy in the air, but an octave lower.

> "Oh, why art thou cast down, my soul?
> What should discourage thee?
> And why with vexing thoughts art thou
> Disquieted in me?"

inquired the Psalmist in noble plaint, only to ring forth in triumphant assurance:

> "Still trust in God, for Him to praise
> Good cause I yet shall have.
> He of my countenance is the help,
> My God that doth me save."

Humbled, rebuked, Hector sang the quaint ancient setting of that noble utterance of defiant faith in the face of adverse fate.

Through the weird mingling of voices—Sandy's thin, high piping, Peggy's dull, tireless chant, and his own bass—came the deep husky voice of the warrior soul of the old lady.

As they rose from their knees, she took his hand between her horny talons in a nerveless grip.

"Thank you for coming in to a poor old crone, spent and beaten with ill fortune," she said.

" 'Spent and beaten'!" echoed Hector. "God forgive me for the miserable coward that I am, Grannie. You have put heart into me."

"Miserable enough, but 'coward' never! Not your mother's nor your father's son. Here, lad!" She turned her cheek to him. "It is crinkled and crackled like a haggis bag, but it is clean, and there was a time—but never mind."

Reverently, tenderly he kissed the "crinkled and crackled" leathery cheek.

"There now, my man, never fear." The great dark eyes glowed with soft steady light upon him. "Heed not the clouds! They cannot dight nor daunt the sun."

He could not trust his voice to answer that dauntless soul. He turned in silence from her.

"You might take a look at yon gawkie's a's and x's to see will she pass her A," she called after him as he passed from her room.

Half an hour later he put his head within her door.

"Never fear. She'll pass her A, Grannie. And, if I mistake not, will win the scholarship as well."

"Huh! Be off with you. It is a terrible liar you are, Minister." She started shaking at him both her bony claws.

But as he climbed the hill again there was a new spring in his step, and at the top, as he paused to look back at the ragged house among the trees and then at the sun sinking in glorious triumph into the sea of gold, he heard again the deep husky voice, "Never fear! Heed not the clouds! They cannot dight nor daunt the sun."

CHAPTER XI

A LIGHT from the kitchen window greeted Hector on his return. Entering he found a fire in the stove, the kettle on the boil and Mary Bella waiting with a telegram for him.

"I thought I might as well put the kettle on," she said, shy apology in her voice.

"You are a good girl, Mary Bella," he said, opening the wire dated St. John.

"Arrived safe—warm night lovely moon—smooth road. Jock slept four hours so pushed through—found all arrangements at Admiral Beatty made ahead by Steve world's best chauffeur—Jock fine—supper bath now sound asleep. Love from all.

Logie.

"Must be a great driver," said Mary Bella.

"What? Great driver? Oh, Steve? Wonderful," said the minister.

"I'll make you some supper, sir," said Mary Bella.

"Thank you, Mary Bella. I think Miss Mary will be expecting me. I shall just run over with this wire. But thank you so much for bringing this to me so promptly."

"It's fine about Captain Jock," said the girl with shining eyes. "Man, won't the people be glad! Everyone loves Captain Jock," said the girl with a little sigh.

"Yes, I think so."

"Indeed and I am sure of it. I hear them talking of the way he used to look after them. And always with a laugh when they went over the top. I often hear them. Good night, sir."

"Good night, Mary Bella, and again thank you." Hector

shook hands with the girl. "It is great news! Great news! Thank you, thank you!"

He ran out of the house, leaving the door wide open, and away to Miss Mary's cottage.

"My, but he's excited! He is as soft as a woman!" said Mary Bella to herself as she carefully closed the damper of the stove and shut the kitchen door. "And yet for all that he can put the fear of God on them too."

Miss Mary's welcome was warm, kindly, understanding. Hector without a word put the telegram in her hand.

"Oh, but that is just wonderful!" she said. "And now we shall just wait and pray for the best. You have had no supper. I was watching for you."

He told her of his visit to the Widow MacAskill.

"She is a great old soul. Quite a wonderful mind. That accounts for her family."

"Sandy?"

"Well, there *is* a slip there. But look at the grandchild. That girl Peggy is rather amazing."

"Yes, I went over her algebra and geometry with her. She had struck a snag. But a dozen sentences and she needed nothing more from me."

"She used to come to me when working for her B."

"Why did she quit the Sydney High School?"

"Oh, the crowds of students dismayed her, and the teachers wearied her with unnecessary explanations. 'Kept telling me things I didn't want to know, or that I knew already,' she complained to me. So she is reading up her work for herself. She has quite a touch of genius."

"Pity she is so dull. She looks so dumb."

"Give her time," said Miss Mary. "I have great sympathy with dumb people. I was terribly dumb when I was her age."

"Indeed?"

"Yes, indeed. Give her time."

"I will. I'll give her ten years," said Hector. "But

still—"

"Not ten years. No. A little time, a little pain, heart pain—and her soul will wake up."

"Forgive me, Miss Mary. Good night."

"Good night. Better come to me for dinner and supper to-morrow. Logie said I was not to let you eat your own cooking."

"I make grand porridge," announced Hector indignantly.

"No doubt. Well, make your own breakfast and then come to me for dinner."

"Very well, Miss Mary, I am coming to dinner and supper," said Hector. "Now for an all-night session at my sermon."

"What is your subject? Don't tell if you don't want to. I understand ministers hate giving advance copy."

" 'The Folly of Making Fortunes.' "

"Oh?" Miss Mary's tone conveyed criticism.

"Well?"

"Nothing. Only, *Experientia omnia docet.*"

"True. Yet surely there is a place for observation and deduction. Besides, though I have never had a fortune, I know people who have."

"I surrender. Go to your sermon."

"I will. It is to be a scorcher."

"Experientia?"

"You just bet. The fortune-maker is a fool, and if he doesn't look out he'll be a damned fool some day."

"Just like that?"

"Well—in modified terminology."

"Poor souls. They all want a little better time. A little finer clothes, a holiday now and then, a book or two and some pictures and a phonograph."

"Why not? Who would say no?"

"Run away to your sermon. Don't make us sizzle."

"It will be a scorcher, I promise you," said Hector.

And a scorcher it was. The theme of the sermon was one

to which the minister had given much thought. Money hunger had been with him a favorite object of denunciation in War days, and more in post-War days, the days of greedy grabbing. To this lust he had attributed most of the industrial, political, economic and social evils in the world. He was quite certain that his unhappy experience with James Cameron had nothing whatever to do with his selecting the theme for his sermon, nor with his treatment of the same. It was this conviction that before the War had wrought in him a disgust at the sordid ambitions of the men he met in business. The eternal quest of the rolling dollar was the thing of important worth in life, the sole dynamic of achievement. Even in professional life success was measured by the size of the retainer, the amount of the fee. To a man of simple tastes massed wealth seemed not a necessity, but an embarrassment, a clog upon the foot of noble ambition. War's glamor, its pomp and circumstance at the first, had filled his eyes with false lights. His later experience of war's cruelty, its wastage of wealth and of human life, its sordid debasement of noble idealism, its futility as a method of international peace and stability turned his mind to the explanation of its elemental motivating urge. The discovery that in nations, as in men, the ultimate objective, the fundamental driving force was in the last analysis, not the noble passion for the things of the spirit, as truth, freedom, honour and the like, but a lust for power to command things material in life, territory, raw material, trade routes and trade concessions, opportunity to exploit secondary peoples. The high-sounding utterances of statesmen and parliaments about national honour, integrity, and freedom, or about international peace and amity, were merely the fanfare of war's trumpets, stimulating the ambitions and passions of trusting and honest souls to the madness of deluded and frenzied devotees of false gods. The madness for money as the *sine qua non* of sense delights, of prestige, of power, he came to recognize as the curse of the race. All this was at work in his soul colouring his thinking, motivating his utterances. His style of delivery, as a rule, was restrained and didactic, but to-day he cast aside his notes and launched his soul upon a turgid torrent of passionate and at times poetic oratory. Though he was not consciously directing his denunciation and appeal to individual members of his congregation, the subconscious reaction to his environment undoubtedly coloured his speech. First, and very impressive, was the cold, unmoved, consciously righteous face of James Cameron. In spite of all he could do the flashing eye, the accusing finger of the preacher were often directed toward his self-assured elder, the very type and protagonist of all money-loving and money-gaining souls. The rest of his congregation—small farmers, fisherfolk, traders, working men, less conspicuously successful but equally devoted seekers after gain—sat enjoying the discourse as being eminently appropriate to Jimmie Hannah, and to one or two others with the taint of money on them. The unexpected presence of the American "towerists"—Mr. Inman and the doctor in fishing garb, and Miss Daphne in alluringly diaphanous array induced by the unseasonable summer heat of this May morning—lent an additional and altogether pleasing tang to the atmosphere of general condemnation induced by the sermon, and indeed stimulated certain subconscious reactions in the preacher.

But even with the most successfully armoured souls among them the effect of the sermon was tremendous. The intellectual power, the clear-cut logic, the lofty idealism, the passion, the burning, penetrating passion of a soul convinced of the truth of its own utterance were overwhelming. With solemn and half-shamed glances at one another the people omitted the cheery greetings and friendly conversations that were wont to follow the benediction. Silently they passed outside the church and stood in silent groups about the door.

Among those who lingered about the door, the first to

greet the minister was James Cameron.

"Good morning, Mr. MacGregor. I am glad to see you so well. A powerful and appropriate discourse. Ay.!" James Cameron's keen eyes challenged and indeed accused the faces about him. "A very powerful and appropriate discourse and one, I will say, much needed in these days."

The minister, who had feared and had been braced for a quite different greeting, was completely nonplussed and confounded.

"I trust, Mr. Cameron, your mother is quite well, and you, Mrs. Cameron," he said, shaking hands with his Elder and rather hurriedly turning to his wife with a greeting.

The other elders, office bearers and members, with faces subdued and even awed, gave him their humble and adoring greetings. With them there was an uneasy sense of condemnation which they could not well define. Definitely convicted of the folly of "fortune-making" they were not, but that they were guilty of many other follies, not to say sins, they were sufficiently conscious to greet their minister with humbled, troubled hearts. Knowing their narrow and straitened resources, their lives of toil, their many self-denials as he did, the minister was suddenly filled with a humiliating conviction that he had missed the mark. Hence, filled with an overwhelming sympathy with them in the daily burden of their lives, he went among them, with both hands busy, his eyes shining with a tender light, his voice warm, kind, genuinely affectionate. Immediately reacting to his mood his people crowded about him, giving him with their hands, their hearts' love and devotion. Many who had been standing aloof and conscience-stricken, when they caught sight of his face and heard the tones of his voice, came near to give him greeting. Suddenly the minister became aware that his people were trying to tell him that they were all with him in his great trouble. They were thinking of Captain Jock. About the gate a number of men stood apart. He recognized them as the comrades of Captain Jock. He waved his hand to them. Immediately one, then another, then the whole body of them came back to the church steps.

"How is he, sir?" said their leader, Ranald Gillis, a tall, athletic, handsome man who had been Captain Jock's lieutenant in the Eighty-fifth.

The thrill in the man's low voice, the eager look in the eyes of his comrades, smote the minister as with a solar plexus blow. For a few moments he stood silent, his lips in a firm, hard line, fighting for control.

"First of all, let me thank you, boys. How Captain Jock is I cannot say. A wire from St. John said he made the journey splendidly, slept four hours on the way, and was feeling fine. But I know he will make a better fight when he hears how you were asking for him."

"He will make a fight of it whateffer," said Ranald Gillis with a determined nod of his handsome curly head.

"Thank you all, boys," said the minister. But still they lingered, shifting their feet.

"Aw now, Danny MacKinnon, just do your stuff," said Ranald.

"Well, Mr. MacGregor, it is just that the boys know that them operations cost like—" Danny checked himself abruptly.

"Are very expensive," interjected Ranald Gillis, hastening to Danny's aid. "And the boys, every man of them, would like to—"

"We all want to have the privilege of standing in with Captain Jock," said Danny. "In fact, here's five hundred dollars in the meantime."

"And more if necessary," said a voice from the rear.

"Of course," said Ranald Gillis.

The minister took the roll of bills, and with a fine sense of the fitness of things made no reference to the arrangements he had made, but with face very white and still, stood looking the men over for a few terrible moments. Then very deliberately he shook each man's hand, speaking not a word, and after long silence he said in a hoarse whisper:

"Say, boys, you are a darned good lot of scouts. You nearly make me swear."

"Let her rip, Minister!" said Ranald Gillis. "We understand fine."

"Get out of this," said the minister, waving them off. "You will have me howling like a wolf in a minute."

With loud laughing they hurried off and the minister went on his way to dine with Miss Mary.

"Splendid sermon, Hector!" was Miss Mary's greeting.

"That is not necessary, Miss Mary," said Hector in a tone of disgust. "I know it's what the boys will call a hell of a sermon. That is what they looked like—all of them except Jimmie Hannah, and he looked like a Pharisee on his way to the gates of Paradise, watching the other fellows on their way to Hell. But the kick in it was that he evidently thought that I was going with him. He praised my sermon, Miss Mary. Praised it as a 'powerful and appropriate discourse,' and then I saw what a sulphurously conceited, self-righteous ass I had made of myself. And when I got among the rest of them and saw in their eyes a kind of humble self-condemnation for their wicked pursuit of massed money— poor devils—and all of them struggling with more or less success to worry a living out of their fishing nets and their hillside farms, and especially when I saw that they were all chiefly terribly anxious about Jock and wanted to tell me so, I tell you, Miss Mary, I wanted to crawl away under the church steps and howl. And then I saw Ranald Gillis and the boys hanging about the gate, and then this happened." He pulled out the roll of bills from his pocket, spread them before her and rehearsed the scene in the churchyard. "Of course, I could not tell them that I had made other arrangements. I will give it back to them—afterwards. Though, mind you, neither Jock nor I would hesitate to take it from them. Keep this for me till I can return it to them without hurting them. Great boys, eh?

"So you know, Miss Mary," he continued, "how I feel now when you say 'Splendid sermon.' 'Splendid sermon,' 'A powerful and appropriate discourse.' Oh, I want to say 'damn'!"

"Why not?" said Miss Mary, with a smile. "That's what I do in the solitude of my chamber whiles. But—"

"But listen, Miss Mary. I have no right to be a minister at all. I ought to be a miner. There I'd turn Bolshevik, like as not. Oh, I don't know what I want. The only man who should orate against the evils and perils of 'massed money' is the man who has masses of it."

"And yet a distinguished philosopher and economist said to me the other day, 'Surely there is a place for observation and deduction.' Besides, the One who said, 'Lay not up treasures on earth,' had nowhere to lay His head—He had not a dollar."

"Yes, but He did not want a dollar. I do. I want a lot of them. I am a plain envious money-lover, jealous of those who have what I have not."

"I don't believe you, laddie. You are just trachled and sore at heart. Come away to your dinner. Go upstairs first and put your head in a basin of hot water which you will find there and don't be too long about it."

The bowl of soup and the lobster did for the minister what psychology and theology could never have done.

"What's your sermon this afternoon at Colin's Cove?" asked Miss Mary as the minister was setting out for his afternoon appointment.

Hector pulled his New Testament out from his hip pocket and read:

"Who was neighbour to him that fell among thieves?"
"He that shewed mercy on him."

"This will not be a scorcher—so much?" said Miss Mary, a smile in her eyes.

"I deserve that, all right," said the minister, with a gloomy face. "But don't rub it in."

"Tut tut! Run away to your folk. But don't forget they just love you and Captain Jock."

"Jock, at least, I know they love," said the minister, going on his way.

CHAPTER XII

MONDAY is supposed to be a "blue" day with ministers, and with Hector this Monday was no exception. The reaction from his Sunday work was heavy upon him. The remembrance of his morning sermon with its flaming denunciation of "fortune-makers" swept over him at times in waves of humiliation that made him groan aloud. He would have gone out among his people but he felt that he could not face them till he had recovered something of self-respect.

Then, too, there was the anxiety gnawing at his heart over his brother's condition. A telegram had arrived to say that a consultation was to be held this afternoon, the result of which it was impossible to forecast.

He attempted to lose himself in a new book setting forth the most modern phase of behaviourist psychology. But he found himself reading a paragraph only to discover that the words left his mind vacant of ideas. In despair he threw down his book, put on his working suit and betook himself to his garden. There was a potato patch to dig for the planting, and beds to prepare for various seeds which ought to be in the ground. He loved flowers but had little interest in making them grow. Gardening was to him mainly a form of exercise.

The day was in harmony with his mood. A dull sky with a chill wind from the sea kept him hard at his digging. As his blood warmed in his veins, the clouds began to lift from his soul and a better mood possessed him. The words of his old professor in philosophy came to him with a modicum of comfort. "When you have done your worst just remember that very likely there's no one thinking about it but yourself."

"Certainly Jimmie Hannah at least will not be thinking about me," he thought. At which point a voice hailed him from the road. Through the line of trees he could see the well-groomed team of the man he had had in his mind.

"Hard at work, Mr. MacGregor. Nothing like it for a Monday morning." Mr. Cameron's voice was kindly and cheery. The minister stuck his spade in the earth and with as cheerful a face as he could achieve he went down to the road.

"Will you not come in, Mr. Cameron?" he asked.

"No, no. I will not be disturbing you at your work." Jimmie Hannah was a firm believer in the wholesome influence of work.

The minister came to the wagon and shook hands.

"I just wanted to tell you again, Mr. MacGregor, how much I enjoyed your sermon."

The minister writhed in his soul, but he had no intention of taking his Elder into his confidence as to his own opinion of himself or his sermon.

"Thank you, Mr. Cameron," he said gravely.

"But it was not for that I came to see you. I have been thinking over your request and I have come to the conclusion that I might be able—"

"Mr. Cameron, I have been able to arrange the matter. I am sorry to have troubled you." It filled the minister's soul with an unholy joy to be able to say this with a pleasant smile.

"You will be annoyed with me, Mr. MacGregor, I fear?"

"Not at all, not at all! It was stupid of me to have made so unbusiness-like a proposition to you, Mr. Cameron."

"You have perhaps been able to borrow it from—"

"No, not exactly, but I have made what I think is a very satisfactory arrangement."

"You have not put yourself out—I mean you have not inconvenienced yourself?"

"Not at all, not at all. Through the good offices of a

friend I have been able to arrange the matter."

"I would be sorry if you have obligated yourself in any—"

"Oh, no, nothing of the sort."

"Well, well, I just wanted to say that I would be quite willing to make the advance—without security—I mean—as a friend—you understand." Mr. Cameron was quite obviously moved out of his ordinary.

"Thank you, Mr. Cameron. I quite understand, and I appreciate your coming to me this morning." Had it been any other man in his congregation he would have offered his hand in token of his gratitude. But somehow his hand refused to move, though he was fully aware that behind that hard face there was some unusual emotion stirring.

Mr. Cameron sat silently for some moments with his eyes upon his horses.

"Well, I will be going. But—" Then suddenly and with a total abandonment of his usual deliberate manner he said: "The truth is, Mr. MacGregor, I was unduly disturbed that morning—indeed I might say I was not quite myself. As a matter of fact, it was Willie George." He paused abruptly.

"Willie George?" The minister came nearer to him.

"Yes, Willie George."

The minister waited.

"He is getting into bad ways."

"Bad ways? Willie George?" The minister's voice expressed his amazement. If one of Mr. Cameron's docile, sleek horses had suddenly been transformed into a bucking broncho of the Western plains he could not have been more astonished.

"Yes. You may look. He is getting entangled with—with—wild ungodly company."

"Wild, ungodly company! Impossible, Mr. Cameron."

"So I would have thought had I not seen them with my own eyes. There was a time when I was thinking—indeed I was hoping—it would be Miss Logie—you will pardon me,

Mr. MacGregor."

"What on earth are you talking about, Mr. Cameron?" asked Hector sharply. "What has Logie to do with it?"

"Nothing at all, and more's the peety. It is that girl in the telegraph office, the bold hussy with her—"

"Mary Bella?" exclaimed Hector in a tone of vast relief.

"Yes, it is what they call her. Though she wants to call herself Isobel. I-s-*o*-bel, if you please, the upstarting creature." The emphasis upon the letter "o" indicated the completeness of Mr. Cameron's contempt. "With her carroty bush on the head of her—bobbed hair indeed it is, like the tail on one of them race horses, and the pent on her face like one of them circus clowns, and not a cent to her name except what she will be putting on her back, and there little enough to cover her nakedness—like the whoor of Babylon that she is!"

"Mr. Cameron, you forget yourself," said the minister in a stern voice.

"Don't I know? There is not a dance nor a rout but she is there, and on a Saturday night, too, at times till near the Sabbath morning itself. And they tell me who have seen her that she is actually seen in the house of that ungodly atheist creature, that Marriott girl, and both of them with a cigarette between their teeth."

The minister started toward him with hand outstretched, paused abruptly, stepped back, and with face white and voice low and husky, said: "Mr. Cameron, you are saying a wicked and cruel thing, sir. Were you a younger man I should exact fitting apology from you for your defamation. You may thank God it was to me you uttered these words. Otherwise you might be called to account in a court of law for your scandal, if indeed you might not suffer bodily injury. Those young ladies are both of them friends of my family and my own friends. They are decent and respectable girls. And if Mary Bella deigns to look at your lout of a son he may think himself highly honoured—and you too, sir, to have such a daughter-in-law."

"My Goad! And you a minister of the Gospel." His lips were all atremble, his eyes glittering as if with madness, his face pale as the face of death.

Slowly he gathered up his whip and reins. "A minister, ay, you may be. But a man of Goad? No, never!" His whip fell upon the backs of his astonished horses who sprang off at a gallop.

"Damned old Pharisee!" Hector glanced hastily about to see if by any chance the interview had been witnessed by any of the villagers.

"God forgive me! But it is what he is," he muttered. "What a damnable slander. By Jove, I will just go down to the telegraph office. He is clean crazy. He may do himself and others great injury." Without hat and in his gardening clothes he set off at a rapid pace toward Mary Bella's place of work. Entering the shop he found Willie George leaning over the counter in deep converse with Mary Bella.

"Get out of here, Willie," he said. "Your father may come in any moment."

"My, my, is that so?" said Willie, terror in his face. "I'll go." Hastily he disappeared by the back door. Mary Bella stood facing the minister, pale and disturbed, but with a kind of fierce defiance in her blue eyes.

"Shall I wait with you, Mary Bella?" said the minister. "He is very wild."

Mary Bella's head went up.

"There is no occasion why you should wait, sir. This is a public office and I am in charge."

"He is in a rage at you, Mary Bella. He may say terrible things. Perhaps I had better wait."

"Huh! Words break no bones," said the girl. "And I think it might be better if you were not here, sir. He is a hard man, and cruel to his son. It is a great shame of him." Hot indignation burned in her eyes. Her whole attitude made Hector think of a mother partridge he had met once

on a woodland path, every feather erect and fluttering de-
fensive fury, on guard for her brood.

"No, Mary Bella, I do not think you require any help
from me," he said with a little smile. "But don't hurt him."

"Hurt him?" exclaimed Mary Bella. "I would like to—
to—"

"Good-bye, Mary Bella. They need fear nothing who
have done no wrong."

"Thank you, sir," said the girl, a quick rush of tears coming to her eyes. "I have not indeed."

Hector went back to his digging, a new respect and wonder in him for women in general and for this slip of a girl in
particular who stood ready to do battle for the man she
loved.

In the late afternoon Mary Bella sent her brother to him
with a wire from Boston. The consultation had resulted in
a decision to operate the following morning.

Study was for him impossible. He determined to go for
a tramp through the hills and return by the fishing camp;
which he did, covering ten miles on his journey and making
half a dozen calls. A half-mile from the camp he came upon
Daphne on her way to a little hillside farm running down by
a succession of terraces to the blue waters of the Bras d'Or,
which at this point penetrated the coast in a deep little bay
with a sand beach. A lovely sunny nook it was, sheltered
from all the winds and fringed with wild plum and Indian
pear, now breaking into bloom.

"How ever did you find your way here, Miss Daphne?"
he cried.

"Angus John brought me here for eggs and milk and butter, and such eggs, such milk and such butter as I never
thought were in the world."

"And the MacDonalds, you know them?"

"Well, I'll say. Aren't they the limit? I didn't know
such people grew on God's earth. Do you know they actually run this ranch, do all the work, without a man?"

"They get help from the neighbours with the plowing, of course."

"But they plant potatoes and beans, carrots and every darn thing themselves, and not a man on the place. Say, I never felt so proud of my sex before. And that little woman cans plums, gallons and gallons, hundreds of them, and berries and currants and every last thing that grows on trees. And did you know she actually cans all sorts of meats, beef and lamb and chicken and pork? What do you know about that? Say, she makes me feel like a tadpole. And that Christine girl. She's only fifteen and she can do any darned thing on the place from nursing lambs to weaving blankets. Did you ever see their blankets? And their homespun cloth, *Claw* they call it. Why, I don't know. I'm going to take a suit length or two home with me—wonderful stuff. Aren't they the ultimate?" Daphne paused from sheer lack of breath.

"They are quite a remarkable family. Have you heard Kenny play his fiddle?"

"*Have* I? I stayed one night till Dr. Wolfe had to come after me—thought I had lost my way and they were wanting the milk and butter for supper. Fiddle? I do a little myself, or used to. The Lord knows Dad spent enough on my violin lessons. I got so that I could chew out the 'Humoresque,' you know, in an agonizing wail. Say, when that boy heard me at it he jumped down my throat, snatched the fiddle out of my hands and went at it! My old Signor Amadi never did it better. He says he heard it on a record at your Miss Mary's. Poor kid, with his crippled leg and his angel face. Look here! It's a crime, a black crime against civilization, that that boy should be shut up here in this hole—"

"Hole! What? This?" Hector waved his arm toward sea and hill and sky.

"You know what I mean—no lessons—hears no music. Oh, hang-dang it all, as Angus John says, that boy should have a master. I'd give him the money, but when I hinted at

something along that line, that woman—his mother— My
heavens! The Duchess of Westoverhamchester couldn't
have chased me into my hole quicker. 'Kenny will be getting his chance in time,' was all she said but it was sign-off
for me, I'm telling you. And the face of him. He makes me
ache in here." Her hand went to her breast. "Say, why
don't you do something?"

"Well, I don't just know," said Hector, rather taken
aback by her vehemence. "He ought to get a chance, certainly."

"Ought to? But will he? When I think of the thousands
of dollars spent by people on all the damn fooleries for their
kids. I suppose I shouldn't have said that to a minister, but
it does get my goat!"

"My dear Miss Daphne, I quite agree. But they'll find
a way somehow. Do you know there's hardly a home in all
this section here but has a son or daughter in school or college or in some good job in the United States or Upper
Canada?"

"And their people at home sweat blood to do it. What's
the use of money anyway? I'd like to give some of the
thousands I waste every year on—on—God knows what."

"Yes, and probably ruin all the finest things in their lives
by it. Money can't do so much after all."

"Oh, there you are. So you said last Sunday, and while
you were speaking I was right with you holding your sweat
blanket, but after we talked it over at camp— Oh, I don't
know—darn it all—I am off in the rough. I wish you'd get
me on the fairway. Somehow—"

"Don't ask me," said Hector emphatically. "I only wish
I knew."

"But you said—"

"Miss Daphne, please do not refer to my sermon again.
And here we are. How are you, Mrs. MacDonald? How is
the planting going?"

"Oh, we have made a beginning. You are wanting the
milk. I am sorry Christine and the lads were late with the

cows. The fence got broke and they wandered off into the bush. But I can give it to you now. I am sorry you will be late for their supper."

"Oh, they can get along all right. I told them I might be late, Mrs. MacDonald. You know you promised me some Gaelic songs to-night."

"Yes, yes, if you can get them at it. Two of the lads have come in who can sing the Ga-a-lic, but they are afraid of fine company."

"Who are they, Mrs. MacDonald?" enquired Hector. "Perhaps I can prevail upon them."

"Indeed you can, but they dislike showin' off. It is Danny Big John and Aleck Morrison. They are good at the Gaelic, but will they?"

There is a delicate technique to be employed and a well-defined ritual to be observed in Cape Breton in the art of persuading singers, even of recognized standing, to perform. All of which was, of course, quite well known to Hector. A frontal attack he knew would be in vain, so with cunning art he began with Kenny and his fiddle.

"How is the fiddle, Kenny?" he asked casually.

"Oh, there is not much time for the fiddle these days."

"Indeed, no," said the mother. "And his fingers are not so soople, with the hoe all day."

"That's so," agreed Hector. "It is too bad. I wanted Miss Daphne to hear 'The Flowers of Edinburgh.' I like the way Kenny plays it. He has turns and quirks of his own. You know, Miss Daphne, every fiddler has his own graces and quavers. For instance, here's the way it is in the book. 'Tee-doo-diddle-dee,' " and Hector went over the tune. "But this is the way that Kenny does it, 'Tow-row-diddle-ow-diddle.' " Aleck and Danny Big John snickered audibly. "What's the matter with you boys? That's the way Kenny does it, 'Tow-row-diddle—' " and again Hector went over the tune.

"Isn't that right, Kenny?"

The boys laughed out loud.

"Well, it is pretty near it," said Kenny, reaching for the fiddle. After careful tuning and a few preliminary flourishes Kenny said, "It is this way." And he was off.

"Yes, yes, that's right. I was wrong," said Hector when the boy had finished. "Now 'The Reel of Tulloch.' " And away went Kenny again. There followed a succession of ancient Highland reels and strathspeys.

"What do you think of that for real music? Not a cheap note in the lot of them," said Hector. "Think of the stuff they are giving us these days!"

"They are perfectly marvellous, especially from Kenny's fingers. And so quaint."

"There, I was waiting for that word," said Hector. "Quaint? What do you mean, *quaint?* Nothing common or slushy like the ghastly stuff we get now over our radios, I hope?"

"No, but different, I mean."

"Different? Well, rather. But now wait till you hear Danny Big John give us a real old Gaelic song."

Danny demurred. He couldn't remember the words. Hector laughed at him.

"Come now, Danny. Miss Daphne must go soon. I want her to hear a real old Cape Breton song. And you are the boy to sing it."

"Come away, Danny," said Mrs. MacDonald. "You might give us 'Ho ro me.' "

"Oh, that one. Aw, that's nothing."

"Come along, Danny, I know that one." And Hector sang the chorus. Danny joined in the last line and followed on into the first verse. Aleck, Kenny and Hector made chorus for him and Kenny accompanied them with wild harmonies on his fiddle. The boys had all good voices, true in pitch and fresh-toned. To Daphne it was a strange performance. Without pause or break the stream of song flowed on. The order was the first verse as a solo by Danny, then the whole company in the refrain, then the first verse repeated by Danny, followed by the refrain. Midway in the refrain the soloist would pause for breath for a line or so, the others gallantly carrying on, but before the refrain was finished he would pick up the last line and swing into the next verse. And so on without pause or break in the stream of music, through the six verses to the end. Then followed "Fear a bhata" and others, songs of the sea and the mountains, of the spinning and the herding and the other life experiences of the Highland folk on the Islands and in the Highlands of Scotland. Wild, weird music, mostly in minor keys.

Daphne was fascinated. It was a completely new experience for her in music. Nothing she had ever heard was like this. Devoted as she was to the mad, cheap, syncopated banalities of most of the modern jazz, there was in this singing something so new, so weird, so wildly beautiful that in spite of herself she fell under its sway.

Then Kenny with a grin on his face called for Danny's masterpiece.

"Give us 'Young Munroe,' Danny. That is the real Cape Breton."

"No, no, Kenny," his mother remonstrated. "That is not Gaelic. Miss Daphne would not like that one. It is not Gaelic at all, but English that Danny sings, and it is the English put on it by a Gaelic man. No, no, Kenny, it is a foolish song."

"Why not, Mother? It is good music, the very best. I played it for Miss Mary and she said it was as good as anything that any German ever wrote."

"You did not sing the words to her."

"But what is wrong with the words, Mrs. MacDonald?" said Daphne, whose curiosity was aroused.

"They are just foolish. You will be laughing at them." Mrs. MacDonald's Highland pride could not bear that.

"Come on, Danny," said Kenny, a wicked grin on his face, while he kept playing softly over and over what sounded like a lament for the dead.

"Tell him to sing it," said Daphne to Hector.

"It will be quite all right, Mrs. MacDonald," said Hector. "Miss Daphne will understand it is a Gaelic song translated by a man not skilled in the English language and with little idea of English rhyme. Come away, Danny, we will give you the chorus."

And Danny, thus admonished, began chanting the chorus in a full, dreamy voice: "Young Munroe Charlie ackum."

YOUNG MUNROE

First Verse:

I was born in Cape Breton.
I was reared on the same.
Oh! I love my native country,
Where I spent my boyhood days.

Chorus:

Young Munroe Charlie ackum
Young Munroe ca thu mo rune.
Young Munroe Charlie ackum,
Handsome Charlie, Young Munroe.

Second Verse:

Cape Breton is an island,
Over a hundred miles long,
And the ocean wash around it,
With its actions, wind and tide.

CHORUS

Third Verse:

Spring and Autumn we enjoy it,
With our little boats at sea.
Small yachts and steamer vessels,
Square rigs and brigantines.

CHORUS

Fourth Verse:

Here I am in a country,
Two thousand miles from the sea.
Briny water and its production
Oh, I love beyond of me.

CHORUS

Fifth Verse:

Here I am in Colorado,
Sitting in the dark alone.
Oh, it's dark and light won't help me,
Till they lay me in the tomb.

CHORUS

Sixth Verse:

By the queeckness of the powder
And the foolishness of me,
I have losted both my ey-es,
And I never shall see again.

CHORUS

Seventh Verse:

It's a cast-iron heart,
Or a heart made of steel,
That would stand the pressure
Of even in my dreams.

Chorus:

Young Munroe Charlie ackum
Young Munroe ca thu mo rune.
Young Munroe Charlie ackum,
Handsome Charlie, Young Munroe.

In the verse Danny's rich, crooning voice carried the music alone, with Kenny's fiddle wailing a deep, low, minor accompaniment; and in the chorus the two boys with the minister assisting took up the refrain with full vigour, allowing the soloist to get breath for the succeeding verse.

Kenny's wicked eyes were on Daphne's face, evidently expecting a grin of derision, but in this he was disappointed. With perfect gravity she heard the song to the end. Then, thanking them, she seized her milk pail, said good night and hurried away.

"My stars! I'll catch it from Dad for being so late. But we have had a grand concert, Kenny. I am sending for some music and you will try it over with Miss Mary for me, eh? Good night. Thank you all a lot." She ran out of the house followed by Hector at a more leisurely pace.

In the bush at the turn of the road Hector caught up with her and found her rocking in a paroxysm of laughter. "What is the matter with you?" he asked, indignation in his voice.

"Oh, Lord, what a song! Say! Could you get it for me? It is priceless!"

"Not to make fun of," said Hector gravely.

"Make fun of? Not for the world. Do you think I would make that woman sore? Not for a million. But that Kenny, he is a young devil. Did you see him on the grin and all the time trying to catch my eye? You must get it for me." But Hector would make no promises. Nor would he later at the camp fire sing the song or recite the words, however much Daphne protested her respect for Mrs. Mac-Donald and her family.

"But that Danny boy is priceless." And Daphne quoted a verse:

> "By the queeckness of the powder,
> And the foolishness of me,

I have losted both my ey-es,
And I never shall see again.

"Young Munroe Charlie ackum—

"What does 'ackum' mean?"
"My darling," said Hector.

CHAPTER XIII

At the camp fire Daphne gave a graphic description of the singing at the MacDonalds'. Hector was none too well pleased. It hurt his Highland pride to have this girl make fun of his people.

"You understand how these songs have come into being, Mr. Inman?" said Hector.

"No, I can't say I do. Never heard anything about them."

"It is an ancient custom of the Highlander to make a song about anything he wishes to give life and wings to. If he has an enemy he makes a song of his wickedness, or folly, so that the story may be broadcast and may live in the memory of the community. So with their virtues, their losses, their griefs, and so on. Then these songs are translated into English by those who, knowing little of English idioms, translate the Gaelic idiom as it stands into English. Scores of these are floating round among the people and are brought out at any social gathering. The music is often really fine and worthy of a place among the finest folk songs of the world."

"They sure do sound swell," Daphne put in, "when that angel-faced Kenny plays them on his fiddle. Say, Dad, I'd like to do something for that boy. Give him a chance with his fiddle. I wish old Amadi could hear him."

"What can you do for them? You can't offer them money. They are immediately insulted."

"Mr. Heggie seems to bear up manfully under the insult," said the doctor dryly.

"He is no Highlander," said Hector.

"Well, tell me, what is the matter with these people anyway? Why are they so poor? Why so many empty farms?"

asked Mr. Inman, voicing the impatience of the successful man of affairs with failure in life's fight. "Are they lazy degenerates like the 'poor whites' of our own Kentucky mountains, or what?"

"Degenerates, sir?" Hector sprang to his feet, struck an attitude and declaimed: "Let me tell you, sir, that during the last fifty years from these little farms have gone forth men who have taken great and honourable parts in guiding the destinies of Canada—yes, and of large sections of the United States as well. Urged by a noble ambition and supported by the sacrificial devotion of fathers and mothers, brothers and sisters at home, they have overcome what might have seemed to others insuperable barriers in the way of training and education, and have won for themselves high honours and positions of power. They have served their country as presidents of universities and of great financial and industrial corporations. They have become professors in colleges or teachers in schools. They have built railroads and directed steamship lines. They have given Premiers to the Dominion and to the Provinces of Canada. They have won distinction as great surgeons, great scientists, great preachers and missionaries. Wherever they have gone they have made life finer, richer, nobler in the communities in which they lived. And at their country's call, with their fellow Canadians they left all that made life dear and adventured forth to meet death on the Seven Seas and upon the bloody battlefields of the Great War, where to-day many of them sleep wrapped in imperishable renown. These, sir, are the men of the Maritimes."

Daphne sprang up with a cry.

"Hurrah! Atta boy! Man, you're grand. That's wonderful."

"Yes," said Hector with a grin. "I was rather proud of that when I delivered it at the Baccalaureate exercises of my University. The boys, however, received it with ribald jeers, ungodly young brutes! But," he added earnestly, "it is all quite true. These abandoned farms and tumbledown buildings about us here mean that ambitious Cape Breton youth seem to think Cape Breton too small an arena for their abilities. The big world outside, they think, offers bigger returns for their life investment."

"But why these deserted farms?"

"Partly shiftlessness, partly lack of organization in producing and marketing."

"Why don't you go after them?"

"I've been thinking about it. It must be done. I am no good at that sort of thing."

"But you have a local market for produce of all kinds?"

"They say there are fifty thousand people in the mining towns within a radius of one hundred miles."

"What of transportation?"

"A railway, good roads and waterways, safe and sheltered, finest in the world."

"And what can you grow here?"

"Anything—everything we need for food. This is an excellent fruit country—berries, currants, plums, apples, all kinds of vegetables. Not even Niagara peninsula can beat us. Then we can raise poultry and sheep—fine sheep, too. We can do a certain amount of dairying. Then besides, our waters salt and fresh are full of fish. Why, these farmers can get enough cod in a few weeks to last them all year."

"Say, are you telling me the truth? Then what in blazes is the matter with these people? You say they are not lazy."

"Not when they have anything they think worth while doing. Wherever they go away from home they take their place among the best."

"Say, young man, why don't you go after them and organize them and get them out of their rut?"

Hector stood nonplussed.

"I really don't know. Didn't think it quite my job, I guess."

"Good Lord! Not your job? Say, I'd like to talk to them. Would it do any good? I know something about organization."

"They would talk to you about Maritime wrongs, confederation and tariffs," said Hector bitterly.

"What the hell has all that to do with producing and marketing their stuff? Say, that's what's killing whole sections in our country. Shootin' off their mouths about their wrongs, when all that's wrong with them is in themselves. That's what held back North Carolina, and whole sections of the South, and other parts as well."

"Mr. Inman, would you talk to a meeting, if I got one together?" said Hector eagerly.

"They'd just tell me to mind my own business, I guess."

But Hector was greatly stirred. It was a subject which had been long in his mind, though he had not given it much definite thought. After long and earnest discussion Mr. Inman agreed to present to them a scheme for co-operative production and marketing.

"All right. Next Sunday, eh?" he said.

"Sunday?"

"What's the matter with Sunday? You too busy?"

"No! But do you think they would talk about marketing on Sunday!"

"Good Lord! Too holy! All right, Monday. You get them there. I'll tell 'em something I know about co-operation."

"Thank you, sir. I shall think about it. They might well have more comforts in life, larger opportunities. But after all—I wonder—"

"Wonder what?" asked Mr. Inman.

"Of course the brightest of them are anxious to get away from these farms, and their parents are ambitious for them, mad after education. They think that the only boys who make a success of life are the boys that get away from the Bras d'Or."

"Guess they are pretty nearly right, too," said Inman.

"I'm not so sure," mused Hector. "Those who have gone out have done well for themselves. They have made money and won fame, but it may easily be that those who have remained have done better. After all, a man's life does not consist in the accumulation of money or of fame."

"No, but money opens the gate to life, to status, power, happiness. What else is there worth while?" said the doctor dryly.

"I'm not certain," said Hector. "Are not these—status, power, happiness—the by-products of life, rather than life itself?"

"And life is—what?"

"Ah, you are asking something. There the greatest of them have been halted. But the great illusion still persists, especially in young men conscious of great power."

"Illusion?"

"That money wins status, power, happiness. And that big money means large life. After all, surely life is that thing in an organism which establishes contacts with its Universe. The more, the finer, the truer the contacts, the larger and better the life. And it is, I believe, the universal experience of the millionaire—you will correct me if I am wrong, Mr. Inman—that his real contacts with men, for instance, arise not from what he has, but from what he *is*. Friendship, fellowship, love, do not come to one because of his money."

"You're damn well right," said Inman with emphasis.

"Of course you're right," echoed Daphne. "Money never got me friendship, fellowship or love. It's perfectly sickening." The girl's voice was full of bitter weariness.

"Hey there, young lady! Why the pessimism?" exclaimed her father. "You've got heaps of friends anyway."

"Have I? Say, Dad, you know darn well that money has nothing to do with friendship or with love either. It's in the way." After a few moments of silence she burst forth again.

"I could make friends with those MacDonalds, with the mother, the girl Christine, with that wonderful boy. But if the shadow of money came into it, the whole thing would be a rotten failure."

"Let me give you an example of what money can or cannot do that came to me to-day," said Hector. And he gave them an account of his experience with James Cameron and Mary Bella. Daphne was quite indignant, her father much less so, and the doctor rather indifferent.

"What has money to do with it one way or another?" he asked.

"The old blighter," said Daphne. "If Mary Bella had scads of money he wouldn't kick."

"A clever young girl," said Mr. Inman. "Getting to be quite an expert in stock-broking. Quite a bright young lady, but I guess money wouldn't make her a better girl, or a better wife for Willie George. She'll make money, though, if she has a chance. By the way, our International Oil is coming on nicely," he added. But Hector was not interested.

"The happiest people I ever knew were quite poor," said Hector, musing. "They had oatmeal and plenty of it, vegetables from their own garden, cod and shad from the sea, and in season trout and salmon and bread and butter, milk and tea."

"What about cake and pie?" asked Daphne. "And fruits and sweets and puddings and ice cream?"

"Yes, they had apples from their own orchard, and plums and rhubarb and berries, wild blackberries. Ice cream? No. I never saw it till I went to college. Everything homemade in food and in most of our clothing, except our Sunday suits. Books too—worth-while books. But we laughed at our own funny clothes and made songs of our hard times, and of our good times too. Happy?" He paused, looked away across the lake and up at the stars. "Yes, while we were all together." His voice sank almost to a murmur.

Daphne, who was standing beside him, put her hand on his arm.

"Sounds wonderful, as you say it," she said softly.

"Wonderful? We never thought—we never knew how wonderful. Money? Good Lord!" His voice was very reverent. "What has money to do with happiness? We need really very little. Now I'm off. There will be another wire to-morrow. Good night."

"Don't be afraid," said Daphne, softly. "He is sure to be all right."

"All right? Yes, he will be all right. Jock will be all right." He moved off quietly into the starlit night, and was soon lost in the shadow of the bush.

"Quite a dreamer," murmured the doctor. Daphne swung fiercely on him.

"Dreamer? Hell! I'm for the hay." Without a good night to either she was off to the cabin.

CHAPTER XIV

BEFORE the minister was finished with his breakfast Mary Bella was at the door with a telegram from Vivien. It read:

> Operation serious but successful. Patient comfortable but very weak. Condition satisfactory on whole. Love from all."

"Very weak," said Hector to himself.

"Yes, but 'condition satisfactory,' " said Mary Bella cheerfully.

" 'On the whole,' " added Hector, anxiety in his tone.

"You could hardly expect better, Mr. MacGregor."

"Thank you, Mary Bella. We must just wait. And now, what about yourself, Mary Bella? Did our friend come in upon you?"

"He did that, and the store full of people. It was better you did not wait, I am thinking," said Mary Bella, relapsing into her native Highland cadences and idioms.

"Was he so dreadful? Did he terrify you?"

"Terrify me?" Mary Bella tossed her head. "It would take more than Jimmie Hannah to scare me. Indeed I was sorry for him before they got through with him."

"What? I hope there was no violence, Mary Bella."

"Violence? Oh, no, there was no violence. That is, not what Ranald Gillis would call violence."

"Ranald Gillis? How did he get into it?"

"Well, you know Ranald's mother was first cousin to my mother. And he just came in when Jimmie Hannah was sayin' things about my character and——"

"Your character, Mary Bella?"

"Well, he might as well as talk about the 'pent on my cheeks' as he said and never a pent on them, but a bit of a rub from a compact as other ladies do, and at that Ranald says: 'How are you, Mr. Cameron?' and takes his hand and holds it.

"'You were talking about my cousin's appearance, Mr. Cameron?' says Ranald, shaking his hand kindly.

"'I was saying she was a— *Ouch!* Let go my hand!' he yells and pulls and wriggles like a fish on a hook.

"'You was going to say what a fine girl my cousin was.' And poor Jimmie Hannah, I was sorry for him and that Ranald made him say the nicest things about me. And all of them laughing like to split. But he said nothing that would hurt me at all, till Ranald led him by the arm and put him out of the door and was that polite to him all the time. Indeed I was sorry for him."

"That was too bad of Ranald," said the minister, but the smile on his face did not indicate any great depth of compassion.

"But that wasn't all of it," said Mary Bella in an anxious voice. "Black Mack MacNeil, a Barra man from the Cove —his mother's cousin is married on to Jimmie Hannah's brother—he speaks up and says: 'You are a great man with old people, I see, Mr. Gillis.'

"'Do you then?' said Ranald. 'And perhaps you may see something else, you or any of your Barrich tribe, if you put your tongues on innocent girls—and you hear me, Black Mack.'

"'I hear you. But I'm taking no orders from any Skeanach bully on the Bras d'Or water,' he says.

"But Johnnie Big Duncan stepped in and smoothed them out. Oh, I am awful feard that something will happen. Those Barra men are a wild lot, and Ranald has a temper."

"I must see Ranald," said Hector.

"Now I must be going," said Mary Bella. "I was very sorry, but—well, he is a hard man to his own. Good-bye, sir. We are all hoping the best things for Captain Jock."

But she did not tell the minister of another telegram sent by Dr. Whitney to his friend Dr. Wolfe, a telegram of more ominous import.

Mary Bella went back to her work and her own troubles, and heavy enough they were and all the heavier because she could share them with no one. Sorely against her will, and resisting at every single step, she had become a stock-broker to a number of her fellow villagers. It was Willie George who was her first client. Innocently enough and with a grateful heart she had confided to Willie George her joy that the minister had been able to escape from his financial *impasse* and was now in a position to provide for his brother, Captain Jock, all the medical care and attendance necessary.

"Is it not a great mercy and Providence that Mr. Inman came just at the moment of his sorest need? And you know his five hundred dollars will have grown to a great sum in another jump. My, but I'm glad." Willie George was keenly interested and drew from her all she knew of the mysteries of the stock market operations.

"But he might lose it all."

"Yes, indeed, if Mr. Inman himself was not behind it. But with him in it and responsible there is no fear of loss."

Next evening Willie George on their quiet walk poured forth a dreadful tale of distress. He was in deep waters financially. His father had advanced him the money for an automobile a year ago. He had paid the full amount, but had borrowed back again some five hundred dollars from the dealer for his own needs. Now the agent was insisting upon payment. Poor Willie George had no regular allowance, but depended solely upon the meagre pittance granted him by his father at odd times. His grandmother also occasionally bestowed a small gratuity upon him.

"It is a shame!" said Mary Bella indignantly. "You ought to have a regular allowance from the farm. You work hard enough for it."

"It is a shame. I ought to have a salary."

"Why not ask your father, then?"

"Yes, and tell him how I spend every dollar? It was my own money I took. But he would make me out a thief if I told him."

"I wish I had it, but I—"

"Nonsense! Do you think I would take it from you? But"—he added with hesitation—"if I could invest it now in Mr. Inman's Oil."

"No, no. I am not going to allow you." Mary Bella was very sharp about it.

"But you took the minister's five hundred dollars from him."

"No, Mr. Inman did that."

"But you own three hundred?"

"That is my own responsibility."

"You won't do this for me, Mary Bella. Oh, all right. I will get it some other way." He looked so depressed, so unhappy that, after long argument and sorely against her judgment, Mary Bella relented and Willie George's two hundred dollars went into International Oil at sixty on a margin of ten percent, and began its pyramidal course to wealth.

The same day Mrs. Heggie stole into Mary Bella's office with the stealth and mien of a dangerous conspirator. "Here," she said in breathless haste and in a throaty whisper, thrusting at Mary Bella a parcel wrapped in brown paper and tied securely with stout yarn. "There is eighty-seven dollars. Thirty-five of it I cached from Hughie in the time he has been driving and doing business for the American gentleman, and the rest I made with my finger-bones. Angus John was telling Hughie about it, how you will be putting it into them stockings and getting hundreds out of them. And the mortgage is past due and the lawyer is for taking the farm off us. And me working twenty-five years on it, but you see Jamus put the money into that automobil business and that was the last of it. I am needing jist another sixty-three, and I would save the place. And I thought—" Here her breath failed her and her voice sank into miserable silence.

It took Mary Bella half an hour to understand the full story of Mrs. Heggie's need, and another half-hour to explain to her the perils of the stock market, and to make clear the danger and folly of her proposed investment. Mrs. Heggie, however, was deaf to warnings.

"But the minister did it, and yourself did it, and you the niece of my own mother's cousin." Mrs. Heggie's strong face was working strangely under the violence of her emotion. Indeed she was in a desperate case. Her very life was threatened. She would soon be on the road.

"I can't do it, Auntie. I can't do it. It is mad folly for you to try this."

"And why not for the minister or yourself? But if you have no bowels in you for your own flesh and blood—" Her voice shook in mingled amazement, grief and despair.

"Oh, well, give it to me," said Mary Bella in desperation. "But I warn you that if you lose your money you need not come to me for sympathy."

"Well, I will be losing the farm whateffer. So why not? But at any rate you will hear no complaints out of me."

The old Highland woman's head went up, her lips clamped hard shut. She might be thrust out upon the road, but Mary Bella would hear no word of recrimination from her.

A few days later Willie George's expansive excitement over his first stock rise led him to confide his great secret to Ranald Gillis, with the result that Ranald had become an investor through Mary Bella.

"How could I refuse Ranald after him standing up for me to your father?" she said to Willie George. "Why in all time did you tell him? And who else did you tell? Not another one will I listen to, if he should die on my doorstep."

But though Mary Bella remained adamant against further solicitations the traffic in International Oil went secretly but briskly on, through the perfectly respectable and up-to-date legal firm of MacGillivray & Stewart in Sydney. Mary Bella was torn between excited and rosy hopes on one hand and gloomy fears on the other. The daily report by wire from her brokers in New York, however, cheered her mightily. International Oil moved slowly but steadily upward day by day. From lip to lip the portentous secret spread with alternating hope and fear, the investors pinning their hopes mainly on Mr. Inman's millions and on the soundness of judgment and integrity of purpose of the minister of Ravanoke.

To neither of these gentlemen, however, did the slightest whisper of these secret and exciting activities make their way.

Both of them were giving all their spare time to preparations for the great meeting called for the following Monday. By Hector, through the schools, by letter and visitation, and by public notices posted at strategic points in the valley, announcement was made of the meeting, while by large use of the telegraph Mr. Inman prepared himself with data in regard to the benefits of co-operative associations in Nova Scotia, of which there existed a number, and of the possibilities and conditions of success for such an association in this community along the Bras d'Or lake.

It was well for the minister that the preparations for the great meeting on Monday became more and more engrossing as the day drew near, for the daily wire from Vivien became more and more guarded in tone, and even Logie's letters were not altogether reassuring.

"He suffers no pain," she wrote. "He sleeps fairly well, but he is strangely dull. He eats almost nothing, though Steve must spend hours in seeking dainties suggested by the dietician, with whom he has made friends. What we would have done without that boy I cannot imagine. We have long since forgotten that he is Mr. Inman's chauffeur and have taken him into our little family circle. He takes either Vivien or me out every day, often each of us in turn, or, if Jock is asleep and the nurse insists, both of us together. He discovers the most wonderful plays and pictures and looks so hurt if we do not use the tickets he has secured. He is always bringing a new book or magazine, and his taste is that of a well-read man. Jock has taken a great fancy to him, and would rather have Steve with him for an hour than either of us."

"What a treasure!" exclaimed Miss Mary to whom Hector read bits of his letter.

"It is very slow improvement," was Hector's reply.

"But remember the serious character of the operation and the long previous diseases. We ought to be very thankful he is not worse."

"I suppose so," said Hector, "but I am just sick with anxiety."

"Nonsense! Jock has the strength of a horse and the courage of a lion."

Dr. Wolfe, however, gave Hector the first cause for serious alarm.

"He might be just as well off at home," he said one evening toward the end of the week when the fishing party had come in to spend the evening with Miss Mary. "Indeed, he might make more rapid progress in his native air here."

"Do you think, Doctor, he is not doing well?" asked Hector.

Miss Mary threw the doctor a warning glance.

"He is certainly not gaining strength as he should."

"Are you anxious, Doctor?" said Hector. "I want the truth."

"That is just what I can't give you without actually seeing him. But don't jump to conclusions," added the doctor with a touch of impatience.

"Don't mind him, Hector," said Daphne. "He is always that way with his patients. He is a perfect nuisance to us all. Don't look like that. Come and listen to Miss Mary. She is really getting me to like Bach. Come and listen to this prelude. Do you know, it makes me think of some of Kenny's Highland stuff." She caught Hector by the arm, dragged him away from the doctor, and set him down upon the piano bench by Miss Mary.

"There now, that phrase is 'the dead spit'—as Angus John says—of one of Kenny's weird Hebridean things."

"Can't get it," said Hector.

"Listen now. Do that again, Miss Mary. Now there, isn't that Hebridean stuff?"

Hector declared his inability to detect the likeness. Daphne strongly insisted and at length managed to inveigle him into a violent argument. But the argument was brief, if violent, and again Hector's face was showing the shadow of pain and anxiety. In desperation Daphne led the conversation from Bach to the approaching meeting, which she protested she was going to attend.

"Why not?" she asked in answer to Hector's dubious look.

"There will be no women there. Our men do not like women to butt into men's affairs," said Hector.

"And that's why their affairs have got into the present jam. Aren't you going, Miss Mary?"

"I hadn't thought of doing so," said Miss Mary in rather a shocked voice. "What does Mr. Inman think?"

"On general principles I should have said no. But this is as much women's business as men's, and I'm not sure it wouldn't be a good thing if they were there."

"Say, who runs the fruit end of the farms round here? Who put up the four hundred and fifty gallons on the Mac-Donald farm? You let the women in on this if you want it to go," Daphne warned. It was not Daphne, however, nor Miss Mary, nor Mr. Inman who settled the matter.

In his weekly visit to the Widow MacAskill, Hector received his final instructions in regard to the meeting.

"Keep out the women?" exclaimed the old lady. "And what will you be having with you? A herd of dumb, driven cattle, with nothing in them but a grunt, and waiting for Jimmie Hannah to tell them what to do. And you know what that will be."

"And what's that, Grannie?" asked Hector mildly.

"Jist nothing," snapped the old lady. "There is no place in that one for any thought but for himself. No, no, Minister, let the women in, and if they can't give much advice they can soon tell the men where they are wrong. That is what they are best at. They have been doing that for hundreds of years. Indeed, you may see me there myself. It is time the women were taking their place. Co-operative work indeed? That is what women have been at all their lives— co-operating; and the man operating and getting the glory."

Hector listened in amazement.

"But, Grannie, I never knew you were that kind of woman —for women's rights and that sort of thing."

"Women's rights?" The dark searching eyes were ablaze. "Look at the women in this part of the country. Take them one by one, in their homes. What is it that is the chief product of the women? Babies. It is inside their very bodies that these souls come into being, it is in the bodies of women that they receive their first shape—the dear lovely things! It is from women's breasts they draw their life; it is by women's hands they are taught to walk. Night and day, and all night and all day, the women have their hands upon them, making and shaping them body and soul. Soul? Ay, the best men are like their mothers. Tuts, man! Here I am saying things I have never said all my life, but they have been here, I am telling you!" The deep, husky voice rose clear, almost shrill, the claw-like hands smote upon the withered breasts. Abruptly she paused. A soft and tender light filled the brilliant dark eyes. "Not but what my men hef been good to me. Every man of them. Ay, good to me!" Her voice grew wistful and tender. "But they were and are rare men." She sank back against her pillows and from her closed eyes two tears ran down the withered cheeks.

"Yes," said Hector. "Good men because they had the hand of a good woman upon them."

"Oh, I do not know," she said wearily. "Himself was a good man to me. And the boys are always good to me. But"—the dark eyes flashed open—"be wise and let the women in to your meeting."

Hence it came that word went out through the schools and announcements were made at the church services that women were expected to attend the meeting on Monday. It was this undoubtedly that filled the church with men. As Hughie Heggie at the church door on Sunday put it:

"Ma gosh, lads, ye'll need to be there. Gude alane kens what they'll be daein' wi' us."

Of course Hughie's word had little enough weight—he was only a South Country man. Nevertheless it was as well to be on the safe side.

CHAPTER XV

THE minister was in the chair and conducted the "opening exercises." The size of the meeting evidently quite surprised and indeed disturbed him. But bravely enough and briefly he made a statement as to the origin and purpose of the meeting.

The origin of the meeting lay in a suggestion made by a distinguished American visitor, Mr. T. Russell Inman, in a conversation with himself—the minister—as to the advantage that might accrue to the people of this community by co-operation in production and in marketing. He himself was no expert in these matters. Mr. Inman was. He had promoted many successful companies. He would ask the meeting to appoint a chairman and secretary and proceed to business.

At this point the meeting had its first sensation. The door opened and, leaning upon the sturdy arm of her granddaughter Peggy and supporting herself upon a stout black staff, came Mrs. MacAskill, followed meekly by her son Sandy. She was beautifully arrayed in a dress of her daughter's providing, soft black voile trimmed with lace. A large black hat, also with lace trimming—likewise the gift of her daughter—shaded the wrinkled face. Slowly, with deliberate and impressive dignity, and followed by her son, she made her way to her accustomed pew at the minister's right, from where she could command a view of the congregation.

The minister, who had stepped from the platform to meet her, placed her in her pew and proceeded with the business. But everyone felt that the meeting was invested with a new importance and significance by the presence of that dignified

and impressive figure in black at the minister's right. The
minister called for nominations for chairman.

"Chairman?" said the old lady impatiently in a low but
perfectly audible voice. "Tuts! Who will be chairman but
yourself?" A slight rustle of assent went through the audience.

"Move it, man," she ordered Sandy, who forthwith
obeyed. The motion was seconded and carried with ac-
claim.

"Now for a secretary," said the chairman. Silence en-
sued. These people were deliberate in their movements.
Mrs. MacAskill moved restlessly in her seat, thumping the
floor once or twice with her staff.

"There is Mary Bella," she said in her hoarse but perfectly clear undertone, pointing to the girl, who sat in a
front seat in the middle aisle. No one moved.

"Tuts, man! Move it, will you!" Sandy was a shy man
whose chief characteristic was indecision. Suddenly she
turned her fierce old eyes upon him. Immediately Sandy
in a hurried voice moved accordingly. A broad smile swept
the audience.

"I move that Mr. Donald MacTavish, the Clerk of Session, act as secretary of this meeting as is appropriate."

The old lady peered from under her hat at Mr. James
Cameron, the author of the motion, who sat across the
church from her.

"Huh! Jimmie Hannah!" she muttered. "And what has
he against Mary Bella? She is very queeck with her pen."

"I second Mr. MacAskill's motion," said Ranald Gillis in
a clear firm voice. "Miss MacRae has the pen of a ready
writer." Laughter and applause greeted the remark.

"It is moved and seconded that Miss Mary Bella MacRae
be secretary," said the chairman.

"I will second the motion for Mr. MacTavish," said Mr.
Malcolm MacNeil from the Cove across the hill. "He is
the Clerk of Session and it is more better whateffer that a

man should be the secretary of a meeting of business."

"Who is that?" asked Mrs. MacAskill of her son. "Oh, indeed! Black Mack, a Barra man," she said. "I know him and his father before him." The tone was enough to condemn Malcolm MacNeil and his ancestors and all their works to deserved oblivion.

Mary Bella in much confusion was protesting to her neighbour,

"I won't be secretary. I don't want to be secretary."

"Whisht now, lassie," said Mrs. MacAskill, reaching forward and tapping her arm with her staff. "Keep your seat." Mary Bella obeyed.

"Any further motions?" enquired the chair.

The vote for Mary Bella was almost unanimous and was greeted with loud applause by all except the Barrich following and the proposer of the defeated nominee.

"Huh! Barrich!" A rippling smile indicated the reach of the hoarse undertone of the old lady's ejaculation and the sympathy of her hearers in her obvious opinion of the Barra element in the meeting.

Organization having been duly effected, the chairman briefly explained the purpose of the meeting and called upon Mr. T. Russell Inman to set forth a plan of co-operative production and marketing for the consideration of the people of this district.

"I confess I am no expert in matters of this kind," said the chairman, "but I believe Mr. Inman has had large experience in these matters."

Mr. Inman's speech was that of a trained promoter and a shrewd judge of human nature.

He was here to-day for three reasons. First, he wanted to make some return to his friend the chairman for his help in time of need. Then followed a humorous description of his first experience of Ravanoke mud. In three minutes he had his audience in his hand.

Second, he was interested in this country. Then followed

an enthusiastic laudation of the beauty of the Bras d'Or land. But there was more than beauty: there were great possibilities in the natural resources of the country.

Third, he was interested in making beautiful homes for people. He had seen the most famous beauty spots on this continent. The valley of the Hudson, the shores of Long Island, the beautiful hill country of his own South land, and California. He had seen the wonderful Niagara peninsula and the Thousand Islands in Ontario, but nowhere had he ever seen a country so rich in the possibilities of making beautiful homes. And beautiful homes were the finest product of any nation. He waxed eloquent over the value to a nation of beautiful homes. All the best people came from good homes. He was surprised and grieved to see so many abandoned farms on these lovely hillsides. He had seen the same thing in parts of his own country—in New England, in the Carolinas, in Virginia. The cities were killing country life and country homes. And yet when men had made wealth they wanted nothing better than to make a lovely home in just such a country as this. He was not talking about making great wealth.

"The minister has been making me see more clearly that the most valuable thing in this world is not wealth but Life. I don't think you can make great wealth. In this section of your country not fortunes but homes, beautiful and comfortable, could be made. The population of this country should be and could be twice what it is. What is needed is intelligently directed energy."

He understood that these hillsides could give the best of vegetables, fruits and grain, and that on these farms, sheep, poultry and hogs could be profitably raised. Then too this marvellous lake could furnish inexhaustible supplies of the finest fish in the world. The people could never be frozen out while these forest-clad hills were at their backs. Besides all this, at their doors were lumber, stone, and lime for building, and—best of all—within a hundred miles there

realized country

was a market of seventy-five thousand souls. Why should not these charming valleys be adorned with beautiful little farms with gardens and orchards and filled with happy families in lovely homes?

"This marvellous abundance of raw material is of no avail unless the people of this country bring to bear upon it three things: Intelligence, Energy, and Co-operation. These three qualities explain the achievements of all great nations. Look at the old land. What has made Britain great? Intelligence, energy, and co-operation. Scotland? The United States? These three necessary qualities."

What was needed was simply intelligent energy co-operatively applied. Intelligence, energy, and co-operation would transform this lovely, wonderful land.

"Study together, experiment together on the best methods of production of your fruits, vegetables, live-stock. Study together the best method of transportation of your products. Study together the best method of securing and holding and developing the market at your doors. Then all work together to bring your products in the finest shape to the people over yonder who need them."

When Mr. Inman had ceased his whole scheme lay like an illuminated moving picture before the minds of his audience. But there was no wild applause—only a quiet and decently expressed approval of a worthy effort by an apparently honest and intelligent man of affairs who seemed to appreciate the undoubted and unsurpassed beauties and excellencies of their country.

The chairman thanked Mr. Inman for his comprehensive and lucid address and invited questions or discussion.

Dead silence followed. They were canny folk. Silence meant safety. The open mouth catches the hook. Don't be the first to try the ice. They had all been carefully nurtured on cautious saws, these Kelts.

Again the minister invited questions. He knew his people, however, and their capacity for masterly inaction.

After prolonged silence the minister was somewhat disturbed to see Mr. Marriott rise in the middle of the church.

"I do not make a custom of speaking in church," he began, "nor do I think my voice will be much welcomed here. But to-day I cannot keep silence. I have waited many years for this day. One of the bitter disappointments we Maritime people have to bear is to see our country—so beautiful, so rich in natural resources—gradually become depopulated of our finest people and slipping into decay. I have studied this question deeply. Here are some statistics to substantiate what I have said." The statistics he had to offer were disturbing to the complacent self-appreciation of Maritimes. "I know it is customary for interested but not too honest or well-informed politicians to wax eloquent over our 'Maritime wrongs,' to harp on Confederation, or to attack violently the fiscal inequities imposed by Ottawa. But whatever of truth there may be in these eloquent fulminations, the honest and fair-minded and courageous thinkers among us know that the causes of our ills lie chiefly in ourselves. Where would our Scottish people have been had they sat down and bemoaned and lamented their political and financial disabilities? The Scottish people hold the proud position which they now occupy in the world largely because with resolute courage and unfaltering faith in themselves they have put into effect that fine dictum of the speaker to-day—intelligent energy co-operatively applied to the raw material lying about us. He is right. We know he is right. Nova Scotia and Cape Breton will reach their rightful place in this Dominion not by ignoble whinings about our 'Maritime wrongs' but by the intelligent and co-operative application of energy to our wonderful raw material. I pledge all I have and am to this end."

Once more silence fell upon the meeting, the silence of conviction and of humiliation. For whatever their opinion of the speaker might be, most of the audience and more particularly the younger generation were quite ready to acknowledge the truth of his courageous words.

"Any questions to ask?" pleaded the chairman.

There was no question.

"Any motion to make?"

Mrs. MacAskill began to fidget. Her piercing black eyes began to dart little flames of light at one and another of those about her.

Finally to her son Sandy she muttered impatiently, "What is keeping them? Bells without clappers." A wide smile illumined the solemn faces. "They are waiting for Jimmie Hannah, I am thinking. Come away then, Jimmie," she said, waving her staff at him. "Have ye lost your tongue?" Thus admonished and fearing he knew not what, Mr. Cameron rose and in portentous solemnity broke silence.

He began with a eulogium of the address they had heard from this visitor to their little village. He was sure they were grateful for this stranger's interest in them and for his desire to help them. They all were delighted with the pictures he had painted of what might be done for them. But they were a quiet folk in this country and he was not sure that they were anxious to have this valley transformed into a Coney Island.

"I was there one time and when I got among the noise and the commotion and—yes, I will say it—the dissipation and wickedness, well—I prayed the Lord if I might get out alive. No, no, I want no Coney Island in Ravanoke. And so I would move that this meeting of the people of Ravanoke and vicinity thank this American gentleman for his kind interest in us and for his remarkable and very beautiful address, and that since we are doing very well in our own quiet way we now adjourn."

The meeting gasped. A due and proper caution was very well but dumb inaction was something quite different.

"I second the motion," came from the rear of the church.

"Huh!" said Mrs. MacAskill quite audibly with a sharp thump of her staff. "The Barrich again!"

Then up spoke Ranald Gillis in an angry voice. "Adjourn? Why did we come here? Is Mr. Cameron insulting us? Let us get to business."

"There is a motion to adjourn, Mr. Chairman," said Mr. Cameron, "which must be put without discussion, I believe."

Again the meeting gasped. The chairman intervened.

"The motion is that we thank the speaker for his kindly interest in us and for his address and that we now adjourn. This is not a straight motion to adjourn and is therefore open to discussion. But I do not wish to stand upon a technicality and if Mr. Cameron wishes to make a simple motion to adjourn I shall accept his motion."

"Thank you, sir. I move that this meeting do now adjourn," said Mr. Cameron promptly.

"I second the motion," said his backer.

Then in wrath rose up Mrs. MacAskill. "And would you be making a fool of me, Jimmie Hannah, me that has sucked you and skepit you, bringing me out with much pain and sending me home again with nothing for it. And you an elder of the church. 'We are doing very well,' you are saying. Yess, yourself may be doing very well, Jimmie Hannah, like the fox with the hen inside of him. Adjourn? Adjourn, is it? My man, if you wish to adjourn, why do you not adjourn yourself and leave decent and kindly people to plan how they may help one another? I am ashamed of you, Jimmie Hannah, and your mother will be ashamed of you when I inform her of your ungodly proposition. Adjourn?" Her voice rose with her indignation. "Go! Out from this place! Out, I tell you. I am ashamed." While she spoke she continued to hobble toward Jimmie Hannah, thumping her stick as she went. The unfortunate man, fearing a scene, seized his hat and passed hastily down the aisle followed by the cheers and jeers of the meeting. "You had better be taking your Barrich collie with you." Again the cheers broke out as huge Black Mack rose up from his seat and, followed by some of the Barrich folk, left the building.

Muttering wrathfully the redoubtable old lady hobbled back to her pew. "Now let us be getting something done, Minister," she said impatiently.

"All in favour of the motion to adjourn will say 'ay,' " said the chairman. Not a sound was heard.

"Adjourn? Man, are you, too—" began Mrs. MacAskill.

"Those opposed say 'no.' "

The no's shook the building.

"Now let us proceed with the discussion," said the chairman.

Immediately with extraordinary vigour and intelligence the discussion was carried on, and with entire unanimity the resolution was adopted organizing the Bras d'Or Co-operative Association and electing the following as the officials of the new organization:

Patron . . . . .Mr. T. Russell Inman
Honorary President . .Mrs. Duncan MacAskill
President . . . . .The Rev. Hector MacGregor
Vice President . . . . . .Mr. Hugo Marriott
Secretary . . . . .Miss Mary Bella MacRae
Treasurer . . . . .Mr. Ranald Gillis

Committee . . . .⎰ Miss Logie MacGregor
⎟ Miss Mary Murray
⎨ Mr. Dugald Morrison
⎟ Mr. William George Cameron
⎱ Mr. Norman MacKinnon

"And now as to the financing," said Mr. Inman.

"Should we not try to get the Government to help us?" said a voice meekly.

"Now I have been waiting to hear that suggestion," said Ranald Gillis, springing to his feet. "That is the curse of this country. The Government! For any sake let us try to do something for ourselves for once. The Government and politics are the ruin of Cape Breton—yes, and of Nova

Scotia. If the Government comes into this I'm out. Let's see what we can do by pulling all together for once on this business."

"Hear, hear!" cried a score of voices.

"I think Mr. Gillis is right," said Mr. Inman. "I advise beginning in a small way. Issue, say, fifteen shares at one dollar par value to start with. You can increase the issue as necessity arises."

This was agreed to.

"You are wanting money, is it?" said Mrs. MacAskill. "I was thinking you would be, and so I am prepared to put down two hundred dollars for my son the doctor, and twenty-five dollars for the professor—poor man, his pay is little enough and he has his own family—and twenty-five dollars for Maisie—she has no family. That will be two hundred and fifty dollars in all. I wish it was more."

"Mr. Chairman," said Mr. Inman, "I cannot allow myself to be beaten by a lady, even so great a lady as our Honorary President, so I am going to ask you to allow me to raise her ante by another two hundred and fifty dollars."

"Your subscription is two hundred and fifty dollars, Mr. Inman?" said the chairman. There was a shout from the youth at the rear.

"I am afraid, Mr. MacGregor, some of your younger members know more about the game of poker than you do. No, sir, my subscription is five hundred dollars, and little enough considering the lead given us."

"Say, can't I get in on this?" said Daphne. "I'd like to stand up beside Mrs. MacAskill if she'll let me." The eager enthusiasm in her voice, her brilliant beauty, her vivid smile swept the audience into a wild burst of applause.

"Look here, boys," said Ranald Gillis, standing up and looking over the young fellows about him. "We can't get into that class but we can all go in for something. I'm going to propose—and Danny MacKinnon here will second it— that we ask Mary Bella for half a dozen sheets out of her book and we will all put down what we can. We want *you* more than your money. So put your names down and opposite them just what you can." This was carried with enthusiasm and in a few minutes the lists showed thirty-seven names with subscriptions amounting in all to six hundred and two dollars, a total of sixteen hundred and two dollars.

The chairman then called the committee to meet the following evening at the manse at seven, and the meeting was dismissed with prayer and the benediction.

"Will you please present me to Mrs. MacAskill?" said Mr. Inman after the meeting had broken up.

"With pleasure," said the minister.

"You certainly are responsible for the very splendid success of the meeting, Mrs. MacAskill," said Mr. Inman as he shook hands with her.

"Me!" said the old lady. "Indeed it is terribly ashamed I am. I want to go away home to my bed. Indeed the minister will tell you I am a quiet old woman. Am I not then?" The old eyes turned on the minister.

"Very quiet, but always effective," said Hector, patting her hand.

"Tut, tut, laddie, you are laughing at me. But could I bear to see any of my own kin doing a thing like that? His mother was cousin to my own man no less."

"Sure thing you couldn't," said Daphne with emphasis.

The shrewd old eyes flashed upon the girl's face. "Ay, lassie, you will be making men march to your drum some day."

"We all thank you, Mrs. MacAskill," said Hector earnestly.

"No, no, laddie. But thank the man that made that picture. No, these eyes will never see it, but my grandchildren will see it. A beautiful picture. Beautiful homes along the Bras d'Or and full of bonnie, healthy bairns."

"Sure you'll see it, Grannie," said Daphne, pressing the claw-like fingers between her hands. The old lady turned her luminous eyes upon the girl's face, drew her down and kissed her without a word.

"Say! Isn't she a corker?" said Daphne as she stood with the minister watching the old lady drive away in Ranald Gillis' car. "Boy! What a peach!" But there was a mist in her eyes as she said it.

CHAPTER XVI

THE whole day Hector gave to the preparation for the Committee meeting in the evening. With his church roll before him, he planned departments of work and groups of workers. Each department was to be put in charge of the person who had shown the greatest success in or fondness for that special work, with a committee to help. The main lines of the plan Hector laid before the meeting for discussion.

"The guiding principle of the Co-operative Association," said Hector, "is that given by Mr. Inman: 'The Association helps each member to serve the whole membership.' If anyone has a specialty he must try to make us all specialists. For instance, for years Mr. Marriott has done wonders with his flowers and vegetables; we make him head of the horticultural department. Willie George is strong on hogs and sheep; he is responsible for that department. Sandy MacAskill's department is poultry. Mrs. MacDonald is mistress of the art of canning fruit, vegetables, meat. Miss Mary and Miss Logie will have charge of the fine arts, music and dramatics. Each head will arrange for a demonstration of what can be done from time to time. Mr. Inman and Ranald Gillis have a very important job: the transportation and marketing department. Each head is empowered to choose suitable assistants to form a committee.

"There will be a weekly meeting of the executive committee till things are going smoothly. Each head and each committee must assume responsibility for the success of its department. There will be a lot of hard work to do, but hard work and full co-operation will bring results. Now I invite criticism. This is only a rough outline. Go to it."

"Some executive, eh?" said Mr. Inman. "Say, if you

folks ever want to fire your minister let me know. He can name his own salary."

"We've got him nailed down right where he is," said Ranald.

Two hours they spent in discussion and the meeting was closed with prayer.

"Well," exclaimed Daphne, "this is the funniest kind of business I ever heard of. Prayers at both ends."

"A survival, my dear young lady," muttered Mr. Marriott. "Superstition dies hard."

"Don't listen to him," said Miss Mary. "He is a dear old pagan and not half so bad as he loves to appear."

At the close of the meeting Mary Bella handed a telegram to Hector. "I didn't want to give you this till after the meeting," she said.

He opened the wire and read: "Arrive Friday evening if weather fine. All glad to get home. *Signed,* Vivien."

"He is no better," said Hector.

"The wire doesn't say so. Anyway the change to this air will do him good," said Mr. Inman, taking Hector off with him for a walk.

"I want to tell you something," said Mr. Inman, after they had walked some distance. "That stock of yours is up to 90."

Hector paid no heed. He had no interest in stocks.

"Look here! Don't you know what that means? If you want to take your profits you must now control some twenty thousand dollars."

Hector woke with a start. "Twenty thousand dollars. I don't want it. I won't have it. Get rid of it. What did I do to get that?"

"You invested a lot of money in International Oil."

"Five hundred dollars."

"Nonsense, you have been investing a lot more, and if you wait till the stock goes to par you will be worth easily twice that."

"Awful! You promised to buy from me at par, Mr. Inman. Buy now! Take it off my hands."

"Don't be a fool," said Mr. Inman impatiently. "In a month that stock will touch par. I know it."

"I tell you, sir, I will not wait an hour. That is more money than I want. Let us go to the telegraph office right away and see about it."

"Very well, Mr. MacGregor. I promised. You are making a very great mistake. I mean that stock to go to par within a month. You will lose twenty thousand dollars. But it is your own funeral," said Mr. Inman in great disgust. "I will take your stock at market value."

After much argument Hector agreed to accept ten thousand dollars in cash and ten thousand in paid-up stock, which arrangement was concluded that night with Mr. Inman's brokers by wire.

While Mr. Inman was dealing with Hector in the matter of stock profit-taking, Miss Mary and the other members of the committee were arranging that Hector should be lured away on Wednesday and Thursday and the manse given a thorough housecleaning, with such refurnishing in the way of curtains, papering and rugs as might be achieved in the time. Ranald and Mr. Inman, who were to spend Wednesday in Sydney on Co-operative Association business, were to make the necessary purchases. Miss Mary and Daphne, with such assistance as could be got from the other women in the vicinity, took this matter in charge.

Wednesday, Hector spent among his parishioners at the Cove some six miles away, returning to spend the night at the house of Miss Mary. The following afternoon he was setting off to visit in his Back River parish, and spend the night there. By land round the deep indentation of the Cove the journey would be twelve miles, but by boat the distance would be cut in two.

"I'll see you off, Hector," said Daphne. "And then I am going up to the MacDonalds' to spend the night there.

I am taking some music for Kenneth, and we are going to have some Gaelic songs. Father and Ranald Gillis are to spend the night in Sydney, you know. Good-bye, Miss Mary. You ought to come with one of us. We would each love to have you."

"Not to-day. I have my classes this afternoon. I shall see you to-morrow after dinner, and you, Hector, some time toward evening."

"No, in the early afternoon, Miss Mary," said Hector.

"Don't hurry. Everything will be quite ready for the homecoming."

"I shall be back early in the afternoon," said Hector, waving a farewell to his hostess.

"I shall see you off, Hector," said Daphne, stepping out with him toward the water front.

The blue waters of the Bras d'Or lay twinkling in the sun. The hills toward Back River lay in a purple mist like humped-up sleeping monsters.

"How long would it take to sail across to those hills?" asked Daphne.

"With this brisk wind about forty minutes, perhaps less."

"I'd like to go across. How about it?"

"Not to-day. I'm busy, and you are due at the Mac-Donalds'."

"They don't expect me. I made no definite arrangement with them."

"Then, too, that bank of cloud in the east there is not too promising, and—".

"And besides you don't want me."

"Oh, I wouldn't say that. But it isn't enough to want to do a thing in order to do it."

"Why, what else?"

"Many other considerations. Is it wise? Is it quite safe?"

"Is it good enough?" Daphne's blue eyes were suddenly turned on him.

"No question of that. It would be delightful. I should love to take you over and back for a sail, but——" said Hector hurriedly.

"You are afraid."

"Afraid?"

"Yes. I might upset the boat if anything happened. If a fish jumped up, say."

"No, I am sure you would be quite steady. You are a different girl to-day."

"Am I? Better?"

"A lot better."

"Hector, take me across and back," she said with shy entreaty. He glanced at the eastern cloud bank. Not too bad. An hour and a half would do it. He had oilskins in his locker, and Daphne in her new soft shyness was very alluring.

"Let's go," she said with a glance in the direction of Mrs. MacTavish's back door. But Mrs. MacTavish, and indeed all Ranavoke, seemed deep in its afternoon siesta this hot May day.

In a few minutes they were away before a humming breeze.

"Oh, glorious!" cried Daphne. "Nothing wrong with this, Hector?"

"Not a thing, except that I feel like a boy playing truant. A lot of people to see, a lot of work to do."

"But a little change won't hurt, and then there's me."

"Yes, there's you," said Hector with a curious intonation in his voice.

"And what about me?"

"I'm not sure—quite. Indeed, not at all sure."

"Now what do you mean? You must tell me."

"You are very attractive. You have lure, you know how to use it, you enjoy using it and——"

"You are a darling, Hector. Do go on——"

"And I am a great deal older than you and——"

"Oh, you delightful baby," thought the girl.

"And I think you might be dangerous."

"Dangerous?" The blue eyes were wide open in their innocent surprise.

"Oh, yes, quite dangerous. And besides, you don't treat the doctor right."

"Fritz? How do you mean?"

"If I were in his place I wouldn't stand it—not for a day."

"Oh. Now you must go on." There was a dangerous flash in the blue eyes.

"Well—I guess I should not have said that—"

"Go on, Hector." The voice was gentle, the eyes were soft.

"Of course I don't know the technique, but do you really love him with your whole heart?" said Hector with sudden vehemence. "Don't answer if you don't want to."

"What right have you—"

"None, not a shred. Forget it."

"I can't forget that—because—well—" with a quick burst of frankness—"I don't know—really I don't know. I am engaged to him. He is clever and bright, and he can be very fascinating. He came along when I was sick of a lot of lounge lizards, and supper-dance Willie-boys. He seemed strong, somehow worth while and—well, I don't know—"

"But he loves you. I can see that."

"Oh, I guess he's got the hook all right," she said with an air of cool indifference. "But don't imagine anything very grand, no 'love me or die' sort of thing. He is quite able to look after himself."

"Let's talk about the weather. That cloud for instance," said Hector. "I started a fool discussion, but you looked, and you have looked often, as if you did not know where you were—and did not care so very much."

"Hector, that's true. You must have had wide experience."

"Never! Know nothing about the mad business, except that I would not marry a girl I didn't love with my soul, body and bones. You make up your mind about that."

The girl sat looking at him for a moment or two with eyes full of intense passion.

"I believe you, Hector. And have you never—"

"Never!" said Hector with emphasis.

A radiant light flooded the girl's face.

"Oh, Hector, she sure will be a lucky girl when you do," she said in a low voice.

"God pity her. If she loved me I would give her all I had, but I would ask all she had, you'd better believe."

"Cave man?"

"Sure thing. That's the only kind of man worth while. No half and half for me. No luke-warm stuff. Hot—boiling hot."

"And if she would only give you mildly warm stuff, quite warm but not hot, exactly?"

"Lady! Good-bye. God bless you. You weary me. In other words get along."

"But if you loved her, Hector. You could not send her off in that nice cool way."

"No? Not nice and not cool. But—send her off? Yes! She wouldn't play with my heart, mind you!"

"Oh, Hector, you would be a splendid lover!"

"I am talking nonsense about things that should not be talked about easily," he said soberly.

"Say, you're absolutely *pre*-Victorian!"

"I'm a fool, I guess," he growled.

"A lovely fool!" she said, arching her eyebrows at him.

"Look at that cloud! And the wind is dropping fast. And here's the rain. Put this slicker on," he ordered, pulling one out of a locker. "Button it close round you." His gaze swept the whole horizon.

"Oh, it is not going to be much." His voice was cheery, but Daphne read his eyes.

"It is going to be a storm, Hector," she said.

"Nothing much, a little blow, but I think we will run for those islands." He pointed to a group of islands a mile away on his starboard bow. "The wind is shifting, but—" His teeth closed down on his words.

"You are afraid, Hector."

"Afraid?" his eyes flashed at her scornfully.

"Afraid of me, afraid that I will act up. But I won't, Hector. I will do just what you tell me, no matter what it is."

He glanced at the resolute little face. "Jove, I believe you! You're all right." His smile breaking over his hard, dour face cheered the girl immensely.

"So are you, Hector," she said with an answering smile.

The Bras d'Or is the home of gales. Gales that come on with slow and dreadful advance and pile up before them everything that floats, everything that they do not gulf down. Gales too that leap out of a bank of cloud like a tiger out of a jungle while the rest of the sky is blue. Little, savage, playful gales these are, that spring at a boat and tear the sails out of her, or fling her over on her beam-ends and leave her a floating wreck with the sun smiling down upon the ruin they have wrought. Hector knew these gales, their tricks and their manners. Had he been alone he would have laughed at the Bras d'Or, as he often had laughed and as Bras d'Or men are wont to laugh. But with this young girl in his care it was different. He cursed his folly in taking her with him. He should have gone about his business and paid no heed to her blue eyes.

The wind dropped to a dead calm, the water moved round them with a sinister and oily heave as if planning something evil. The clouds had, with amazing swiftness, blotted out the sky, and were hanging low in bellying balloons over the sea.

"Here, Daphne, sit and hold this tiller—so—"

With swiftly moving fingers he took up a couple of reefs

in the sail.

"All right, thank you. Now let her come."

And she did come across the slate-grey waves, a line of white water in her wake. Hector edged his boat round to meet the gale bow on.

"Hold steady now, here she is," he said quietly, as wind and wave struck them before they could make way.

"Oh!" gasped Daphne, as a wave of salt water drenched her.

"Wet?" he shouted with a laugh. "There'll be a lot more of it too. Sit tight and enjoy it."

Terrified at the wholly new experience she sat with white lips and looked at his face.

His eyes looked twice their size, his jaws were set in a hard line, but there was a gay laugh on his lips as he shouted at the driving spume.

"Come along then! We will be going with you, and as fast as you like." In a few minutes the boat, yielding to the tiller and the drive of the gale, went plunging through and over the whitecaps, shipping buckets of water.

"Do you think you could bail her a bit?" he asked her in a few minutes.

"Bail her? How do you do it?" she gasped.

"See that old can? Can you throw out the water?"

"I guess so," she gasped, and went to work gingerly enough.

"Scoop her out!" shouted Hector. "You are doing fine. A little more pep!"

"Pep?" she gasped. *"Ouch!"* A wave caught her full in the face.

"Scoop her out! You are doing fine. Scoop it out. One! Two! Three! Four!"

"What are you talking about?" she asked.

"The water, you idiot. Scoop, scoop, one! two!"

"Oh, I see," she shouted back at him, getting down to her job with all her power.

"Splendid! Keep her going! Little more speed! One! two!"

"Oh, I see!" Down into the bottom on hands and knees she began flinging cupfuls of water overboard with all her might.

"Hurrah! Now you are doing it! Scoop her up! Keep your head down! Let her go! Good girl!"

With cheery shouts of encouragement, with snatches of song, with taunts flung into the teeth of the gale, Hector kept his boat on her course, making steadily for the line of islands still half a mile away.

"Take a rest," he ordered.

But seeing the water gain upon her she refused.

"Take a rest! Do you hear?"

"But the water—"

"Do what I tell you. Take a rest!"

"But—"

"Shut up! Sit down at once!"

"Brute!" she gasped and sat panting for breath.

"All right! Sit there, I tell you."

Almost in tears with rage and terror she sat gazing with staring eyes at the white waters rushing at her like furious wild beasts.

"All right now! Go at it again! Scoop her out! One single motion! Scoop and throw! That's better! Fine! Let her go."

They were now a few yards from a line of heavy breakers. An opening appeared before him. Could he clear it? He was doubtful, but he dared not let her into the wind. She could not carry an ounce more.

"We are going through here, Daphne," he said quietly. "Listen carefully, will you?"

"I'm listening," she said, still bailing for dear life.

"Throw down your can." Down clattered the can into the bottom of the boat. "Take your breath quietly now, we are going through a smother of water. Hold tight to the edge of the boat. Hang on like grim death, no matter what comes. When I call, take a breath, and then keep your mouth tight shut as long as you can. And don't be afraid. We are going through to quiet water where we will be all right. Understand?"

"Yes, Hector." She was very white and very still. "All right."

Quietly he let his boat into the wind. Like a hound she leaped. With a quick thrust of the tiller he set her straight at the gap. A plunge, a bump, a deluge of water and she was through, half-full but floating quietly in the shelter and in shallow water.

"All right, old girl!" called Hector. There was no answer.

Across the thwart lay Daphne still and white. With a quick leap he was at her side, lifted her out of the boat, carried her to land and laid her on a bit of sandy beach in the lee of a large cliff. Carefully he loosened her slicker, felt her heart.

"Thank God!" he muttered and, dipping his handkerchief in water, wiped her face and hands. In a few moments she revived, opened her eyes, smiled at Hector's anxious face, closed her eyes and lay still with a little sigh.

"Hey! Don't go off again!" he cried anxiously, beginning to chafe her hands vigorously. Hastily he ran to his locker, searched frantically and found a flask. Empty! Confound it! No, a teaspoonful. He found a cup, darted toward a little rivulet dropping down the face of the rock, brought back a half-cup of water, emptied the flask into it and held it to her lips.

"Drink this, old girl!" he said, lifting her head on to his breast. "You are a brick! A regular hero, by Jove! Easy now! Just a sip—that's right, now a little more. Fine!"

With a long sigh she settled herself down into his arms and lay still with closed eyes.

"Any pain, Daphne?" he asked anxiously, bending over her.

She opened her eyes, smiled at him, then reached her arms up about his neck, drew his face down and kissed him on the lips.

For a moment or two he held her close while she clung to him. Once more the blue eyes opened slowly upon him and again the lips quivered in a little smile.

"Any pain?" he said.

She shook her head, still holding his eyes with hers. Slowly he drew her up to him and kissed her gently, then again with a swift hard pressure upon the smiling lips.

"That's better, Hector," she said. "I was afraid you wouldn't and that would have been terrible. Do you really love me?"

"Love you? Good Lord, no! You belong to Dr. Wolfe."

She shook herself free of his arms, staggered to her feet and exclaimed indignantly, "Then what do you mean by kissing me that way?"

"I—don't—know. You looked—so—I don't know. I guess because you looked—somehow—oh, I can't tell. I just did it."

"Then you didn't mean anything?"

"What do you mean?"

"You don't love me?"

"Do you want me to?"

"Of course I do—"

"And Dr. Wolfe?"

"Well? Oh, never mind him."

"You are finished with him?"

"I don't know—exactly. It depends. What would you do if I were finished with him?"

"My dear girl, forget it. I kissed you because you were very kissable and you had shown yourself a brick, and I was proud of you—and—well, I had no business to. If you want me to apologize I will grovel to you. I'm not the kissing kind. I was off guard, and you were—well, you were rather pitiful and very lovely and—there you are!"

"Are you sorry?"

"On the whole, no. If you feel I behaved like a cad then yes. But I really don't think you do. No, honour bright."

"You *are* a cool one."

"Supposing we forget it. Or if you like I shall apologize to Dr. Wolfe when I see him, explaining the circumstances and taking full blame." Hector's manner was portentously grave.

"Oh, you are a darned idiot, and if you ever hint such a thing to Dr. Wolfe I'll never forgive you."

"And if I don't, we call it quits?"

"Oh, let's get home. I'm sick of you."

"No wonder. I am sick of myself. I was an ass."

"You were not. An ass to kiss me, indeed?"

"Well, what would you say—unutterably weak?"

"Weak? To kiss me?"

"What then?"

"Oh, I don't know. But I am very angry."

"Angry because I kissed you? Or because I don't love you?"

"Now you're a brute."

"I agree. Suppose we finish at this point of agreement and see about getting back. First, I will salvage my boat. Meantime you are getting chilled. See, I shall build a fire against this rock, and you will get yourself dry and warm. Can you gather some birchbark?"

"I'm afraid not. I am—rather—faint. I am hurt, I think." She sat down suddenly.

"Oh, confound me for an idiot." He laid her down upon the sand, covered her with his slicker and rushed about gathering birchbark and dry pine branches, and in a few minutes had a fire going.

"Now, you poor little thing, you have been hurt. Why didn't you tell me? Where is your pain?"

"My side—here—not much—"

"Wait, I may have some grub and tea—at least I generally have." He rummaged in his locker, found a tea pail and inside some tea, sugar and biscuits.

"Glory be! It pays to cultivate good habits. We always aim to have supplies in this locker. Now I shall make you tea. Then a bed. Then you shall sleep and when the gale moderates I shall take you home to Miss Mary. And tomorrow you will be your old self."

"My old self?" she muttered. "Huh! My old self."

Soon he had a blazing fire going and before long a cup of black hot tea ready for her. Silently she drank the tea, and then snuggling down into the sand near the fire fell fast asleep. Hector meantime was keeping his eye upon the progress of the storm. He had found his boat with a hole in the bottom, but with birch bark and gum and a few stray tenpenny nails found in his locker he had patched it up.

Their temporary camp was hard against the cliff quite sheltered from the storm. The gale was still lashing the Bras d'Or into whitecapped, racing, mountainous seas. No chance of getting home for some hours yet. As he sat there smoking, his mind went over the events of the last half-hour. He had acted like a silly modern fool. Kissing a girl! Faugh! He might have been one of the ordinary night-club-haunting, "necking" fraternity. This girl? How would it affect her? Well, he rather imagined she would not take it too seriously. She knew her way about. But a minister acting in this silly way! He grovelled in utter abasement before himself. At this point he lost his train of thought, and was holding to his breast this girl, and feeling once more the clinging arms and the soft resistance of her lips.

"Oh, darn it all! What has come to me? Love? Nonsense. This American society girl with her loud, cheap, crass vulgarity!" In a moment, by some subtle, subconscious trick of his soul he found himself thinking of another girl: Vivien, and her last kiss. Vivien, honest, fearless, wholesome, out-of-doors sport. Sound of heart and clear of mind. Fine in every sense of the word. And yet in that kiss no thrill, not in the least like this last kiss. Faugh! Disgusting! He was growing a crass sentimentalist. And yet— He got up from his place and stood looking down upon the sleeping girl. What a child she was! A sweet, pure, lovely child, with an utter absence of the shrewd sophistication of the young lady, so completely self-suffi- cient, so eminently mistress of herself and of her environ- ment, especially her menfolk. He found his heart full of a gentle protective pity washed clean of all passion. God forgive him. He would take care of this child.

An hour, two hours passed, and still she slept. She must have been exhausted. The storm had abated its fury, but the sea was still running high. A slight fog was coming up, a threat of rain moved him to action. He went into the woods, cut down some birch saplings, and laid them up against the rock for a shelter, then gathering a great heap of spruce and balsam branches he began to construct a rain- proof pent-house against the rock. In the midst of his opera- tions Daphne awoke, sat up and gazed about, her blue eyes still heavy with sleep and more than ever with a child won- der in them. Hector's heart again smote him with a sense of shame.

"Well, my dear," he said gently, "how is the pain now?"

"Pain? What pain? Oh, in my side? Gone, I think."

Hector offered her his hand and lifted her up.

"That's fine. Rested, I hope, and recovered from the shock of shipwreck?"

"Quite! Oh, I feel so well, so fresh. How long did I sleep?"

"A couple of hours."

"And you? Have you slept? No, of course you would not. You must be tired out, Hector."

"Me? Tired? Nonsense! But you must have had quite a shock. I ought to have known. You never went through any such experience in your life, I venture to say. I should have taken better care of you."

The blue eyes were turned questioningly upon him. "Better care?"

"Yes, Daphne dear. Should have treated you better. You were in my care."

Slowly the blood came up into her cheeks. Her eyes fell. "It was my fault," she said in a low voice. "Oh, Hector, I am ashamed of myself." Her lips were quivering a little.

"My dear young lady," said Hector, taking her hand, "you were not yourself, you had just come out of a swoon. But I—I hope you can forgive me." He lifted her hand to his lips, with a bow as to a great lady.

She said not a word. Her lips were quivering like those of a child about to cry.

"Come now!" said Hector briskly. " 'Nuff said? Both sides?"

She nodded.

"Then let me show you your house if it rains."

Swiftly she responded, and in a moment was in full command of herself.

"Oh, lovely! What a darling little house!"

"Rainproof too. Now I am going up on top of this rock to take a look at the weather, to see just what the chances are of going home. Shall be gone about fifteen minutes. So don't be alarmed. Then we shall have tea."

"Good-bye," she said softly.

From the tops of the rock he could command a view of the Bras d'Or. The sea was still running high, the clouds still threatening with angry banks at the southeastern horizon, promising another storm. The situation was grave. Unless the sea subsided it would be risky making the crossing in the dark. Were he alone he would not hesitate, but with this girl? No, he would take no such risk. He returned, to find Daphne looking into the fire with a face more earnestly serious than usual.

"Hungry?"

"No, I don't think so. But now you mention it—a good

juicy beefsteak with mushrooms—"

"Ah! Hold on! We might do better." He ran to his locker and fished out a troll.

"There is just a chance in this quiet pool—only a chance, but still a chance."

He made his way to a jutting rock overhanging a bit of quiet water in the shelter of the island, swung his spoon, flung far and began rolling in. Immediately there was a flash, a sharp slap and away went the line.

"Oh, glory!" yelled Daphne, running up to the rock beside him. "What is it? Oh, what do you think it is?"

"Cod, I guess. But, by Jove, he fights better than a cod. Say! boy, you have no chance with this tackle. Not a ghost of a chance. No use playing you."

Hand over hand he rolled in his line, and soon had the fish on the sand.

"Hello! A salmon! Jove, what luck! Early for them. And especially in this water. He was getting away from the storm. Well, a noble destiny awaits you, old chap. Food for angels—an angel, I mean."

He killed the fish, rolled him in a thick covering of clay, covered him up in a bed of coals. In twenty minutes he drew out the red, glowing mass, threw a can of water upon it, causing it to explode with a bang, and removed the brick-like covering.

"There you are! Sherry himself couldn't equal that! Now with hardtack and tea we are all set."

It was indeed a feast for the gods. Never had Daphne tasted such fish! Never such tea! Never such biscuits! Never had such a meal in her life! There her exclamations stopped short.

"Never such company!" cried Hector enthusiastically. But in spite of great efforts on his part there was little talk, and no hilarity, no jollity. The sea was still running high, night was drawing down her darkest curtains, and a drizzling, driving rain was beginning to fall.

"Must get inside," said Hector, carrying slickers and oil-skins within the shelter. He drew the fire toward the door of the little hut.

"Now get inside, Daphne. You must not get cold."

"And you?" said Daphne.

"I'm all right in my slicker. I'll have my smoke out here and then I shall gather some wood. We don't know how long the gale may last. Fortunately they won't be anxious. Miss Mary will think you are at the MacDonalds'. And no one knows where I am anyway. So we needn't worry about anyone but ourselves."

"There are no animals about?"

"Nothing more dangerous than a rabbit."

"Anyway, I don't care. I feel quite safe."

"Thank you, my dear. You are safe—safe as God can make you."

"Yes, I guess so. But I was thinking of you."

"Thank you again, my dear. Well, you are safe enough anyway. Homesick? Lonely?"

"Lonely? What nonsense, Hector!"

"I don't know. I am considered very dull company for young ladies. Now I shall get some wood."

"Let me come! Do. I have a slicker, and my shoes are heavy. Do let me!"

"Come along."

Together they gathered the wood, making great fun of it and establishing an atmosphere of thorough good comrade-ship. The wood gathered, they once more sat together in the door of the shelter. Whatever may have been Hector's reputation as "company" he showed nothing of dullness this night.

He began with old tales of the Bras d'Or during the French régime. Tales of gallant fighting, of heroic daring, and splendid sacrifice they were. Then he went on to sto-ries of his own life as a boy in these woods. Stories of life in the manse, of the jolly times they all had together. Spoke of his father, of his splendid self-sacrifice in the service of his people. Then of his mother—not much about her, but in tones of tender and reverent pride, till Daphne listened with tears in her eyes and an ache in her throat. He told her a little about the War. He hated the War. It had done cruel things to them all. He began to talk of his young brother Alistair. But when he came to Jock, he abruptly paused and, saying, "Must take a look at the weather," climbed up to the top of the rock.

When he had gone the girl put her face in her hands and groaned. "What has this man done to me? Why did I never meet a man like this? Or why do I meet him now? God help me—what can I do?"

.   .   .   .

The first grey of the morning was coming up over the distant hills when Daphne entered Miss Mary's boudoir, worn, wan and in the last stages of exhaustion.

"Hush! Let me get into bed," she said, falling into the arms of her friend. Without a word Miss Mary undressed her and put her between cool, comforting sheets.

"But why so wae, my dear? You had a lucky escape, but of course he is a good man with a boat."

"A good man? Yes, a good man, a damned *good* man! Oh, hell!"

"But what's the matter, Daphne? What's all the grief about?"

"Are you a woman? Did you ever kiss a man?"

Miss Mary flushed a brilliant red.

"Well, then perhaps you understand. I kissed him. Yes, with my arms round his neck. And he kissed me. Yes, twice—you may look! and then—"

"What then?" asked Miss Mary in deep anxiety.

"What? That's what I'm telling you. That's all he did. He stopped right there. Treated me like a dear little sister. Oh, hell!" She hid her face in the pillow and groaned aloud.

Miss Mary suppressed a smile.

"Well, my dear, I wouldn't worry about that. Besides, there is the doctor."

"Oh-h!" groaned Daphne. "That's just it—that's what he said."

"Go to sleep, Daphne. I'll bring you breakfast in bed."

"No!   Think I'm going to play the wan and woeful maiden? Darned if I do! I'll be down for breakfast, and let him look out for himself! Darn his goodness!"

CHAPTER XVII

Mrs. MacTavish was paying an early call on Miss Mary, before breakfast indeed. Mrs. MacTavish had had a bad night, what with the storm and Mr. MacTavish's rheumatism and Mariah. Mariah had been most annoying, out and in all night. There was something uncanny about Mariah. At times it was as if she was possessed.

"Them cats will be knowing more than many of us," said Mrs. MacTavish with an air of mystery. "It was her mother—no, her grandmother—yes, her grandmother that was a queer one. Jemima they called her. The very devil would be in her at times. And that wise. Don't I mind her lepping and tearing at his nightcap one night and him poor man with a toothache, till I had to put her out. And there if you please was the kindling on fire in the oven where himself had put it for the morning fire. We would have been burnt in our beds. Oh, them cats, they know! Oh, they know! That Jemima now, I got her from Granny MacPhail, she was a Barra woman, and one of them wise women." Here Mrs. MacTavish lowered her voice. "Is the minister in? No? Well, she had cats, lots of them and she would be talking with them. And they would be telling her things. What? Why not? Was not the ass telling Balaam, and the angel of the Lord there telling the ass? Well, so they were saying whateffer. But Jemima now. Well do I remember the night, and an awful storm, and the wind howling like wolves at the door, and voices. What? No! I am not saying what voices. Jemima was wild to be out, fleeing about the house and tearing at the door till I was terrified. And when I opened the door, out she was like a sperrit from the pit, and the cries of her! And that very night my old mother died. They will be telling me the cats will not stay in the house when there's going to be a death. Oh, they know! What? Oh, yes, it is a fine morning. But I hef had no sleep since the break of day. No, I was quite well. It was Mariah. She would be out. And I opened the door, and there—" Mrs. MacTavish paused abruptly, then with a fierce rush went on. "Will you be telling me, Miss Mary, what was the minister doing with the besom at that hour of the night? What sort of goings-on is that for a godly man?"

Miss Mary took the matter lightly.

"Oh, Mrs. MacTavish, I'm afraid Mariah had been eating too much cheese. Miss Inman and Mr. MacGregor went for a sail across to Back River in the afternoon. They were caught in that terrible storm. Fortunately they made the Pirate Island and took shelter there till it was safe to return. Indeed they had a narrow escape. Their boat was broken, and indeed we may be very thankful. Poor Miss Inman was quite exhausted. Won't you have a cup of tea?"

"No, I'll not be waiting. A storm, was it? And them on the Pirate Island all night in the storm?"

"Yes, Mr. MacGregor built a little shelter against a big rock so they were quite safe and snug there."

"Snug? Huh! Well, them cats knows, is what I always says."

"Yes," agreed Miss Mary with a cheerful smile. "They know about mice and rats and all that vermin, ugh! I don't like cats much myself, Mrs. MacTavish."

"But did not that ass know about the angel of the Lord, and did he not warn the prophet of the Lord against his destruction?"

"The Lord may be trusted to look after His prophets, Mrs. MacTavish," said Miss Mary gravely. "He does not need cats to help Him."

"He will that. Oh, yes, He will that," said Mrs. MacTavish in a voice hoarse with passion. "But if she hurts a hair of his head I would tear the eyes out of her."

Miss Mary's face grew very grave.

"You are speaking of your minister, Mrs. MacTavish. We all love him, and we are all proud of him. He proved himself a brave and capable man last night! As we would expect. He saved himself and his companion from drowning, and saved her from getting her death of cold by providing fire and shelter from the storm. Miss Daphne told me all about it."

"I am wondering! But—well, good morning, Miss Mary. But Mariah was awful queer last night—"

"Good morning, Mrs. MacTavish." Miss Mary shut the door. "Cats indeed! Why does the Lord make them? I wonder now. But what nonsense!"

The day was full of preparations for the homecoming of Captain Jock. The interest and excitement attendant upon the organization of the Bras d'Or Co-operative Association were quite flooded from the minds of all who were waiting for the coming of the sick man. Dr. Wolfe, who had come specially for the occasion, however, would allow no gathering of the people.

"No strangers, only his own family and immediate friends," said Dr. Wolfe. "He will be nervously exhausted. No greetings. No excitement. We will carry him upstairs and get him to bed at once and as quietly as possible."

All this was carried out to the letter. The homecoming of Captain Jock was marked by an utter absence of emotion. A quiet greeting by Hector, swift deft manipulation by Steve and Hector of the stretcher upon which the white-faced patient lay, and Captain Jock was lying quietly in his own bed. The rest of the company with the exception of Vivien, who remained upstairs, were gathered in the dining-room taking supper, talking quietly over the events of the past weeks.

Upon Logie fell the task of giving in detail the history of the operation with its results. It was a pathetic story of high hopes fading into drab disappointments and then again deepening into anxiety and fear.

"He wanted to be home so terribly that it hurt him, and put him back. He wanted the Bras d'Or, its air, the smell of the sea. He was weary for his own room, and he was aching for the sight of kind faces and the sound of their voices. And so were we. Not that they were not all kind, oh, so kind!" Logie's voice faltered here. "And Dr. Whitney, oh, he was so good to us all. And the nurses." Here Vivien slipped in.

"But we never could have done without Steve, Mr. Inman," continued Logie. "He was like a brother to us all. He was always thinking before us, and planning some new thing for Jock. And Jock really came to depend on him and love him. His stories helped Jock through many a weary night, and his drives helped Vivien and me through many a terrible day. You did us a good service, Mr. Inman, when you gave us Steve and the car. Never, never can I forget that." Again her voice faltered. "I am sorry, Doctor. I am rather foolish and weak."

"Quit that, Logie," interposed Vivien sharply. "Don't be lying to these people. If ever there was a rock to lean against it was that girl there. Weak? God knows and I know there wasn't a weak hair on her body. We have come through a hard time, but without that little black-headed, white-faced creature we would have all blown up many a time. And Steve! She is right about Steve. Cool-headed —he would make a great bandit. Cool-hearted—"

"Oh, Vivien!" protested Logie.

"I didn't say cold-hearted. He never slopped over, never lost his head, never was unfit or unready for any kind of emergency. Oh, yes, he would be a darned good bandit, or a great over-the-top man. And he always kept his place."

"And now, Doctor, what is your opinion? You may as well tell us frankly. It is better to face the truth," said Hector.

There was a deep silence while the doctor hesitated.

"Yes, truth is always best in the long run if you are dealing with the right kind of people, as we are here," said the
doctor. "So I say first, he looks a very, very sick man."
Hector's face grew grey. "But I cannot give an opinion
till I have observed him for twenty-four hours and until I
have read Dr. Whitney's letter, which Nurse Marriott
brought me. I will say that though there is reason for anxiety, for grave anxiety, there is no ground for despair. Further let me say, and say very definitely," the doctor's voice
grew almost stern, "that an atmosphere of despair would
be fatal to the patient. Let us be resolutely cheerful. A
little noise, a lot of jollity, won't hurt at all."

"Jollity! My God!" murmured Hector indignantly.

"Jollity, sir!" said the doctor. "That's the way your men
went up the line. Is that impossible?"

"Impossible?" said Hector. "Doctor, pardon me, I am
sorry. No! It is not impossible. With God's help it is
possible. And with God's help it will be so." His voice
was steady, his face composed. The whole company felt
that what was necessary this man would do, even to the
point of jollity, and the whole company resolved that in
this effort it would do its utmost.

"Carry on," the good old military phrase, was the order
of the day.

To the Inman family this meant the continuing of their
fishing operations during the few days which remained to
them. But their interest in the manse family had become
so deep-rooted that the fishing became a quite secondary
thing. The doctor frankly placed the observation of his
patient before everything else, his interest being both professional and personal. Daphne, never an intensely ardent
devotee of the angler's art, lost interest in it almost completely as the doctor became more and more absorbed in his
patient. However, they still made the camp their habitat,
which the car, now available, brought within a few minutes
of the village.

It was Mrs. MacTavish's extreme solicitude for the moral integrity and the reputation of the minister that precipitated an explosion that shook the whole community to its very foundation. To others less prudent than Miss Mary she confided the revelations brought about through the agency of her cat Mariah. The unsavoury rumour reached at length the Barra community in the neighbourhood of the Cove, and in particular the ears of Black Mack MacNeil.

In Black Mack's soul there was a festering sore of irritation against Ranald Gillis of long standing, reaching back indeed into War days. There was a rankling memory of a boxing tournament in his military division in which he suffered a humiliating defeat at the hands of Ranald Gillis. The bitterness of this experience lay in the fact that he knew well he had gone into that contest when he was just emerging from a prolonged spree, and was consequently by no means at the top of his form. That a man of his "heavy and his queeckness" should be beaten by Ranald Gillis, twenty-five pounds the lighter man, was not to be borne. Ranald's devotion to his minister was well known. Black Mack though an adherent of the same church had little practical interest in its affairs. Furthermore Ranald's championship of his relation Mary Bella against Mr. James Cameron's adverse criticism had recently deepened the feeling of irritation and hostility in Black Mack's mind. He was only waiting for "the day." Indeed he had recently made a habit of haunting the village in the hope of running across his enemy. The defamatory rumour in regard to the minister in due course reached the ears of Mary Bella, who in her acute distress confided it to Ranald Gillis.

"And they say that Miss Mary knows all about it," said Mary Bella, almost in tears.

"Mary Bella, I am ashamed of you, that you should let such a thought enter your mind."

"I am not believing it, Ranald Gillis, if that is what you mean, and the more shame to you to think it, but that is what they are saying."

"Let them say it to me once. They will say it no more, I warrant you." And away went Ranald straight to Miss Mary for the truth of the story, who gave it to him in the sweet simplicity of her own pure soul.

"And immediately she came to me with the whole story and then went to her father and her fiancé, both of whom took particular pains to express their gratitude to the minister for what he had done: only what any gentleman would do, seeing her safe through the storms and keeping guard at the door of her shelter till it was safe to return home," said Miss Mary, her gentle face pale with indignation.

"But, Ranald," she added, "we will say or do nothing about it. Anything else would be just silly."

"Of course," said Ranald. "What else? Would I be a fool?"

But alas for Ranald's excellent resolution. Indeed, within twenty-four hours, walking into the store where there were half a dozen people waiting for their mail, among them Willie George Cameron, Black Mack, a little under the weather, and his cousin Hugh MacNeil, as big as himself, Ranald heard from Black Mack's lips the words:

"Yes! On Pirate's Island with the young lady all night—and that's the minister for you!" and a cackle of ribald laughter.

At this point in walked Steve with a telegram from Mr. Inman which he handed Mary Bella.

An ominous silence fell upon the group. With face white, hands trembling as with ague, Ranald walked slowly toward Black Mack, stood in front of him and in a voice choking with fury said slowly,

"Were you saying something about our minister?"

"Yes, my lad," said Black Mack with a laugh. "I was saying what I have good reason for saying—that he spent the other night on Pirate's Island with the young American lady. That's all."

"Men," said Ranald, with a tremendous effort command-ing his voice, "I have heard the story from Miss Mary, and later from the young lady's father, and from the man she is going to marry. And the story is this: the minister was taking the young lady for a sail across to the Back River and back. A storm drove them on the Pirate's Island. By good seamanship he made through the channel and saved the girl and himself. He made a fire, built a lean-to against the cliff, and put her into it and sat at the door till the storm was over. Then he took her back to Miss Mary's. Would any of you have done anything else? Not one of you. And if Black Mack MacNeil or any other man has said a word against our minister for what he did that night, then he is a black-hearted liar from hell and a dirty coward who will slander a lady and a minister behind their backs."

"And if any man here has anything to say against the young lady in question I am here to deal with him as a slanderer and a liar," said Steve, taking his place beside Ranald Gillis and speaking in a voice that cut like a knife-edge.

"I do not need to answer to you, Ranald Gillis, or to any man in this room for what I say, I am telling you."

"Unless you say something against the character of our minister. Then you answer to me."

"I say what I said. And as for the minister—well, per-haps the less said the better." The laugh died in his teeth, driven into his throat by the back of Ranald Gillis' open hand.

Half a dozen men threw themselves between the two. Black Mack, tearing off coat and waistcoat and shirt, brushed the men aside.

"Come out of this, Ranald Gillis, where I can get at you. It is the day I haf been waiting for long, and now, praise the Lord, it has come. Come out where there is room! My Goad, do not keep me waiting!" He was panting like a man after a race.

To a little glen surrounded by trees a quarter of a mile from the store the company of excited men repaired. Vain were all efforts to compose the quarrel. The two men were powerfully built, Black Mack, the heavier by twenty-five pounds, with tremendous muscles, fists like a blacksmith's hammers, legs like pillars, was truly a terrifying picture of a man. Ranald Gillis was slighter, with longer reach, with the lither limbs of an athlete. Both men were stripped to the waist.

"Who will keep time?" said Steve, who also was present, stripped to his shirt.

"Time?" yelled Black Mack. "What in hell do I want of time? All I want is let me at him!" and with a yell he rushed blindly upon his antagonist, his arms going like a windmill. A quick side-step, a sharp smacking sound, and Black Mack plunged headlong to the ground, rolled over on his back and lay quivering.

With a wild gasping cry his cousin rushed forward and threw himself beside the fallen man. "Water! Some water for Goad's sake!" he cried, lifting Black Mack's head upon his knees. Soon the water came, but it was some minutes before the stricken man opened his eyes.

"What is it?" he said thickly.

"Nothing at all. Lie still awhile," said Big Hugh. "A bit of an accident, which I will be putting right in a meenute. Lie you still."

But Black Mack struggled to a sitting posture and gazed stupidly about. His eyes finally rested on Ranald.

"Wass it—yourself—Ranald—that gave me this? It wass a deevil of a belt—whateffer." He struggled to his feet and swayed toward Ranald. "I am not—seeing—you—well, Ranald. Will you—excuse me—for the present? To-morrow—we will be—putting a feenish to it. But—just now—I will say to you, Ranald—I am sorry—about the meenister. He is a man—of God. There—is nothing—wrong with him—at all. But—we will be—putting a feenish—to it—to-morrow—or the next day perhaps."

"No, no! Mack. It is over between us. You know the minister did nothing wrong. That's all I want. Let us call it quits."

"Quits? Man—yon was—a deevil of a belt! It will be—necessary to put a feenish—to it," insisted Mack.

"All right, Mack. If you say so. But I don't want to. I wish you would let it go," said Ranald.

"Let it go?" shouted Big Hugh. "Not while I am alive. You took him unawares. What he said I stand for. The minister and that damned she—"

Smack! went an open hand upon his cheek, making his teeth rattle.

"Will you take that back?" said Steve, facing him quietly.

With a roar, Big Hugh sprang at him, but found nothing. Again came that jarring smack on his cheek followed by two more. Smack! Smack! One on each cheek. In vain Big Hugh rushed frantically at his elusive enemy.

"Say, you fight like a cow!" said Steve. "Going to take it back? I'll give you half a dozen more while you are thinking about it." And he did. In quick succession, six hard, jarring, open hand-blows, till Big Hugh stood actually dazed and breathless blinking at his slim, lithe, elusive foe.

"Going to take it back?" said Steve, coming nearer. It was a fatal move. For a second or two Big Hugh stood blinking like a cat, then with a swift leap he had his enemy in his powerful grip.

"Ha!" he cried in triumph. "I haf got you! And now I will break your back to you."

Quickly Ranald sprang forward. "Let him go!" he shouted.

"Keep out of it!" ordered Steve sharply, yielding limply to Big Hugh's crushing grip, as they swayed from side to side.

"Now then! I will be—breaking—every bone in your body," grunted Big Hugh, crushing his foe to his broad chest. With a swift, serpent-like movement the slim body shifted its position. One long arm slipped round the huge shoulder up to the neck where sinewy fingers buried themselves behind the ear. The other hand slid up under the chin. A few moments and Big Hugh's head began to go back. Slowly but surely the great head went back and back and still back. "Look out, Steve!" cried Ranald. "You'll break his neck."

Suddenly a choking scream came from between Big Hugh's clenched teeth. The huge body collapsed in a formless heap upon the ground and there lay. Over him stood Steve waiting.

"Next time you grip me, I'll break your neck. Do you want to try? Get up, you big slob!"

Big Hugh struggled to his feet and stood bewildered.

"Have you enough? Are you going to apologize?"

"No!" yelled Big Hugh, suddenly letting drive in a fierce blow at the pale, impassioned face in front of him.

Only the head moved, but with incredible swiftness up from below flashed a terrific upper-cut to the chin, from the right a swing to the jaw, then a sickening straight-arm to the throat. Without a sound the great form spun round and fell prone upon the ground. Steve walked back and forward before the group of astonished men, his face pale as that of a dead man, his lips drawn back over his teeth in a snarling grin.

"Any other man want to say anything about my young lady or her friends? I hate handling a clown. Gentlemen, I have trained with world champions. But no man can say things about my young lady. Sorry I hit the big slob." Then to himself he said, "And that minister is a good man! He is a good man. I'll kill the man that says he isn't." For some minutes he waited, walking back and forth before the fallen man. "Well, I guess that's all," he said.

"Yes, that's all, Steve. Let's put on our clothes and get away," said Ranald Gillis. "I hardly think anyone here has

more lies to tell. Danny, you bring my car up here. Mack,
you are coming home with me."

"Not with you, Ranald. I am not feeling very good. Yon
was a deevil of—"

"You are coming home with me, Mack. I see Big Hugh
is all right again. He can look after himself. Steve!
Where's Steve?"

"Guess he's gone," said a bystander. "Holy terror, isn't
he? And the size of him!"

"Come get in, Mack. Hurry up!" Mack, still more or
less dazed, got into the car and was driven to Ranald's
home, where he spent the two following days under the care
of Ranald's mother. His remembrance of the particulars
of the encounter was never very clear. But as a result of
his stay at Ranald's home he lost all desire to "put a feenish
to it." The affair was ended. Also, after some further conversation with Miss Mary, Mrs. MacTavish's concern for
the good name of the minister straightway evaporated. Her
confidence in Mariah, however, as a medium of communica-
tion with the world of spirits remained unshaken. The interpretation might be faulty, but "them cats was queer."

It was to the credit of the community generally that no
word of either the rumour or the fight ever reached the ears
of the minister or his family.

CHAPTER XVIII

DR. WOLFE'S requisition of cheerfulness to the point of jollity for the patient at the manse appeared to be productive of good results. Captain Jock was certainly better. The head jollity organizer turned out to be Daphne. Her first introduction to Captain Jock, on the second day after his return, gave him a shock. Deliberately she dressed for her part, "with all her war-paint, head feathers and bells on," rather to the disgust of Hector.

"This is Miss Inman, Jock," said Hector as the young lady followed Logie breezily into his room.

"Hello, Rip!" she cried. "My stars! Why don't they give your face a chance? If I had a face like yours I'd give the public a good time."

Jock stared at her with a puzzled little smile. "My face? Oh, I see! Couldn't be bothered," he said weakly in a tired voice.

"They ought to run a mower over you. Say, Logie, why not give that schoolgirl skin a chance to radiate? It's a shame, Captain Jock."

In ten minutes she brought to play a barrage of her most expert and most effective vamp artillery upon the invalid. Her beauty, her daring, her swift play of fancy, her humour, aroused interest and amused Captain Jock in spite of weariness. Her account of her experience with her first fish was extraordinarily funny. She had them all in gales of laughter, not excepting Hector himself.

"Caught me by the ankle! A minister! Offered to spank me! Good thing I couldn't swim that day! Oh, he is a wild man!"

"Better get out now, Daphne," said Hector. "Go."

"All right. But, Captain Jock, get a shave or a permanent. I'll send Steve. Good-bye."

"Come again!" murmured Captain Jock, with a smile.

She danced out of the room blowing him a kiss as she went, but in Logie's room she flung herself into the girl's arms in a passion of tears.

"My God! What a shame!" she sobbed. "Oh, that smile of his! And at my fool nonsense."

"Hush, dear," replied Logie, herself in tears. "He hasn't smiled like that for months."

That was the beginning of it. Five minutes again in the afternoon, five minutes the following morning, and ten minutes in the afternoon, and Daphne's visits became a recognized and important feature in the jollity course of treatment prescribed by the doctor. Later on she introduced impromptu numbers by Miss Mary and Kenneth, in the living-room downstairs, to Captain Jock's immense delight. The doctor was astonished at the effect of the new treatment.

"Perfectly sound," he declared. "Good psychology and good therapeutics. Keep it up, but don't overdo it. Don't rush him."

"Rush him? Say! If I had only half a chance to go into action, I'd show you something!" said Daphne, making eyes at Hector.

"Go to it," said Hector. "You have my permission."

"Huh! Your permission? I guess so," she replied, making a face at him.

Hector however had his hands too full to give more than casual attention to Daphne's technique. The Co-operative Association was absorbing his energy to the full. He had long consultations with members of his committee and very especially with Mr. Marriott, the vice-president, with whom he was beginning to develop a close friendship. The vice-president's practical knowledge of horticulture proved to be both sound and extensive. He made a trip to Nova Scotia in order to study at close range the methods of co-operation

successfully practised in various centres there. His enthusiasm for this new enterprise drew him away from his books
and brought him into closer contact with humanity.

"You are looking better, Mr. Marriott, than I have ever
seen you. The work is doing you good."

"It is the open air."

"Yes, and something else," said Hector.

"Yes?"

"Religion. Practical religion, I mean. No! Now don't
get all worked up. You are the most religious man in
Ravanoke. The religion of the highway. The religion that
makes a man help his neighbour. The only kind worth
talking about."

"By the way, Mr. MacGregor, that reminds me—you will
allow me, seeing it is Captain Jock—what of the expenses?
Please listen. I am your neighbour. I have some money
idle in the bank. Why not put it to use for me? You
won't rebuff a friend?"

"No, Mr. Marriott, I would not. I do thank you with all
my heart. But—well, I will tell you about it." And the
minister proceeded to give a full account of his stock transaction with Mr. Inman.

"Ten thousand dollars?" said Mr. Marriott in amazement. "Splendid!"

"Splendid? I am not so sure," replied Hector doubtfully.
"I wish I were. But I have been so worried and so busy
I have not really given time to the study of the question.
But thank you all the same. And you will keep this to
yourself."

"Yes. It will be as well. There are those who might not
understand. But I am really much relieved, and very
thankful."

"And I am thankful to you, sir. You are doing a great
work among our people, and as I said that is true religion."

Mr. Marriott shook his head. "I fear not much religion
in that."

"I. have the highest authority on my side. 'Who was neighbour to him that fell among thieves? He that had mercy upon him. Go thou and do likewise.' And mind you, the story shows that the discussion was about eternal life. Now don't get mixed in theology and ritual. The lawyer in the story was word-perfect in his theology, and the priest A1 in his ritual but neither one had any religion. He was no good to the man half-dead on the highway. Mr. Marriott, you have made me think a lot. I am afraid I have been living too much in books or creeds and rituals and not enough on the highway."

"Books? Books? Yes, books worry us. Especially the Book. To be quite frank, Mr. MacGregor, that does bother me. It grieves me to the heart to say it. And more especially these days, when I am getting near to such fine people. The Book. Oh, I really cannot accept it as truth. Now before the tribunal of your conscience and your reason, Mr. MacGregor, can you accept that Genesis statement of origins for our universe?"

Mr. Marriott was deeply moved. Gone were his usual flippancy, his scornful arrogance, his contempt. He was a simple-minded, earnest man, deeply anxious in his search for truth.

"Do you mean the Genesis story as literal scientific truth? Mr. Marriott, you insult my intelligence and my religion. No, I do not. The Genesis writing sets forth truth, deep, marvellous, eternal truth. But as a scientific statement of world origins? No!"

"And all those miracle stories, angel visitants, signs in the heavens and wonders on earth, and—and—all that?"

"As historical accounts of actual happenings? No, Mr. Marriott. I am no child!"

"Will you wipe out all miracle from the Book?"

"Mr. Marriott, if I said 'yes' you would misunderstand me. If I said 'no,' you would equally misunderstand me. Give me a day for this with you. Meantime, let me say, my faith is not based on what are called 'miracles,' but upon a conception of a God that approves itself to my mind, my conscience and my heart."

"But—but—not on miracles?"

"No, certainly not. No man of modern thought and intelligence does."

"But—you amaze me. Then why in God's name don't the leaders of religion tell the truth to their people? Why don't they? I dare you to." Mr. Marriott was much excited.

"I take you. I will begin next Sunday. Will you be in church?"

"I will."

"And with fair and open mind?"

"Who can promise that? I know my prejudices and preconceptions, but I give you my word I will do my best."

They shook hands on the compact.

"You may get into trouble, Mr. MacGregor. Perhaps you had better think twice."

"Dodge trouble, or dodge truth, eh? Thank you, Mr. Marriott. You have offered me the eternal alternative."

The minister went away carrying with him a new and weighty sense of responsibility. It came as a shock to him to discover that a man of Mr. Marriott's intelligence and reading should attribute to him a theory of Scriptural interpretation discarded more than a quarter of a century ago by every Biblical scholar of any importance, certainly in Britain or in Canada. How many of his own congregation held that same opinion of him? And how many still clung to that old and discarded theory? And whose fault was it? Afraid of disturbing people's minds? Afraid of shaking the foundations of their faith? He had often heard that from his professors in college, and from wise leaders in the church. How long was this to go on? How long must the church bear the contempt of thinking men for its adherence to theories of interpretation which it had long since discarded?

No longer would he be guilty of this cowardice. Truth was its own defence. He would speak the truth as he saw it.

On his way home he paused to let his eyes rest on the blue waters of the Bras d'Or, upon the forest-clad environment, upon the sky overhead, all bathed in the glory of the golden sun.

"And God said let there be light, and there was light."

He had got his text. He went at his sermon. He had material in abundance—on his shelves the newest and most authoritative works on Biblical criticism and interpretation. He soon found that his only embarrassment was that of riches. He could make his sermon only a mere introduction to the subject and a challenge to further study. Having prepared his outline he determined to experiment with his American friends whose theology he suspected would be of a pronounced Fundamentalist type. With Daphne he walked up to the camp to spend the evening with his friends there, taking with him the outline. The subject of the sermon came up in natural sequence from a reference to Mr. Marriott's fine work in the Co-operative Association.

"Fine old boy that," was Mr. Inman's comment. "And mighty well versed in a lot of things."

"Kind of Free-thinker, I guess?" said Daphne. "Atheist, they say."

"Agnostic would describe him more accurately," said Hector.

"Well, they're all the same to me, all poison snakes, I reckon," said Mr. Inman.

"Not the same," said Hector, "and not all poison. He challenged me to preach a sermon on it. He was in such downright earnest that I took him up. He is really a fine and honest soul."

"I'll be there. What are you going to give us?" Mr. Inman enquired.

"Well, I have my outline here, if it wouldn't bore you."

"Try it on the dog, eh?" said the doctor.

"Go on," said Daphne. "We represent three classes. There's Dad, the hard-headed, worldly-minded millionaire. Dr. Wolfe, the sceptical modern scientist. Me, the shallow-minded society traditionalist."

"A fair cross-section of a modern American congregation perhaps. But what about your folk?" asked the doctor.

"To tell the truth, I am ashamed to say I don't know, but we are all pretty much the same. Travellers in a strange country, following a trail none too clearly marked. Well, here goes."

The outline set out, in a series of crass, stark, unrelieved propositions, the central position of the modern view of Biblical interpretation with the main argument for it.

"Say, boy, they'll carry you out," said Daphne. "Better have a gun on you."

"You don't leave us much of the Bible, eh?" said Mr. Inman soberly. "Sort of takes the whole works out of the machine."

"Is that the extreme modern view? I mean, what about our theological professors?" asked the doctor. "What about what's his name—the opposition to the Co-operation?"

"Mr. Cameron will reject it *in toto*."

"And Miss Mary?" asked Daphne.

"For it."

"And the dear old lady, our Honorary President? Say, boy, I wouldn't hurt her for a good deal," said Mr. Inman.

"She will surprise you. She is quite up to date."

"And those young fellows, Ranald and the MacDonalds and that gang?" asked Daphne.

"I wonder," said Hector.

"After all, the question is, I imagine, not 'How will they take it?,' but 'Is it true?,'" said the doctor.

"Say, boy, if they need a purge, why, give 'em raw castor-oil. Why not a pill, with a sugar coating, eh? For instance, you've given *me* a hell of a jolt. If what you say is true my religion is all up in the air. What I mean is you want 'em to take it and keep it and use it. You're not after a riot. As a practical man now, why give kids—and that's what we are—why give 'em a dose for a horse? Isn't that so, Doctor? You're not talking to a lot of young theologians."

Hector folded up his outline and put it in his pocket.

"I believe you are right," he said doubtfully. "I'm glad I tried it on you first. I see your point of view. I guess I am an amateur practitioner, eh? But this is the way I look at it, if I may bore you still further?"

"Go to it," said Daphne. "They need it, and me too."

It was far into the night when Hector had finished his argumentation.

"Well, I have given you an awful dose," he said, rising to go. "And I am more than grateful to you for letting me try it on you."

"Well, I begin to see some sense in it, now," said Mr. Inman. "If you're right, then by the jumpin' Jeremiah I'm goin' to look into this thing. You'll have to give me some A B C books on this thing. All the same I believe in pills sugar-coated for kids, not horse-medicine."

"I will remember that," said Hector. "I feel you are right."

"If you are right," said the doctor slowly, "and if that is the position of—I won't say your most advanced—but your soundest thinkers, then for God's sake why not give it to us? It would make a difference, a damned big difference, to a lot of us."

After Hector had gone the others sat in silence about the fire, busy each of them with his own thoughts. The reactions were characteristic in each case.

"Interesting, eh?" said the doctor. "Of course I ought to know more about this. The air is full of that kind of stuff, but somehow this chap makes it a real and practical thing."

"Say, if what he says is true about the Bible, then why

the hell don't our preachers tell us about it? Why keep
the cards up their sleeves? Why don't they play the game
according to the rules? Makes me mad clear through," was
Mr. Inman's reply.

"They have, Dad. I've heard a bit of this right along.
They all talked about it at college. But I guess we have
been too busy with the stock market, with jazz and supper
dances."

"My God, girl, don't rub it in," said her father with a
kind of groan. "Good night. It's horse-medicine I've got,
and, well—good night, Daphne. You might have a lot better father," he said, kissing her.

She put her arms right round his neck, and whispered in
his ear: "There isn't any better dad. Don't be a darned
fool."

The following day in the course of her wonted "jollity
treatment" Daphne gave her own version of the minister's
proposed sermon and of the reactions of the camp dwellers.
In spite of her racy and humorous account there ran
through her tale a note of real feeling and of anxiety.

"Me, I'm packing a gun. They aren't going to rush my
minister if I can help it."

"That will do, Daphne," said Vivien, who was in attendance in the sick room, and whose patience with the American girl was short enough at times. "You need have no fear
for your minister. You'll find he is quite able to look after
himself. Get out now."

"All right! Good-bye, Captain Jock. You haven't often
met a crazier kid, have you?"

"And never a more charming," said Captain Jock, as he
returned the kiss blown to him.

But on Sunday morning when Hector came in to say
good-bye before going into his pulpit, with face set and eyes
aglow, Captain Jock arrested him, holding his hand a moment.

"Going to give 'em hell, eh?"

His brother stopped short as if he had been struck, and turned his glowing eyes in wide surprise and something of dismay upon his brother.

"Hell? No-o-o! No, not hell! God forgive me, not that!"

"Of course not!" said Jock, still holding his hand. "Say, old chap, you remember that sermon of yours, a year ago— the Shepherd coming on to that damned fool sheep in the thorn bush and tearing his hands getting it free? Say, could you work that in somehow?"

For a long moment the minister looked down upon his brother, nodded and turned away.

He went back into his study and closed the door and there remained.

"Hector, it is past time, dear," said Logie, knocking at the study door some minutes later.

When he came forth the glow was still in his eyes, but the face was set in softer lines. He was going to work in somehow that damned fool sheep and the Shepherd tearing his hands getting it free.

CHAPTER XIX

THE congregation were slow in dispersing, dazed, stunned, bewildered. Regarding one another doubtfully and saying little, they slowly emerged from the church and stood in groups waiting for they knew not what. Some with eager, anxious faces were waiting for a word with the minister. Others had withdrawn toward the line of vehicles near the shelter of the trees. Prominent among these latter was Mr. James Cameron, who by his gesticulations was manifestly much excited. Indeed his voice could be heard in explosive ejaculations—"Myths and legends! Fables and fairy tales! Songs and stories!—Lies—mostly lies! God help us! What have we?"

The minister standing on the steps caught an echo of the words and turned his eyes upon the group. For a moment he listened, then made a movement toward the group.

"No, Mr. MacGregor, not now—wait." It was Mr. Marriott, who with Vivien beside him was keeping his hand on the minister's arm. "Let me thank you from my heart for your sermon. You have given me a new point of view. A new conception of the Book. Come and see me. Again thank you. A wonderful exposition. Do come."

"Yes, come," said Vivien, edging him off to one side. "Come soon—he needs you." The girl's grey-green eyes were swimming with waves of warm glowing light. Come soon," she whispered, giving him her hand. "*I* want you too, Hector." The firm strong fingers closed on his hand with a soft, clinging pressure.

"Yes! What?" Hector glanced at the vivid face, now with a faint flush showing through the brown. "Yes, certainly I'll come, Vivien." A radiant little smile was his answer. He was conscious of a disturbing quickening of his heartbeat as he turned away to meet the Inman group.

"I want to thank you, sir!" boomed Mr. Inman's voice over the throng. "A very remarkable discourse. A very powerful presentation of new aspects of truth. Thank you, sir." He shook hands with the minister. "Sugar-coated all right," he added in a low voice, "but a drench, sir, a regular horse-drench."

"It was all right," said Dr. Wolfe quietly. "Makes a reasonable proposition out of what was an impossibility."

"I loved it, Hector," said Daphne, in a quiet tone. "That Shepherd! Oh, that was—say, that broke me up!" Her eyes suddenly filled. "It does yet. I'll never forget it."

The Marriotts caught up to Mrs. MacTavish at her gate.

"Lovely day, Mrs. MacTavish," said Vivien, "and a wonderful sermon."

"Oh, yes, the day is not so bad, and"—here Mrs. MacTavish's head went up with a perceptible jerk—"the sermon may suit some people. I was glad to see you in your place in God's house."

"Yes, I was glad to be there," said Vivien quite humbly.

"Yes, it is a preevilege that some folks despises in these days."

"Good-bye, Mrs. MacTavish," said Vivien with eyes downcast.

"Good-bye then."

Mrs. MacTavish lingered at the gate. "I am afraid," she said in a troubled voice, "the minister is not himself these days. What with his brother—and—and—his visitors and other trials."

The invitation to a gossip over the gate was obvious, but Vivien, knowing the lady's penchant in this direction, declined to be drawn. "Yes! But we hope Captain Jock is improving."

"It will be a great relief to have a quiet house again," said Mrs. MacTavish.

"It looks a little like rain, Mrs. MacTavish. But rain will do good to the gardens. They seem to need a great deal of rain just now," said Vivien over her shoulder as she hurried on after her father.

"Huh!" muttered Mrs. MacTavish. "It is not rain you are after, I am thinking, my young lady." But just what it was the young lady was after, Mrs. MacTavish did not specify.

At the door of their home Vivien and her father paused as was their custom before entering. Along the main road east and west, up over the hill roads, the people were making their way homeward.

"I wonder what their various reactions will be," she said. "What a devil of a job a minister has, anyway."

"God only knows," said her father. "But it is a big job for a man that can handle it."

Vivien glanced at her father's face. It was full of trouble.

"He'll handle them all right, never fear. Say, Dad, he's got some guts, hasn't he?"

"My dear, your English is unnecessarily Shakespearean," he said. "But," he waved his hand toward the blue arc in its setting of azure hills, "what a beautiful world it is with this light on it. Light? Ah! Light!"

He turned wearily into the house.

The reactions to the morning sermon were characteristic enough in the MacAskill home. After the dishes of the midday meal had been disposed of, it was the old lady's custom to extract from the members of her household the "heads" of the sermon, with such "particulars" as she could elicit by keen questioning.

"And what was the text to-day, Sandy?" she began.

"The text I don't mind well, but—"

"Let there be light and there was light!" replied Peggy supplementing, as was her custom, the frequent *lacunæ* in her father's report.

"A grand text indeed. And the 'heads'?"

"Heads?" said her son with a distinct snort. "Heads nor tails! Indeed you need not be asking me. Though there was plenty of 'tales,' and queer 'tales' at that," replied Sandy.

"Tales? And what does the man mean? Tales?" inquired Mrs. MacAskill in a severe tone. "Is that any way to be coming home from the church?"

"You need not be blaming me then. For it was the queer 'tales' the minister was giving us to-day." Sandy's voice was bitterly flippant.

"It was about the Bible, Grannie. And he told us how it was made, and what its message was, and how we were to make use of it," said Peggy.

"Say that again, Peggy. Thank God, *you* have a head on you at least."

Peggy repeated her answer.

"Ay, that was a grand division. And then what?"

"Well, he told us that the Bible was full of lies, for—" said Sandy with more spirit than was his wont.

The old lady sat up in her bed.

"Be silent, sir! God forgive you. You cannot help the head on you, though where you git it the Lord only knows. But there is no need for your slandering of your minister. Who is that at the door?"

"It's just Kenneth," replied Peggy with almost exaggerated indifference.

"Give him a drink of milk and bring him in."

"Come away, Kenneth. Sit you down. You were at the preaching?"

"Yes, I was there. I was at the back."

"You would be, and a lot of loons with you, I'll warrant. And behaving yourself none too well, I am afraid."

Kenneth grinned pleasantly at the old lady, of whom he stood in little dread.

"And what was the sermon about?"

"The Bible," said Kenneth promptly, "and it was a dandy.

Wee Hughie Heggie kept awake. Indeed there was no sleeping to-day. And he is going on with it to-morrow night. And I'm going. So is Archie Morrison, and Danny Mac-Dougall, and—"

"That will do, Kenneth. Now what did he say about the Bible? Man, I wish I had been there."

"He said it was not one Book at all, but a whole library of seventy-six books, and made up of a lot of songs and stories and things, and it kind of grew and—" Kenneth paused.

"Well. I could have told you that much myself about it. And then what?"

"Oh, I don't know. He said—"

"He said it was made up of a great mass of fragments of literature," said Peggy, taking up the story. "At first they were in the form of old songs and tales—"

"Ay, tales! Didn't I tell you? And queer tales too. Some of them lies," said Sandy triumphantly.

"They were not lies!" said Peggy indignantly. "They were not always exactly history, but they told the truth that God meant them to tell."

"Ah! That is different," said the old lady. "As you ought to know yourself, Sandy. Have we not many old songs ourselves that may not be—indeed could not be—history, but they tell you the kind of people they were about. Go on, Peggy. I wish I'd been there."

"He said it was never intended to be a book of geology, or astronomy, or even history itself. And what good would it be to those people at that time? And it would be queer geology—when there was not any in the world."

"Never you mind arguing about it, Peggy. You go on with it. And what did he say about the message? And now who is that?" The old lady was impatient at the interruption of what to her was a thing of compelling interest.

"It is Ranald Gillis and Black Mack," said Kenneth in intense excitement.

"Well, what of it? Bring them in, Sandy, and mind your manners, Kenneth."

The two stalwarts came in like King Agag of old, "treading delicately."

"Come in, lads, and sit you down," said Mrs. MacAskill. "It is myself that was wanting to see you both. And now will you be telling me why men of your age will be carrying on like two kids, like Kenneth yonder?"

"Oh, that is all past, Grannie," said Ranald. "It is something else we want to talk about."

"Oh, indeed. I was just thinking you were perhaps wanting to fight it out before myself, seeing that I could not have the privilege of being with the company that had the honour of seeing two men carry on like brute beasts the other day. I am surprised at you, Ranald Gillis. And what would your mother be saying?"

"My Goad! Mistress MacAskill, they would not be telling on us to Ranald's mother!" exclaimed Black Mack.

"It would serve you both right, only it would be too big a shame for Mistress Gillis. And you, Callum Mohr," she went on in Gaelic because of the young people, "how were you shaming your lips with lies upon your minister?"

Black Mack fairly covered his face with his great hands and groaned in Gaelic.

"Ochone, have pity upon a man who had lost his mind."

"It was not the minister," said Ranald, hurrying to his friend's aid, for the lustrous eyes were blazing with indignation. "It was me he was after. But it is all over. Will you not forget it, Mrs. MacAskill? And we want to ask you about something else of some importance, indeed of great importance."

"Well, well, if it is over, it is over with me. What is it now? Is Callum Mohr going to take a wife? Indeed it is himself would be the better of one."

"God bless my soul, it is not as bad as that," said Black Mack in devout gratitude.

"No, it is the sermon this morning, and what can we do about it?" said Ranald.

"And what was the sermon about? I have been hearing that it was a wonderful sermon upon the Bible. How we got the Book, and what its message was. We were just at that part of it. Perhaps you will tell me that, Ranald?"

"No, I am not sure that I could. But it was that the Bible was full of mistakes."

"He did not say 'full of mistakes,' " spoke up Peggy.

"Well, one or two is enough," said Black Mack.

"Tuts! And where have you been, and what have you been reading for the last twenty years, not to know the difference between the Bible and a geography book or astronomy book, or any other kind of school book? Is that what is troubling you? Indeed then, I am surprised at you. Have not I been hearing from the Doctor and the Professor and the others that same ever since they went out from home? And what did he say about the message of the Book?"

But this Ranald, and of course Black Mack, could not answer.

"What was it, Peggy, then?"

"It was the message of God to man. He said it was like a Father sending a message to His children telling them what they were to do, and how they were to get home to Him."

"Yes, yes, he said that," said Ranald eagerly, "and indeed that was very fine indeed."

"Mrs. MacTavish herself was crying," said Kenneth with a grin.

"Whisht you now, Kenneth, where is your manners?" said the old lady sharply.

"It is not the sermon, Grannie," said Ranald harshly. "It is James Cameron we are thinking about. The sermon, I will confess, was a little too much for me, but I know the minister is all right."

"And what is Jimmie Hannah busy about! The Ark of the Covenant, I am thinking."

"He was mad about Willie George and Mary Bella, I guess," said Kenneth with a wicked grin. "They were sitting together in the church."

"Tuts now, Kenneth, hold your tongue about your elders. And what would Mary Bella have to do with the sermon and the minister?"

"Well, I don't rightly know, but Mary Bella told the minister about Willie George, and the minister was pleased enough."

"Indeed? And so that's what is wrong about the sermon?" said the astute old lady.

"Yes, and I am pretty sure he is going about. We saw him with a lot of folk this morning at the church. And he is out among the Barra men this afternoon. And we were thinking it would be easy for him to make a lot of trouble. And of course, Mrs. MacTavish—"

"Tuts! man! Where have you left your brains? Mrs. MacTavish indeed! Not but she has a clackin' tongue. But the Barra men? They still put the Bible at the door to keep out the witches. I am hearing that they are stubborn cattle."

"I could soon settle the Barra men," said Black Mack with grim assurance.

"Ay, Callum Mohr, you could easy beat the senses out of them, but could you beat any sense into them? No, no, my man. You keep those big hands of yours in your pockets. Do you hear me?"

Black Mack promised obedience. "We will need to think about this, Ranald," the old lady went on. "Ay, and Mary Bella and Willie George are making it up? And the minister is for it. No wonder Jimmie Hannah is in trouble for the Bible. Well, we must think about it. But, Ranald, I am surprised you know so little about your Bible, my lad. I will give you a wee book that Maisie sent me long ago.

Peggy, you were reading it to-day.　Get it for Ranald.　Now be off with you.　I must rest and think."

"And there is a meeting to-morrow night for Bible study."

"And who called that?　Jimmie Hannah?"

"No, the minister."

"Tuts.　If he had let them alone for a week they would forget all about it.　Well, Ranald, you and Mack will go to the meeting.　And mind you do not get too concerned about the Bible.　The Book was doing its work and giving its message in the world a long time before either you or Jimmie Hannah were thought of, and it will be here long after you are both away—where, I will not be saying.　So do not show yourself anxious at all.　Indeed it would do for Jimmie Hannah and Mrs. MacTavish, and perhaps Hughie Heggie and the other theologians in the congregation."　At this the old lady went off into a series of deep-throated chuckles, in which first Kenneth joined gleefully and then Ranald, and finally Black Mack in a low rumble.

Peggy alone remained unmoved.　Her face was sullen and her eyes dark with what Kenneth knew at once was deep anger.

"Huh!　And they never heard a word he said about the Shepherd going after the foolish lamb, and tearing his own hands to get it free from the thorns," she burst forth in passionate rage, and ran hastily from the room.

"Now what is wrong with the lass?" asked her grandmother.

"It's the story he told about a lamb in a thorn bush, and about a boy that went away from home and—"

But Kenny himself for all his mischief and laughter was suddenly choked into silence.

"Come here, laddie," said the old lady, her piercing eyes growing soft.　"Hand me that box."　She put a handful of bull's-eyes into the boy's hands.　"Now go and get Peggy to give you a scone and jam if you find her.

"Good-bye, Ranald, and thank you for coming.　Never

you fear for the Book. It has a rare fashion of looking after itself. And as for the minister, I wish he would laugh more, but—there is not much for him to laugh at just now, poor Hector! With Jock lying there. Ah, well, God knows about it. Good-bye, Callum Mohr, and keep your hands off the Barrich."

After they had left she lay back on her pillow with a heavy sigh. Her face seemed to shrivel into a little patch of wrinkles. She folded her claw-like fingers upon her heart, her lips began to move and from her closed eyes two big tears ran down unheeded among the wrinkles.

CHAPTER XX

THERE was wide divergence of opinion and feeling throughout the congregation in regard to the proposed meeting for Bible study. Mrs. MacAskill was strongly of opinion that it would have been much wiser to postpone the meeting for a week or two, by which time "they would have forgotten all about it." But seeing that the meeting must be held, someone from the house must attend.

"You will be going, Peggy. Sandy, you will make nothing of it and will neither do nor get any good. Peggy will bring me an account of what will be going on. You will go with the MacDonalds and stay the night with them, Peggy, and mind you keep your ears open."

With face sullen and unmoved, but with a deep and secret joy in her heart, Peggy accepted the order. There would be "a doing" in which her soul delighted. And the MacDonalds were nice enough, except Kenneth, who thought himself too smart forsooth, because he could play the fiddle with the best of them.

In the manse there was a slight contention between the two attendant nurses as to which should put in an appearance at the meeting in the church.

"I really ought to be there. Of course I know Hector's theory of Bible interpretation. Most people do."

"Well then, I don't. So I am going. Besides my father is going to be there and he will need a guardian, poor dear. He gets so excited, and says things."

In a private room of the store and telegraph office, the matter was debated by Willie George Cameron and Mary Bella from a slightly different point of view.

"I am not going," was Willie George's decision. "My father is going to raise the devil, and he has a lot of the Barrich lined up with him. He really feels terribly about the whole thing, and of course does not agree with the minister."

"I am going," said Mary Bella definitely, and very firmly. "I don't understand what he was saying yesterday, and I want to."

"Oh, pshaw, you can get it from the books. There are lots of books."

"I am going. You need not come. My cousin Ranald will be there. Of course he is only my second cousin."

"Your cousin Ranald! Indeed that will be enough of your cousin Ranald."

"Well, he will see that I am—"

"Indeed he will not—"

"Oh, just as you like of course."

Willie George decided that the meeting for Bible study was indicated for him that evening.

Daphne was keen to go to the meeting. But her father put his foot down.

"I'd like to go all right. But I hear our minister is in for a row, and I guess he'd rather that strangers weren't present."

"Quite right," agreed the doctor. "I hate being mixed up in family quarrels."

Daphne reluctantly decided her men were right. "I'd like to say something to that old guy that the old lady calls Jimmie Hannah."

"I gravely doubt whether your contribution would be of any considerable value to the old gentleman," said the doctor.

"I'm thinking of Hector."

"Or to the minister."

"Darned old crank. It isn't the Bible that's troubling him. It's the minister backing up that mooncalf of his and Mary Bella."

"All the more reason for keeping out."

"Well, I wish he'd pull out of this God-forsaken country and come to a church where he'd be appreciated. Couldn't you get him a church somewhere down in our country, Dad? In six months, after he'd get polished up a bit—"

"Polished up? I like that."

"Well, he'd fill the biggest church in New York. He's got brains, and—and—something else that a lot of ministers need."

"And what is that, daughter?"

"Darned if I know, but anyway it's something I want in a minister and have never seen before. Do, Dad—you could fix it."

"Fix it all right, I guess, but—"

"What would happen to a minister who preached that sermon of his down in our country?" said the doctor. "What would our Fundamentalists do to him?"

"They'd give him hell, I guess," said Daphne. "No, it wouldn't do. They'd crucify him, damn them."

"He is much safer in his own country, believe me. They have got past all that in this country, I understand."

"Not in Ravanoke, apparently," said Daphne gloomily.

"Don't you worry. That young man can look after himself," said the doctor. "Or I have read him wrong."

"But just now, when he is in such trouble. It's a damn shame!"

"Well, we will keep out anyway," said her father, settling the question.

"Feel badly?" asked the doctor, with a keen look at the girl's troubled face. But Daphne made no reply.

At the meeting in the church after the opening exercises the minister made a brief statement as to the plan of Bible study which he proposed to follow.

"First, we must know how the Bible has come into being. Its sources, the material out of which it grew, the people to whom this marvellous revelation first came, their history, political, social, religious—all this will give us the background of the book. Then we will examine—"

"Pardon me, Mr. MacGregor," interrupted Mr. Cameron, "I may be wrong. I am no scholar, but just a plain ordinary man, a member and an elder of this church. But it seems to me that there is a preliminary question that ought to be settled, especially in view of what we heard yesterday in this church. And that question is this: Is the Bible true? Is the Bible the inspired Word of God? Or is it a collection of myths and fairy tales, mostly lies? If the Bible is not true, if it is not the inspired and infallible word of God, why bother about it? For my part if it is not true, I will not be taking trouble with it."

A burst of applause from the northwest corner of the church, where the speaker's friends had gathered, greeted Mr. Cameron's speech.

The minister waited till the applause had ceased and then said pleasantly:

"It is quite true that Mr. Cameron's plan of study might be followed. He proposes to begin with the content of the book. But I think that the better method is to begin with the origins, the sources. If we know something about how the book has come into being we shall be in a better position to discuss its content."

"Will the minister answer us plainly? Is the Bible the inspired and infallible word of God?"

"Mr. Cameron is not asking one question but three: Is the Bible the Word of God? Is the Bible inspired? Is the Bible infallible? I might truly answer 'yes' to all three questions, and yet might be terribly misleading you."

"Can we not get a straight answer to a straight question without quibbling?"

The minister's head went up.

"Quibbling? A straight answer?" Then very deliberately he added, "Is Mr. Cameron asking his minister whether he is an honest man?"

An ominous rumble came from the northeast corner

where Ranald Gillis, Black Mack, the MacDonalds and their friends were gathered.

"No, no, Mr. MacGregor," said Mr. Cameron hurriedly. "I am not asking that. No, no."

"It would be better not," said a deep voice from the northeast corner.

"But I will ask one thing: Is the Bible true?"

"I will answer in my own way. The Bible sets forth a true and noble conception of God, and a true and noble ideal for man."

"That is what I mean," said Mr. Cameron impatiently. "I cannot get a straight answer. For me the Bible is true. Every statement, every word, cover to cover." Great applause from the southeast corner.

"That is what I believe myself," came from the middle of the church in a loud strident voice. It was from Mrs. MacTavish.

"Hear, hear!" came a low voice, with a chuckle, from the northeast corner.

Mrs. MacTavish rose to her feet. She was impressive in size and forceful, even truculent, in manner. Her attitude breathed threatening. Her speech flowed like a river in spate. She had a nimble wit and a biting tongue. It was dangerous to cross her bow.

"The book, the whole book and nothing but the book, the inspired and unfailable Word of God. That is my belief, and my father's before me. A godly man he was. I mind well when he had the headache and couldn't sleep he would be putting the Bible, many's the time, under his pillow, and would be asleep like a babe sucking its mother." (Delighted giggles from the northeast corner.) "And I am the same way." (Increased giggles.) "And I will tell you why. Wan time I was in Boston, I was only wance, my daughter Betsy paid my passage. She is married on a barber in Boston, and he has a fine shop with a Ladies' Parlor" (here

Mrs. MacTavish became friendly and intimate) "and all that—"

"Manicures, too?" inquired an earnest voice.

"Yes, I heard them talk about many cases, but I did not ask what they were curing. I was attending to my own business," added Mrs. MacTavish in a cutting aside. "Indeed I did not approve of that part of it. Them hussies! If they had less paint on, and more clothes, it would set them better." (Delighted approval of the sentiment from the northeast corner excited Mrs. MacTavish.) "Oh, I know well enough what you are thinking of. But as I was saying there was two men in Boston, evangelists Torrey and Alexander—oh, they were the lovely men, and the big church, it would hold a dozen of this church." (Mrs. MacTavish's contempt was withering.) " 'The Temple' they called it. And the galleries were filled with thousands of people, and the big organ and the big choyer, and the singing—oh, it was heavenly!"

"But what has that to do with the question before us?" asked Mr. Cameron impatiently.

"Amn't I jist telling you? Well—and the man on the platform was asking, 'And what was the hymn your mother put you to sleep on?' And they would get up and sing a verse, and some of them was not much at it. 'And what was the hymn your mother put you to sleep on?' And he pinted up at me, right in the front gallery. And I rose up and said: 'I cannot sing good since I had the pewmonia, I hav only one string in my throat.' 'Well,' he said, 'word it out to me.' And I did.

> "There is rest for the weary,
> There is rest for the weary,
> Where the tree of life is blooming,
> There is rest for you.

Oh, it is a lovely hymn, and then they sang it. And I won the prize, too." (Great cheers for Mrs. MacTavish's triumph from the northeast corner.) Mrs. MacTavish glanced suspiciously at the corner, but forbore threatening.

"But perhaps, Mrs. MacTavish—" began the minister in a courteous voice.

"Wait a meenute," answered Mrs. MacTavish in a soothing tone as to a fretful child. "I am coming to the pint. Then that man Mr. Torrey—oh, he was a great and godly man—he began on the Bible and he said, I mind like it was to-night: 'The Bible is the inspired Word of God, true and unfailable, the chart and compass on the voyage of life.' And then he holds the book to his heart and says: 'The book, the whole book, nothing but the book. Every word necessary, every word true.' And then he said, 'It is like a necklace of pearls: break the string and the whole necklace is lost.' And that is what I think. One lie in the Bible, and there is no Bible for me." Amid thunders of applause from both northeast and northwest corners Mrs. MacTavish resumed her seat.

"May I ask," said Mr. Marriott, who with his daughter was sitting just behind Mrs. MacTavish, "whether the excellent Mr. Torrey was considered an expert, a really critical Biblical scholar?"

"Bible scholar, is it?" said Mrs. MacTavish in great indignation. "He could quote the Bible from wan end to the other."

The minister interposed. "Charley Alexander I knew and loved. He was a princely leader of sacred song. Mr. Torrey was a great evangelist, but he never claimed to be a critical Bible scholar."

"That is just what the matter is with us. The Bible is God's word for plain people, like us in this room. Why all this nonsense about critics? We have too many critics. Yes, and atheists." The audible interruption from Mrs. MacTavish wakened a sweet smile on Vivien's face.

"Let us get to particulars," continued Mr. Cameron. "I will ask the minister a plain question. Did Moses write the truth when he wrote the story of the Creation in Genesis?"

"Mr. Cameron does not pretend to be a Bible scholar. The question illustrates the necessity for Bible study," said the minister. "My answer is first: There is not a competent scholar in the world to-day who would say that Moses wrote the first chapter of Genesis, not one. Second, the story of the Creation is not scientifically accurate, was never intended as a scientific statement, and would have been of no use to the people for whom it was written who knew nothing of science."

"Then it is a plain lie?" came a voice from the northwest corner, followed by angry applause.

"No. It sets forth in dramatic form the essential truth that this Universe did not come into being of its own accord, but by the creative power of God."

"And the account in Genesis of man's creation, in the first chapter the twenty-seventh verse," said Mr. Cameron, reading from his Bible, "is also a lie?"

"But in the second chapter and the seventh verse," said the minister, "there is quite a different account of the making of man, and further on, in the twenty-first verse, still another account of the origin of woman, where we read that the woman was made from the rib of a man."

"And the worse for her, poor soul," said Mrs. MacTavish savagely. "It was there she got her first crook."

(Shouts of laughter and applause from the northeast corner.)

"Here again you see the need of study," urged the minister. "We have two accounts which come originally from two different sources. We must study these origins."

"Origins indeed! Origins, we are hearing much about origins. There are some of them critics will be telling us that men are from the monkeys. Monkeys? Well, they may not know themselves who their fathers were—indeed, by the ways of them they might well be from the monkeys."

(Shouts of applause from the northeast corner.)   "But I know my father was no monkey." (Renewed cheers.) "And the men of Skye were no monkeys." (Wild cheers.)

"Order, order!" sternly cried the minister. "This is unseemly."

But Mrs. MacTavish had not finished. There was still a root of bitterness in her soul.

"They were great days, and great and godly men in them days. The Bible is true for me, and every word in it, no matter what of origins or sources. Yes, the rib and all, though it is my opinion she would be better with her own ribs."

"What about the ass and Balaam?" asked a very respectful voice.

"The ass and Balaam, is it? Why not? If the Lord can allow a man to speak like an ass why should He not allow an ass to speak like a man? No! the Bible for me, and the Confession of Faith and the Catechism. And that is all that I will be saying to-night. Indeed I am saying too much, except may God have mercy upon us. And may God have mercy on you, sir. And that is what I will be praying day and night for evermore."

With a sudden catch in her voice she gathered up her Bible and gloves and walked like a sergeant-major out of the church. There was no cheering, not a sound till the door had closed behind her.

Then Mr. Marriott spoke.

"Perhaps I have no right to speak in this meeting. I am here because of my interest in the subject. My studies, I confess, have led me away from Bible studies. But the sermon yesterday, and—and other things"—his voice trembled a moment—"have wakened in me the hope that perhaps deeper study might give me back my Bible again. I suggest that we might adjourn now and those who wish to take up this study might meet again next Monday evening."

"I second the motion," said Willie George, who with Mary Bella was near the front of the middle section of the church.

Whether it was because Mr. Marriott, a well-known sceptic, had made the motion, or because it was his son who seconded it, Mr. Cameron seemed to lose control of himself at this point.

"No! Let us have done with this wickedness and folly. I am not going to see God's Holy Word torn to pieces before our eyes."

"Tuts! If it is God's Word, who can tear it in pieces?" It was Peggy. The exclamation, the deep hoarse voice, the impatient scorn were all reminiscent of her grandmother.

"Listen to that!" said Mr. Cameron. "The very children are losing their reverence, not to say their manners. I give notice here and now that I shall bring this matter before the Session of this church for consideration and action."

"And next Monday the class for Bible study will meet at eight o'clock," announced the minister, and closed the meeting by pronouncing the benediction.

Mr. Cameron stood waiting in his place till his son and Mary Bella came near him.

"Willie George, you will come home with me. I will be requiring your services."

"Yes, Father, I will be right home," said Willie George with alacrity.

"You will come at once!" The old man was trembling with passion.

"I cannot go till I have taken Mary Bella home."

"Go, go," whispered Mary Bella. "I can get home all right."

"You will come now, or it will be the worse for you."

"I will be with you in a few minutes."

"No, *now!* Now or never!" thundered his father, turning away.

"Willie George, go with your father," said the minister, who had come up. "I will take Mary Bella home."

"I will not."

"Go, Willie George. Go, or I will never speak to you."

"Willie George, I command you. Go with your father. And at once," said the minister.

The combination of these various influences was too strong for Willie George.

"I will go then, Mary Bella, this time," he said in a voice thick with rage and shame. "But, as God hears me, never again."

On his way back from taking Mary Bella to her home the minister was striding through the dark at a good pace past Miss Mary's gate when a lithe little figure sprang at him from the shadow of the hedge.

"Daphne," he cried, "you little devil, you scared me to death. What are you doing here?"

"Waiting for you, but I dare not let Mrs. MacTavish see me or your character would be gone." For the rumour of the great fight and its occasion had reached Daphne's ears.

"You are staying the night with Miss Mary. I'll go in with you."

"No. Logie is in there getting the report of the meeting, and I want to talk to you."

"What about?"

"What about?" Her hand went through his arm. "Why, about the weather, and the crops, and the markets, and—and any other darn old thing. Hector, you are a queer chap."

He was acutely conscious of her weight hanging on his arm, he caught a waft of the perfume on her hair, and a gleam of the starlight in her eyes. He was man enough to feel within him a quickening of his pulse beats. But he was thoroughly master of himself. This was a very lovely girl, a child in years, but with the experience of a woman of the world, and of a world whose ways were not at all those of this quiet countryside. She had made a fool of him once. But not again.

"Yes, I am queer, and very queer. But it is time you were in your bed and asleep. And so I am going to give you into the care of Miss Mary forthwith."

"We are going away in a few days, Hector," she said quietly.

"I thought you would be. Your father has not had much of a fishing holiday, or the doctor either. I feel guilty over it. I am awfully sorry. But I—we all are more grateful than we can say. Never have I known or heard of such kindness."

"Oh, shucks! Talk sense! What have we done? What in comparison with what you have done for. us?"

"Well, I have showed you a good fishing pool, but—"

"Oh, Hector, don't be a darn fool! Can't you understand? You have made the whole world new to me. I never knew there were such people as you in the world. You are all different—you, Miss Mary, and Logie. You are just wonderful, and that darling Captain Jock—oh, he just breaks my heart."

"Yes, Jock is fine. Ah, if you had only known him before his sickness." Hector's voice failed him.

The clinging hands tightened on his arm. "And you, Hector, you are—oh, I can't tell you what—"

"Nonsense. I am a very dull and very commonplace, and at present a rather harassed minister. Not much good to any one, I fear."

"Oh! oh! oh! You are so hard, so—so stupid! Do you know what I want you to do?" she said in a low voice tense with passion. "I want you to put your arms round me and kiss me—and—kiss me."

"Yes, it would be very delightful," said Hector pleasantly. "We might play the fool for half an hour, and then what? Feel like a pair of traitors all our lives. Don't look at me that way. I tell you, young woman, you are dangerous. Quit it! Do you hear?"

"Am I?" Her lovely face was lifted to his. "Oh, if I only were."

"You are most horribly dangerous, so dangerous that I feel I must take you in to Miss Mary's, and at once. How could I look your doctor in the face?"

" 'My' doctor? My God, that's just it! He is not 'my' doctor! And he wouldn't care much. Oh, you are a beast —a cold-hearted beast. You shame me!" Her breath was coming fast.

"No, Daphne," he said, very gently and very quietly. "You are a very dear, a very lovely, a very fine—"

"Fine? Oh, hell! Fine? And me throwing myself at you like a—a—"

He put her hand over her lips.

"Listen! A lovely, fine little girl of whom I am very fond, and who will be a splendid and noble woman one day if—"

"Oh, Hector, don't! Don't. You are killing me! I am a damned little fool!"

"Stop it!" he said sternly.

"Damned is the only word, a damned little fool." Her breast was heaving with great dry sobs.

He put his arms round her and held her close to him.

"Daphne, my dear, do you see that light up in that room? There is a boy waiting for me there. That's where I ought to be. He will not sleep till I have seen him. He is very fond of you. You have worked in him a wonderful thing. If he gets better it will be because of you. We have all seen it and we all love you for it. That is why I could not kiss you a little while ago, and that is why I am going to kiss you now, if you will let me."

"Captain Jock? But I have done so little for him. Oh, I am glad if I have helped the least little bit. Poor dear boy. Yes, you may kiss me, Hector. . . . Now we will go in to Miss Mary, and you are not a bit queer, but are a

man all through. Forget my foolishness, Hector," she whispered.

"What foolishness? Come along, my dear. You are a
brick. If the doctor gets you he will be a lucky chap."

"No, no. Don't talk about him. After all, he is a good
chap—but—don't talk about it—I can't bear it."

CHAPTER XXI

"THERE they are! I see them!" Logie sprang to her feet and dashed downstairs two at a time.

"What's up?" said Captain Jock.

"Dad's back, I guess," said Daphne, going to the window. "Yes, there he is. My stars! Will you *look* at the way he is kissing Logie? You certainly ought to be over here watching those two!"

"*Logie?* She's rather careful with her kisses, too. But she is so happy that she is hardly herself these days—she thinks I'm out of the woods."

"So you are, Jock," said Daphne, coming back to him. "You're a new man."

"Am I? I don't know. If I am, Daphne, it's your work, old girl."

A flush came over the girl's face. "Me? Tuts, as dear old Mrs. MacAskill would say."

"You're a wonder, Daphne. You are so vital. You ooze life. And you are a lot more than that, too."

"I wonder what they are doing now," said Daphne, going back to the window. "Say, that girl is crazy. She's doing a cancan on the grass. Oh, boy!"

"You ought to see her in her glad rags. None of the others can touch Logie. She used to turn the boys' hearts to water. Poor old girl, I've taken the life out of her."

"You are giving her life back again, then. Now she's vamping Steve. I'd hate to let her loose on any boy friend of mine."

"Yes, that's always been the way with Logie. She had them all dizzy. And mind you, she's the same to them all, old or young. From the colonel to the cook. She loves them all."

"What is it, I wonder? And she never tires. And she never gets burnt herself."

"There is only one Logie," said Captain Jock quietly.

"I wish I had her secret," said Daphne, coming back again to Captain Jock.

"She loves people—that is her secret. She never thinks of herself."

"And she is so darn clever," said Daphne with a little sigh.

"What are you grousing about? You've got enough, I guess. You needn't worry. Why, dash it all, Daphne—come over here."

"Here they are!" said Daphne, running to the door. "Hello, Dad! How are you? And how is the little old burg?"

"I was just telling Logie I was glad to be back here again. When I saw this green little grove with the spire pointing up through the trees, says I to Steve, 'There's *home*, Steve. Let her go!' And he did. I guess Steve was as glad as any of us to be here again."

"He would. Steve hates New York, and of course like everyone else he's nuts on Logie. I saw you, Dad, just now. I told Captain Jock that I'd have to keep my eye on you!"

"You'd better," said Logie with a gay laugh. "It was good to see Mr. Inman again. Just think—four days away from us."

"Glad to see you're better, Captain," said Mr. Inman. "You certainly look better."

"Why not? Everyone is either pulling or pushing," said Daphne.

"Yes, I'm better. Your daughter is a great psychologist, a regular pep artist."

"She has pep all right. I suppose the doctor is up at camp. Well, I must see him. I guess I'll have Steve run me up. Want to come along, Daphne?"

"You go, Logie. I'll keep on pepping up the Captain. And here's Hector—he will be next door for chaperon."

"Run along, Daphne," said Captain Jock. "You are losing all your good looks, some of them at least. You're losing colour."

"Smartie! It's Logie and Miss Mary. They've hidden my rouge pot. All right, Logie, come along. Back in an hour? Hector, you look after the baby!"

"Get out. I'll have a chance to sleep," said Captain Jock with a grin at her.

"Stop at the telegraph office," ordered Mr. Inman.

Mr. Inman found Mary Bella deep in conversation with Willie George, who was leaning far over the counter.

"Well, Miss MacRae, and how is the market?"

"Very good, sir, I think," said Mary Bella, who was a great friend of Mr. Inman's. "Here are some wires for you."

Mr. Inman read the wires, stood for some moments in thought, then said: "I'll be in again within an hour. Meantime, young lady—" He lowered his voice, and Willie George moved off to another counter. "Listen to me carefully. Your stock has been pyramiding pretty lively. You have now more than you want, a great deal."

"Yes, sir."

"Now you wire my broker at once to sell. Do that tonight. Be sure!"

"Yes, sir. Thank you, sir. Oh, I do thank you, sir!"

"All right, do what I say."

"Yes, sir," said Mary Bella, looking at him earnestly, with shiny eyes.

"All right, my dear," said Mr. Inman, patting her hand and nodding to Willie George as he passed out.

"I'm sitting with you, Dad. I'm not taking any chances of having Logie as a stepmother," said Daphne, springing out from the front seat.

"That's right. You can't be too careful!" said Logie, getting in beside Steve.

Meantime Willie George was eagerly discussing the market with Mary Bella.

"Well, he said 'sell' and I'm going to wire to-night," said Mary Bella with decision. "You get into your car and bring Mrs. Heggie and Ranald here right away. No, don't argue. Get right away. I will be glad enough to get this responsibility off my shoulders. I'm sick of it. Now get right away. No! Do what I say."

"But the stock is going up every day, Mary Bella."

"Do what I say, and right away. I won't speak to you till you do." And so resolute was she that Willie George was forced to obey.

On the way to camp Daphne kept up a brisk fire of questioning as to New York, its people and its doings. But in the front seat there was little conversation. Steve was busy with his wheel, for the road was none too good, and besides, when he was at the wheel he was strictly a chauffeur. But as they were nearing the camp, Logie said in her wonted cheery, kindly voice:

"It was a lovely drive, Steve. I always feel so sure with you."

"Thank you, Miss Logie," replied the chauffeur. "I shan't have many more drives with you. I am leaving this service very soon. I am done with chauffeuring, thank God."

"Oh, and what next, Steve? Shall we not see you any more?" There was dismay in her voice. "I hate to lose touch with friends," she added.

"That is kind of you, Miss Logie."

"Where will you be?"

"In England—once more." The suppressed note of triumph caught Logie's ear.

"That is your home, Steve? You will love that. I did love England. The English are so sure, so very understanding. I mean somehow one feels safe with them, just as I always feel with you, Steve." As she spoke the lovely dark eyes were turned trustfully on the thin hard face.

Steve's foot came down hard on the accelerator, and the car leaped half its length.

"Yes, but if you fail them once it is good-bye forever."

"But of course. You couldn't trust people who disappoint you, could you? I mean it would be hard to." Again the kind eyes turned straight to Steve's face.

"No, of course not. No never!" Steve's teeth came hard on that "never."

"But of course you would be sorry for them," said Logie.

"Miss Logie, I believe you would forgive the devil himself."

Logie seemed to think this over, then said: "Do you know, I often feel sorry for the devil."

Something like a groan came from the thin hard lips.

"There's the camp. Oh, I always love the look of this lake through the screen of trees, and that high rock away beyond looking like an ancient castle, and the dark line of trees on the other side." She glanced up at the face beside her. Its distortion startled her.

"What's the matter, Steve?"

"Tooth!" said Steve, setting his foot down again on the accelerator.

"Say, what's the matter with this car anyway?" cried Daphne. "It's bucking like a broncho."

"Accelerator sticking a little, Miss," said Steve.

"Can't we do something, Steve, for your tooth?" said Logie, trouble in her face.

"Please don't," said Steve, in an imploring whisper.

The doctor came eagerly forward to meet them. Hughie Heggie was busy with the fire.

"Hello, Mr. Inman, glad to see you. Hello, Daphne. You did come up, did you? How's the patient?"

"Oh, well enough to leave, as you see. Hector is in charge and Vivien will be over for tea. And Miss Mary will look in. I guess he'll pull through till we get back. How are the fish behaving?"

"Well, one of them behaved rather well this afternoon, after about thirty-five minutes' persuasion. Look at this."

The doctor uncovered a little nest of balsam boughs and lifted up a magnificent fish.

"My stars and all the angels!"

"Jumpin' Jeremiah!"

"Oh, what a beauty! A salmon! Oh, doctor, I am so glad! I was just wishing you would get a salmon!"

"He *is* a whale. What does he go?" asked Mr. Inman, a touch of envy in his voice.

"Just over twenty-eight pounds. And he almost played me out. He was a glorious fighter. But I got him at last, just a little after five. I had been thrashing the water for an hour or so, getting little chaps and throwing them back."

"Yes, isn't it just sickening?" said Logie, her dark eager face all aglow with as much excitement as if it had been her own catch.

"And then I made a cast off that point into the little bay beyond, when z-z-z-i-p—splash—whoop—and he was away."

"Gone?" exclaimed Logie. "Oh, what—!"

"Gone! Not on your life, but—" and on went the epic through all the nerve-racking phases and climaxes of the Homeric struggle. "And then Hughie made a sweep at him with his net and missed."

"Oh! How awful!" Logie's voice rose in a delighted shriek.

"But next time, I was reeling him in nice and slow, and he turned over on his side, and again just as Hughie raised his net—flip—z-z-z-oo-oo-oo-m! Off he was."

"Oh, Doctor!" Logie was fairly dancing in her anguished excitement.

"Look at her!" said Daphne *sotto voce* to Steve, whose eyes had never left the girl's face. "She's fighting it all over, herself."

"That's right, that's just right," said Steve, his pale face tinged with two spots of red.

"Next time, however, Hughie slipped his net under him and had him."

"And man alive! He was like to drag me oot into the deep wi' him. Ay, he was a fair deevil!" said Hughie, shaking his head solemnly.

"Poor chap!" said Logie.

"Say! She'd pity the devil himself," said Daphne.

"Just what I was saying," said Steve, almost as much excited as the girl herself.

"What?" said Daphne, glancing sharply at him.

"A great fight! And splendidly told," said Steve quietly.

After the excitement had somewhat subsided Mr. Inman called the doctor to one side and engaged him in what apparently was a deeply important discussion.

"All right!" finally said the doctor. "You're the boss. What you say goes."

Mr. Inman proceeded to write out some telegrams.

"What can I do with this fish?"

"Hector can distribute it where it will do most good," suggested Daphne.

"Seems a pity to cut it up," said the doctor.

"No! Never!" said Logie. "Tell you what, send it to Dr. Whitney. Steve can run it over to the West Harbour. Mr. MacKinnon can pack it in ice. He does it often, and by to-morrow night it will be in Boston in Dr. Whitney's hands. Let me first make some photos, will you?"

The suggestion was enthusiastically accepted. And three days later there appeared photographs in the *Boston Herald* showing Hughie with the fish in the landing net, and the fish with the whole party (Steve excepted) along with a graphic and highly imaginative sketch of its capture.

"It will take us all our time to catch that train," said Logie after the photographs had been made. "I wish I could stay for supper, Doctor."

"We have some trout. Of course they are not so lordly a dish as Mr. Salmon would supply, but—"

"But really ever so much finer," said Logie. "I am sorry, Doctor, and I am so glad you got the fish. It would have been too bad if you had gone back without landing a salmon. I would have been so disappointed. You have lost so much time from your fishing—I mean—"

"My dear child, I know just what you mean. And you are an angel to think of it, as you always are," said the doctor with warm appreciation in his voice.

"Now, Doctor," she said with arching eyebrows, "there are really no angels about here, you know. But you have really been so—"

"Tuts!" broke in Daphne, "as friend Mrs. MacAskill would say. Let's adjourn this meeting of the Ravanoke Mutual Admiration Society and do something."

"Yes, we must hurry," said Logie. "You have your supper here. I will go down home with Steve, and then Hector will get the fish away at West Harbour and—are you coming down to-night again, Daphne? You really don't need to. You would love to stay up here this wonderful night. And you might catch Mrs. Salmon in the morning."

Daphne looked at the doctor, who made no sign.

"Yes, Daphne, we will stay," her father said. "I really want to do some deep breathing of this marvellous air, after four days and four nights of—well, other air. And I want to tell you a lot of things."

"All right," said Daphne rather listlessly.

"You take these telegrams, Steve, and get them off."

"Yes, sir," said Steve.

After supper, which with some bull cook aid from Mr. Heggie, the doctor prepared, they lay stretched at ease upon beds of balsam in the light of the fire, the men smoking, Daphne dreaming, but with little talk.

"No cigarettes with you, Daphne? I can supply you,"

said the doctor.

"I'm off cigarettes," said Daphne shortly.

"Hello! For how long!" said her father.

"I don't know. I hate the damn things."

"Say! Not feeling well, daughter?"

"I'm all right," she snapped.

For some moments there was silence, then Daphne burst forth.

"Say, Dad, can you tell me what in hell is wrong with the women and girls in our country? How have they come to be as they are?"

"What exactly do you mean? There are lots of lovely girls and women in our country, as fine as any on earth."

"Man, where are they? Why don't I meet them? I tell you, Dad, I never in my whole life met girls like these girls. Never a woman like Miss Mary. And as for Logie—I guess she's in a class by herself, and Vivien too. They are no hicks! They are better educated than I am. What do I know anyway? What have I read? Some damn fool rotten sex, murder, detective stuff. They have something—oh, I don't know—something fine, lovely, clean. I tell you that girl Logie makes me think of—of—some lovely flower in a grass meadow."

"She is indeed a lovely girl," said her father, "but I guess they don't grow many like her in this country either."

"When I think of my crowd," went on Daphne, "ugh! With their cocktails, with their cheap, loud, smart talk, with their night clubs, and their rotten minds and hearts, it makes me sick. Hearts? They wouldn't know a real woman's heart if they met one."

"Oh, come now, Daphne, there's a fine lot of girls in your crowd."

"Oh! It's myself, I guess. I am sick of myself and sick of my crowd too, sick—sick—sick to death. My God! When I think of going back to that life again, I feel like taking poison or jumping into that lake. At least it would be cool and clean. Hell! What in God's name are we living for anyway?"

The doctor made no reply.

"Of course, as you say," continued her father, "those girls—Logie and Miss Mary and Vivien—are mighty fine girls. But I guess they'd be rather rare in any country."

"No! There's that dear old lady Mrs. MacAskill, and Mrs. MacDonald. Yes, and a lot more of those women in the Co-operative. Not so much culture—but something fine about them, and clean—and—and—oh, I don't know. I know I'm sick of myself. Sick to death."

"You want a little change, I guess. We'll be going home next week."

"I can't bear the thought of going home! What is there to go back to! All that silly damn fool round of dinners, dances, theatres, suppers, night clubs, movies. My Lord!"

"Why, you're dead keen on the movies, Daphne!"

"Yes! I suppose I *was*. Why? We are all bored stiff. But these people? Why, they're happy. That girl Logie is happy. If she were sure her brother Captain Jock was going to be all right again, she would be as happy as a lark, never ask for another thing. My God! If everyone else is happy she is in Heaven. Did you see her when Fritz was telling about his fish? She was thrilled to death, every bit as much as if she had the line herself. What is it? What is it? My God, what is it?"

"Guess you've got it there, Daphne, or at least a bit of it," said the doctor gravely. "She is interested in other people. As you say, if they are happy, she is happy. She has a heart at leisure from itself. That's not all, but it is a big part. I noticed that girl's face, now that you speak of it. She was absolutely thrilling to my experience. And then, besides that, she has a lot to do."

"Housework! Ugh!"

"Yes, but work for other people. There you are again."

"Work for other people?" said Daphne as if to herself.

"Yes, perhaps if they were your own, and if you really cared. But there it is again. Logie cares for everyone. Every damned soul about her. Not only her brothers and her dear friends, but Hughie Heggie. She is desperately interested in that nitwit. And in the MacDonalds, too. She adores Mrs. MacAskill. I don't wonder at that. And that granddaughter Peggy with a face like a pig, Logie thinks is wonderful. Oh, she loves every hick in the place. And Steve—she treats Steve—why, she treats Steve as if he were a gentleman of her own class. And Steve! Well, Steve would shiver with delight if he felt the heels of her boots on him."

"Daphne, you are on to *my* job, now. Nine-tenths of my patients are ennui-ridden females. The primary symptom of neurosis is extreme egoism, no interest in other people; the next, no interest in work."

"Well, I guess a good sleep would help us all, so I'm off. Good night, Daughter. Better get off to bed. Things will look better by morning light."

"Want to have a talk, Daphne?" said the doctor after Mr. Inman had gone.

"No! I don't want to talk to-night. Some other time. Not to-night, Fritz. I'd say things to-night I might be sorry for."

"Just as well perhaps to wait. I want to say things too. But not to-night, dear. So we'll just say good night."

"Thanks, Fritz. You do understand a fellow. And you are a dear." She put her arms round his neck and kissed him. For a few moments he held her close to him, then kissed her—but not, she knew well, with a lover's kiss.

"Good night," she said and hurried away. But not to sleep till the pale light of morning had begun to wipe out the stars. With her the doctor kept unconscious vigil.

CHAPTER XXII

NOT in her lifetime would Logie ever forget the ride to West Harbour that night.

"I am afraid we will not have time to go for Hector. Drive right to the telegraph office," she said.

To their dismay they found they had just twenty-nine minutes in which to drive ten miles, pack and ship their fish.

"We can't possibly do it," said Logie.

"Jump in!" said Steve, springing to the wheel. "Good road, good light! Sit tight!"

Logie sat with her eye on the indicator. Inside of a minute the dial showed 45—then crept to 50—to 60—with a creeping back on the curves and hills to 45—then on nice long straight reaches to 60 again, and once for a few breathless seconds to 75.

"Glorious!" she breathed, and still sat tight. Next breath —it seemed to her—and West Harbour lighthouse showed far down by the water. "Oh, Steve!" she cried, clutching his arm in an ecstasy of rapture. "What a race! Just twelve minutes!"

"Eleven and a quarter," replied Steve, pointing to his clock dial. "Those curves slowed us down."

"You are quite a driver, Steve! Now for Mr. MacKinnon. We can't expect too much speed here, I fear."

"You get him. I'll look after the fish."

In a few minutes Mr. MacKinnon materialized out of the shadows of his own doorway with Logie behind him, talking in high excited tones.

"A box!" said Steve crisply incisive, "two feet six."

"A box?"

"Yes! Two and a half feet in length."

"Yes, I think there is one in the baggage room. Wait! My key—" He felt in his pockets. "No, it will be in my other coat, I think. Yes, I remember now—I will be getting it in a minute."

"Oh, please hurry, Mr. MacKinnon," pleaded Logie, dancing on her toes about him.

"Hammer and nails too," snapped Steve.

"Yes, there is a hammer somewhere. It will be in the office, I think. I will get the key." He moved off toward the house with deliberate step.

"Oh, isn't he dreadful?" whispered Logie.

"Blasted glacier!"

Several hours, or so it seemed, elapsed and Mr. MacKinnon appeared with the key in his hand, and strolled toward the baggage room. With patient care he proceeded to manipulate the lock, but with no result.

"Hut!" he said with a touch of impatience. "Will you believe me? It is the wrong key! Wait you now!"

"Here! I can kick that door open. Stand back," said Steve, preparing for the charge.

"No, no! Not at all! It is quite unnecessary," Mr. MacKinnon said severely. "I will be getting the key in a meenute." After a further lapse of time Mr. MacKinnon was back with the proper key and promptly opened the door.

"There!" he said in a tone of triumphant satisfaction. "That is the right way. Wait now till I find the light."

Steve snapped on his cigar lighter.

"Man, them's the handy things!" the other exclaimed, examining the lighter in admiration. "I often thought I would get one of them."

"The box?" said Steve.

"It will be over yonder, I think," pointing to a pile of rubbish in a dark corner.

"A hammer! For heaven's sake, a hammer," said Steve, hurling himself at the rubbish heap. Trunks, harness, egg-

crates, barrels, machinery, Steve flung out upon the floor.
Mr. MacKinnon looked on with unmixed admiration.

"Man! He is the worker now!"

"The hammer!" shouted Steve. "And nails!"

"Yes! yes! There is a hammer somewheres."

"Oh, where, Mr. MacKinnon?" implored Logie.

"Well, let me think now. Will it be——? Yes, I think it
is in one of them drawers."

"Let me look, Mr. MacKinnon. Can you get some ice?"
"Ice?"

"Yes! Ice! I told you, for the fish! We are sending it
to Boston on this train."

"Fish? And what kind of a fish will——"

"A whale!" yelled Steve in his ear, "a whole whale.
Here," he pulled out a five-dollar bill, jerked up his watch
and held them both under Mr. MacKinnon's eyes. "Have
your ice here in five minutes and this is yours. Five minutes!"

"Five minutes? Yes, in three of them!"

Mr. MacKinnon stepped briskly to a door, opened it and
pointed to a pile of sawdust.

"There is your ice," he said, "a ton of it."

Steve flung the bill at him.

"Here is a hammer," said Logie in triumph.

"Here is a box that will do," said Steve.

Seizing the hammer he clawed at the lid of the box, ripped
it off, half-filled the box with sawdust and seized the fish.

"Paper!" he yelled.

"What for is the paper then?"

"To wrap the fish in, you darned idiot!"

"And who will you be calling an eejiot?" said Mr. Mac-
Kinnon in a quiet voice, straightening up his tall lank form
to its full height. "I will not be pairmeeting any——"

"Oh, Mr. MacKinnon, it is only a joke!" said Logie,
dancing up to him and catching his arm with a gay laugh.

Mr. MacKinnon looked at her laughing face in doubt,

then smiled slightly.

"Of course a joke," cried Steve, with a loud cackle. "Where is the paper, old man? Can I get it?"

"A choke?" muttered Mr. MacKinnon. "It is a quare choke. Indeed there is some chokes—"

"Will this be all right, Mr. MacKinnon?" said Logie, pointing to a roll of newspapers.

"Sure!" said Steve, leaping at it knife in hand. A swift swipe and the roll lay open, and a couple of copies of the *Halifax Chronicle* snatched from the pile were wrapped round the fish.

"Now! Now! What are you doing?" remonstrated Mr. MacKinnon. "Them's the *Chronicles* from the postoffice. That's Government property and—"

But the fish was already wrapped and in the box in its bed of sawdust. Steve leaped at the ice pile with an axe which lay at hand, and hacked a lump into fragments.

"There's the train," he shouted. "Get the waybill made out, Logie. You know the address."

"No, no! Not at all," said Mr. MacKinnon, a touch of impatience in his voice. "That is Number Six. The Express will not be on for some time."

"Two minutes!" cried Steve, jerking up his sleeve.

"No, no! Not at all! The Express is an hour and a half late," said Mr. MacKinnon.

"My God!" gasped Steve, and sat down weakly upon his box.

"Oh, Steve!" cried Logie, swaying and rocking in a paroxysm of laughter.

Slowly Steve rose from his seat, drew from his pocket another five-dollar bill.

"Mr. MacKinnon, I apologize! Have you a wife?"

"I have that," said Mr. Mackinnon with emphasis.

"Give her that with my sympathy."

"Thank you, sir," said Mr. MacKinnon.

"And now what will the cost of this box and ice be?"

asked Steve gravely.

"Huh! What's that between us?" said Mr. MacKinnon.

On their way home, the car, purring quietly like a contented pussy-cat, took curves and hills at a very moderate speed. There was no need for haste. The night was young, the moonlight lay like silver on the hillside and, mirrored in the glassy waters of the Bras d'Or, the silent pines like ghostly sentinels stood stiff at attention as they passed. For the first miles with gusts of laughter Logie kept rehearsing the scenes with Mr. MacKinnon through which they had passed.

"Shall I ever forget your face, Steve, when he solemnly announced: 'The train is an hour and a half late'? Oh, I could have died."

"Never in my life have I been so completely sold," said Steve. "You could have bought me for thirty cents. It is a safe rule never to take things for granted. I have had lessons enough in my life. But some lessons are hard to learn."

"You said you were going back to England, Steve. Are you going soon?"

"Within a few weeks. There are some things to do in this country—America—first."

"That will be lovely for you, Steve," said Logie warm interest in her voice.

"Not so lovely. My people, most of them—all that matter—are gone."

"Do you mean your father and mother, Steve?"

"Yes. Mother died five years ago, during the War."

"Oh, did she lose—were any of your brothers killed?" Logie asked.

"No, it wasn't grief—it was shame. I was the cause."

"Oh, no, Steve. I won't believe that," said Logie firmly.

"Shall I tell you? Do you want to know?"

"Not if you don't want to tell, Steve. It really doesn't matter. I am quite sure you never—I mean—it must have been a mistake. Was it something awful, Steve? If so, please don't. Because unless it is necessary why should you? I mean—I am rather stupid—but it is such a perfect night, and we are having such a lovely drive. And after all, why not forget the ugly things and go right on living with the lovely things?"

"Quite right," said Steve. "It is a lovely night, and I shan't have many more—I mean here with you."

"That's just it. You are quick at understanding, Steve. I noticed that about you on the very first evening. Don't you remember? We were all so sad and distressed about Jock, and you were so helpful. You knew just what I wanted and you were so quick and understanding. And that is why I liked you so much. And you have been like that all along."

"It was you, Miss Logie—"

"Now don't begin *Missing* me again. You are not my chauffeur now, but just my friend."

"Well, you were so human, so friendly. You treated me like a human being. And that was what I hadn't had for a long time. And it is really a joy to be just a man again."

"And why shouldn't we be just human and kind and friendly? There is so much real pain and sorrow in the world that we can't very well avoid. And you were really like a brother to us in Boston. Vivien and I felt so safe and sure with you, and Jock too. Oh, you were good to us. But I found that out in the army. Almost everyone is nice, don't you think?"

"Everyone would be nice to you. I rather think we do make our world, don't we?"

"That's it!" cried Logie enthusiastically. "I am sure that's true. All the men at the front were that way—the officers and the men, the nurses too, and the doctors and the orderlies and the poor wounded soldiers."

"But didn't they sometimes swear at you? They weren't all angels, I fancy."

"Oh, sometimes at first when they were suffering terribly. But they couldn't help that, poor boys. And very soon they were all just fine. They behaved like gentlemen. Do you know it was just wonderful how good they all were just as soon as you got to know them."

"You mean just as soon as they got to know *you*, Logie."

"Well, that's the same thing, of course."

"Hardly. But let that pass. I understand."

"And they were so brave and so patient. They tried so hard to hold in. Of course sometimes they just couldn't— could they?"

"It is hard at times."

"And if you treat people nicely they always treat you the same, don't they? Almost always."

"Great heavens!" said Steve softly.

"But you are coming back again, Steve? I mean to Canada? To this place?"

"I don't know," said Steve. "It depends—"

"I do hope so. I don't like losing friends. I am such a bad letter-writer. Somehow I don't seem to be able to answer all my letters."

"Funny, too," said Steve between his teeth, "with all the time you have on your hands, after you've put the house tidy, and looked after your sick brother, and Hector and all his odd jobs, and all the troop of folks who come in at all hours of the day and night, and all the meals and the extra cups of tea, and the slices of bread and jam for all the kids, and the visits to the old ladies, and the Sunday School classes, and now this co-operative stuff. Oh, damn it!—I beg your pardon—I mean you are just the packhorse for everyone's burdens. It makes me rage within—and never a moment left for your own things. Don't you ever get any fun?"

"Fun? Oh, if only Jock were all right! Do you know, we used to have the jolliest times in the world." A faint little sigh came from her lips. "And when Jock gets better we will have such good times again. You can't imagine how happy we all were, but now"—again there was a deep sigh—"I think it's fine to be busy. And it is fun to keep things going nicely, don't you think?"

"Wonderful! Oh, just marvellous!"

"Now you are being sarcastic, Steve. And you get so much in return. You know, I have the loveliest friends."

"Hughie Heggie!"

"Poor Hughie. He does try hard. But he really doesn't like work. And then his wife, who is a splendid worker, gets so cross with him."

"Poor man!"

"Now, Steve, you are making fun of me. Now *you* talk for a while. That's my fault, I always talk too much."

"Never too much for me," said Steve. "Of course you don't know how wonderful you are."

"Of course not! Now don't be mean."

"I have met lots of girls."

"Do tell me about them. English girls?"

"Yes."

"I like them so much. So reliable. Any American girls?"

"Lots of them, mostly hot ones, as Miss Daphne would say."

"I met such a lovely American girl in France. She was a volunteer nurse at Étaples. Rich and clever and so jolly. And so capable. Do you know, the American girls are so much more capable than we are!"

"Are they? I hadn't specially observed," said Steve.

"Smart? Yes, and quick. Yes, and really so frank and easy to know and so very kind. They are always giving you things. I was ashamed to take all the lovely things this American girl insisted on giving me."

"Why not? You gave her ten thousand times as much as she ever gave you," said Steve vehemently.

Logie laughed delightedly.

"That's just where you're wrong. I had nothing to give

her. Not a thing. But you haven't told me about the girls. That's the way I go on. Jock calls me the 'Tennysonian rivulet.' Now that's my last word till you have told me."

"The girls? All kinds?" asked Steve.

"Yes! No! The nice ones first. Though the others were often more interesting."

Steve shouted his laughter. "There, I am certainly forgetting my manners. I haven't laughed like that for years."

"Do it again, I love it. Go on with the girls."

"All right, I will tell you about the best of them."

And for many minutes Steve in a low quiet voice told Logie about "the best of them."

When he had finished, with a deep-drawn breath Logie said:

"She must have been a darling."

"Oh, she was!" said Steve with a little laugh. "She married my brother. He had money and a—and everything."

"And yet she must have been—she must have been very fond of you, Steve."

"Oh, she was!" His laugh was not too pleased. "She told me so herself," and again he laughed.

"How could she do it?" said Logie.

"She was a wise guy, as Miss Daphne would say. That's why." But this time he did not laugh. "And I am thankful she did. Yes! That's one good thing *le bon Dieu* did for me. One good thing! And it is a lovely night. And the stars are shining. And the moon. And it is a lovely world, Logie, and full of good things, and you are the best of them all. And that's the best thing *le bon Dieu* did in letting me know you. And now I am going to begin again when I leave here next week, and never, never, never while God gives me breath will I cease to thank God for you. I know now there are good people in the world, and that means new life to a man."

For a long time there was only the soft purring of the engine, and then Logie said in a very quiet voice:

"I shall always think of that, Steve. It was good of you to tell me. It makes me very—oh, so very happy—because you have done so much for me—for us all."

"For Heaven's sake don't," groaned Steve. "Don't make me feel like a crawling worm."

She put her hand in his arm, and gave him a little pat.

"And don't touch me, for God's sake! And thank God we are home," he added as they drew up at the telegraph office. "I must hand in these wires. Do you mind?"

"Not a bit, Steve. We have had a lovely drive, haven't we?"

Swearing deep oaths Steve pushed into the office and handed the wires to Mary Bella.

"Hello, Miss MacRae. How is the market?" he said.

"Splendid. I am selling out."

"What? Selling out, and it climbing every day?"

"Yes. He told me to sell," said Mary Bella in a low voice.

"Told you to sell? You're sure?"

"He was very strong about it. What is this 'Arriving next week'?"

"Let me see? 'Arriving next week campaign follows almost immediately. Have all arrangements completed.' And you are sure he said 'sell'?"

"Didn't I tell you?"

Steve pulled a pad toward him and wrote rapidly.

"Send that right off."

It was to his Wall Street brokers and read:

Sell International Oil immediately judiciously without delay and without reserve.

"You are selling?" said Mary Bella.

"You can read good writing? Do you want me to spell it for you?"

"But in Sydney they are all buying."

"Who says so?"

"Well, a friend of mine."

"My dear child, open your ears to me and do what my chief told you and what I tell you now—sell. Do you get me? Sell before you sleep!"

"I can't before to-morrow."

"All right, my dear. Good night. When you are weeping and wailing and gnashing your teeth think of me. Good night."

"I will sell, I will," promised Mary Bella passionately. But she didn't.

CHAPTER XXIII

MARY BELLA was in great distress. She had done her utmost to persuade the little group that formed her clientele in her stock-broking operations to sell.

"He told me to sell and I promised I would," was her one argument.

"Pshaw, he's not selling himself," protested Willie George. "And all those men in Sydney are not selling and they are in touch with the market every hour. Sell? No, sir."

It was Mrs. Heggie who interjected the determining factor for holding. "Of course, I am wanting to lift that thing that is breaking the back of the very soul of me. But I do not know. One thing I am going to ask, that I haf neffer asked, and it is this: has the minister sold his stock? He is the smartest man of the lot of you."

No, Mary Bella had not heard of the minister selling. He had been getting money and he had paid money to the doctors in Boston. But she had not heard of his selling.

"Then I will follow him," said Mrs. Heggie firmly.

Hers was the determining word. They would follow their minister. So weighty is the load the shepherd must carry.

The load on the minister's shoulders was heavy enough. In spite of the cheering symptoms in Captain Jock's case, Hector could not rid himself of foreboding. Captain Jock's spirit was high and carried a note of victory, but his physical condition did not keep pace with the march of his soul. He was pathetically resolved to live, and this was the obvious effect on him of the influence of the gay and buoyant spirit of the young American girl, who had taken command of the sick-room.

But Hector had not failed to note that in spite of diplomatically optimistic utterances, the doctor had never committed himself to a definite assurance of final victory in the gallant fight the soldier was putting up.

"If I didn't know Jock so well, I would be happier about him. He is never so cheery as when he is at his last ounce of fighting strength," he said to Vivien and her father as they sat in their arbour where it had become his daily habit to spend an hour.

"But he is certainly stronger," said Mr. Marriott, upon whose spirit the last few weeks had wrought a remarkable change. "Surely we must not allow ourselves to lose our courage and our faith."

Hector looked up sharply at the word.

"Yes," said Mr. Marriott. "That is a new word on my lips, I do admit. How it has come to me I am not going to analyze, but it would not be fair in me to deny it. But one thing I want to say to you, Hector, that the world does not seem to me such a lonely or hopeless place as it did a few weeks ago. And this I owe to you. Yes, you have done something to me. Not so much by arguments, though they are not without reason, but by the way you live, the way you carry yourself with these people of yours."

"You knock me out, Mr. Marriott. If I didn't know you, I would say you are—well—just talking sheer nonsense," replied Hector.

"Oh, I am not saying you are perfect. But anyway it has helped me much just to come into close quarters with you."

"Dad, you have got a lot, too, by going around among the folk, working with them and that sort of thing," said Vivien.

"Quite right. They are really rather fine. Their patience, their courage, their—yes, I must say it—their steady faith, all these things have changed my outlook. Humanity for all its pettiness has something noble about it. These women with their little families about them, well, they amaze me."

"And, Dad, be honest now. You know you've got a new 'Book.' And so have I. There is so much in it that you don't need to swallow."

"Yes, that is true too. Now I must go. Don't wait tea for me, Vivien. I am taking tea with Mrs. MacAskill, a most wholesome person."

"Don't be too late, Daddy, and watch your step with that old warrior. You know your weakness. He is a frightful gossip."

"Vivien, this is a great day for me!" said Hector, when they were alone in the arbour. "I am completely knocked out. Do you know I was just wondering how I could decently run away from this job?"

"I don't wonder. That old devil Jimmie Hannah. I can't stand the old hypocrite."

"No, not hypocrite. A hypocrite is a man who is consciously playing a false game. Cameron is quite sincere."

"All right, he is none the less a devil. And he is all over the place working up a bunch against you. I'd like to twist his neck."

"Forget it, Vivien. This is a wonderful thing about your father. That makes it all worth while."

"Yes. I can't tell you how glad I am. He is so different," said Vivien. "Oh, I just love you for it."

"Say! What's coming to the world?" said Hector with a laugh.

"Hector, it is true. He was terribly lonely before this change. He had nothing left to him except me. Mother gone and gone forever. A blank wall before him. You can't imagine it. He has somehow got her back again. He feels he going to see her again." The girl's voice broke suddenly. "I don't care whether it is true or not. No, I don't mean that—I mean even if it is sheer delusion, it is, oh, it is a dear delusion. Can't you understand? No, you can't. You have never known that awful blankness. Your father, your mother, Alistair gone, but not obliterated from your soul's horizon. Your world is still peopled with them. And then there was Victor! Victor was the centre of Father's life, more than Mother even. His pride, his hope, his everything was built up in Victor. The shock to his heart, I think it was, that killed his faith. You know he couldn't bear to look at their pictures. He actually cleared them out of his bedroom. The other day, I found them back in their places again. And he stands looking at these for whole minutes at a time, and in his eyes such a happy light, where there used to be only black, blank despair, and almost hatred. Oh, Hector, now you know how I feel about you. I would do anything for you."

She was sobbing wildly! Vivien, the gay, hard, reckless, heartless, creedless Vivien!

"You have done this for him and for me, too. Though I never quite got so far away as Dad. I am younger. Oh, I wish I could show you how much I love you for it. Love?" she continued. "Yes, love! There! I guess that will do."

She suddenly wiped her eyes. "Don't think me a fool, Hector," she said, recovering her tone of voice. "I meant to tell you this, but quite quietly and properly. But the picture of Dad before those photographs always gets me."

Hector sat for some time gazing out over the Bras d'Or to the purple hills in the distance. "Besotted fool! Darned besotted fool!" he muttered. "And I was beginning to wonder where God was."

Again he sat silent still with his eyes upon the purple hills.

"You know, Vivien," he said, his words coming in a hurried rush, "I don't believe Jock is going to get well. Somehow I can't believe it! And I was terribly bitter about it. I have lost so much out of my life, Father, Mother, Alistair, and almost all my old friends—except Logie. Of course, there's no one like Logie."

"Only one Logie!" said Vivien fervently.

"And Jock!" He steadied himself a moment. "And Jock

more than any of them. Of course, you can't understand
this. No one can. And I was most terribly afraid of what
would happen to me—to my faith, to my heart, if he went.
But that terrible picture of your father with his lonely heart
and the blank wall before him, and his taking down the
photographs. Oh, my God! No, I must not do that! No,
I won't do that! God," he cried, "don't let me do that!"

"No fear, Hector," said Vivien, and rising hurriedly she
went to him and, taking his head in her arms, she held it
close to her warm soft breast. "No, no, dear," she whispered, pressing her lips to his hair. "God won't let you,
and I won't let you."

"There now, I must get back to Jock," she said, giving
him a little pat. "Daphne will be all in. She is a brick, but
a sick-room is a trying experience for one not trained to it."

"I am going up to have a talk with Mr. Cameron," said
Hector.

"No, not to-day, Hector. Get Steve to take you and
Daphne for a long drive, and take the camp in on your
way. Mr. Inman is quite set on a final blow-out before
he goes. Keep him within bounds. He is spoiling our people with his reckless throwing of money about."

Hector took her advice and went after Daphne to take
her off with him.

"We will take Miss Mary along," she said. "If we are
to have a fête Dad will swamp us. His standard of simplicity is a New Year's Eve celebration in New York. Besides, Miss Mary has not yet visited our camp once. Pretty
exclusive, I call it."

When they called for Miss Mary, they found her full of
work and of excuses. But Daphne followed her out of the
room for a private talk.

"You must come, Miss Mary. I am not going on a tête-
à-tête ride with Hector," she insisted. "You must come.
Besides, I have just been telling him that you have not once
been to our camp. I know we are only vulgar Americans,

but all the same—"

"Nonsense, child. You are just very charming people, but— Well, I will go and let the work wait."

Forthwith they drove to the camp and were warmly welcomed by both the fishermen, who were tired of their sport and were quite ready to sit quietly by the lake in the cool of afternoon and talk.

It was as Daphne had said. Mr. Inman had in his mind a stupendous affair to which the whole Co-operative Association was to be invited, with a brass band from Sydney and a truckload of provisions with fireworks for a grand final blow-out.

"You people have been so mighty good to us. I never had a holiday like this in all my life, and I want to show you just how I feel about it." The combined efforts of the whole party were barely sufficient to persuade him to a modified program.

"Just the two families and the executive of the Co-ops," said Daphne. "Kenny with his violin. Fritz will send for a banjo. We will have races and swimming, and Logie and Miss Mary will perform."

"And you, Daphne," said Miss Mary.

"No! No jazz! This is all high-class, and a little supper in the evening by the moonlight."

"And some Gaelic songs," said the doctor.

"Sure thing," agreed Daphne. "Kenny will bring the boys."

And with this modest program Mr. Inman was forced to be content.

CHAPTER XXIV

A WIRE from New York which Mr. Inman found waiting for him when they all drove into the village that night upset their plans.

"I must go day after to-morrow," he said, profound regret in his tone. "I hate it like the very—like everything. But it can't be helped."

"And the fête, the big party?" exclaimed Miss Mary.

Mr. Inman looked at her with gloomy eyes. "Yes, and you have only been once at our camp. And I was planning a long talk with you."

"I'll come to-morrow night, and then we will talk," said Miss Mary penitently.

"Of course, Doctor," said Mr. Inman, "you needn't come with me. Steve will run me to the station, and I'll take the train. You and Daphne finish out your week."

"No, I shall go with you," said the doctor. "I am away beyond my holiday. But, Daphne, you can stay. There is really no reason why you should return to New York."

"Not a reason in the world," said Daphne with marked emphasis.

"What I mean is—"

"Oh, don't tone down the bitter truth. New York will neither need me nor miss me."

"What I mean is," the doctor explained, "there is nothing doing in New York just now. Everybody is gone or going away. I shall be terribly busy and—well—you have no special engagements, I suppose?"

"Not one, and don't much care to have one," said Daphne promptly. "I am sick of New York, and all its engagements."

"Oh, how splendid!" cried Logie, putting an arm round Daphne and drawing her close. "So you can stay with us. You know how much we love to have you, and how much good you will do us all."

"Yes, indeed, a real boon to us, Daphne," said Hector. "Besides, you are such a splendid nurse, you know."

"And it will be a very real charity," said Miss Mary, "to a lonely old maid, if you would spend some time with me."

"Do you know, I really believe you all mean it. You are the darnedest dearest angels in the world. I could weep buckets on your necks." Daphne's eyes were very shiny.

"And aren't you the lucky girl? I only wish I could take your place," said her father.

"Oh, now, Dad—you know—that's rather—"

"Oh, darn it all, don't be so all-fired smart. You all know—"

"Of course we know, Mr. Inman," said Miss Mary. "She is a rude little child!"

"Well, that's settled," said the doctor.

But Daphne, keeping her eyes on his face steadily for a few moments, said: "We will talk about it to-morrow, Fritz. I must think."

"Yes. We will talk about it to-morrow," he replied. "We will have our talk while Miss Mary and your dad are having theirs, eh?"

"Yes, indeed," said Miss Mary, a little touch of color in her face. "We will let these young people go off for their talk, Mr. Inman."

"Sure thing, and we'll find a place for ours, you bet."

The following day there was little fishing at the lake. After packing up his own things the doctor strolled off down toward the village in the afternoon, and made his way to the Marriotts' home, where he found Vivien alone. She received him with cool friendliness, invited him in, and frankly waited till he should explain why he had come.

"I have come to do what I can to atone for a wrong I once did you, Vivien," he began.

"You did me no wrong, Dr. Wolfe, thank God—though perhaps it was not of your will that you did not. But I will confess you did hurt me—yes, dreadfully. I have found out, however, that it was my pride that was injured more than anything else."

The doctor sat with bowed head.

"Please go on," he said very humbly. "I want to suffer. I want someone to flog me. And I have learned better too, I hope. This visit, these people, the whole atmosphere of this place has—well—Vivien," he burst forth: "I feel my-self a cad! My very soul is writhing in your presence. That is all I can say. Good-bye." He made no offer of his hand, but simply turned to go.

"Good-bye," said Vivien.

When he reached the door she spoke again.

"Dr. Wolfe!"

He turned again toward her, leaving the door open. "I am going to say I am glad you came in to-day, for I wanted you to know that I have forgiven you."

"You—you—you really couldn't do that, Vivien?"

"Yes. You are a different man. You are a better man. But especially it is because of what you have done for these people, these dear, dear people."

"What have I done for them?" he said in a thick husky voice, making no movement to take her hand. "I could kiss the ground they walk on." He looked down at her hand. "No, no, Vivien!" he said vehemently. "I cannot take your hand. I did like you. I tried to make you love me. I made you think I loved you. I might easily have loved you. But I was poor and terribly ambitious. And now I think per-haps I am going to get some of my own medicine—if that is any comfort to you."

"No, it would grieve me. I hope you are mistaken, oh, I do hope so. Good-bye." Again she offered her hand.

Standing in the doorway he took her hand, held it in his for some moments looking steadily into her grey-green eyes.

Suddenly she smiled at him, a warm kindly smile, vivid with friendly good comradeship.

"Vivien, you make me feel that you have really forgiven me. That is how you used to smile." He drew her toward him. "I kissed you once, Vivien, when perhaps I should not have. Do you remember?"

A quick flush dyed her face. "I do," she said quite frankly. "And now you may kiss me again."

At that instant, as he kissed her, Vivien looking over his shoulder saw Hector come in through the gate, stand transfixed at the scene in the doorway, turn hastily and go away.

"Hector! Good Lord!" she exclaimed, drawing herself quietly from the doctor's arms.

The doctor gazed aghast at Hector's disappearing form, then turned toward her again. Her face was pale and disturbed.

"He—saw me. I shall explain the whole thing to him," said the doctor eagerly.

"Dr. Wolfe, you will explain nothing," she said. "You will never mention this thing to Hector. You give me your word?"

"Certainly! But—"

"You understand? You will never mention it to him!"

"As you wish, Vivien. But really—"

"Good-bye, Dr. Wolfe. It is good to be friends again."

"Good-bye, Vivien. I can't tell you how very glad and thankful I am. You are a brick."

When he reached the gate Hector was nowhere to be seen.

With head bent low, conscious of a hot fury choking him, Hector was crashing blindly through the underbrush, going he knew not and cared not whither. After some miles of strenuous walking, physically and emotionally exhausted, he came to rest on the top of a hill, where in a grassy glade he flung himself down. His first fury spent, he proceeded to analyse this extraordinary experience. Why, in the name of all reason, had he been crashing through these thickets like a bull with a bell on? It took only a few minutes to abandon all his safe lies and face the stark facts. It was not that the doctor was playing a traitor to Daphne. Nor was it that Vivien was a traitor to Daphne. He looked back with amazed dismay at that sudden devastating flood of passion that had swept his soul. He understood now as never before how people could commit murder. It would have given him a mad delight to batter in the doctor's face. With the mad fury there had been a vague but very real sense of loss. That pain was still acutely present. It was Vivien that had hurt him so. He had thought that he came first with Vivien. He was her oldest friend, her dearest friend. Friend? Well, there was no girl like Vivien. Logie and Vivien were in the same category. And yet no. Vivien! What did this mean? The doctor was evidently cool to Daphne? Was Vivien the cause? Vivien had for more than a year been associated daily with this man in work. They had many things in common. Besides, he was a coming man. He would be a famous doctor. He would give Vivien everything a girl wanted. As for himself— Nonsense, he had never thought of Vivien that way! Was he quite sure about that? Marriage? He had never thought of it. Why not? Many reasons. There was Logie. Besides, would Vivien look at a minister of a little country parish in a back township of Cape Breton? She was too clever, too ambitious for that. Besides she had no interest in his work. Rather despised it indeed. He could not think himself out of his maze. On one thing he had resolved. He would leave Vivien strictly alone. This resolve to his dismay did not ease his pain, but rather deepened it. He was surprised to find himself conscious of an overwhelming sense of loneliness. But what else could he do? Vivien was not thinking about him. She was a trump of a friend, sympathetic and all that. Thank God, there was his work to do, and in that connection plenty, especially at the present time, to occupy his mind and strength. He sprang to his feet, squared his shoulders and faced up again to his immediate duty. Work, after all, was the big thing in life.

In the evening Steve drove Daphne and Miss Mary to the camp. As they reached the point at which they could catch the first gleam of the lake through the screen of trees, Daphne cried out: "Wait a moment, Steve. How lovely this is, Miss Mary. And how different! I remember well my first night here. Beautiful and all that, but, oh, so lonely, so forsaken. Nothing but water and trees! I wanted to get right away again. Now it just makes my heart ache to think I must leave it. Everything is changed. Oh, Miss Mary, I am changed in here." She laid her hand on her heart.

Miss Mary was a wise woman, and wise especially with young girls.

"Yes, you are changed, Daphne. Very greatly changed."

"Oh, I just crawl inside when I think of that first night at the manse. Oh, how could you stand me—loud, cheap, vulgar, rude—ugh!" She shuddered. "Disgusting little beast!"

"But I liked you that night. You were so very sincere and—"

"Oh, don't speak of it! Thank God and thank you people I at least see myself a little more clearly. And now! Oh!" she clutched her friend's arm, "I don't know where I am or what to do."

"May I say something, Daphne?" said Miss Mary gently.

"Oh, do, do! I do so want advice."

"Just this, my dear. First, we have all learned to love you."

"But no one—no girl, I mean—ever said that to me the way you say it!"

"And then, you know, these people of the manse are quite unusual people and—"

"As well as Miss Mary, their friend," interjected Daphne.

"And then, and perhaps most of all you have been doing a really fine bit of work—I mean in that sick-room—in quite a difficult situation. So you are really a different girl this evening from the girl I saw that first night."

"Really? You're not just kidding me? But of course you wouldn't—"

"And the doctor is different too, Daphne."

"He is! He is!" groaned Daphne.

"I feel he is going to say something very definite to you. My advice is, don't make any decision to-night. Do not say anything final. You understand?"

"I do. Oh, yes! I'm sure you are right. Well, I won't. I'll stall. I promise you. Drive on, Steve, please."

They received a vociferous welcome from Mr. Inman.

"This is too bad now—we're not looking our prettiest just now. Too bad, for your last visit, too."

"Perfectly horrid!" cried Daphne. "I hate all this packed-up appearance."

"Still, all *that* is very perfect," said Miss Mary, sweeping her hand toward the lake.

"But look at this!" exclaimed Daphne in a tone of disgust, pointing to the packed-up baggage. "Back to the pavements and the noise and the heat, and the jazz—ugh! I hate it all."

"Yes, but after all that is life, isn't it?" said Miss Mary. "Camping to-day and breaking camp to-morrow. 'We have here no continuing city,'" she quoted softly.

"Here, Doctor, take this girl away. She's just in the road," said Mr. Inman. "Miss Mary is going to say some lovely things to me."

"Well! I like that!" grumbled Daphne. "My stock is certainly on the toboggan slide to-day."

"Come along, Daphne, where you are fully appreciated," said the doctor, taking her arm in his.

"Now, Miss Mary. Here's a good spot. Now just talk

to me. I love to hear you talk. What's that you said about
the city?"

"The city? Oh, yes! That was a quotation: 'Here we
have no continuing city. We seek one before us.' An
echo, I suppose, of the longing in the hearts of a nomad
people on the march."

"On the move, eh? Yes, that is life, sure enough. On
the jump from one thing to the next."

"One campground to another. And always with the
dream of a city with foundations."

"Say, Miss Mary, I've got a queer, sick feeling inside me
to-night. A kind of doubt whether there is anything in the
whole thing after all, anything worth the whole darn everlasting fight."

"I think I understand," said Miss Mary.

"Do you? No, you can't. The other night I listened to
Hector talk about how the boys used to feel on the last
night of leave when they were going up to the front next
day. Say, that boy gets me all worked up. Wouldn't I just
like to have a boy like him? He just does this with me."
Mr. Inman's fingers went through the motions of tying a
knot.

"He is a fine boy, Mr. Inman. He is hardly himself these
days. He is terribly anxious. We all are."

"I know. Guess you're all worried. And you are 'carrying on,' as the soldier boys used to say. Well, as I was saying, that's the way I feel. Leave is over, back to the fight
to-morrow. Next week I'll be sitting in my office, coat off,
busy with plans, schemes, getting ready to beat 'em."

"Beat them?"

"Beat 'em," repeated Mr. Inman, driving his fist into the
palm of his hand. "Every time my office door opens my
mind asks, 'Friend, or foe?' I'm ready for 'em. Dodge,
duck, sidestep, strike, but never to run! No, sir, not yet."
Mr. Inman's jaw was set like concrete. "And all day long
it's fight, fight, fight."

"But why fight?"

"Why fight?" echoed Mr. Inman. "Why fight?" he repeated with the air of a man facing a distinctly new proposition. "Well, Miss Mary, when you put it up to me that way, darned if I know. Money? Got more now than I can ever decently use, or Daphne either. Why fight, eh? Well, the main reason, I guess, is that I can't quit. You can see that, Miss Mary?" he pleaded with pathetic simplicity. "You couldn't quit till you'd licked 'em, could you? You see, the whole bunch of us are organized and set for fighting."

"But why for fighting?" persisted Miss Mary. "I can't see your reason. You don't hate people?"

"Bless you no! I don't hate anybody. I never see most of the people I fight with. Wouldn't know 'em from an applecart. No! Good Lord! I don't hate any of 'em."

"And yet you want to beat them?"

"Sure! Want to lick hell out of 'em. You'll pardon me, Miss Mary, you've got me all het up."

"Supposing you followed one of them home one night and heard him tell his wife—the children upstairs asleep in bed—that you had beaten him, and that they would have to leave their home—you would be filled with glee?"

"My God, woman! What do you think I am? A damned tiger?" Mr. Inman glared at her out of furious eyes.

"No, Mr. Inman, I know you are a tender-hearted gentleman, somehow by your system condemned to be a man-eating tiger. Why? You apparently can't tell me."

"Darned if I can."

"I suppose in this dreadful fight some people are ruined every year?"

"Hundreds of 'em—and in a few months, if I know the signs, thousands of 'em."

"Only the tigers will win? And not all of them?"

Mr. Inman sat silent.

"And many of them quite decent people?"

Mr. Inman rose and towered over her in speechless wrath.

"And with lovely little children. And some of them in despair will take their own lives."

Still Mr. Inman glared in silence.

"And the only reason is that somehow they can't out-tiger the tigers?"

"Hang it all, Miss Mary, what sort of a hell-born devil do you think I am anyway?" he gasped at length.

"That is the sad part, Mr. Inman. Your system transforms dear, good, tender-hearted Christian men like you into tigers, only more ruthless. Tigers kill to eat. Those men kill, they don't know why."

"Say, I guess you don't want to talk to me any more, eh?" said Mr. Inman helplessly. "But what in—what can a fellow do? Be a quitter? Stay on the side-lines? What? Tell me!"

"Mr. Inman, I am only an ignorant woman. I—"

"Ignorant? What the—"

"You say you are organized to fight? Why not organize to fight tigers and save their victims? Organize to help men?"

"Help men? Oh, Lord! Now you *have* said something. Do you know I pay a secretary twenty-five hundred a year —not very much, I know—to dish out help?"

"Too little!"

"Show me how to make it go and I'll make it ten thousand."

"Too little, Mr. Inman."

"You come to me, Miss Mary—as secretary, I mean," he hastened to add, "and I'll double it."

"Too little."

"For Heaven's sake, how much would you want?"

"Not money. Yourself, a bit of your life."

"My God!" he muttered, "I'd give that quick enough, only—" Then aloud he asked: "How did you learn all this, Miss Mary?"

"In a hard school, Mr. Inman." Miss Mary's voice sank to a deeper note. "I was in New York till I was twelve years old. My father," a shudder shook her body, "died in the panic of 1891."

Mr. Inman stood rigid, as if turned to stone, then slowly he sat down beside her, took her hands in his, kissed them again and again, murmuring brokenly: "You poor child, you poor child, oh, you poor little child," while tears streamed down his face. "Miss Mary, come to me!" he pleaded. "Let me try to make up for the crimes of men like me. I will do anything, anything—you hear me?—anything you ask."

"Hush, my dear, dear friend," she said, "I see them coming." She hastily rose and began pointing out the beauties of lake and sky in the scene before them.

"I'm not going home with you, Dad," Daphne announced. "Fritz thinks it would be better if—I—" her voice faltered.

"Miss Mary, I think—and Daphne agrees—that in the very critical stage of Captain Jock's condition, she might just give the touch necessary to his recovery if she remained a few weeks longer," said the doctor.

"Yes," said Daphne, "it sounds foolish, but Captain Jock —poor dear—really does kind of take to me, you know."

"Not foolish at all," said the doctor decidedly, "but sound therapeutics. I should hesitate to deprive the patient of any interest in life he may have just at this particular stage."

"I do think you are both very wise—and both very dear people," said Miss Mary, kissing Daphne very tenderly.

"Well, that suits me," said Mr. Inman. "As far as I can see I'm not going to have much spare time on my hands for the next two weeks."

Had he known all the facts awaiting him at his broker's office he might well have asked himself whether he might expect to survive the tornado that was to sweep Wall Street and indeed all the financial centres of the country. For he found a market palpitating with a fever of expectancy that within twenty-four hours developed into madness, which drove men to undreamed-of speculative adventure.

International Oil was among the leaders of a runaway market. From par it leaped fifty points in a single day. After a pause of a day of breathless anxiety the market went wild again, and within forty-eight hours Wall Street found itself bewildered, exhausted, stunned, desperately trying to recover sanity, and idly toying with a flood of "new money" that reduced all values to mere babble. To three hundred International Oil went.

A twenty-four-hour period of vacuity was followed by stealthy but very definite efforts to "get from under." The older captains of the pirate gangs, with the wisdom of experience, began first to consolidate, then to unload, very gingerly. At once, as if by a plunge in an ice-water bath, the fever heat passed. Sane normality asserted itself. Men began to ask themselves questions beginning with such words as What? How? Why? with various qualifying phrases attached. For a few days the market hung dizzily poised on Alpine peaks, then almost imperceptibly began to subside—to slip—to hold fast—to slide again—to check desperately—to fall definitely—to disintegrate—to slither— to topple—to plunge headlong. Then followed scenes of panic so appalling, so overwhelming, as to threaten the sanity of the coolest heads, the steadiness of the soundest hearts. The day of doom and damnation had arrived.

CHAPTER XXV

"We will have a nice cup of tea ready for him. He will be tired after his hard day," said Miss Mary.

"He really is looking ghastly these days. I could cheerfully boil that creature Jimmie Hannah in oil," said Vivien. "I hear he has got the Session quite worked up over the Fair."

"The Fair?"

"Well, of course, the tremendous success of the whole Co-operative Association is gall and wormwood to him. So he has fastened upon your play with the Greek dancing and all. If it had been a Highland reel, now, it wouldn't have been quite so bad. But 'Church members dancing in the House of God,' as Mrs. MacTavish said. 'All this lepping and skipping like he-goats upon the mountain! It's no sort of goings on for the Church.' The old devil, though she is a lot better than most of them. I hear Jimmie Hannah is getting the Session to demand a Presbytery inquiry. I only hope they get one."

"Yes, it would really be a good thing—that is, if they got the right members on it."

"Oh, old Dr. John Murray would be on. They always put him on these things. If he comes I shall most certainly be there. It will be a grand show. I only hope they will come out on a Sunday and see the congregation and then stay for the Study class on Monday. That would open their eyes."

"Oh, by the way, what is the matter with Mary Bella these days?" continued Vivien. "To-day she was like a ghost. She looked terrified and weepy. I wonder if that old wolf is worrying her to death. He was in the office

to-day and was talking to her. If only Willie George were
not so much of a sheep. I do despise a man that won't
fight."

"But he did stand up rather well, you remember, the night
of the organization meeting."

"Yes, he made me think of a rabbit standing up on its
hind legs and barking."

"I see by the *Post* that the New York Stock Market is
having a sad time with 'the bears,'" said Miss Mary, with
her eyes on the headlines of the evening paper.

"Bears?"

"Yes, the Stock Market 'bears.' 'Unparalleled collapse,'
it says."

"Oh, I don't know anything about stocks."

"Mr. Inman will be in it, of course."

"Why sigh about him? He has millions and he's a
fighter."

"Yes, he is a fighter. But millions vanish in a night. It
is a cruel shame. It looks dreadfully serious, too. Securi-
ties are tumbling. The Federal Reserve is issuing a warning and raising the rates. A lot of Sydney and Glacé Bay
men are heavily in the market." Miss Mary was evidently
disturbed.

"I suppose that means they will lose a lot of money.
Serve them right, too. Well, we shan't lose any in Ravanoke, eh? Good thing to be poor little country mice sometimes."

The next day, however, if Vivien had known all the facts
she would not have been so easy in her mind about the country mice.

There was a gathering of her clientèle in Mary Bella's
office looking at one another with stricken faces. Their International Oil shares, which for a week had been deliriously
advancing from one dizzy height to another till they had
reached the unbelievable peak of three hundred, there hung
one brief twenty-four hours and then began an appallingly

swift descent into Avernian glooms.

In vain Mary Bella kept sending frantic wires to Mr. Inman. She received one curt answer.

"Situation very grave. Doing utmost to sustain market. Sorry you did not obey my orders."

Finally in desperation Willie George appealed to his father for aid.

"And how did you get into this gambling?" enquired his father.

Willie George did not answer this directly. "If I had only sold last week I would have made big money," he groaned.

"Yes, it is a robber's old plea. Every convicted thief has an 'if' in his story," said his father, with grim lips.

"I believe we could save something yet," suggested Willie George timidly.

Mr. Cameron acted promptly. He drove into Sydney and consulted with his lawyer.

"Tell me, as an honest man, Mr. MacGillivray, not as a stock gambler, is this stock really worth the price? Or is it a mere war?"

"Mr. Cameron, I examined International Oil very carefully when I became interested at the first. I am convinced that the value at which I invested is there. But in a panic all values vanish."

"Is it worth while trying to save something out of this mess?"

"That, neither I nor any other man can answer. It is now no longer a question of values; it is merely a question of who can guess best."

Mr. Cameron pondered long. "My son put in a thousand dollars, borrowed on his automobile," he said bitterly, "when the stock was at sixty. It is now forty. If he could get his own back I would ask no more. I would not help him to make a dollar out of the sinful business. But a man has a right to his own. I will give you a thousand dollars. Mind you, I would not touch one of those dirty dollars. I only want my own—for it *is* my own. The boy had no money," he added with a groan. "Oh, woe is the day when my own flesh and blood would do a thing like this. Mr. MacGillivray, you have known me for many years. I am a hard man, they say, but I am a broken man this day. I have one child and he is a thief and a fool."

"A thief? Nonsense, Mr. Cameron!" said Mr. MacGillivray sharply.

"He put a thousand dollars into this gambling thing which he borrowed on an automobile. The automobile was not his. It was my money paid for it."

"Sit down and listen to me." Mr. MacGillivray's voice was stern. "I face ruin to-day myself. I am putting up my last dollar hoping to save all my estate. I was a fool. So was your son. But a thief? That is an ugly word."

"And an ugly thing."

"Let us look at the facts. That automobile now? I mind when the boy got it. He showed it to me in pride and glee. He said his father gave it to him. He thought it was his."

"It was not. It was mine."

"You kept a string on it, eh? A mean trick. He thought it was his. He drove it. And now because he raises a thousand dollars on it you call him a thief. Whose fault? Do you pay him wages? No. Does he have any money of his own? No. A young man of twenty-two, and you treat him like a child. If he is a thief, you are the cause of it. Don't talk to me, I know you well. You are an honest man. And deep down you have a heart, but what the world sees of it is hard as that oak." Mr. MacGillivray's open hand came down on the hard desk. "Go home and ask God to forgive you and change your heart. That's my advice."

"Huh! And that is your advice? Well, I am not asking you for it. Good day." And with a pathetic effort to walk erect Mr. Cameron stumbled from the room, muttering, "My Goad, what a world!"

Arrived home he called his son to him.

"You have done a foolish thing," he said, speaking like a judge. "But worse, you have committed a crime. The money you put into this thing was not yours. I am trying to save you from the consequences of your crime. But now you will tell me on whose advice you went into this thing."

"Mr. Inman was doing it himself," said Willie George.

"And how did you know that? Who was telling you what he was doing?"

Willie George refused to say.

His father waited a short time, then suddenly cried: "Aha! I have it! It was that—that girl! She it was! Answer me."

Willie George remained silent.

"She it was that led you astray."

"She did not!" said Willie George angrily. "She tried her best to keep me from doing it. I thought it would be safe to follow him. She tried to keep me back."

"As God lives I will have her out of there!" said Mr. Cameron in a voice trembling with rage.

Willie George slowly and for the first time in his life faced his father man to man. Deliberately and very quietly he spoke.

"Father, when I raised money on the automobile I did not think I was doing anything very wrong. I can see now I was. I am sorry for that. When I bought that stock I thought I was safe. It was Mr. Inman stock. Mary Bella begged and prayed me not to do it. I wouldn't listen to her, none of them would listen. She is not to blame. I am to blame first and last But, Father, the day you do anything to injure that girl"—here he raised his hand in the Scots way of making affirmation—"as God above hears me, that day you will lose a son and I a father."

"I hear you," said his father. "That girl has no right to be in that office. It is a public trust. I will do my duty."

The next day the village was humming with the news that some of its citizens were among those who had suffered in

the stock-market crash. The knowledge, it must be con-
fessed, did not greatly distress Ravanoke. Indeed, Ravanoke was conscious of a new dignity, a new sense of being
involved in great events. None but the innermost circle,
however, suspected that the minister was implicated. That
would certainly have shocked and deeply grieved the people
of the village.

It was Hughie Heggie that hurled the bomb. As the Bible
Study class was dispersing next Monday evening, a voice
sounded down the road in hilarious triumphant song upon
the still night air.

> "If ye can say it's a braw, bricht, munelicht nicht,
>   Ye're a' richt, ye ken."

Through the dim light of the moon a swaying figure could
be discerned making past the church gate for the village.

"That's Hughie," said the minister. "I'll just take him
home."

"I'll look after him," said Ranald Gillis. "I have my car
right here."

"Thank you, Ranald. I will go with you. Hughie is a
little difficult at times," said the minister, moving toward
the swaying figure.

"How is this, Hughie? Are you not ashamed of yourself?" The minister's voice rang out in stern reproof.

Mr. Heggie drew himself up and with outstretched arm
and pointing finger exclaimed dramatically and with
drunken gravity:

"Thou art the man! In the words of the holy prophet of
old, 'Thou art the man'!"

"Cease this nonsense and come home at once. What will
your wife say?"

"The wife, is it?" A fiendish glee came into the drunken
voice. "Heh! Heh! Heh! The wife's no sayin' much
these days, I doot. Oo—ay, she's terrible humiliated under
conveection o' sin. Ay. It's a sair fall for the wife!" mused

Hughie sadly. "A professor, a communicant and a gambler!" With a solemn and sad eye Hughie gazed about upon the company.

Light suddenly dawned on Ranald Gillis. Like a terrier upon a rat he was upon the little man. Shook him till his teeth rattled.

"Come on home out of this," he said, dragging Hughie off to the car.

"Easy, Ranald," said the minister.

"And wha is responsible?" shouted Hughie, pointing a swaying finger at the minister. "Thou art the man. He can-na—de-ny—it. He—was the shep-herd—that shep-herdeerred—her in-til—the sin o' gambling—the meenister —her ain—meen-is-ter—"

In broken but perfectly audible accents punctuated and syncopated by Ranald's shakes, Hughie's announcement fell upon the ears of a perplexed and horrified company.

"Ay! She followed him," shouted Hughie.

"Shut up! You drunken fool," said Ranald, clapping a hand over Hughie's mouth.

"Wait a minute, Ranald," said the minister in a calm voice of authority. "What is this he is saying?"

"Just some drunken nonsense," said Ranald, hurriedly struggling with his gears.

"Nonsense, is it? Come awa' an' tak' a look at her! Humbled in dust and ashes. Ay!" Hughie's voice was full of malicious glee. "Why is she no at the meetin' the nicht? Conveection o' sin! Ay! Thou art the man!"

Under that terrible accusing finger and under the menacing terror of that nameless charge, the whole company cowered in horror. Ranald's open hand swung hard on Hughie's side face and tumbled the little man whimpering into the bottom of the car.

"Drive on!" sternly ordered the minister, taking his place beside Ranald.

Before throwing in his clutch Ranald turned toward the

amazed and horrified company, and said in a voice that cut like cold steel:

"Is there anyone here darned fool enough to think there is anything wrong with the minister?"

There followed an appalling silence of a single moment; then Mary Bella stepped forward. "No, Ranald!" she said in a clear, firm voice. "I am going with you. I know all about this." She opened the car door and took her place in the compartment beside the whimpering Hughie, leaving behind her an indefinable but very real sense of relief and confidence.

CHAPTER XXVI

THIRTY-SIX hours later Hector stepped out of a train at the Grand Central station, New York, in a somewhat dazed condition. To his amazement he was met by Steve, who carried him off to an apartment on Riverside Drive, overlooking the Hudson. The last few weeks had wrought a marvellous transformation in Mr. Inman's former chauffeur. He had shed his uniform and was now faultlessly dressed in a light grey summer suit, and more, he wore his clothes with the ease of an English gentleman.

Steve let himself into the apartment and was met at the elevator by a man in uniform.

"Just bring up the things, Pipps," said Steve. "And we will have breakfast shortly."

"Very good, sir," said Pipps. "Everything is quite ready, sir."

"Thank you, Pipps. This is your room, Hector. But you will first have a bath."

"I surely will," said Hector. "But this is gorgeous, Steve. Now tell me, what? whose? why? and all the rest of it."

"Hadn't you better wait, sir, till breakfast?"

"Oh, hang it all, Steve, cut out that 'sir' business."

"All right, Hector, that goes! By the way, any message home? I am sending a wire."

"What? I say you are a reckless beggar. Here, give me a pad. How many words?"

"Never mind the words, say all you want."

Hector wrote a few words on the pad and handed it back to Steve. The telegram read:

Feeling fine stop met at station by terrible English swell apparently living in clover.

HECTOR.

"All right," laughed Steve. "May I add a bit?"

"All you want," said Hector. "I am not paying for it."

Steve wrote a few words and handed the message again to Hector. The wire now read:

Feeling fine stop met at station by terrible English swell apparently living in clover.

HECTOR.

Don't believe the above stop no English swell only a humble and devoted retainer of the clan MacGregor.

STEVE.

"All right, Steve, you certainly have me tangled up, but let her go."

When breakfast was over Hector pushed back his chair and said, "Now, Steve, let's have it."

"Very well," said Steve gravely. "Here are the *fasti* concerning your present host. To begin with, an English gentleman—of sorts—soldier—officer—broke. Emigrant to Virginia—broke again. Chauffeur at an impressive salary to an American millionaire in stocks.—Observed and imitated in a small way his methods and movements for two years. Following a pointer received at Ravanoke, plunged into International Oil, pyramided till par—sold out—quite a strong killing. Trip to England—three weeks there straightening things out. Returned to New York—wire day before yesterday from—er—Miss Logie. And here I am at your service. Any questions?"

"Not one, Steve," said Hector, reaching across the table. "I think I know a man and a gentleman when I see one."

A little flush came into Steve's hard thin face. "Thank you, Hector." Steve was troubled with an awkward cough for a few minutes, and then he added, "All that I have and am is at your service. Now you tell me."

Thereupon Hector poured forth his tale of the devastating effects of the stock crash on Mary Bella and her clientèle.

"And what do you propose to do now?" asked Steve.

"I propose to lay the facts before Mr. Inman and ask what reparation he is prepared to make. He is an honourable gentleman."

Steve smiled a smile of gentle pity. "He is also a stock manipulator, and furthermore this thing has gone far beyond the limits intended or expected."

"Intended? What do you mean?" asked Hector.

"You don't imagine stocks just happen to rise or fall?" asked Steve. "Personally I do not think it would be the least bit of use seeing Mr. Inman. At present he is being crowded by the biggest oil trust in the world, which is after his oil or his hide or both. International Oil to-day is at thirty."

"I am a baby in this business, Steve," said Hector. "Can you give me any pointers, anything to read up?"

"The main principles and rules governing stock manipulation are very simple. But I have lived in the thick of it all for two years and I feel as much of a baby as you do. But all that I have I shall gladly give you."

"Go to it, then," said Hector.

For three days and three nights while Steve vainly sought for an appointment for his friend with Mr. Inman, Hector swatted reports, pamphlets, articles, books dealing with stock lore, principles, methods, till Steve declared his pupil a far greater expert on stocks than he himself.

"You are certainly a wonder, Hector. All you want now is a season in the market, and after that a little toughening up of the resistance muscles in your moral and emotional organisms. Then you ought to become a regular stock pirate, outfitted to kill."

After another day's ineffectual waiting, Hector decided to "crash the gate" of Mr. Inman's stronghold. "I am sick of all this waiting," he said. "I only want ten minutes. I am going into his office."

Pursuing this determination the following morning, Hector, with Steve in attendance, approached the outer precincts of Mr. Inman's sanctum. "I wish to speak to Mr. Inman," he said.

"Sorry, sir," replied a weary-eyed clerk. "Mr. Inman's time is fully taken up this morning. He has a meeting of directors at ten seventeen."

"Where is that meeting?" asked Hector quietly.

"In the office," said the clerk, turning away to his desk.

"We will wait here," said Hector, leaning up against a window ledge.

"What are you waiting for?" asked Steve in a low tone.

"I am going into this meeting," replied Hector.

At ten-fifteen precisely two men with brisk step reached the door of Mr. Inman's sanctum, and opening it passed in. With two strides Hector was through the door with them, leaving Steve behind.

Mr. Inman, at the head of a long table of polished oak, was busy with some papers. The men present, some fifteen in number, took their places about the table. Hector remained standing at the table. At ten-seventeen precisely, Mr. Inman looked up from his papers. His eyes fell upon Hector standing at the foot of the table.

"Hector?" he gasped in a strangled voice, passing his hand over his eyes.

"Mr. Inman," responded Hector.

"Thank God!" said Mr. Inman. "I thought I was seeing things." He rose as if to come round the table.

"Keep your seat, Mr. Inman," said Hector in such a tone of command that Mr. Inman sank back into his chair. "Mr. Inman, I have come from Cape Breton on behalf of some friends of yours and mine." He read a list of the names of Mary Bella and her clientèle. "You know these people?"

Mr. Inman nodded.

Hector then proceeded to tell the story of how it had happened that Mary Bella and her friends had become interested in International Oil stock, and to give in detail the story of the losses sustained by Mary Bella and Mrs. Heggie. He spoke in a low voice but it reached to the heart of every man in the room. His words were simple and unemotional, but somehow when he had done, that group of New York stock manipulators had a vivid and heart-moving picture of Mary Bella taking her three years' savings and investing them under Mr. Inman's direction with the purpose of educating her young brother. To Mrs. Heggie's story he imparted a touch of humour which made the pathos of it no less effective.

"Mary Bella has lost all her money and every hope she had of educating her brother. He will now go to work in the mines. Mrs. Heggie, whose pitiful little savings she had worked out with her finger bones, will now lose her little farm. Mr. Inman, she is a Highland woman and you know these Highlanders, their pride and their independence. This loss will humble her pride and break her independence and her heart."

Up to this point the men present had listened with faces indicating amused interest. They rather enjoyed seeing their chief squirm and wriggle under the grilling of the weird young minister from the North country.

"I ask you, Mr. Inman, what you propose to do in the circumstances."

"Not a thing," replied Mr. Inman in an angry voice. "In the first place I told Mary Bella to sell out when the stock was at ninety. She promised she would. In the second place, I knew nothing whatever of these investors. They went in to make money. They made money. Because of their greed they got caught. It is their own fault."

"Yes," replied Hector sadly. "It is their own fault. They suffer because of their ignorance and their greed. But also, Mr. Inman, they trusted you. They felt that in following you they could not possibly go wrong. Let me ask you two questions. First: did International Oil go to three hundred as a result of your manipulation?"

"Well," said Mr. Inman, "I certainly didn't try to keep it down."

A grin overspread the faces of the group round the table.

"It was war, Hector, plain, bloody war. Some of our enemies jumped in to smash us. They got what was coming to them, and serve them right."

"Thank you," said Hector. "My second question: when International Oil went down to thirty, was it by your manipulation?"

"Well, that was war too. Our enemies needed another lesson in short selling and I guess they got it."

"Then, Mr. Inman," said Hector, and his voice took on a deeper tone, "all those tens of thousands who have lost fortune, health and some of them life, owing to the manipulation of International Oil, owe their ruin to you and your associates."

"Say," said Mr. Inman, with angry impatience, "you don't seem to understand this is a war. Men were out to ruin us; we beat 'em. That's all there's to it."

"Yes," said Hector. "That is the usual justification of war. In war all the worth-while things in life must go—truth, honour, justice, pity, mercy, love. All these dearest things are forgotten. The difference—the difference is this: a real war has the bare excuse of devotion to country and to kindred, while in *this* war, no such motive is suggested—the sole motive is gain. Mr. Inman, thank you for your time. I am thankful to be able to tell your friends and mine, however, that when you were conducting this war, when you were exploiting the people's ignorance, folly and greed, you did not know you were destroying your friends in Ravanoke. That will take some of the bitterness out of the pain. And now let me take a little of the bitterness out of your pain, for I am sure you must suffer with them. Let me tell you that they will not suffer. They will not make any money, but all their losses will be made good to them."

"What do you mean?" asked Mr. Inman sharply.

"Mr. Inman, they went into this stock gambling because they knew that their minister was in it. They did not know that I was fortunate enough to get out and take my profits with me. I thank God that it is in my power to restore to them the money of which you and your associates have robbed them. Good-bye. I cannot wish you success in your life work. I cannot bring myself to wish you ruin."

Sadly, slowly, Hector turned from the table and moved to the door.

"Just a moment, sir, if you please," said a sharp voice.

Hector returned to his place at the table and waited.

"Mr. Hirsch, Mr. MacGregor," said Mr. Inman, indicating a pale, hatchet-faced man.

"You have been asking us questions, Mr. MacGregor. Allow me to ask you some questions in return."

Hector bowed.

"You know something about stock transactions?"

"Very little, sir."

"You know perhaps that it would be impossible to carry on the industrial and financial enterprises of this or any other country without stock operations?"

"I do," said Hector.

"Is there anything wrong then in the buying and selling of stocks?"

Very deliberately Hector made answer. "To sell stock at a price that represents intrinsic reality in value is a legitimate and necessary transaction. To sell stock at a price which the seller knows exceeds intrinsic economic value is a fraud and the seller is a robber."

"You remember the Roman dictum, *'Caveat emptor.'*"

"I do. That is a dictum of a pagan people governed solely by legal maxims. It doesn't relieve the seller of responsibility for robbing the buyer."

"Perhaps you will be good enough to explain what you mean."

"Certainly. International Oil went to three hundred.

No gentleman round this table will honestly say that three hundred represents intrinsic reality in value, either present or prospective. In the last ten stock booms in this country not one tenth of one percent of maximum prices represented intrinsic value, and with the leading stocks the maximum prices never represented intrinsic economic value at all."

"Excuse me, Mr. MacGregor, can you or any man here definitely indicate the point at which intrinsic value was left behind in International Oil during these last weeks?"

"There will be differences of opinion among all of you here, but there is a figure at which every man in this room will agree reality was abandoned. That figure may with some be one hundred and twenty-five, but I doubt if anyone here would set it higher than one hundred and fifty. Beyond that point trading in International Oil ceased to be speculation in oil and came to be merely speculation in chances.

"Let me repeat, the business of buying and selling of stock is an honourable and perfectly legitimate business, and is necessary to a country's industrial development. There is a point beyond which it becomes robbery, and robbery which may end in murder. The man who sells what he knows is not value is a robber, he is exploiting the greed, the fears, the needs of his brother man, and when he drives that man to death he becomes a murderer. The papers report this morning that a man, driven to desperation by his losses in the stock market, took his own life in this city. Gentlemen, who killed that man?" For a moment or two Hector looked away from his audience and stood looking out through the window into the far distance.

For a short time there was silence. Then they fell upon him, questioning, challenging, scorning, deriding him. But the last word was his.

"Gentlemen, I am ignorant of many things—"

"Not so damned ignorant," said a voice.

"But one thing that I know and that you know is this.

The basis of all honest exchange in business is value for value. The man that knowingly sells wind for money is a thief. The man who knowingly buys wind with the purpose of selling for money is a thief. In this war as in all war, honour, justice, truth, pity, mercy, love, are all abandoned. Yet believe me honour, justice, truth, pity, mercy, love, will abide because God abides. Gentlemen, pardon my intrusion. Thank you for your time."

Without further word he again moved slowly to the door. An old gentleman rose quickly from his seat and followed him.

"Where are you going, Mr. Craigie?" asked Mr. Inman in a shaking voice.

"Are you still holding a meeting, Mr. Inman?" said Mr. Craigie.

There was a general movement of members to their feet.

"For my part I want to have a further talk with that man," he said and passed through the door.

CHAPTER XXVII

LATE that evening Steve's phone rang.

"It's Hector speaking, Steve. I am in East Orange with Mr. Craigie. He wants me to stay with him to-night. He is perfecting my education in stocks, and he wants me to preach in his church Sunday. His minister is taken suddenly ill. But I can't see myself preaching to Mr. Craigie and his friends."

"Of course you know your own business best. But it seems to me what you would designate a clear call. Yes, a lot of Craigie's friends will be there, you bet. I know him. He is a fine old chap, but a devil when it comes to a stock market fight. I suggest you preach for them and give them hell. The Lord knows they need it."

"No, I wouldn't give them hell. But you have given me an idea. Yes, I'll stay and preach for them. And I shall start Monday for home." The Highland minister from the Bras d'Or found himself out of his element in the beautiful stone Gothic church at Craigmont. The elaborate service with its bewildering ritual made him nervous. But when he stood up and faced the congregation to deliver his message he found that he was master of himself and of them. Mr. Inman was not present; somehow he had no heart for a sermon from the minister from the Bras d'Or country that Sunday morning. It was young Fred Baker, junior partner to Mr. Craigie, and a great admirer of Mr. Inman, that brought a report of the sermon to that gentleman.

"Well, how did you like your Cape Breton preacher?" asked Mr. Inman.

"Why, I don't know. He makes a chap most decidedly uncomfortable. Makes you feel you ought to quit almost everything you specially like to do—most unpleasant."

"What was he preaching about? What was his text?"

"There you are—right at the start he gave you a jolt. He read that parable, and boy! Can he read! His voice with its funny Highland cadence. I know it well—my grandmother was from Skye. His face, his eyes—a regular prophet outfit."

"I know—a kind of other-world business. Go on."

"Well, it was that parable—rather ghastly—sheep and goats business. By the living jingo! I saw the whole show. You remember it?"

"Sure, I do! What kind of a heathen do you think I am? I was brought up a Methodist. Go on."

"Well, when he got through reading, your Tom Seabright sitting next me gave me a nudge and said, 'We're going to get hell, I guess.' And I bet you Mr. Craigie and that bunch of hard-boiled friends of his were thinking the same thing. But that boy is full of surprises. His first word got us on the flank. 'I may say at once,' said he, 'that I do not believe in the doctrine of hellfire. Hell is much more terrible than hellfire.' Say, that congregation shook itself awake!"

"I know," said Mr. Inman with a chuckle. "It's a way he has. Go on. Didn't he give those 'stock market rotters and murderers' some hot stuff?"

"There you are again—another of his surprises. Not a thing—not a word of abuse—no hard names, but everlastingly rubbed in that terrific sentence, 'These shall go away.' Just as if he were most terribly sorry for them, poor devils. Go away, away from everything worth while—the finest people, the finest things in life, all your own best folk, and with Heaven and God and all that thrown in. Then with a straight solar plexus, he fired the question at us: 'And why? Why must any go away?' You know! My mind went hurdling over all my past villainies—but not one of them did he spot. 'Not for any of the things they had done,' he goes on, 'not one, but for this only—they didn't give a hoot.' Of course not in those words. For all the poor unlucky devils—hungry, thirsty, sick, prisoners and that outfit. I can't stand them myself personally, find 'em most unpleasant. I send a cheque now and then, but personally—well, I don't see them much, as a matter of fact. Then he nailed me right there: 'You give money,' he shouts at me, 'but your money won't save them nor you—that's too cheap.' "

"Yes," said Mr. Inman to himself, "that's what she said, too."

"What? Who said?"

"Nothing!" said Mr. Inman shortly. "I was thinking. Go on."

"Oh, that's about all. He kept rubbing that in. The things not done. The poor devils we forget—the people He cared most for—the people He spent His life trying to help."

"Help? Trying to help," muttered Mr. Inman. "She said that too."

"What? Who?"

"Nothing. Go on. Did he say anything about organizing help?"

"Why, yes? Who told you? Then he ran over a string of names. The people whose names the world can't forget. And then he told about a girl he knew in the War—a corking girl too, used to sing, dance and play for the sick and lonely soldiers and get them all crazy about her. Say, he got the hydraulics at work right there. She must be a lovely girl all right."

"She is. I know her," said Mr. Inman with fierce emphasis. "Finest girl God ever made."

"What? You know her? Say, I'd give several grand to meet her."

"Oh, go on. Did he say anything about a friend of hers?"

"No! But I tell you, Mr. Inman, I felt sick of all this damn scrambling and fighting. 'What is it all for anyway?' I said to myself."

"Say, young man. He's right. I'm too old to change.

But you, for God's sake, listen to him. Don't be a cursed fool. It's all no good!"

"Eh? What do you mean?" Mr. Baker was startled at the tone and look of his friend.

"What? I'll tell you." Mr. Inman started to his feet and began to pace the room. "If I was starting again I'd organize to help those poor forgotten devils—Lord, what a host of 'em! Organize to fight the man-eating tigers I am palling up with now. This is one hell of a game. Get out of it, Baker, while you can. Was that all?"

"Yes, just kept rubbing it in—quietly, not like a minister —kind of friendly, like a big brother. That's about all."

"And it's enough! Get out, Baker! Why in hell did you come round and tell me all this? Get out!"

"I beg your pardon. I—"

"Oh, get out! Do you know what I am? A man-eating tiger sharpening my teeth and claws for the biggest man-hunt of the century. Get out!"

Young Baker got out and drove furiously to Mr. Inman's oldest friend, Mr. Craigie.

"Say, get into this car. Old Inman is going off his nut. Get the preacher and take him along. Anything may happen in the next hour."

Within half an hour Mr. Craigie and Hector were at Mr. Inman's hotel. They found him smoking quietly.

"Come in, gentlemen. Come in, Hector my boy. How are you, my dear fellow?" He put his arm about Hector's shoulder and placed him in an easy chair, taking his place beside him.

"When are you returning home, Hector?" he said with a certain solicitude.

"To-morrow morning. I have been here too long."

"Yes, to-morrow at nine-thirty is your first train. It is a long trip."

Hector looked at him with startled eyes.

"You have heard something, Mr. Inman?" he said.

"Steve was phoning me half an hour ago. There was a telegram. No. Nothing wrong. Jock is not quite so well."

At that moment the phone rang.

"Yes, he is here. Quite right. Come on up."

"Steve is coming right up," he said and sat close to Hector.

In a few minutes Steve entered and handed Hector a telegram. Hector read it and began looking for his hat.

"My car is at the door. Your bag is in it," said Steve.

"Good old boy, Steve. I knew it. Good-bye, Mr. Craigie. Thank you for your very beautiful hospitality, and good-bye, Mr. Inman."

"One moment, Hector." Mr. Inman took from his desk a signed blank cheque and handed it to Hector. "For our friends up there," he said.

"No, Mr. Inman, thank you. I really don't need it."

"Hector! Don't disappoint me. I can afford to give money, but I can't afford to lose friends. Especially"—he swallowed hard—"not friends like those people of yours."

"You won't lose your friends, Mr. Inman. I'll see to that. And if I need this, I'll use it."

"Thank you, thank you! My Lord, that helps. And my love to Captain Jock and Logie—and to Miss Mary. Tell her I'm thinking of hunting tigers. She will understand. Love to Daphne—that dear little girl of mine, and to that bright little nurse, Vivien. And God bless you, my boy. Safe home to Jock and all."

CHAPTER XXVIII

THERE was still an opalescent glow over the Bras d'Or hills when Steve drew up at the manse door. A light burned in the kitchen, but upstairs the windows were almost dark. Both men alighted from the car.

"Wait here, Steve," said Hector. He made his way to the kitchen door.

In a moment a girl came running out.

"Vivien! Jock?" he asked, a great dread in his voice.

She put her arms about him, drew him close as if he had been a child. "This morning at dawn he went quietly away," she said.

He swayed in her strong arms.

"Gone!" he echoed. "O God, could You not let him wait?"

"He tried to, so hard, Hector! He said, 'Tell Hector I tried my best,' and he did—oh, he did."

Again the door opened and Logie came out. Like a bird in flight she ran to him, hands outstretched before her, fell into his arms and clung there quivering, tearless, voiceless.

Together the three walked toward the house where Miss Mary waited in the open door.

"It was all peace, Hector." Her calm clear voice steadied them all. "He was content, yes, glad to go. Oh, yes, glad to go. The doctor said it was God's mercy for him and for us that he should go. So we are not grieving, Hector, dear boy. The doctor will tell you himself."

From within the room came the doctor and supported by him Daphne, very white, very wan—tearless and composed.

For an instant they stood gazing at each other, then Hector moved toward her and took her into his arms.

A visible shudder shook her. "I loved Captain Jock," she said, lifting appealing eyes to Hector. In silence he nodded. He had as yet utttered no words to them.

"And yes! Oh, yes, he wanted me. But he wanted you —you most of all, Hector. Oh, Hector!" Her voice rose in a cry. Then controlling herself, she said resolutely: "No! I will not cry. It was best." Quietly she released herself from Hector's arms and went to the doctor, who placed his arm round her and held her steady.

"It was best, Hector," said Doctor Wolfe.

Again without a word Hector nodded. About the circle his eyes wandered and finally rested enquiringly upon Logie. "I will get him, Hector," she said, and passed into the kitchen. There she found Steve, standing alert like a soldier on guard. Something in his face stayed her steps. The hardness was gone, and instead a look of mingled pain and passionate appeal. The cold grey eyes were warm, tender, compassionate. Slowly she moved toward him, a questioning wonder in her dark lovely eyes.

"Steve, we want you," she said in her gentle voice.

"Logie," he said, his voice deep and vibrant, "I would give my life to help you."

"Would you, Steve?" A shy surprise dawned in her eyes.

"You know I would, Logie."

She came quite close to him and lifted her dark lovely eyes to his. "We want you, Steve," she whispered.

"And I want you, Logie. Oh, more than everything else in life."

"Yes, I know, Steve," she whispered. "And I want you just the same way."

Quickly her arms went up and about his neck. With a swift movement he caught her to him and kissed her on the lips.

"Steve, they are waiting for us," she said at length. "Come, dear."

Hand in hand they entered the room.

"Shall we go upstairs, Hector?" she asked with a little smile. "We thought you would like to see him in his bed."

Hector motioned them upstairs. Daphne and the doctor hesitated. But Hector motioned them to follow.

They stood in silence about the bed where Captain Jock lay as if in sleep. A dim light filled the room. Hector went and turned up the lamp.

It was as Logie had said. Captain Jock looked rested. The lines cut by suffering and weariness were all gone. It was the face of one who had fought and conquered, strong, beautiful, nobly content. There was no place for tears here. Steadily, almost critically Hector leaned over and looked upon the face of his brother. After some moments a great sigh as of relief breathed from his lips. He looked down into Logie's eyes and smiled. Quick came her answering smile.

"We know this is the best, Logie, for him—and—for us." It was his only word. There was no need for more.

In the living-room downstairs they recounted to one another the doings of the last week. Miss Mary, in her calm, controlled voice, told of Captain Jock's last hours, of his quiet courage and his cheerful acceptance of the inevitable as the best.

"The doctor helped him amazingly," said Miss Mary. "He was so straight with him, and so strong. He seemed to call up all Captain Jock's store of courage."

"Courage!" said Hector. "That was the very heart of him."

"Courage and confidence," said the doctor, deeply moved. "I have seen many men go, but never with such a fine realization of what was happening, and with such superb assurance that everything was just right."

"You were splendid, Fritz!" said Daphne, the tears quietly running down her cheeks. "Oh, just fine! You made it so easy, so kind of natural for him to go. You know, Hector, I wired for Fritz last week and he came at once. He has been wonderful to us all."

Hector put his hand on the doctor's shoulder.

And then Steve told of the doings in New York, of Hector's meeting with Mr. Inman's Board of Directors. A different Steve it was speaking in that company from the Steve they had known. With his chauffeur's uniform he had laid aside the whole manner and bearing of the servant. He was one of themselves now, quiet, considerate, confident, and with the indescribable charm of speech and manner that marks the well-bred English gentleman.

"I am afraid they gave Hector rather a bad half-hour," he said, "but I fancy he gave them something to think about." And then he told of Hector's sermon in the Craigmont church. "You would all have been proud of your minister," he said as he finished.

"Of course we would," said Logie, pride shining in her dark eyes, and a new and wondering pride in this new lover of hers.

"And your father sent his love to his dear little girl," said Hector, "and—" he paused a moment or two to steady his voice—"and to Jock and to you, Logie. He sent a special message to you, Miss Mary. I was to tell you that he was preparing to hunt tigers. He said you would understand."

For the first time that night Miss Mary gave a sign of emotion. There was a quick flush in her cheek, a suspicion of tears in her eyes.

"Yes, I understand. Oh, I am glad," she said. She looked as if there was something beautifully sacred in her mind.

And then they planned the order of the funeral service.

"We want everything very simple," said Hector.

Logie made quick response.

"Oh, yes, very simple, but not sad. Jock would not want it to be sad."

"No, no, not sad. Anything but sad," said Miss Mary. "Something of triumph in it."

"Ranald said the men of his company would be there," Logie added, "and they want to come in uniform."

"Certainly, quite appropriate," said Hector, "but not the pipes."

"Oh, not the pipes," said Logie. "That would break our hearts."

"Nor the Last Post, nor any firing party."

"Oh, no! Something fine and high, something warm and cheery and kindly, like 'I to the Hills,' and 'O God of Bethel.'"

"Just right, Logie. That is the word. Fine and high and cheery," said Hector with a smile at his sister.

"We wired the Principal, Hector. He came to-day."

"Oh. That is good. Everything will be safe in his hands. That is all, I think. Steve," he continued, "I want you to see Mary Bella to-morrow morning and arrange for the distribution of these cheques. You will find all that is necessary here," said Hector, handing him a large envelope. "I want all that thing to be wiped off before the funeral."

"I shall see to them personally," said Steve.

"I think that is all," said Hector. "It is good to be with you all again, and to find you all so brave."

Then Vivien rose to go.

"I would stay all night with you, Logie, but father is not so well. He is feeling very lonely to-night."

"I shall go with you," said Hector. "I wish to see your father."

They walked slowly through the starlit night, Vivien with her arm through Hector's, her heart warm with the mother love of pity for him. For that hour Hector forgot entirely the turmoil of suspicion and pain that had filled his heart only the week before.

"How good you have been to me—to all of us, Vivien, ever since Jock came home. How could we have carried on without you? My heart is somehow numb in me. I can't say what I would like to say. But you will understand.

You always understand."

"I understand, Hector," she said, holding his arm close to her breast. "Don't try to tell me. I know. And you know too how much more I would do for you if I could."

There was no answering pressure on Hector's part. His heart was, as he said, numb and capable of no other emotion than his grief. But somehow that firm warm clasp brought him help and comfort.

They found Vivien's father still in the doorway, for the night air was kindly and there was still a glow over the hills. In silence the men shook hands. And when they spoke there was no note of sadness. For only a few moments Hector sat with the old gentleman. As they said good night Mr. Marriott pointed to the soft glow in the sky over the hills. "A great gathering over there," he said, and named them one by one. "What a meeting!"

"And they shall go out no more for ever," quoted Hector and took his departure.

CHAPTER XXIX

WHEN Mary Bella reached her office next morning she found Steve waiting her arrival.

"May I see you in your office, Miss MacRae?" asked Steve in his finest manner.

"Certainly, sir," said Mary Bella, greatly impressed with the change in his manner and appearance, and led the way to the back room.

"This, I think, is the list of your investors with their investments in International Oil stock."

Mary Bella ran her eyes over the paper.

"That is correct," she said sadly. "It was a terrible mistake that I did not take your advice, sir."

"No use crying over spilt milk," said Steve. "Mr. MacGregor is arranging for the repayment of your investments with a slight addition in the way of compensation for services and other things. In Mrs. Heggie's case it will be difficult to explain the amount, but we will pass that lightly over. There is sufficient to meet the full payment for her mortgage. With Ranald Gillis and Willie George, the amount represents only their investments, with costs and interest. In Mr. Cameron's case the repayment is simply of the amount which he advanced to save Willie George's investment, without interest or costs. You understand, Miss MacRae?"

"No! I do not understand one word of what you have been saying." Her eyes were wide with astonishment, her lips quivering, her voice trembling. "Whose cheques are these? And why should they come to us?"

"You know your minister well, Miss MacRae? He has a sense of responsibility for his people. He has the feeling

that you all invested because he invested. Hence these
cheques."

Then Mary Bella put her head upon her desk, sobbing
bitterly.

"Oh, I cannot do this! Please! I cannot do this. It
would be a sin and a shame to take his money."

"Neither sin nor shame, Miss MacRae, but just because
he is the man he is you will take this cheque. I am rather
hurried. I must see each one of these to-day. By the way,
I should be glad to have you go with me. It would help
me greatly. So please sign this receipt and come along."

Steve's manner was perfectly courteous, but carried with
it an air of authority that Mary Bella found quite irresistible.
Without further words she did as requested.

Mr. Heggie was sitting outside of the door of his house,
smoking quietly with an air of serenity quite unusual with
him.

"We would like to see Mrs. Heggie," said Steve.

"Indeed she is no that brisk these days," said Mr. Heggie,
shaking his head sadly. "No ill," Mr. Heggie continued, a
grave compassion in his voice, "but low in her mind. It
was a sad fall."

"Fall? Did she meet with an accident?" asked Steve
anxiety in his voice.

"Accident? Na, na! It was no accident. Deleeberate—
an' wilfu'. Ay, a sair fall! Under severe temptation, I
grant ye—a severe temptation."

Steve was thoroughly perplexed.

"Where is she, Hughie?" asked Mary Bella impatiently.

"In the kitchen," said Mr. Heggie, "at her wark. Though
what's the use o' wark if guid money is to be flung aboot in
a wicked gambling ploy?" said Mr. Heggie. "Ay, it's a sair
fall. And a deserved judgment foreby."

"What is he talking about?" said Steve thoroughly mysti-
fied.

"Come in," said Mary Bella angrily. "Leave this old

fool out here."

"Auld fule? Auld fule, is it? Wha is the fule the noo,
I'm askin' you? You that confederated with her in her sin!
Huh!" Mr. Heggie's voice became shrill with indignant
reprobation.

"Come awa' ben," he said, leading the way to the kitchen
where they found Mrs. Heggie busy setting the room to
rights.

"Here's some of your freens tae see ye!" Mr. Heggie's
tone dissociated him entirely from Mrs. Heggie's visitors and
from any purpose they might have in view.

Mrs. Heggie was indeed sorely changed. Her former
brisk, almost truculent air of authority over her husband
was gone, and in its place a meek and humble spirit suitable
to one "conveected o' grievous sin."

"Oh, it is you, Mary Bella," she said, heaving a deep
sigh. "And your friend. Come away. You will excuse the
house. Indeed I am not that well."

"Indeed no!" said Mr. Heggie with sad severity. "And
it is small wonder conseederin' her experience."

Steve explained his errand in a few clean-cut sentences.
"So if you will, please sign this receipt. That will be all."

"Wumman, I forbid ye!" exclaimed Mr. Heggie. "We'll
hae nae mair o' these on-goin's. Nae mair gamblin' for me
or mine."

Mrs. Heggie in a dazed state of mind said humbly, "No,
Hughie, there will be no more of that."

Then Mary Bella explained that by Mr. MacGregor's
kind intervention her losses were being made up without
further obligation or responsibility.

"Allow me to see yon paper!" commanded Mr. Heggie.
"As the head o' this hoose I demand a full exposeetion o'
the proposed action."

"Listen to me, Heggie," said Steve. "Mrs. Heggie was
unfortunate enough to lose some money. Through the kind
offices of her minister the money with all costs and interest

is being restored. She signs a receipt for the amount. Sign here, Mrs. Heggie, please," said Steve.

"And what does it mean, Mary Bella? Who sends the money? And what right have I to any money?" asked Mrs. Heggie in tearful perplexity.

"Ay, what right?" said Mr. Heggie with emphasis. "Ye may ask!"

Again Mary Bella explained that it was from the minister.

"The meenister, is it?" cried Mr. Heggie, his voice shrill with indignation. "Ay! An' weel he micht. Wha was it led her astray?"

This was for Mrs. Heggie beyond the limit of endurance. The insult to her minister, together with the dawning sense of her emancipation from crushing debt and from the guilty consequences of her sin, loosed the floods of wrath in Mrs. Heggie's bosom, held in check for the past weeks of humiliation.

"Led me astray?" she exclaimed. "How often have I told you! You will be keeping your tongue off the minister. Indeed it is time you were out of here, and at your work." Angrily she seized the broom.

"Woman, listen tae me!" shouted Mr. Heggie.

"Hut! You will listen tae me!" said Mrs. Heggie. "Will ye not be going, or must I—?" She raised the broom over her head. Without further parley, but with indecent haste Mr. Heggie scuttled from the room. His brief hour of dominance had passed.

As they drove back past the store Mary Bella's eyes fell upon a car parked near the door.

"It is Ranald Gillis," she said.

The interview with Ranald was brief. He positively and definitely refused the money.

"I went into this thing on my own," he said. "I was caught like all the other fools. Why should any man, least of all the minister, pay for my folly?"

"Ranald," said Steve, "your minister feels this to be his

duty. You must let him judge of this. I know how you feel and respect you for it. But you must help him out. Besides, he has enough to bear to-day."

"Yes, yes—God knows he has. I don't understand. But if it will lift a single ounce of the load on his heart—say, I'd lick the boots of him. Give me that damned cheque. Here take your receipt. But not for any other man would I take the shame I am taking to-day," said Ranald, with a sudden choke in his throat.

"You are a man, Ranald," said Steve, gripping him by the shoulders. "What else can you do?"

"What else? I know not. But tell me what else and I'll do it. I'd go through hell for him." He passed the back of his hand over his eyes and strode from the room cursing deep oaths to himself.

With Willie George there was little difficulty. Mary Bella had decided that the thing must be, and, this being made clear to Willie George, there was nothing left for him but submission.

When it came to James Cameron, Mary Bella said: "I will not go. He hates me, and I don't think much of him." And that settled the matter.

Steve was ushered into Mr. Cameron's best parlor and into the presence of a somewhat distinguished company. Besides James Cameron himself there was the Principal from Halifax. With Presbyterians in Cape Breton there was only one "Principal." He had come the previous evening with a twofold purpose in his heart. First he was to take charge of the funeral of Captain Jock, a warm personal friend and the son of the minister, who during his life had held the highest place in the Principal's affection and esteem. But besides this he had received a letter from Mrs. MacAskill some two weeks ago in reference to the trouble in the congregation, which had greatly disturbed him.

"You will just make visit with my cousin James Cameron," she had written, "an honest man, but with nothing new in his head for the last twenty-five years, and when you have finished with him he will no longer be troubled with Adam's rib and such-like mysteries."

It was Mrs. MacAskill too that had suggested to her cousin that he should invite the Principal to be his guest. "And who knows but I may look in upon you myself?"

The first suggestion Mr. Cameron had accepted with great good will. He held the Principal in high esteem both personally and as a sound theologian. In regard to the second suggestion Mr. Cameron had made a gallant effort to be cordial, but the shrewd old lady looked at him through eyes half shut.

"Very well, Jimmie, if it will be giving you all the pleasure you say, I may come. Besides, it will make the day of the burying a little easier for me to be near at hand. I will be needing all my strength, I am thinking."

The previous evening and most of the morning the Principal had spent in converse with his host. There was no man in the Canadian church more thoroughly equipped with the qualities of heart and endowment of mind necessary to the initiation of a man of Mr. Cameron's type into the broad principles of Higher Criticism. Refusing to debate the minute details of questions of Biblical interpretation, he spent his time and strength describing at great length how he himself had got his New Bible, and how his new view of the Holy Scriptures had liberated his mind and enriched his spiritual experience.

"After all, Mr. Cameron, the Bible is God's revelation of Himself, not because of the miraculous element in it, but because of the noble concept it gives of Him, of His purpose in His universe, and above all of His love for His children." And all this with the marvellous charm, the insight into human mind and heart, the warmly human sympathy that had won for the Principal his place in the confidence and affection of the church.

Into this company and into this atmosphere was Steve

ushered.

"Ah," said Mr. Cameron, "Mr.—er—you are Mr. Inman's chauffeur."

"No, Mr. Cameron, by happy fortune I was Mr. Inman's chauffeur during a time of stress. My home is really in England. At present I am here acting as a friend of Mr. MacGregor in a matter of some importance."

"Principal, let me present Mr.—"

"Wyndham is my family name," said Steve, shaking hands.

"How are you, Steve?" said Mrs. MacAskill, offering her clawlike fingers. "Whateffer the name and whateffer the place, there are those who will be holding you in high regard in this place. And there are others, but the less said of them the better—"

With a low obeisance Steve took the old lady's hand.

"I have the pleasure and honour of a much fuller knowledge of Mrs. MacAskill than she has of me," he said courteously.

"And do you want us to leave you?" asked the old lady.

"Not at all, as far as I am concerned," said Steve, with the quick perception that his cause would not be injured by the presence of these two friends of the minister.

"Sit down, Mr. Wyndham," said Mr. Cameron coldly.

Briefly Steve told of the minister's adventure in International Oil, then followed with the story of how the minister's friends had become involved and of the disastrous consequences. "To save his son's investment Mr. Cameron came to the rescue with a thousand dollars, which was also lost. The minister fortunately had sold his shares when they had reached a fairly profitable figure."

"I wish I had done the same," said the Principal with a rueful smile.

"You, Mr. Principal?" said Mr. Cameron, horrified.

The Principal nodded.

"And that's what my son the doctor wishes," said Mrs.

MacAskill, "but you will all be learning."

"Mr. MacGregor feels a certain responsibility in this matter. The investments in this neighbourhood were made following his lead."

"No," said Mr. Cameron hotly, "it was that girl, she lured them into it. My son and others."

Steve paused a full quarter-minute, then very gravely and courteously said: "Mr. Cameron will be glad to be corrected and saved from making a statement which I know to be incorrect." Thereupon Steve made clear the limits of Mary Bella's responsibility. "That, however, is by the way. I have here a list of investors and a statement of their losses. They have all been made good."

"By whom?" asked Mr. Cameron sharply.

"By the minister, such is his sense of responsibility in the matter. This is your cheque, Mr. Cameron."

Mr. Cameron took the cheque and examined it. "This is the minister's money?"

"It is."

"Has he any left?"

"I am not fully in his confidence. But after he has met the expenses of his brother's sickness and—and—" Steve's voice shook a little—"and of his death, it is not his intention to retain any of the money made in International Oil still in his possession."

"Ay, the lad!" said Mrs. MacAskill, a proud flash in her wonderful eyes. "I could have told you that same, Jimmie."

"I cannot take it," exclaimed Mr. Cameron, rising in his excitement. "No, not a dollar!"

"It will only add to his burden to-day if you refuse, Mr. Cameron."

"I tell you no!" said Mr. Cameron. "I love money, God forgive me! But I would rather cut off that hand than take any of that money off him."

"There is no taint on that money," said the Principal.

"I cannot take it! I am telling you. It would be as fire

in my bones. It would drive sleep from my eyes. No! It is my fault! It is all my fault!"

"Tuts, Jimmie man!" said Mrs. MacAskill. "What are you saying?"

"What am I saying? I will tell you. I will confess my sin unto the Lord. It has been a consuming fire. My sin is ever before me, and I will confess to you as well. It is my fault! The boy came to me desperate for money to pay for his brother's operation. I refused him." He paused and glanced hastily about the circle of faces. "Yes, God be merciful to me! I showed him no mercy that day. Then his American friend came with an offer, which he accepted. There it is! Now you know. And since then I have been seeking to find justification for myself in persecuting him— him with his load of pain and sorrow." The iron face was distorted with grief. "Him I love as my own, and his father before him. Take that money? The Lord do so to me and more also if I touch a penny of it." He sat down with his head in his arms upon the table.

Mrs. MacAskill rose, hobbled to his side, placed her hand upon his bowed head: "Tuts, Jimmie lad! It is a hard heart that you have gotten to yourself. You did a cruel thing that day to our lad. But you have suffered for it, and down deep in you the heart was sound. And it is that heart we are seeing now. It is God's mercy that sent this young man to you to-day. What could you do to-morrow with that in your heart? How could you look in the face—the dead face of the lad you refused to help?"

"But I did try," groaned James Cameron bitterly. "I went next day to offer it, but I was too late."

"Did you now, Jimmie? Then kiss me, lad, for that." She lifted his face and kissed him. "And thank God I can say my prayers to-night without passing your name. And now, lad, you will do what I tell you. I am an old, old woman, near to the Gate, and I am seeing your way to-day, James. You will not grieve the lad's heart by refusing that money. You will take that money and do with it what you like. The Principal here knows what to do with money," she interjected shrewdly. "You will take that money—it will hurt your proud hard heart—but the hurt will heal you of your pain. And to-morrow you will be done with all your bitter persecution and lay the healing of your love upon the lad's sore heart."

James Cameron rose from his seat. "You have the word! God gave you the word. I will take it. And here it is." He handed the cheque to the Principal. "Do with it what you will. And to-morrow—no, to-day—this hour—I will go to him. My God! Hate is a hard and bitter companion. Come! Thanks be to God! Oh, thanks be to God! I must go to him. Oh, but he has the sore heart. And me pouring vinegar on it! Now, I will pour oil upon the wound. I think—I believe—I know—I know by the heart in me, he too will be glad."

With Steve Mr. Cameron drove to the Manse.

"I would see himself alone," he said as they neared the door.

"I shall arrange that for you," said Steve.

And thus it came that no one was there to see when James Cameron humbled himself before his minister and poured upon the sore wounds of his heart the healing oil of love. But it was for all the world to see that thenceforth all problems soever, social and critical, were easier of solution.

ppl still prob
wanted b believe
in God ask
her so tly
had some
comfort that
their lad was
now @ peace

CHAPTER XXX

NEVER had the Bras d'Or worn a lovelier dress, all gold and blue, and never for a nobler parade than when for the last time Captain Jock led his men.

With no pomp or circumstance of war, with neither wail of pipe nor tuck of drum, the men of his company in their old worn khaki marched behind their Captain to his last campground. The service was held on the greensward upon which stood church and manse, with its encircling pines, the green hills in the distance and just below the blue waters of the Bras d'Or shining in the sun.

With the beautiful simplicity characteristic of him the Principal read the noble words of the Christian's hope. With fine restraint he spoke of the gallant soldier they had known and loved, of his courage, his cheery spirit and his faith. Then he spoke of the father and the mother and the young soldier brother all lying near. Lovingly he commended to the comfort and sustaining grace of the Heavenly Father the remaining members of the family circle. And that was all.

In the kindly earth they laid him, under the pines, a band of his comrades led by Ranald Gillis doing for their Captain this last service.

There is in the Highlander an instinctive courtesy, and with it a fine sense of dramatic values.

After the benediction had fallen, the little group of the family and more intimate friends stood close about the grave; Hector with Logie on one side and Vivien on the other, next to Logie, Steve, then Miss Mary, Daphne and the doctor and the Principal. About them at a little distance the guard of honour in khaki, under the command of

Lieutenant Gillis, formed a half circle, and just inside the line of the guard the Session with Mr. James Cameron as senior elder.

Then one by one the elders, led by James Cameron, came forward and gave to their minister their hands in token of loyalty and loving sympathy. There was a general forward movement of the people. They were eager to follow the Session's lead. But at a signal from the doctor, whose eyes had been upon the women of the minister's household, the guard of honour closed ranks, and the crowd slowly dispersed.

The dreaded ordeal was over. The little group were alone and near them the new-made grave. They hardly dared look at one another, much less speak. Spent emotions, worn bodies, tired nerves, left them a prey to a heart-sickening sense of loneliness and loss. The moment too had come, one of life's terrible moments, when they must leave there alone their dead. With a convulsive shudder Logie put out her hand and caught her brother's arm. They two alone were left of that happy group alive with them only three years ago. A desolating fear and loneliness fell upon her soul. She was at the end of her strength, on the verge of collapse. Her long watch night and day, and every night and every day for the last six months, had drained life from body, spirit, heart. It was Steve who noted and moved to the rescue. A few quick steps led to a slight mound from which through a break in the tree line the sea was visible.

"Look, Logie!" he said, pointing through the trees. All moved toward him, welcoming relief. There, reaching away between its rampart of green hills to a low line of misty purple twenty miles distant, and climbing by cloudy terraces to a city glorious with spires, minarets, pinnacles and towers, lay blue as the Heaven above and touched with the gilding of the setting sun the Bras d'Or, The Arm of Gold.

"Ah!" said Hector, a note of triumph in his voice, and

with hand outstretched toward the golden city among the clouds. "Thank the good God there, not here," pointing to the mounds of earth about them, "they abide, 'And they go out no more for ever.'"

CHAPTER XXXI

EXHAUSTED physically and emotionally as she was, Vivien passed a restless night. Back of her grief for Hector, quiescent at present, but as real as her very soul, was her love for him. He had never referred to the unfortunate contretemps in the doorway with the doctor and herself. But she knew his pride. Never would he share the love of any woman with another. Never would he acknowledge by word or sign that he had in any degree been supplanted by another. Besides this, her heart was torn with a very real doubt as to her place with him. Friend, family friend, Jock's friend, old-time comrade, all that she was—but anything else?

"He isn't thinking of me. I am nothing to him," she said to herself, as she tossed on her sleepless bed. "His whole soul is preoccupied with his grief. And why not, poor dear? And distracted with the problems of his work, though Jimmie Cameron has apparently come round.

"Oh, he doesn't care for me. I am nothing to him. I am second and a bad second to Logie. And I want to be first! Oh, I want to be everything!"

If she could only go away somewhere, but leave her father she could not. There was nothing for it but to carry on.

She rose and looked out over the Bras d'Or. The light of dawn shone pearly grey in the eastern sky, but toward the southwest dark banks of clouds. She would go out to her nets. Angus John had been attending to them for the last week. The sooner she got back to normal the better.

When she reached the pier the whole sky was overcast and the wind was beginning to kick up the sea horses. She was none too sure of her old boat.

"That old mast of mine is rotten, the rigging is rotten, the whole darned thing is rotten. I must get a new boat. However, she is good enough for this little blow, I guess," she said and cast off.

Daphne, too, had had a bad night. The last six weeks had brought her a new and quite startling experience. For the first time in her life she had been forced to give herself, her strength, her heart, her very soul for others than herself. For the first time in her life she had caught glimpses of a world where altruistic motives played a dominant part. Her experience in the sick-room had wrought a greater change in her than she knew. Never before had she come into contact with sickness. Never had she faced the solemnity of death. It had amazed her to discover that her former horror of sickness and her dread of death had somehow gone. Under the compulsion of her affection for Captain Jock, and her sympathy with those who loved him, she had entered into the grief without a thought of herself.

Her new friends too had released in her heart new tides of emotion. Logie, Miss Mary and Vivien had wakened in her heart a depth of affection and admiration which utterly amazed her. And then there was Hector. What Hector meant to her she was unable to say. His strength, his complete selfless devotion to his brother and sister, his high conceptions of life, and duty and service to humanity, all this puzzled her, excited her. Then too, those flashes of deep passion in him, which now and then had startled her, stirred in her a vague longing for a fuller exploration. What a lover he could be, if he would only let himself go! She had moments when her whole body grew hot at the thought of what it would be to lie in his arms and feel his kisses on her lips. She was startled at the possibilities of response in her to such an experience. But it was not in her to kindle into a flame this passion in him. She had made men love her before, madly. Why not Hector? That she had interested him, stirred his heart, she was woman enough to know. That great moment on the Island! And yet that was a mere upleap of passion. He had remained master of himself. Why? Was it Vivien? Vivien was such a splendid girl. So strong, so self-contained, so deep-hearted, anyone could see that. Did she love Hector? That too puzzled her. Oh! These people were so strange, so different! She had no standards in her past life with which to compare them. Vivien so clever, daring, cool, effective and with such a heart for love.

Daphne was too exhausted for sound sleep. As the dawn looked in through her window she rose and sat looking over the Bras d'Or, grey under grey clouds piling up in the southwest. As she sat dreaming over the varied experiences of this strange visit, she saw Vivien loose her boat, trim the sail and beat out against a partially head wind. She had more than once gone out with her to her nets.

"She should not go out alone against that head wind, and in such rough water. If I were only dressed I would go with her."

Without thinking just what she was doing she threw on some clothes, donned a sweater and a slicker, pulled a tam over her hair and raced off down toward the pier.

"'Tis the watcher gets the roughest water,'" she had heard one of the Bras d'Or lads say. And sure it was that she, more than Vivien, felt the heave and climb and pitch of every wave. The nets were set out in the lee of a small island in mid-channel of the southeastern gap. Behind this island the boat disappeared. Long she waited for its return in growing fear and anxiety. What had happened?

"Ah! There she is, thank God," she breathed as the bow of the fishing boat showed itself from behind the island. "But this gale has gone wild. I wish to Heaven Hector were here. He would go out to meet her."

Meantime with a starboard gale on her third quarter Vivien was coming down the wind at racing speed. Her boat seemed to leap from the white mane of one sea horse to that of another. Nearer and nearer came the boat. About three-quarters of the way across the open stretch Vivien caught sight of her and waved a gay salute. At that instant something happened, what it was she could not tell, but as Vivien waved the boat's head yawed wildly and caught the full force of the gale. There was a wild leap forward, and then to her horror Daphne saw the sail come tumbling down athwart the boat, hiding Vivien in its folds.

Without an instant's pause Daphne flung aside her raincoat and raced off to the manse, dashed in through the door, upstairs and into Hector's room, shrieking, "Hector! Hector! Come quick, for God's sake! Vivien is out there and her sail's down."

"Where?" he cried.

"Out in the bay."

With one leap Hector was on the floor, seized his dressing gown, pulled on his running shoes and was off with Daphne following. On the pier he stood a moment glancing at the boat now tossing helplessly in a welter of white water. Then darting toward his own boat, which fortunately was also moored to the pier, he jerked her free.

"Keep back!" he cried to Daphne, as he leaped. But quick as he was, the girl was in the boat beside him. Seizing the tiller she cried: "Get up the sail, Hector. I'll steer."

"Oh, you are the darned little fool!" he cried, but did as he was ordered, and in less than a minute the boat was headed out to sea.

"Get down into the bottom," he ordered, taking the tiller in his own hand, and tacking out toward the floundering boat.

"Are you sure it's Vivien, Daphne?" said Hector, his voice hoarse, his black eyes staring wildly out of a face ghastly white.

"I saw her from my window go out more than half an hour ago."

"Blasted little idot! In that rotten old tub of hers! If she ever gets out of this I'll break the thing to bits. My God, help us now!" he groaned in a voice of agony, his eyes fixed upon the pitching boat.

"What is she doing? Oh, what in blazes is the girl doing now? She's monkeying with that sail. Can't she cut it adrift? O God, give her sense to do the right thing!" Hector's frenzied voice came in choking gasps.

At every tack his boat neared the labouring craft.

"She's not rising! She's filling up! Oh, God! She is filling up! She can't make it."

"She has got her sail overboard, Hector. It's dragging behind her," said Daphne.

"Good girl! By Jove, she's using it as a riding anchor. If only she were not so waterlogged. What now? What? She's rigging up her jib! Oh, Lord! She *is* the sailor."

It was true; somehow she had got her jib set and was beginning to make way through, plunging heavily.

But now Hector was able to tack down upon her at a tremendous speed.

"Cut loose your sail," he roared. "We'll pick you up."

She did as she was ordered. They could see her slashing at the ropes and finally cut the sail and broken mast free.

"Swing into the wind now. I'll come alongside!"

"Pick up my sail, Hector!" she cried gaily, waving her hand at the derelict sail and mast.

"To the devil with you!" said Hector wrathfully. "Swing into the wind and come aboard. We'll take you in."

"Not on your life. I'm all right now."

"Now why did God ever make such everlastingly confounded fools? Come on in, Vivien!" he pleaded.

"I'm perfectly all right, Hector, and riding fine."

"You are filling up. That's what."

"Not a bit. Not now. I'm doing fine. I am really. Don't worry. Hello, Daphne! Having a good time?"

"O my God, keep my mind from leaving me," Hector

groaned. "If I had you in this boat I'd wring your neck," he roared at her as he kept tacking from side to side, keeping as close to her as he dared.

"She seems to be riding all right, Hector," said Daphne, who had become more or less familiar with the ways of boats. "And she'd hate to come in with us. I know she would."

"Yes, you would," snapped Hector. "You're another just like her. Stubborn little mule."

Meantime running on the jib before the wind, her boat steadied by its ballast of water, Vivien was evidently in a state of wild exultation.

"Why not come in with us, Vivien?" said Hector in a last desperate entreaty.

"But I'm all right, Hector. And even if the old tub founders you could easily pick me up."

"You could too, couldn't you, Hector?" suggested Daphne meekly.

"Oh, damnation and blazes! What things women are! God forgive me! But who could help it?"

"Oh, Hector, I think she is magnificent! Just look at her handling that boat. You couldn't do better yourself, though you are the best sailor on this water," said Daphne.

"Oh, shut up, will you! You both are enough to drive a man to madness."

Together they approached the pier, Hector holding off and on. Trailing behind came Vivien with her little jib pulling hard and gallantly riding the sea horses like an ancient Viking.

"Oh, splendid, Vivien!" cried Daphne with a shriek of delight, as Vivien swung her waterlogged old tub into the lee of the pier.

"Oh, Hector, listen dear, don't be cross with her." Daphne spoke in hurried, low, fierce accents. "Oh, my dear, my dear, be tender and kind with her now. Love is sometimes cruel, oh, very cruel." The tears were streaming down her face. "Oh, Hector, you love her. This rage is love! Hector, Hector, my dear, I am saying good-bye to you. Do you understand? Love her. She is worthy even of you."

Sobered by the poignant pathos in her voice and by her flowing tears, Hector brought the boat to her mooring, caught the pier and made fast.

"What is it, Daphne?" His voice was full of perplexity and very gentle, as he steadied her in the tossing boat.

"Nothing, nothing," she whispered hurriedly. "Take her home and tell her you love her. And, oh, boy! don't be a fool! Hold her in your arms and kiss her till it hurts. That's what she wants. It is the only thing. Good-bye, Hector. Let me go."

Hector lifted her to the pier still in a maze of wonder.

"Oh, you brave girl!" cried Vivien, running to Daphne, holding her close and kissing her. "You dear splendid girl!"

"For God's sake take him home and give him a chance," whispered Daphne madly. "Don't fence. Oh, give him a chance—make him tell you."

With a wild little laugh she waved her hand in farewell, crying, "I must get away—home—"

Vivien stood waiting till Hector had secured both boats. Then he came to her still pale and with his dark eyes alight, but not with rage.

"My fish, Hector, please," she said with a tremulous and very tender smile.

Without a word he climbed down into the boat and lugged up out of the water the sack of fish.

Still without a word on either side, they walked together to the house.

Quietly she opened the door, her finger on her lips, then closed it softly. They were in the little hallway together. Daphne's words were sounding in her heart like a bell. "Give him a chance! Make him tell you." Suddenly she resolved she would do both. Slowly she came toward him, her lips parted in a brilliant smile. Into her grey-green eyes she allowed to flow the full hot tide of her heart's passion, and turned them full upon his.

As from a stupor his eyes awoke, a single step he took.

"Vivien!" he whispered. "Does it mean you love me?"

She raised her arms a little. Then Hector took his chance.

Daphne rushed home to Miss Mary's, every nerve in her body tingling. As she was slipping upstairs Miss Mary, who was a light sleeper, came from her room.

"Let me come in with you, Miss Mary. I have had the most thrilling experience! Wait!" She dashed into her bedroom, undressed and reappeared in her kimono, crept in beside Miss Mary and proceeded to give her a most vivid account of Vivien's peril and rescue.

"Oh, she was a corker! Gosh, what nerve she has! Oh, I am so excited. I am wondering what has happened."

"What do you mean?"

"Hector! I do hope he won't be a darned dumbbell. He is the— Miss Mary, you cramp my style so. He is so difficult—stupid—dumb. And Vivien is such a darling. Oh, I wonder whether she can bring it off."

"What are you talking about, you silly girl?"

"What? The greatest thing in life! Oh, will he be a darned oyster or a real hot-blooded man? Vivien is such a cool-headed beggar too. Oh! They do want some pep. What the—oh, hang it, my vocabulary is horribly hampered."

Miss Mary looked puzzled and a little shocked.

"I wonder if he has got home. If he has it's all off. If not, I guess everything will be all right. Oh, I do hope so. Now that I—" She paused abruptly.

"Oh, isn't this the darnedest skewgee world? And yet . . ."

"Now, Daphne, I'm going to send you straight to your bed for your beauty sleep unless you can talk sense."

"Sleep? Miss Mary! Sleep? And the world afire! A bit of my world at least! Come here!" She leaped out of bed. "Come here!" She dragged Miss Mary to the window. "See that house among the shrubbery?"

"Yes, of course, the Marriotts'," said Miss Mary rather impatiently.

"Yes. Well, in there somewhere—likely in that little back den—is that boy Hector!—And he is holding Vivien in his arms, and kissing her—oh, kissing her madly—as if he could never get enough. And she is just swooning for the joy and pain of it and hoping like hell—can't help it—that he will never stop. And—and—oh, Miss Mary—I wish —I wish— Oh, I don't know what I wish! I wish I were Vivien for an hour, only one little hour! And then she could have him." She flung herself into Miss Mary's arms sobbing wildly.

"My poor darling, you are worn out. You have been so splendid. But it has been too much for you." She carried her to the bed, got in beside her, took her in her arms and held her in her warm embrace, soothing and petting her as she might a child. And like a child Daphne sobbed herself into quietness, and at last to sleep.

When she awoke she found Miss Mary and the doctor beside her bed.

"Hello, Fritz, you old graven image. I have had the most wonderful sleep. You might kiss me good morning."

"Take this tablet," said the doctor quietly.

"What for? If it is to make me sleep I won't. If it's to give me pep I don't need it. I am right on top of the world!"

"Take it!" ordered the doctor.

"What I want is breakfast—porridge, fish, eggs, toast, marmalade and tea."

"After this tablet," said the doctor.

"Oh, all right, you darned big bully. Now get out. I'm getting right up."

"After breakfast," said the doctor, "which is ready and which I shall bring up to you."

"Isn't he the cave-man brute? All right. Only get a move on."

When the doctor left the room she dashed into her own room, rushed through her toilet and reappeared in a most fascinating negligée. "This ought to help," she said to Miss Mary. "Now just watch me vamp that old Bluebeard!"

And it was to Miss Mary an amazing exhibition. She told the story again of Vivien's rescue, picturing Hector's baffled and futile fury in such humorous fashion that she had both her hearers in gales of laughter.

"And then I sent them both off to Vivien's home to make love to each other. They give me a pain in the neck, these darned love-sick idiots, like a pair of pigeons on a roof." Then she added abruptly, "When are we going home, Fritz? It's time you were at your work again. And me? Well, I must have a talk with this wise one," jerking her thumb at Miss Mary.

"Would to-morrow be too soon?" said the doctor eagerly.

"Do you know what I should really like?" said Daphne, her eyes shining like stars, her cheeks tinged with a sudden flush of red.

They both waited her next word.

"I should like to be married before I go home—in the manse here, with Logie for bridesmaid, and by Hector; and have Mrs. MacAskill here, and Kenny."

The doctor's eye critically scanned her flushed face. He slipped his finger on her pulse.

"Say, boy! Don't you want me?" she asked, looking up shyly into his eyes with a slightly tremulous smile.

"More than anything else in this world, Daphne," said the doctor, a rapturous gleam in his eyes. "If—but—that is—"

"Say another word and it's all off," said Daphne, holding up a threatening finger.

"May I not even say 'Yes'? It is rather sudden, you know."

"Will you excuse me?" said Miss Mary, hurrying to leave the room. "Back in an hour."

"One moment, Miss Mary," said the doctor. He wrote rapidly with steady fingers. "Give this to Steve, please. Want to see it?"

"Sure," said Daphne, taking it from him with shaking fingers.

It was a wire to her father.

Married here day after to-morrow please come at once.

Daphne.

"Great stuff! Read it, Miss Mary."

Miss Mary read the wire.

"Good-bye—for an hour," she said, hurrying from the room.

"Isn't she a wise guy?" said Daphne.

"Solomon was a dumbbell compared with her," said the doctor with solemn emphasis.

.   .   .   .

The great news thrilled the whole manse group into new life. First Logie came running wild with joy.

"Oh, Daphne, you lucky, happy girl. There is no one so worthy of you. I am so happy for you both. He is such a splendid man."

Steve followed more sedately. "Lucky beggar, I call him, what?" he said.

When Vivien came Daphne ran to her and as she kissed her whispered in her ear, "Did he?"

Vivien nodded.

"But I know it," said Daphne. "I have only to look at you both. You lucky things!"

"I owe you something, Daphne. You gave me the nerve. But mind you, not a word to him."

"Oh, shucks!" said Daphne. "He is a cold-blooded—"

"Cold-blooded?" gasped Vivien, with a little reminiscent smile. "Cold-blooded? Hector?"

When Hector heard the news he came to Daphne, caught her in his arms, kissed her once, twice.

"For me—and for Jock," he said very gently. "It was Jock helped to make you the lovely girl you are."

"Lovely? Not very, I fear. But yes, Jock helped me. And you too, Hector, and the Bras d'Or and its dear people —but you, Hector, most of all."

Within an hour of the despatch of the wire to Mr. Inman, an answer came:

> Great going daughter stop some speed artist stop watch my smoke.
>
> *Dad.*

The same afternoon toward evening the dwellers of Ravanoke were startled to behold a seaplane emerge from the haze over the purple hills to the south, circle uncertainly over the Bras d'Or water, finally drop into the bay and taxi to the little pier, there to be received by the assembled village with tumultuous welcome.

Miss Mary, however, received Mr. Inman in her home.

"Your message made me very happy," she said.

"Happy? I'm glad. Me? I have been having a—well— I haven't been any too happy, I can tell you. What you said and what that preacher of yours said knocked all the punch out of my fight. I've been seeing man-eating tigers in my sleep."

"You are looking tired, Mr. Inman," said Miss Mary, putting her hand out to him.

He caught her hand and held it fast. "Miss Mary," he began impulsively.

"Oh, did you hear all our exciting news?" she said, withdrawing her hand with quiet dignity. And then she told him of the love affairs within the manse circle.

"Well, isn't that just great? What I say is they deserve what they're getting. Every last one of 'em. But say, those Craigmont people are coming after your minister. Bound to get him too—offering him ten thousand dollars, I hear."

Miss Mary's head went up a bit.

"Tell them not to trouble themselves. He's not for sale."

"Nor you either," muttered Mr. Inman. Then he added, "I've found there are two things can't be bought for money."

"Yes? And what are they?" asked Miss Mary.

"Love and Life," said Mr. Inman.

"True, they are to be had only for two things."

"And what are they?"

"Life and Love—and so our young people have found."

"Look here, Miss Mary," he burst forth in an eager voice, "I want—"

"Oh! Here's Daphne," cried Miss Mary, running to the door.

"Oh, darn Daphne," said Mr. Inman heartily.

The wedding ceremonial was shorn of all its customary appurtenances. Flowers there were in the room in greater profusion than usual; the windows were wide open upon the Bras d'Or; and there were none of the going-away barbarities.

"It's a simple thing to mean so much, isn't it?" said Logie, a gentle tenderness in her voice, as they all stood at the manse gate watching them drive away up the first rise.

"Simple?" said Mrs. MacAskill, her deep luminous eyes alight with the vision of the seer. "It is God's mystery, lassie. It has Life in it, and Death and Life again and all eternity."

"And Love, Grannie, too," said Logie, awed by the old lady's "lifted" look and tone.

"Love? Ah, yes, my lassie, Love and Love and more Love—that never dies."

At the top of the first rise Daphne touched the doctor's arm. "Stop, dear," she said gently. "Let's get out."

They stood upon the top of the rise and looked back. There in the slanting rays of the westering sun lay the little hamlet nestling up to the Bras d'Or, and there behind the rows of pines the white church amid its quiet graves, and beside it the manse and at the manse gate the little group standing.

"There! They see me!" cried Daphne, waving frantically. "Oh, good-bye, you dear, dear people! Good-bye—good-bye," she exclaimed in a breaking voice, the tears running unheeded down her cheeks. "Oh, you darlings, good-bye, good-bye. Oh, *what* you have done for me! Good-bye, once more, you dear darling things. Good-bye. Come, Fritz, I can't bear it." One last wide wave, a last whispered "Darlings, good-bye," and she stumbled into the car.

"They are great people," said the doctor, after they had taken the road again. "They have certainly done great things to me."

"And to me," said Daphne. "They made me all new inside."

"That Hector is a great man."

"He is a great man," said Daphne. Then she snuggled to him and putting her hand through his arm she said with a happy little chuckle, "Huh! You are just as great a man as he is. And to me a lot better." ·

"Little liar," he said tenderly.

"To me, Fritz, a whole lot better."

He stopped the car short.

"Say it again," he threatened.

She said it and took the consequences. At the top of the second rise they stopped the car for a last look.

Hidden from their eyes were village, church and manse. But far down below, winding in loving curves about its wooded hills, in all the matchless glory of its gold and blue, lay the Bras d'Or—The Arm of Gold.

THE END

FORMAC FICTION TREASURES Also in the Series

By Louis Arthur Cunningham
Fog Over Fundy traces the adventures of a young non-conformist French Canadian woman who returns from Europe to the Tantramar in New Brunswick to fulfill her duties on the family estate and her obligation to the "peasant" workers there.
ISBN 10: 0-88780-710-0 ISBN 13: 978-0-88780-710-7

By Frances Gillmor
Thumbcap Weir
Gid Wyn and his fiancée, Debbie MacQuarrie, are counting on getting her father's fishing weir when they get married in the spring; but there is one villager, Tony Luti, who thinks it's his weir and that it has been stolen from him. Luti sets out to destroy the young couple's dreams and his hatred gets greater with the passing months until one day, under cover of fog, he and his son take revenge.
ISBN 10: 0-88780-645-7 ISBN 13: 978-0-88780-645-2

By Evelyn Eaton
Restless are the Sails
Paul de Morpain, a prisoner-of-war in New England, overhears a plan to send an expedition against the French fortress at Louisbourg. He knows he must do whatever he can to warn the governor. It is 1744 — a dangerous time to attempt a 500-mile journey by sea and overland along dangerous forest trails.
ISBN 10: 0-88780-603-1 ISBN 13: 978-0-88780-603-2

Quietly My Captain Waits
This historical romance, set during the years of French-English struggle in New France, draws two lovers out of the shadows of history — Louise de Freneuse, married and widowed twice, and Pierre de Bonaventure, Fleet Captain in the French navy. Their almost impossible relationship helps them endure the day-to-day struggle in the fated settlement of Port Royal.
ISBN 10: 0-88780-544-2 ISBN 13: 978-0-88780-544-8

The Sea is So Wide
In the summer of 1755, Barbe Comeau offers her Annapolis Valley home as overnight shelter to an English officer and his surly companion. The Comeaus are unaware of the plans to confiscate the Acadians' farms and send them all into exile. A few weeks later, the treachery unfolds and they are sent to an unknown land as pawns in the Anglo-French conflict.
ISBN 10: 0-88780-573-6 ISBN 13: 978-0-88780-573-8

By W. Albert Hickman
The Sacrifice of the Shannon
In the heart of Frederick Ashburn, sea captain and sportsman, there glows a secret fire of love for young Gertrude MacMichael. But her interests lie with Ashburn's fellow adventurer, the dashing and slightly mysterious Dave Wilson. From their hometown of Caribou (real-life Pictou), all three set out on a perilous journey to the ice fields in the Gulf of St. Lawrence to save a ship and its precious cargo — Gertrude's father. In almost constant danger, Wilson is willing to risk everything to bring the ship and crew to safety.
ISBN 10: 0-88780-542-6 ISBN 13: 978-0-88780-542-4

By Alice Jones (Alix John)
The Night Hawk
Set in Halifax during the American Civil War, a wealthy Southerner — beautiful, poised, intelligent and divorced — poses as a refugee in Halifax while using her social success to work undercover. The conviviality of the town's social elite, especially the British garrison officers, is more than just a diversion when there is a war to be won.
ISBN 10: 0-88780-538-8 ISBN 13: 978-0-88780-538-7

A Privateer's Fortune
When Gilbert Clinch discovers a very valuable painting and statue in his deceased grandfather's attic, he begins to uncover some of his ancestor's secrets, including a will that allows Clinch to become a wealthy man while at the same time disinheriting his cousins. His grandfather's business as a privateer and slave trader helped him amass wealth, power and prestige. Clinch has secrets of his own, including a

clandestine love affair. From Nova Scotia to the art salons in Paris and finally the gentility of English country mansions, Clinch and his lover, Isabel Broderick, become entangled in a haunting legacy.
ISBN 10: 0-88780-572-8 ISBN 13: 978-0-88780-572-1

By Evelyn Richardson
Desired Haven
Mercy Nickerson's father returns from a voyage to the Caribbean with a young Irishman he has saved from a shipwreck. Mercy and Dan are instantly attracted to one another. Rather than go to Boston, Dan decides to stay and turn his ambition to the fishery and ship supply. But his desired haven becomes a more dangerous place than he intended when he turns to smuggling and his wife turns against him.
ISBN 10: 0-88780-675-9 ISBN 13: 978-0-88780-675-9

By Charles G.D. Roberts
The Forge in the Forest: An Acadian Romance
Jean de Mer, an "Acadian Ranger," returns, after three years' absence, to his lands on the shores of Minas Basin to find his son Marc in trouble with the Black Abbé, a French partisan leader. Marc is waiting to be tried as a spy. Together father and son make a daring escape but Marc is wounded and Jean must endure a perilous canoe journey with a young English woman to rescue her child from the Black Abbé.
ISBN 10: 0-88780-604-X ISBN 13: 978-0-88780-604-9

The Heart That Knows
She was abandoned just hours before her wedding. Helpless and shocked, she watched her "husband" sail away without so much as a word of explanation. When her fatherless son grows up he sets off to sea, determined not to return to his New Brunswick home until he has sought vengeance on the man who treated his mother so heartlessly.
ISBN 10: 0-88780-570-1 ISBN 13: 978-0-88780-570-7

By Margaret Marshall Saunders
Beautiful Joe
Cruelly mutilated by his master, Beautiful Joe, a mongrel dog, is at death's door when he finds himself in the loving care of Laura Morris.

A tale of tender devotion between dog and owner, this novel is the framework for the author's astute and timeless observations on rural living and farming methods, including animal care. This Canadian classic, written by a woman once acclaimed as "Canada's most revered writer," has been popular with readers, including young adults, for almost a century.
ISBN 10: 0-88780-540-X ISBN 13: 978-0-88780-540-X

Rose of Acadia
One hundred and fifty years have passed since the Acadians were sent into exile; now Vesper Nimmo, a Bostonian, sets out for Nova Scotia's French shore with the intention of carrying out his great-grandfather's wish to make amends with the descendants of Agapit LeNoir. Nimmo finds himself immersed in the Acadians' struggles to preserve their culture and language and meets Rose à Charlitte, the innkeeper at the hostelry where he makes his temporary home. Their romance is thwarted by her past, but he cannot leave.
ISBN 10: 0-88780-571-X ISBN 13: 978-0-88780-571-4

By Frederick William Wallace
Captain Salvation is a little-known novel of Maritimers at sea, now brought back into print in this new addition to Formac's Fiction Treasures collection. It is an exciting tale of a young reprobate who works his way up from able seaman to mate, skipper and then ship owner. His strength and intelligence pull him through the violent life aboard ship. Finally, shipwrecked off Cape Horn, he has to face his demons.
ISBN 10: 0-88780-676-7 ISBN 13: 978-0-88780-676-6

Blue Water
Set in the early 1900s, *Blue Water* traces the adventures of "Shorty" Westhaver from boyhood to young manhood in the dangerous and often tragic world of the Grand Banks fishery.
ISBN 10: 0-88780-709-7 ISBN 13: 978-0-88780-709-1

Marquis Book Printing Inc.

Québec, Canada
2007